Boy, Son

A Classic Southern Gothic

Paul David

Table of Contents

Dedication

I would like to dedicate the book to my family.

Acknowledgement

I would like to acknowledge God, my wife and children, Steryl Jones, Ruth Farmer and Carl and Joyce Montgomery.

About the Author

Paul David lives in Washington State where he enjoys hiking, travel and spending time with friends and family.

Chapter 1

Broken men and broken bones only ache in the wet, the rain, the wind, and cold. Peter stared at the slick concrete floor that lay before him, wiping his moist palms on his pant legs, that subtle, sharp pain beginning to pulse through his right hand like a cool shock. He unconsciously rubbed his dry skin, trying to soothe the pernicious little bite. Thunder outside, as he patiently waited for his final paperwork to be completed. Peter had learned to count on that pain like he had counted on morning chow, automatic like a heartbeat, like recreation time in the afternoon, and dinner, and work in the computer room, where he replaced cables and keyboards, and other hardware, day in and day out, one after another, his work all stacked up like an endless inventory of dull, necessary units of random what-not. The work was consistent and dictated like a child's life, or at least how a child's life should be, or maybe even an old man's, for that matter.

Peter could almost feel the lift of a cool breeze as the vast plains outside pulled the heavy purple clouds from the western sky.

"Dernovish...Peter!" the man shouted as if Peter sat mingling across a crowded room.

Peter grabbed his twisted, wooden cane and stood up, motioning toward the officer in his little box.

"Don't go past the orange line, Dernovish." Peter replayed the outcomes of seeing his father a million times over in his head. Was the bastard still alive? Would he recognize the guy?

He thought about spitting on the cop who lethargically sat in the dingy little space, filling out his exit paperwork. Maybe punching the next trustee that he saw sweeping the floor would keep him safe and sound in the familiar so that he didn't have to leave the prison and go out into that big, bad unpredictable world. He could stay right where he had lived for a good chunk of his past years a little bit longer, maybe pay back a little more debt to society, while he waited for the old man to die. He could always perform kitchen work, or take classes in a technical school, or fix computer hardware issues on all of the junky machines inside the stark prison walls. Again, systematic and predictable. Comfortably numb might even come to mind if one were to work at it real hard, focus a little. But then again, no matter where he went, the fear would be right there with him, intimate like that damned neighbor you can't stand. Fear like a throbbing appendage, terrorists and natural disaster, rednecks and the government, or death itself maybe, or of suffocation or being trapped under a collapsing structure or overall obsolescence in general.

Does a person really ever change?

Peter hadn't seen his father in nearly twenty years, the crazy old bastard with his Army-issue Colt .45 and beer-belly. Peter rummaged his mind for anything good to hang onto about the old man but could only see his thinning, graying hair back then and the way he spoke with that manufactured, thin confidence in his vain attempt at masking a life of regret.

Peter stood at the line as the sergeant gathered the plastic bags that contained the remaining items that he hadn't sent to Fr. Ligero. Peter had been allowed to change into a pair of jeans, some white socks, and a white t-shirt, along with his black DOC boots before his final exit processing. The cop behind the window prodded each bag, subsequently checking the sheet in front of him. Jesus, they must have an underground bunker full of these guys to work the prisons of America, Peter thought. They all look the same, talk the same, and have the same red, pasty tint to the surface of their flesh as if they might just pop if they ate one more pork rind or had to pop one more out-of-line punk with the silly stick before lights-out.

Peter wondered if the suit that Grammie had bought him still fit. He could almost smell the wrinkled, musty mess inside the plastic bag from the other side of the thick glass. The once-designer suit looked like moldy roadkill in a miniature body bag. The cop gathered all four of the personal property bags and slid the clipboard through the slot in the scratched, bullet-proof window.

Peter reached for the ledge so that he could sign the property paper.

"You can step up now, cowboy."

"Thanks," Peter said.

Peter signed the paper, pushed the clipboard back through the window, and stepped back. The cop crammed the bags through the long, narrow slot in the window toward Peter.

"You need bus tokens to get to town?"

Peter shook his head 'no' and then grabbed his belongings from the ledge. "Enjoy the world out there," the cop said and laughed. "If you can still recognize it, ya know?"

Peter remained silent for a moment longer, looked at the remainder of his life in his hands, and finally looked back up to say, "Yes, sir. Thank you," and walked down the orange line, to the thick security door that slowly buzzed open as he stood there before it like an eager, yet out-of-place child, staring out the back door into the pitch-black night.

Peter walked down the next concrete hallway, the same one he would walk down to go to the recreation yard, and came to another door and waited for it to open.

As he walked through the door, he noticed an officer's outline up ahead, waiting by the door separating him from the outside world. Peter could tell by the officer's pear-shape who it was and laughed to himself at the fact that he and the guy didn't get along too well and that he could be crossing that particular guard's path for the last time, in fact. Peter felt a pang of premature longing as he approached the guard. Not for the guard himself, probably, but for that familiar day-to-day, as he now plodded into something so very unfamiliar. Peter's knuckles turned white, clutching the plastic bags.

"Outta here, finally?" the guard said, bowing out his chest, the shadow around him receding to show his puffy, pink face.

"Yes, sir," Peter said and shook the guard's hand. The guard smiled as if he'd been waiting all those years to show that he actually had a heart. "I won't miss any of you guys, though."

"Ah, shit, son. I watched you through the best years of your life. You gonna miss me, alright. I'll be looking for that Christmas card."

"You do that," Peter said and then looked straight ahead as the next door began to open.

"Dernovish."

Peter took his eyes off of the widening door, looked back at the guard, and said, "Yeah?"

"I'm sorry you had to spend the prime of your life in here. That's tough, kid."

"Sarge, I ain't hit the prime of my life yet."

"Alright, Dernovish," the guard said, laughing now. "I hope you get it done out there. It's pretty good, ya know?"

"I'm gonna find out...take care," Peter said and walked out into the bright, summer sun. No pomp, no press, just him, his cane, and his bags, out onto the sidewalk, leading to the friendly side of all that razor-wire.

Peter hugged the bags to his chest, went through two successive security gates, and stopped at the little booth on the inside of the last razor-wired fence.

The little lady in the booth slid another clipboard through another slot in yet another scratched-up slab of bullet-proof glass. Peter looked at the paper and found his name. The deputy didn't look up at him. She kept her eyes on the clipboard, and the remainder of what looked like a blueberry muffin in her hand, as if someone might snatch them right out her hand, had she taken her eyes off of them for one split second. Peter said, "Thank you," and pushed the clipboard back through the slot. "Good luck," she said and turned to buzz the gate open, never making eye contact.

Peter walked through the gate like a dream, head buzzing, hands tingling. He ambled a couple steps further out onto the road that led away from the prison grounds. Then, as if the weight of the moment had just been given gravity out of the blue, him finally arriving within the earth's atmosphere, he fell to his knees and kissed the ground, crying. Crying for all the years that had drifted like curls of smoke out and away from him. Mourning…elation.

Groans poured from his belly and out into the hot Oklahoma wind. He poured sweat and snot and tears like a crazy hot rabid baby. He kicked the ground, and slapped the ground, and writhed a little bit, this way and that, until he had gotten it all out, for the time being.

Peter lay splayed at the edge of the road, settling down a touch. Any passer-by might have thought that he had just been mugged or bludgeoned, perhaps, the way he kind of rocked back and forth, spread-eagle and slightly dug into the ground.

He stared at the sky for a moment longer, totally still now, and then closed his eyes and breathed the summer air in. He didn't ever want to see a concrete floor again. No painted lines or bars or cafeteria trays. He opened and closed his eyes a few times, as if he had just regained sight - his slight little way of tempting reality, just to make sure that he had indeed landed on the outside of those prison confines, once for all.

Peter gingerly gathered himself, scooting back away from the little muddy spot of drool and tears where he had just wallowed. He opened one of the Ziploc bags and pulled out his old Timex.

The thing hadn't kept on ticking, but he put it on just the same, loving the feel of cool metal on his achy wrist. The time read 8:02, but the second hand had stopped somewhere in the last eighteen years.

Peter closed the bag and got to his feet. He looked out over the rolling plains dotted with cattle and oil rigs.

He had looked out onto those fields every day that he had gone outside for recreation. All but the rainy spring and autumn days when they had to stay inside and clean the kitchen. No fence now.

No more reminders of his captive bad choices.

The sound of the blowing wheat and ragweed slowly gave way to the rumble of a car engine in the distance, coming in waves like breeze itself. Peter could see a black dot on the horizon get larger as the sound of the engine's crescendo mounted about.

Peter looked at his watch. 8:02.

He sat his bags down on the ground, took the watch off, wound it up until it would wind no more, and threw it out into the field across the road, where the cattle had come closer to the fence, grazing and swishing tails. The cows looked indifferently at him as if they had no use for the broken watch, chewing their cud, biding cow time. The noise of the natural gas engines on the oil pumps clung to the gusts of wind to and fro, up and down. The noise climbing and falling like so many locusts in the trees, as the engine of that black BMW M5, rumbled over it all, pulling right up next to Peter and stopping abruptly.

Chapter 2

Peter felt as if he floated down that old highway, surrounded by the kind of silence you feel in the wake of a loud explosion.

Everything passing by in slow motion, under an ubiquitous haze of amber light. The subtle vibration of rubber on the road swirled inside his stomach as he sat back, staring into the dusty heat. Peter closed and opened his eyes a couple times to make sure that he wasn't dreaming. Outside, the Indian paintbrushes left streaks of bright red-orange up the sides of the ravines that ran along the highway, rising into the vast golden plains that stretched to the end of the earth, under the promising blue sky. A swath of blue and gold, majestic in its simplicity, swallowed up everything Peter had ever known.

"Boy, we're gonna have a good time! Do you like fishin'? I like fishin'. I mean, a real man likes to hunt and fish, ya know?"

Peter didn't really have an opinion one way or the other about fishing or hunting.

Being five years old, his desires and dislikes were few. All he knew right then was that he didn't know where and when his mom had run off.

Peter already had issues with her leaving, being flighty in general, and the thought of her bailing on him was enough to make his stomach ache even more than the van ride.

"You don't talk much, do you, boy?"

Peter shook his head a little.

"We'll get that straightened out too."

Peter thought that he heard words come out of his father's mouth, but that road kept humming below, haunting him from beneath like some subversive act of cruelty bubbling up to the surface.

"Where are we going?" Peter said.

"Fishin'."

They drove for hours on end like that. Peter's eyelids became heavier as he sat in dull wonder, listening to his dad's stories about people that he'd never met, the sound of the transistor radio fading in and out of reception through curls of static. Peter sporadically jerked out of his imminent slumber to look down at the radio to make sure that it was still propped up against the engine compartment between the front seats. Still good…check.

The weight of sleep hovered over him until he finally slipped into a short-lived dream, where he and his mom were riding in the back seat of a black Camaro, laughing, with the wind in their hair, like slow-motion, dreamy and movie-like. The folks in the front seat were talking loudly over the music, and smoking cigarettes and drinking out of red plastic cups. The driver spontaneously belted out the lyrics to the song on the radio, and then stopped to spark up a shouting conversation again. Peter didn't know what lucidity meant, but he knew that he was in a dream and that he liked it.

A rough, rutted road jarred Peter out of his little impromptu escape into the great unknown. He rubbed the heaviness off of his eyelids. A preacher ranted on the radio like a man yelling at a bunch of unruly boys tearing up the living room. Darkness surrounded the van like a storm as Peter sat up tall, trying to see over the dusty, metal dashboard. The road, two dirt tire tracks made from previous vehicles, stretched out in front of the van into the blank, black night. The grass hump in the middle of the tire tracks scraped beneath the panel-van, headlights fighting to cut through the darkness.

"Where are we?" Peter said.

"A fishin' hole."

Peter imagined that every word his father spoke was a variation on the word "fish," as if the old man had come up with his own language, simply utilizing that one simple noun to satisfy his limited communicative needs.

"You alright over there, boy?" Verlin said. *Fish, fish, fishing, fisherman, fish-ity, fish, fish...*and on and on like a blathering madman on sabbatical from giving a damn.

They came to a stop, and Verlin turned the lights off and then the motor.

Peter could feel his dad looking at him in the darkness. Peter thought that the gaze didn't feel like the warm eyes of affection of Grammie's as he awoke from his afternoon naps back home. He couldn't see his father sitting next to him because the black in the van seemed to have spilled in from the black outside. No dash lights, no moonlight.

"This damned preacher don't know shit about shit," Verlin finally said in the dark.

"Do you have a flashlight?"

"Ya scared, boy?"

"No," Peter said, feigning his best manly tone. He squinted out of the passenger window. "What's that sound?"

"Them's cicadas, boy." A bright wedge of light shone in between the boy and his father. After a second or two, Peter's eyes adjusted, and he noticed that his dad had an uneasy, serious look on his face. "Are you having fun yet?" the old man said.

"Sure."

Peter didn't want his dad to feel bad because he could tell that the old man was really trying hard to make him feel comfortable. He tried too hard, though, Peter thought. A father shouldn't have to think so much around his son, shouldn't be so damned self-conscious. Peter guiltily looked over at his dad and forced a smile. The old man didn't smile back. Peter looked down at the floorboard, at the radio, and then back up at his dad, feeling that floating sensation overcome him once again. As if the tension of the moment had somehow forced him out of his body, where he floated, looking at a mere rendition of himself, a much older version, full of piss and fear and doubt.

The man on the radio carried on about how everyone has the power of God at their disposal if they only go to Him for their solace and answers. The crackle of the radio is like some otherworldly transmission.

Verlin reached down and turned the radio off. "That's about the stupidest fuckin' thing I ever heard, boy," Verlin said.

"Let's go, gitter done."

"Okay." Peter didn't really want to leave the van, but he figured that he should be safe enough with his dad.

Verlin went to the back of the van and opened the side-by-side doors. The creak of the hinges was somehow familiar in a distant way. Peter felt good about that familiarity and stumbled his way to the back of the van.

The dusty, oily smell back there reminded Peter of his grandpa's garage. Peter could see him out there on Saturday afternoons, tinkering around with random parts and odd gadgets, fixing everyone's broken stuff under the bright florescent shop lights he had hung from the ceiling on rusty chains.

The beam from Verlin's flashlight bounced around in the back of the van. A Yamaha motorcycle stood in the center of the floor, strapped securely to the interior walls. There were two toolboxes and neat little stacks of wire in the corner near the doors. On the other side, near the back doors, there was an old Indian blanket covering a heap of something. Peter wondered what was under the blanket but didn't want to bug the old man while he rummaged for his gear. Large, red metal gas cans lined both sides of the van walls. Peter's dad shined the light further back into the van and grabbed a tackle box and three fishing poles that lay on the floor, and handed Peter the tackle box as he started to shut the doors.

"Verlin," Peter said.

"Dad.

I'm your dad, boy," Verlin said.

"You understand, son?"

Peter nodded that he did understand. "What're all those red tanks?"

"Fuckin' rag-heads, boy."

Peter nodded as if he understood as if his dad's ethnic slur had made perfect sense to him. He tried to see out into the darkness to make sure there weren't anymore 'rag-heads' running through the woods carrying large, red tanks, doing God-knows-what.

What Verlin meant in his own special way by "fuckin' rag-heads" is that OPEC was responsible for having imposed an oil embargo on the U.S. back in October of the previous year and that he had to stock up on fuel for his little road trip, because fully relying on gas stations for fuel needs wasn't the surest way of getting to where you had to go at the time. Most gas stations had a ten-gallon limit per day, some were totally out, and most didn't even sell gas on Sundays.

"I know I haven't been around much, but I've been busy...and your mom don't like me too much, I guess." He shut one of the doors, put the last of his fishing gear on the ground behind him, and then shut the other door.

Verlin turned to shine the light out in front of them as they followed the fuzzy beam through the pitch-black. The beam bounced up into the rustling trees above and then way out ahead over the still water. That black water, like the black night, felt lifeless and lonely but hopeful in a weird way. After perusing the area, Verlin lowered the light to shine out in front of them, so that they didn't trip over a rock or fall into a hole.

"Are we gonna go home soon?"

"We just got here. Anyway, we have a long drive tomorrow, so I think we'll just camp here tonight. Ever been campin'?"

Peter shook his head 'no.' He didn't really want to start that night either, but decided that he didn't want to protest more than he didn't want to camp. Peter squinted hard, trying to bring something out there in the black night into focus, but to no avail, as he thought about the bugs and the rain and the dirt. Not to mention the 'rag-heads.'

"Fishin's better at night."

"Really?"

Peter didn't know the difference between a catfish and a dogfish, night or day.

He sat on a rock near the edge of the water, settling his tackle box down next to the poles. The weight of the night had begun to lift a little as Peter sat near the pond listening to the wind tousle the leaves above, tiny little waves splashing against the grassy shore of the pond. The cicada's buzzing drone faded in and out like the sound of the static on the transistor radio had earlier. Peter took deeper breaths as his heart began to beat more slowly.

Just as he started to feel comfortable in his own skin, however, a rotten odor flooded his nose and mouth like road-kill. He started to gag on the offensive smell.

"Gross!" Peter pinched his nose off. "What is that?"

"Stink bait, boy!"

Peter thought that the stuff had been appropriately named, for sure. Nothing had been more fittingly named in all of God's good creation. Birds, check.

Cow, check. Fish of the sea, check. Stink bait, yes! Brilliant!

The big guy upstairs had most likely said to himself.

Verlin shined the light on the plastic container of pink-orange balls that looked like chunks of clay. He put a ball on his hook and then handed Peter the container. Peter held the container out at arm's length and quickly put the lid back on.

"Here." Verlin grabbed one of the poles on the ground, pulled the line taught, and took the hook between his thumb and forefinger. "Get a piece of bait, and I'll show you how to bait your hook."

Peter balanced the plastic container on his leg, slowly taking the lid off.

He held his breath and pinched a little ball of the bait out of the cylinder, which he quickly tried to give to his dad, but the old man said, "No, you put it on."

"That thing's sharp."

"Come on, be a man."

Peter grabbed the hook at the end of the line and began to push it through the soft ball of stink bait very slowly.

"Oww!"

A shiny bead of blood percolated on Peter's fingertip as Verlin shone the flashlight where Peter had been working with his hook.

The bait fell from Peter's leg and into the dark grass underneath him.

"Dammit, son! Watch what the hell you're doin'! That shit's not free!" Verlin said with a violent excitement and quickly got up off of the tree stump that he'd been sitting on. "You're off to a really bad start, son. That's bad luck to dump the bait on your first fishin' trip. Ya know that, boy?!"

Verlin took the flashlight and went to the van. He came back with a small ice chest and put it down on the ground next to where Peter sat wiping his hands on his jeans. Verlin stood up straight, smoothing back his greasy hair, and lit a cigarette. Verlin then got down on the ground on his hands and knees next to Peter. "Come on, ya little shit," Verlin said. "Help me pick up your fuckin' mess, will ya?"

Peter didn't really remember his dad from before. He had left some years earlier when Peter was about two or three years old. He did, however, remember or recall how to be still and quiet in the face of potential disaster. His mom had taught him well, and he had been the unwitting student. The tools had been laid at his feet. Knowledge and survival.

Chapter 3

"I can't believe this is finally happening," Peter said.

Perky sat back on the couch, reading a collection of poetry by Sylvia Plath.

Peter couldn't stand Sylvia Plath.

Not what it did to Perky anyway.

She would read those beautifully dark and hopeless poems aloud and then ask what he thought of them.

"That's good," Peter would say. "You didn't even listen, did you?" Perky would invariably press. "That's a nice one," he always assured her. Sure, he felt a bit romanced by the delicate despair of Plath's poetry, right up to the point of too personally identifying with that despair, after which he had nothing to say but a deflated, "Yeah, that's great, honey."

Perky always had to remind him that her friend Neider thought that she read beautifully. She told Peter that he just didn't appreciate her and that Neider was the one who believed in her artistic abilities. "Neider's a nihilist, Perky. He doesn't believe in anything," Peter would have to remind her after yet another weak and thinly veiled attempt at getting under his skin. "He's your drug dealer, anyway. Come on."

As far as artistic abilities, any grade-schooler can read a damned book out loud, he thought. Whenever the Plath debacle took place, Peter not giving her appropriate kudos and such, that is, she would usually end up storming off to their bedroom, sobbing uncontrollably, throwing herself onto their oversized bed. That not-so-delicate despair.

"I haven't seen my dad since I was a kid," Peter said from where he stood over the couch, his tie undone and his belt dangling.

He sat down on the couch next to Perky, her body in the process of slowly being swallowed up by the saggy, greedy cushions.

"Why do you have to wear that suit all the time?"

"I haven't seen him in years," Peter said again and got up to walk over to the hallway mirror. "And I don't think that went so well. I don't really remember much about him, except that he was a little crazy...bi-polar, sort of." Peter glanced at Perky in the mirror.

Peter began to feel a little cloudy-headed as he spoke from the hallway. Peter had quit smoking pot the year before, trying to clean up his act for the military, and there sat Perky, puffing away oblivious to anyone but herself and her sad sap poetry.

Peter couldn't go to college without money and without being a minority, so he figured the military would be the next right step for his future. He knew that his dad had been in the Army, and he couldn't wait to share the good news with the old man. Peter had experienced a fair amount of success working with Perky's dad in the B and C credit racket, but he wanted more out of life than selling shitty loans to none-the-wiser people who were buying overpriced, dilapidating houses, which would probably be lost anyway, once the first balloon payment was due.

"Do you want to go with us?" Peter said to Perky as he put the finishing touches on his tie.

The question felt forced, a bit awkward, as he began to get a little edgy knowing that his dad could show up at any given moment. Peter didn't want him to walk in the door, Perky smoking weed with her dreary book in hand. He walked over to the couch, hooking his belt, as he stood over her, waiting for some recognition in any form. A *"Fuck you"* or a *"How do you do?"* would have been sufficient, at any rate. Perky continued to sit, ignoring his presence, as if he were a not-so-bothersome fly in the periphery.

Eventually, she looked up and said, "Okay.

What? Do you need something?"

"Do you want to go with us?"

"Come on, Pete." She put her book face down on the wobbly coffee table, got up from the couch, and went to the bedroom. She came back out of the room with a cellophane from a cigarette pack in her hand.

"Here." She handed him several little blue pills. Ten milligram diazepam, for the nerves.

"Thanks," Peter said, blankly looking at the cellophane in his hand, like a young boy getting clothes on Christmas.

Peter went to the kitchen, got a beer, popped the top, and chased two of the pills down for good luck. He sat the beer bottle down on the counter and accidentally tipped it over the edge, startled from the loud, rapid knock on the front door.

He grabbed the air freshener from under the sink and the dish towel hanging from the stove handle. He threw the dish towel over the little puddle on the floor and went into the living room to spray the Lilac Fresh Scent, hoping that his dad wouldn't smell the pot smoke in the air.

Peter lit two cigarettes and gave Perky one as she lay indifferently on the couch, reading her Plath again, becoming one with the cushions. Peter slowly walked to the front door, staring at Perky over his shoulder, hoping she'd just look up and smile at him, but she kept her nose buried in the book as he answered the door.

Peter turned the doorknob, nervous to see who was on the other side of the door. He knew that his dad would be standing there sure enough but flirted with the idea that it was just the mailman, or maybe Grammie, who often liked to come by unannounced.

"Damn, boy," Verlin said as Peter opened the door.

"You're a skinny little shit, ain't ya?"

Peter stared at his dad for a second and then said, "Yeah...come in." Peter stood in his dad's way, looking at him as if he were an old missing friend who had recently come back from the dead to say hello.

"Ya goin' to a funeral or somethin'?"

Peter thought that his dad's good cheer and seeming familiarity felt awkward, like shoes on the wrong feet or unanticipated sarcasm. The discomfort passed quickly.

"Maybe...I guess..." Peter said as he moved over to let his dad come into the living room, Perky still reading her dreadful book.

Keep it light, Peter. There could be no talk about the years that had passed– the birthdays and Christmases, all of those Little-League games that had been missed.

Everything in the apartment silently crystalized in Peter's field of vision, as if his life were caught in a sculpture or a portrait of a sculpture rather, the anticipation of meeting his father still palpable in the air, even though the man stood right before him in the flesh as real as the day.

Peter's dad laughed nervously and stepped into the silence, scanning the living room, as Perky finally sat up on the couch and pulled herself together. She put her book back on the coffee table, suddenly standing up to hug Peter's estranged father. Verlin hugged her back firmly, smiling.

"Verlin McDash," he said to Perky as he pulled his head back to look at her.

Perky laughed and patted Verlin on the arm, as she pulled away.

When Verlin quit ogling at Perky, Peter leaned into him to get a hug too, but Verlin quickly stepped back and stuck his hand out.

"Do it like a man, son."

Peter shook his dad's hand, breaking eye contact.

"You look good," Peter said, looking up again, not knowing what else to say. He hadn't seen the guy in years. He could have looked like a dumpy replica of the guy he had seen so many years before, for all Peter knew. Small-talk and niceties sometimes have their place.

"Shit, fatter'n balder's all." There was something melancholy and remiss about the old man's bravado, like he'd been rehearsing what to say the entire trip to Peter's house, yet had forgotten his lines under pressure, only to rely on the old bullshit banter that he'd always known how to throw around. Peter wanted the old man so badly to be the hero that he needed. That rogue celestial body that would come into Peter's life and sweep all of the mundane over the edge, giving Peter a chance at something new and meaningful.

Some perspective, perhaps.

"Are you hungry?" Peter said.

"Let's get the hell outta here, boy."

Peter's stomach fell back into place. A change of pace. A new setting with sunlight and air and noise is what Peter needed to help him take it all in. Somewhere outside of he and Perky's claustrophobic little house, where nothing changed, and nobody but Grammie and Neider came or went on any regular basis.

"Do you need anything while we're out?" Peter said to Perky.

"Get some beer," she said, her nose still in the book.

"Just like his old man," Verlin said, slapping Peter on the back. "I should'a known."

"Yeah. Hold on a second," Peter said and went to the kitchen. He got into the cookie jar where Perky kept her stash of pot. He put a couple pinches in a baggy that he got from the drawer below and put Perky's bag back in the jar. He opened another drawer and grabbed one of her little pipes that she had hidden behind the spatulas and wooden spoons. Just in case he got cornered and stranded in a bad spot, he thought. Something to further take the edge off. Peter grabbed a couple beers from the fridge and walked back out to the living room.

"Okay, let's go. Bye, babe." He grabbed his blazer from the back of the chair and shook free any random cat or dog hairs.

Perky looked up at Peter from her book with a forced grin, like she had misgivings regarding his reaching into the cookie jar, but only said, "Have fun," putting her book up again, as the guys walked out the front door.

Peter was closing the door when Verlin patted him on the back a little too hard for his liking and said, "Whattaya think?"

Peter turned and followed Verlin out to the old man's white, 1953 Chevy pick-up. A beautiful specimen. "Totally restored," Verlin added proudly, like he'd just shown off a picture of his first-born.

"Nice."

They got in either side, and Verlin started the engine. He pushed the gas pedal a couple times and looked over at Peter to gauge his reaction.

"Sounds good, don't she?"

"It does."

The red vinyl interior smelled rustic, like a dusty Western store. The spotless interior felt good to a fellow anal-retentive. Peter realizing his penchant for severe cleanliness didn't fall too far from the tree.

"I'm gonna get you one of these," Verlin said.

"What do you think about that?"

"Sounds good."

"You didn't have to go and get all dressed up for me, son."

"Gotta look good for potential business."

"I ain't never had no job with a suit," Verlin said. "Shit, I've only had three jobs my whole life."

Peter couldn't imagine how someone could have only had three jobs in their lifetime. Especially someone Verlin's age. He had to be pushing fifty. Peter had already lost count, and he wasn't even twenty-five years old. The mere thought of staying somewhere longer than a year or so made him squirm in his seat.

Verlin and Peter drove for a while, neither one knowing what to say to the other, an awkward silence wrapped in ongoing questions.

Familiar places passed by like old memories. Peter quietly stared at his dad's profile. The man had materialized out of nowhere on a whim. Peter caught himself looking in the side mirror and then staring at the side of his dad's face again. Peter stuck his head out the window and scrunched his mouth up to make it look more like Verlin's, and then pulled his head back into the truck and stared at his dad again.

"Damn, boy, how old are you now?" Verlin finally said.

"Twenty-three." The number hung in the air a quick minute. Peter had to shake the feeling that his dad's questions were coming from somewhere outside the truck, from another time altogether.

"You look pretty good, boy."

"Thanks."

They pulled up in front of a house on Twelfth Street.

"Remember this place?"

"Aunt Bitty?"

Verlin slapped the seat between the two of them and smiled. "Come on, let's go inside."

Peter opened his door and stepped out onto the sidewalk. The light was a golden oblique like Fall had just occurred all of a sudden. A solar eclipse? Clouds gathering above? And then Peter suddenly remembered the pills he'd popped at the house and how sedatives dim everything a little bit. The whole point, Peter thought, embracing the warm whim of the sensation, feeling safe in his protective little psychological coating.

Peter followed his dad up to the front door of the faintly familiar house, perusing the clear blue sky above, smiling to himself and the bulging shrubbery. The soft edges of life becoming more enjoyable with each step further.

"Grandma!" Peter said, moving quickly past his dad to the porch. Grandma was his dad's mom, better known as Grandma McDash.

"Peter," she said. "It's been way too long."

"Little shit, huh?" Verlin said, coming up behind Peter.

"You look real good, Peter," Grandma McDash said as another familiar face came up from behind her.

"Is that Peter?" the other woman said.

"Aunt Bitty!"

Grandma McDash released Peter so that he could bend to give the other woman a big hug too.

"You guys get in here outta that heat," Bitty said, holding Peter out by both arms like an oversized baby.

"You boys want something to drink?"

"We got a twelver in the truck," Verlin said as they all went in through the front door.

Verlin stopped next to Peter, giving him friendly elbows and a goofy grin.

Grandma McDash looked at Verlin and sighed. She looked tired for a moment but then quickly brightened, turning to Peter. "Do you still live here in town?"

"I just came back not too long ago."

"My lands. You sure look nice in that suit. What are you all dressed up for."

"He's a big-timer now," Verlin said.

"I'm just trying to look nice for my dad."

"Well, isn't that a sweetheart?" Aunt Bitty said.

Peter looked down at the ground, a little embarrassed by his own B.S.

Aunt Bitty stood behind Peter's grandma, beaming like the Pope had just come to visit. Aunt Bitty was one of the warmest, kindest ladies Peter had ever known, and he hadn't seen her in too long, unfortunately. Actually, Peter hadn't seen either Aunt Bitty or his grandma since he was a kid, as if they had defected to some obscure land of refuge, far and away from any and all family drama.

Peter really loved those two women, but his mom said that they had just quit trying to get in touch after Verlin had been ordered to stay away from Peter and his mom through legal means. Peter's dad's dad, a cantankerous old detective, died when Peter was only three or four. Peter's grandma said she had remarried. A real nice man, she said. Someone who was good to her.

Verlin passed them all and went to the kitchen.

"Is there anything in here to eat," he said.

"Hold on, Verlin," Aunt Bitty said, smiling at Peter and then hesitatingly turning to go to the kitchen.

"Forget it," Verlin said, coming out of the kitchen, almost running over Aunt Bitty. "We've got cold beer to drink. We'll pick something up at The Hot Doggie."

"Oh, Verlin," Grandma McDash said. She looked at Peter with an earnest curiosity and smiled, putting out her arms, grabbing him by the hands. "Peter, I'm so glad to see you again."

"Me too," Peter said. The sweet, familiar smell of Aunt Bitty's house was a time machine.

The smell of must, butter-mints and fresh-baked dinner rolls couldn't be duplicated.

"Come on, boy, we got shit to do."

"Verlin!" Aunt Bitty said.

And just as quick as they came, they were leaving.

Peter scribbled his phone number down on a little pad that was on the end-table by the door and handed the whole thing to his grandma. "I love you two," he said, as he followed his father out the front door. "Bring him back, Verlin," Grandma McDash said.

"You hear?"

"Yeah, okay!" Verlin yelled halfway out to the truck.

When Peter got outside, Verlin told him that he could only handle a couple minutes of the old bitches rambling on and on and that they had better things to do than sit around and hold hands with fucking old ladies. Peter nodded, smiling to himself, wondering why in the hell they even stopped by Aunt Bitty's if they weren't going to stay for a while. Verlin started the truck, put it in gear, and squealed the tires, tearing away from the curb.

A few blocks down the street, they pulled up to the front of The Hot Doggie. The place was a drive-in burger joint that Peter had passed a million times but where he had never chosen to eat. Their reputation didn't really sell the place, but Peter was open to new ideas and didn't mind a free meal if nothing else.

"What do you want?" Verlin said.

"I'll take a cheeseburger with fries," Peter said.

"Everything?"

"Yeah."

"That's my boy. You need to put some meat on them bones. You don't work out, do you?"

"Sometimes."

"Yeah, right."

Verlin ordered the food, they waited in silence and then they ate when it came. When they were finished, Verlin lit a couple cigarettes and gave Peter one. Peter pulled a can out of the twelve-pack that was between them and popped the top. The sweat from the cold can felt good in his clammy hand. The light outside had become dimmer yet, Peter in his rounded, soft little head buzz.

"Gimme one of them," Verlin said.

Peter popped him a beer and they toasted low, so that the cops eating lunch in their cruisers across the parking lot couldn't see them.

"Fuckin' cops," Verlin said.

Peter looked over at the officers, not recognizing either of them. He didn't feel scared sitting there with his dad. The old man somehow legitimized Peter in some unexplainable way, as if being reunited with one's father somehow abolishes all of the petty little rules in life. Peter felt warm and cool at the same time. Comfortable.

"What do you want to do?"

"I don't know."

"Wanna go fishin'?"

Peter wasn't a fisherman, but he had been out a handful times just to pass the boredom with a couple friends. He remembered his dad liking to fish and thought that the time alone would be good. It could give them just enough to do around each other so that things didn't get too awkward.

"Let's just cruise around," Peter finally said.

"Sounds good."

Verlin started up his truck and pushed the gas a couple times, looking over at the cops, giving them a little wave. They slowly waved back, chewing their food, watching Verlin like an old shop merchant might watch some unruly street kids snooping in the aisles.

"Tax dollars hard at work," Verlin said, pulling out of the parking lot.

Peter sat back in his seat and smiled.

They drove down the back roads, the dirt roads, and all the others that Peter had never traveled before. He had lived in that town his whole life and had been out drinking beer on weekend afternoons with buddies, cruising away the day, but hadn't seen the places they saw that day. An old school house here, where the old man said *his* dad had gone to school. They passed a dilapidated church building. "Looks like God closed up shop there, boy."

Remnants of generations past. A time gone by when things were simpler and when families prayed together and stayed together through thick and thin. Back when people worked to live, not the other way around.

Peter killed his beer and threw the can in the bed of the truck.

Verlin pulled up in front of an old bait shop out in the middle of nowhere in particular. The dirty fluorescent poster board advertised, "BUD $6.99 12-pk," and "CAMEL LIGHTS cartons $12.99."

"They never have Coors on sale."

"Coors Original?" Peter said.

"Boy, when I started drinkin', there wasn't no light bullshit," Verlin said as if he were passing on some ancient wisdom that only lived in the canon of their family oral tradition.

Verlin got out of the truck and went into the store.

Peter got out and went behind the building, where he sat his cigarette on a rock and unzipped his pants to go pee.

Peter pulled the little baggy and pipe out of his pocket, loaded it, and took a couple deep hits as he relieved himself.

He knocked the burnt dregs out of the pipe when he was finished and put the pipe and pot back in his pocket after he zipped up. He picked the cigarette up off the rock and took a couple big drags to cover up the smell of the lingering marijuana smoke.

"Hey boy, good idea," Verlin said as he came around the corner, holding a brown paper bag in his arm, looking around to make sure the coast was clear. "They ain't got no pisser in there, boy."

"I had to go," Peter said, feeling light-headed.

"You smokin' weed, boy?"

"Hell no."

"Fuckin' hippies," Verlin said, looking around the place again as if a group of random hippies was strewn about in the bushes over by the old, rusty propane tank behind the convenience store. Stray pot-smokers from the fringe who had lost their VW bus in a dope deal gone bad.

Peter looked around, too, as he puffed on his cigarette. He didn't see anybody around. When all else fails, blame the hippies, he laughed to himself.

"You wanna go out to grandma's land and shoot a little bit?"

"Sure," Peter said, as his dad zipped up and they got back in the truck with fresh beer and cigarettes.

Chapter 4

Peter fell to the ground screaming after his dad opened the door again.

"Be quiet," Verlin said. "Come on boy, get up!"

The young boy continued to lay on the ground, crying and drooling all over himself. His smashed, swollen right hand made him feel nauseous and crazy inside.

Verlin told Peter that he was lucky his fingers didn't get cut off, sticking them in the hinge-edge of the door from the outside like he had. Peter didn't feel too lucky right then, slowly getting up, as the old man brushed his pant legs off.

"Come on, son, we'll get you fixed up," Verlin said and carried Peter up a damp sidewalk to the side of a brown clapboard apartment building.

"Where are we," Peter said, his sobs beginning to simmer to a mild whimper.

"A friend's house," Verlin said as they went around the back side of the building and came to a door. "Now, be quiet. I don't want this woman gettin' all fussed up."

Verlin knocked on the door and then looked around impatiently as if they had been waiting for hours.

A woman opened the door and smiled.

"Verlin," she said.

"Can we come in? Got a man down." She smiled and waved them in. Verlin sat Peter down and led him by his good hand. He told Peter to sit at the kitchen table as he went to the freezer and opened it. "Do you have any Popsicles?"

"No," the woman said.

"Will you get some ice for his hand?"

The lady took a rag out of a kitchen drawer, wet it, and went to the freezer to put some ice in it. She made a little bundle out of the wash cloth and ice and handed it to Peter, telling him to put it on his hand where it hurt and that it would make it feel better.

"Here." Verlin pulled some money out of his front shirt pocket and gave it to the lady.

"Will you get some beer and cigarettes too?"

"Did you guys eat dinner?"

"And some fuckin' Popsicles, alright?"

"Excuse me, Mr. Cranky," she said. "You still drink Coors?"

Verlin looked at the woman as if she had just asked him if he had a penis or a vagina.

"I'll be right back," she said, grabbing her purse and car keys from the Formica counter-top and left.

"It's cold," Peter said.

"Keep it on there, boy."

Verlin got up to rummage through one of the lady's cabinets for a minute and then pulled out a medicine bottle and tapped a couple pills out.

"Here you go, son."

"What is it?"

"It doesn't matter. Come on...and keep that ice on that hand. You want it to get better, don't you?"

"It hurts."

"You gotta be tough. Keep that ice on there."

Peter took the dark red capsules out of his dad's hand and put them in his mouth. Verlin went to the sink and poured Peter a glass of water, handed it to him, and then went to the other room. Peter took a slow, deliberate drink of the water and then looked around the apartment for telling pictures, board games, or toys lying about. Peter thought the place was too dark for kids to have lived there. The room smelled spicy, like his uncle's house. His uncle smoked a lot of cigarettes and burned a lot of incense 'to keep the bad spirits away,' he had always said. The woman's probably a hippy-like, his uncle, Peter thought.

"Are we going to the doctor?" Peter said when Verlin walked back into the room.

"No."

"I don't have to get a shot?"

"Your old man here's a doctor. I'm gonna fix you up and you won't even have to get any shots. How's them apples, huh?"

Peter looked down at the crude ice pack pressed against his throbbing hand. "Who's that lady?"

"A friend."

"She's pretty. Does she know mommy?"

Verlin laughed and then said, "I don't think so."

Peter pulled the ice away from his hand for a minute, but his dad told him to put it back on or that it would get worse, dammit.

After some time, Peter staring at the floor, and Verlin rummaging the place like a detective on a homicide scene; the door finally opened, and in walked the pretty lady. Verlin got up from the table and grabbed the brown paper bag from her arms before she had a chance to put it down on the counter, pulling the box of Popsicles out. He put the bag on the table, then opened the box and the wrapper to one of the frozen treats inside the box. "Here," he said, handing Peter a lime-green Popsicle.

"Hi there," the lady said to Peter. "Who is this little guy, anyway, Verlin?" she said, bugging her eyes out. "Are you going to introduce us, or what?"

"My son, Peter," Verlin said. "We're on vacation together."

"Sounds like fun." Peter nodded as the woman turned to him with a look of concern.

She looked down at his hand. "You poor dear. Does it hurt?" Peter nodded again.

Peter already felt better having the Popsicle.

His dad pulled three more out of the box and gave the lady one. "Here."

"I don't like Popsicles," she said.

"Just eat the damned thing," he said. "We're on vacation." Verlin opened the other two and quickly ate one, cold bite by cold bite. "Damn, these are cold."

"They're frozen," Peter said.

"Look at the little rocket-scientist," Verlin said.

"Do you want to go ahead and take care of yourself, there little Einstein? Huh? Since you know every damned thing in the world?"

"No, sir."

Verlin ate the second Popsicle a little more slowly, neither Peter nor the lady saying a word. The lady sucked on her treat gently, smiling at Peter between little bites off of the end. Peter smiled back at the lady as she looked at the ground and then back up to Verlin intently, as if she awaited her next set of instructions on how to care for the injured, maybe not even knowing what to do with the rest of her life.

"Are you guys about done?" Verlin said, slapping the tabletop with the palm of his hand.

"What's the big deal?"

"I need the sticks so that I can fix the boy's hand, Carla."

"Aren't you gonna take him to the emergency room?"

"He don't need no doctor. My old man used to fix our fingers with Popscicle sticks."

Verlin held his hand up for her to look at.

The woman gasped as if he had held up a bloody stump. None of Verlin's four fingers looked like the other. The index finger bent one way and the other three the opposite. They looked like the hands of a seasoned wide receiver, gnarly and crooked and covered in parched skin. Peter imagined some delirious old coot, bent over sweating under some crude hanging lightbulb in a basement somewhere, trying to tape some little sticks to his dad's hands when *he* had been just a little boy.

"Oh," Carla finally said, looking at Verlin's hand kind of sideways, like she didn't have the nerve to tell him his hand was not a good example of great orthopedic care.

"Don't worry, he's a tough one," Verlin said.

"Ain't that right, boy?"

Peter nodded.

"You have any medical tape?" Verlin said.

She went to the bathroom and came back with white medical tape in her hand. "Here. Are you sure you don't want me to take him?"

"Sit down."

Verlin picked up one of the Popsicle sticks and went to the sink to rinse it off. He held it next to Peter's index finger, then broke the stick off to be about the same length, and taped it to his finger lengthwise. Verlin went to the sink and thoroughly rinsed the other three sticks off.

"You'll get another one after we get done, okay?" Verlin said as he came back over to where Peter sat.

Peter nodded. Verlin got into the grocery bag and pulled out a can of Coors Original and a pack of Marlboro Reds. He popped the top and lit up.

"Could you get me an ashtray?" Verlin looked at Carla, who watched the whole ridiculous affair with an animated incredulity.

"Would it kill you to say please?"

"Pretty fuckin' please." Verlin stared at her, his face hard and insensitive, yet eventually softening, as if he realized that she wouldn't budge one bit, as she stood there staring at him pitifully. "Please, honey, my dearest compadre."

Carla left the room, and Verlin went back to work getting all of Peter's fingers taped up. Peter's pain had faded somewhere in between Carla leaving for the store and his dad's 'Please, honey…' Peter felt like he was in the middle of a lucid dream, but one of which the course could not be changed, one he couldn't awaken from. He watched his dad as he carefully taped the hand with the precision of a watchmaker. Every strip of tape and every little stick the appropriate length, leaving no extra, unnecessary pieces. The old man wasted no time on talk and coddling, focusing on the task at hand. The old man finished up and told Peter to lay down on the sofa.

Sometime later, Peter woke up in the dark. He rubbed his eyes with his smashed hand, life slowly creeping back into his consciousness, as a moaning sound came from somewhere around him in the dark. Peter stayed put. He felt a little sick, even scared a little, because of the return of that sharp pain accented by the dull thud of his pulse in his fingers. And that muffled moaning. He couldn't tell if it was inside or outside, whether it was night or day.

He thought it sounded like someone had a real bad stomachache. He wondered if they had the flu like he had last winter, not able to keep anything down, not even Sprite.

The moaning got louder for a few more seconds, to an inevitable crescendo, and then it stopped suddenly. Peter could see a faint outline of a lamp on a table next to the couch once his eyes adjusted. He tried to reach over and turn it on but knocked the lamp to the floor.

He slowly got up off of the couch and bent to pick up the light, even more slowly placing it back on the table, where he then turned it on.

When Peter's eyes adjusted to the light, he noticed that he was still in the strange woman's apartment. She came out of her bedroom in a robe. She looked like she had just gotten half way into the shower and then went to bed, and then had suddenly remembered to do something out in the living room, maybe a little flustered.

"Are you okay?" she said.

"Yes."

"How does your hand feel?"

"It hurts."

She went to the kitchen and came back, kneeling next to the couch where he lay. Her sweet and savory smell and thick blonde hair fell all around her.

She handed Peter some little orange pills. "Here, chew these up. I have them for my niece when she comes over and she's sick. They'll make the hurt go away."

"Thank you."

Peter felt better just having her next to him.

He could see inside her robe as she bent over him, her breasts large and smooth, with little sunspots dotting them all over. Carla noticed him looking down her robe and quickly pulled the top closed against her tan chest.

"Do you know my mommy?"

"No, honey, but I've heard a lot about her.

She sounds like a real nice lady."

"Where is she?"

"Hey, you guys, what's going on in here!" Verlin shouted as he came out of the bedroom in his underwear. "You feeling better, bud?"

Peter nodded 'yes.'

"Do you feel like another Popscicle?"

"Sure."

Verlin went to the kitchen and got Peter another Popsicle and some more ice for his hand. "Here you go, son."

Peter said thank you, put the ice on his hand and handed the Popsicle to Carla to open.

"We better get goin', son," Verlin said. "We gotta get back 'fore too long."

"Can't you leave in the morning?" Carla said, handing the Popsicle to Peter.

"Shit, woman. It is mornin'," he said and went into the bedroom. He came out a few minutes later, dressed and primed to go.

"Can we get some supplies for the road?

I don't have time to stop at the store."

"You just got here, Verlin."

"Yes," Verlin said, staring at Carla for a minute and then taking a cigarette from the pack in his waistband to light up. "I've gotta go load the bike up, can you help me?"

She got up from the side of the couch and went into the bedroom. She came back out wearing short shorts and an old Mississippi State football jersey.

Peter couldn't help but stare at her tan legs. His stomach felt funny as he watched her slip her sandals on by the front door.

Carla and Verlin went outside as Peter lay on the couch eating his Popsicle, staring at the front door that had closed behind them.

Peter could hear shouting coming from outside the apartment and wondered if they were fighting about him. He knew that his mom and dad used to fight about him all the time and that he was probably the reason they got divorced. Peter's mom always looked hurt and sad after his parents fought, and then his dad would just leave for a couple days, only to come back to more of the same shouting and madness.

Then came the fear.

Peter got up and got another Popsicle from the freezer and then went to the bathroom. He lifted the seat and went pee. He set the orange Popsicle down on the edge of the sink so that he could zip up.

He grabbed his half-eaten Popsicle and looked into the mirror. When he stuck out his tongue, it looked brown because he'd eaten a green Popsicle and then an orange one.

"Yuck."

He turned the light out, as a huge bang and a crash came from the front room. Peter stayed put, quickly turning the light back on and shutting the door. Before he could sit on the toilet, his dad started beating on the door.

"What're you doin' in there?! You better not be beatin' off, boy!"

Peter could hear Carla trying to calm the old man down but then heard a thud and a higher-pitched slam against the hallway wall right outside the bathroom. Peter pulled his knees to his chest, where he sat on the toilet, frozen solid, rigid with fear now. He noticed that he had started crying, rocking back and forth on the cold toilet lid, not knowing if he had been there a minute or a day.

Then, as if mounting pressure in the hallway had reached its limit, the door burst in, sending splinters and pieces of door trim toward Peter in slow motion. In that same moment, his dad had him by the collar, dragging him out into the hallway, through the dark living room, and out the front door.

Verlin held Peter's face right up to the gas tank of the motorcycle. "See that?!

That's what bad people do to hard-working people's stuff!" Verlin still held the gas cap in his other hand from when he had been outside just few minutes earlier. "They stuffed leaves in there!"

The motorcycle had been parked right outside the door of the apartment on the sidewalk after Verlin and Carla had gone for a late-night ride. "Dammit!

Fuckin' leaves!" Verlin let go of Peter's shirt and stormed back into the apartment.

"It's okay, Peter," Carla said, standing next to the front door, staring hard at where his dad had just gone. "He's just a little mad that someone vandalized his motorcycle."

"I didn't do it."

"Oh sweetie, I know, he's just a little mad."

Nevertheless, Peter almost felt like he did do it, that somehow he was responsible for someone else's vandalism. If the old man hadn't had to come get him and stop and doctor him up and go for a motorcycle ride to relieve the stress of the whole thing, the motorcycle would have been safe inside the van in the first place.

Peter glared at the side of the motorcycle, trying to suck up the tears from coming again, fighting it, bracing himself like a frigid walk in the rain. He didn't want to show his fear. He knew the danger that might bring as if he had suddenly been uploaded with some deep, intuitive knowledge from the depths of the collective unconscience. He remained silent as best he could, waiting for the storm to blow over, as he stared at the open gas tank, waiting for his dad to come back outside to put the cap back on.

"Really, honey, don't worry," Carla said again and went inside.

Chapter 5

At five years old, passing state lines is like going to some far away, exotic country for the first time. And time, yes time, is like a long, wide valley where only shooting stars could break the monotony of its repetitive expanse. They passed the sign for Arkansas, The Natural State…they drove over the biggest bridge expanding over the biggest river that he had ever seen…and then…he just realized, all of a sudden, that his mom sure had been gone for quite a while. She must have decided to stay out there in the country, hunting wildflowers by the lake, maybe getting some sun. Peter thought that he should have stayed with his mom, even though he hated hunting wildflowers. Vacation didn't seem to be all that great.

They traveled on another endless highway, yet shrouded by dense, dark green trees at that point. The Spanish moss clung to the branches like dusty green stalactites, hanging nearly to the ground, where their reflection rippled in the shimmering water at the sides of the road. For the most part, Peter had gotten used to the long, silent driving with his dad, in between the static on the radio and his father's tirades about Bible-thumpers and fuckin' sand-niggers and crazy, bra-burning kidnaped bitches.

There was no lack of entertainment via the news lately. Patty Hearst had been kidnaped from her apartment in Berkeley by some crazed hippies, the Arabs were putting the screw to the West, and the preachers and advertisements filled in the gaps where there was nothing else to report. Peter thought that his dad sure knew a lot about a lot of stuff. He had a lot to say about all of that stuff.

Peter stared at the radio on the floor that Verlin had turned off. He said that the news is all a bunch of bullshit anyway and that they needed to hear the sound of the road, the wind. That was good, boy.

Peter stared at the hole where the radio used to be in the middle of the metal dashboard. Peter imagined that some other vandal had stolen his father's radio when he had been inside the house. Peter tried to keep himself busy gazing at the reflections in the water on the side of the road. Light and shadow with the hum and wind.

"Son!"

Peter jerked in his seat, quickly looking over at his dad. "Yes, sir?"

"I like that boy," he said. "You have respect. You're a little light in your loafers, but dammit, you really know how to talk to your old dad," Verlin said and lit another cigarette.

"Where are we going?"

"We're almost there."

"Really?"

"You ask a lot of questions, boy." Verlin threw an empty cigarette pack out the window.

"You shouldn't litter," Peter said. Back home, Grammie would slap his hand if he threw candy wrappers out the window of the car. He knew better.

"That's bullshit, boy. This shit heap's gonna go up in fuckin' flames someday anyway," Verlin said, looking earnestly at Peter. More timeless wisdom. "Get with it, son!"

"What?"

Peter saw images of his house back home burning to the ground, large pieces of framing falling into the flames, sparks and debris flying, as the smoldering grass in the yard spread into large, blackening patches like tentacles. He could see the fields and trees consumed by an endless conflagration – the earth a hurling ball of fire, spinning into the bleak black of the universe.

"Never mind, son. We'll be there 'fore you can shake a stick."

Verlin reached down between them, one hand on the wheel, the other searching for the radio. Peter could hear the radio click on as Verlin tuned it to that familiar voice again, this time a little less static.

"Roland Stacks!" Verlin said, smiling. "That fucker thinks he's gonna save the whole damned world. I oughta shoot that bastard and save us all from *him*, ya know?"

Peter looked over to his dad, not knowing if it was a real question or not. Whether it was a question at all. If Peter had known what rhetorical meant, he might have believed the question to be so.

Nevertheless, he tried to gather the gumption to chime in on the old man's comment but couldn't quite muster the chutzpah that it took to stay in the ring with his dad.

"Jesus this, God's grace that," Verlin said.

"It's all a big line'a shit, if ya ask me."

Peter wondered why his dad listened to the preacher so much if he didn't like him. There were other things to listen to on the radio. Like Paul Harvey. That's what his grandparents back home always listened to. Peter liked Paul Harvey's voice. Familiar.

"Do you like Paul Harvey?"

"Can't stand the faggot, boy. You don't listen to that shit, do you?"

"Grammie does."

"Figures."

Peter didn't really know what that meant and just figured the conversation was over. Better safe than sorry.

It was getting dark outside when they turned onto a little dirt trail, almost like the one they'd driven on the other night, by the fishing hole. The trees and the smell of the air a little different, though. The live-oaks draped with Spanish moss were mingling with all of the tall pines. Fresh pine smell like when mom cleaned the bathroom at home, but better, lighter, and without that burn in the nose. Natural.

He thought that maybe they were still in the Natural State.

"Where are we?" Peter said.

"Home, for now."

Peter rubbed the inside of his hand, right below the fingers that were still taped to the Popsicle sticks. He thought that those things would be on there forever, browning tape and all. He tried to sit up tall to see over the dash, to see where they were going, but night had fallen as they tunneled through the thick, black trees.

Verlin stopped the van and turned the ignition off.

Peter thought that it seemed louder with the truck off, the cicadas chattering all around them, competing for the stage with Roland Stacks. *Do you know where you're gonna go when you die?* The man said through the radio.

"Come on, son," Verlin said and turned the radio off.

"Fuckin' Roland Stacks. I'll bet he's got stacks. Stacks'a money. That's all them billy-goats do all that yappin' for is money, ya know?" Verlin said, staring at Peter to make sure everything was registering properly.

Peter motioned to get his door open.

"Hold on, I'll get the door, boy." Verlin got out and went around to Peter's side of the van to open the door. "Come on boy, we don't got all day."

"Can you turn the lights on?"

"There ain't no lights."

They walked to the back of the van, where Verlin opened the side-by-side doors. "Here."

Verlin handed Peter a duffel bag, which he quickly let fall to the ground because of its surprising weight.

"Here." Verlin turned it on and handed Peter the flashlight.

"Thank you," Peter said as he turned the flashlight toward the old, dilapidated mobile home they were parked next to, streaks of green and brown mold and dirt running down the aluminum siding.

"Right here, come on," Verlin said, obviously irritated. Peter didn't want to make him mad again, so he quickly shone the light in the back of the van where Verlin continued to rummage around. "Right there...good...okay." Verlin moved the dusty Indian blanket off of the curious heap in the corner and grabbed a soft shotgun case and a couple boxes of shells.

"Let's go."

Peter felt a pang of fear and excitement at seeing what he knew was a gun inside the case. He didn't want to ask why they might need a gun, so he just let his imagination take over. A couple boxes of shells. Too many questions. It was time to be quiet and malleable.

They walked to the side of the trailer, where the wet grass grew up around the rusty skirting and over the bottom two steps going up to the door. Peter kept the light ahead of them lest he got yelled at again. He mustered all he had not to start complaining about the dark and the wet, the bugs and slime. The waves of cicada chatter, loud and soft, loud and soft, almost silent, then their aggressive crescendo again, like the yappin' of that preacher man on the radio.

"Can we go eat somewhere?"

"I got fish in the cooler, boy," Verlin said, opening the front door. "Come on.

I can't see where the hell I'm goin'."

Verlin grabbed the end of the flashlight and pointed it ahead of them to light the way.

They walked through the door, as Peter instantly got smacked by the stench of mold and gasoline. The place smelled sweet and musty, like a basket of rotting oranges, but scary in how overwhelming the sensation of it all felt in his throat and eyes.

"Dad!"

"What?"

"What's that smell?"

"Country, boy," Verlin said. "Why you always gotta go sniffin' everything? Come on. I'll show you where you're gonna sleep."

Peter had been in the country a lot before and had never smelled anything quite like that. He thought about riding horses at his uncle Lenny's in the heat and the dust, the wind nearly blowing him off his favorite old black mare.

"Dad, there's big roaches everywhere."

"Them's beetles, boy. They like it hot and wet, ya know?" Verlin started laughing out loud. "Get it, boy? Hot and wet?

Shit, son! You gotta lot to learn."

Peter stared at his dad's glowing profile as if he had just materialized out of thin air.

Peter followed his dad to the back of the trailer, where he stopped at a door in the hallway. Verlin opened the door and told Peter to shine the light in there.

"Boy, look down under that hot water tank and get that key."

Peter aimed the light beam at the scurrying beetles on the floor of the closet and then slowly moved the light from the bottom of the rusty, old water tank to the top of the tight quarters.

"Go on, boy. I need that key. Bend down real good, ya hear?"

Peter bent down once all of the beetles had cleared out of sight, slowly getting down onto his knees, where he could get a better look. All of a sudden, Peter felt a swift kick in the ass, and he fell into the closet, banging his head against the hot water tank, rust and grit falling into his hair and eyes and mouth from up above. Verlin shut the door and banged on it a couple times for good measure.

"Dad! Let me out!

Dad! Dad!" Peter banged on the door with his left hand, his good hand, but quickly stopped as he landed the side of his palm on a finishing nail that stuck out of the door.

He aimed the flashlight at his punctured hand, blood trickling out, but could barely see because of the rust that had fallen into his eyes from raising his head under that decaying hot-water tank.

Peter could hear his dad laughing on the other side of the door. Then breathing heavy.

Peter shined the flashlight at the door. There was just a small round plate where the doorknob should have been. He could see the little nail sticking out, shiny with his own blood.

"Oh, what, do you need your old man now?" he said.

"Is that it, boy? Your mommy's not here to save you now, is she? Well, you just sit tight. Don't want you runnin' off or nothin', got it?" Verlin walked down the hall and came back and put something up against the door. "There.

That should keep you safe in there, boy.

Don't you go messing with the door, ya hear?"

Peter slumped back against the cool metal of the rusted water heater, the air around him thick and gritty. Peter kept the light shining on the ceiling above in a tight, bright circle so that he didn't have to see the bugs that probably crawled all around him where he sat. Peter could hear his dad working to get gulps of air on the other side of the door again as if he had been holding his breath until he could tell that Peter was safe and secure inside the closet.

Peter began to cry quietly, nevertheless, not wanting to provoke his dad to further anger. Peter didn't move and didn't beg but just listened to the slowing tempo of his dad's ragged breaths from outside the little closet. Then, just as Peter had found a little comfort in the calming repetition of his dad's slowing breaths, Verlin began to walk back down the hallway toward the front door, where Peter assuredly knew that his dad would take his leave.

Peter heard some banging around in what must have been the kitchen. Then silence.

Then noise again, and then it got silent for a good minute while Peter focused on the spot of light on the ceiling. He could see particles floating in the air through the beam of light.

Peter began to panic, his breath thick and his chest dense with tension. He honestly thought that his short life had run its course. Five short years of confusion and wonder, leading to such a dismal end, right there in that filthy little closet, in a shitty trailer, out in the middle of God-knows-where. Where was God now, he thought. The one with all the beloved children and all that happy crap that he had heard repeatedly about in parochial school.

Peter tried to imagine what Roland Stacks looked like. Probably a fat, sweaty man, up on a stage somewhere telling everyone what they should and shouldn't do so that they could get to heaven. *Do you know where you're gonna go when you die?*

Peter didn't want to die. He didn't want to go anywhere but home. He wanted to see his mom and grandparents and nice people, normal and happy. People that seemed to love him despite his stupid mistakes.

Peter imagined his dad rummaging in the drawers and cabinets to find the gnarliest, most grotesque butcher knife available.

Peter knew his dad would come right back to the water heater closet and gouge his liver out with that damned thing, twisting it in his belly, hypnotized by his own handiwork, the glimmer of the blood, until Peter had given his last futile resistance under the old man's cold anger. Peter had dreamt about such things.

Stabbings in dreams are surreal, to say the least.

First, there's that dull tension of the actual entrance wound, which lingers like swelling beneath the skin, spreading outward, folding over and into itself, creating a thickening sensation with each passing second, until eventually, you become comfortable with the reality that your bodily tissue has indeed been mutilated. Then, right when you think all is well, that you've lucked out somehow, that you are recovering without issue, you feel the slow draining of your life seeping from you in the form of a warm pool of blood, below where you lay, soaking your pants, horrifying, yet warm and comfortable like an opiate haze. But then it's comfort, then warmth, then the light...and then you awaken.

Verlin's footfalls traipsed back to the closet, where Peter held still in near shock.

"Boy, I think we have a little pest problem." Verlin stood on the other side of the door for a long minute, and then, as Peter imagined the door bursting in on top of him, leading to his inevitable death, he heard a hissing sound come from the bottom of the door. It wasn't until Peter shined the light toward the hiss and saw the stream coming in under the door that he realized it was roach spray.

That sweet-acrid chemical smell, which can almost be enjoyed in small, fleeting doses, somewhere outside, with a slight breeze. But in tight, closed-off quarters? Not so nice.

But there it came, ounce after choking ounce of the deadly aerosol, to the point of Peter's lungs beginning to seize, his thighs tightening as he braced himself in that small space.

"Dad, quit it! Dad!"

"Calm down, son, I'll get rid of them roaches," Verlin said in mockingly good spirits. "Just relax. Don't be such a party-pooper."

Peter covered his face with the collar of his dirty shirt, moving his head as far back from the door as possible, that devious hiss persisting. "Dad," Peter said, losing heart, but knowing that he had to fight until he could free himself, that hiss slowing, slowly...until...steadily and more slowly...Peter...fell...asleep.

The next morning, Peter woke up with a sore throat and dying of thirst. He sat up as the pins and needles burst into life through his legs and butt. A sliver of light slipped under the door, so he knew it must have been morning or daytime anyway. Peter began stretching out, but the confines of the room were not permitting. He had been crammed in the closet all night long, more rust and dirt in his eyes upon awakening.

A dim hue of yellow light glowed from the end of the flashlight that lay between his legs. Peter picked the light up and shook it. He'd seen someone do that before to get the light a little brighter.

No such luck. At that point, he fully realized that the night before wasn't a dream or a nightmare rather and that he had actually been put in the water-heater closet against his will. Peter's eyes became thick with tears as he stared up at the dim, yellowing circle cast above him on the ceiling.

Peter could hear footfalls coming toward the door, and then the door opened, daylight flooding into the little closet.

"Boy, what're you doin' in there?" Verlin said, smiling as if he'd discovered a surprise visitor. "Come on. I got breakfast ready."

Peter looked up at the inside of the door, noticing the little plate marking where the doorknob should have been and the nail with the dried blood.

Was he joking? Peter thought, not moving for a second, fearing that his dad was just going to kick him in the face or spit on him if he tried to get up. Verlin moved toward Peter and put his hand out.

"Come on, fella. I ain't gonna bite," Verlin said as he helped his son out of the closet.

Verlin led Peter out the front door and down the mossy, wooden stairs into the yard. Not much of a yard, but a little clearing amongst the Spanish moss-covered trees. Blue skies shining through the leaves. The air swallowed Peter like the mouth of a warm, wet monster. The white panel van looked like it had been moved. Peter thought that his dad went to town to get some supplies, maybe even some soda or good snack food for a change. Peter sat down on one of the lawn chairs that were set up next to a little fire ring with a metal grate over it.

"You like crappie?" Verlin said, bent over the little cooking fire.

"Yes," Peter said, although he couldn't be sure if he had ever had crappie. It wasn't on his favorites list anyway, like pizza or spaghetti. He had simply learned to agree with everything the old man seemed to like or say or do and that he would be relatively safe if he did that.

"Boy, I got some work to do today." Verlin turned the fish on the grate, little pieces of flesh sticking to the warped metal grid, as he hunched over the fire, sweating. "I want you to come help me out. Ya know? So you don't get yourself into any trouble out here. Ya hear me, now? I don't you want to become some kind of fag out in the woods, boy. You understand?"

Peter shook his head 'yes,' and looked away for a second. Peter didn't want to make his dad angry by not being interested enough, so he turned back to the grill and watched intently as the old man poked at the sizzling fish on the hot grill. Verlin looked as if he were the proudest father in the world, sitting there cooking fish by the campfire, talking about the good old-fashioned day of work ahead, yukkin' it up like the old guys at Peter's grandpa's hardware store.

Peter gently browsed the area to see if he could see anything other than moss and trees and fallen timber. He couldn't see a road, houses, or any other buildings.

No cars, no life, but trees and dirt.

And that God-awful suffocating, moist air. Peter sat still looking at the smoking fish, hissing like the roach spray under the door.

The subtle whisper of cicadas and sizzling fish somehow made Peter feel human, nevertheless, as if he were connected to a benevolent reality, as if he really were alive, like hope itself.

"Here you go, son," Verlin said, handing Peter an old army mess plate with a browned piece of fish on it. Peter gladly took the fish and sat it on his leg. Both of his legs were still stiff from being crammed into the closet all night, and *both* hands hurt now since he had landed his good hand on a rogue nail sticking out of the closet door. Peter knew better than to complain. He looked at his fish as if it were the most interesting thing he had ever seen, and then he looked down at the tape coming unraveled around the Popsicle sticks and then at his other hand. The dried brown blood had begun to flake off, revealing the redness around the actual puncture, healing as he sat there contemplating the day ahead.

"Don't let that get cold, boy. You don't wanna waste good food, son."

Peter closed his eyes and said *Bless Us, O Lord* like he'd heard his grandparents say a million times before every meal. He started to say the prayer to himself, though, silently.

"What the hell are you doing, boy?"

"Thank you," Peter said, opening his eyes to look at his father, and then he started eating. Verlin got up and went inside.

Bless us, Oh Lord, for these thy gifts... Peter kept one eye on the fish in front of him and one eye on the door to the trailer...*which we are about to receive...* he didn't want his dad to get mad at him for talking to God like that crazy fool on the radio...*from thy bounty, through Christ, our Lord. Amen.* Raised a good Catholic boy, Peter recited the words to that prayer like an unconscious mantra.

The fish tasted like a gift for sure. Peter could almost feel the protein course through his blood, rebuilding the decay from the noxious gas of the roach spray from the night before. He devoured the wide, thin strips of fish like an unruly dog. Verlin said that they had to go to work, so Peter hurried to finish his breakfast. He would try to make dad proud.

Later that morning, after Verlin had checked his cargo and put all of the supplies away, he and Peter packed themselves into the van and took off. The main road at the end of the narrow grassy driveway turned out to be another one-lane dirt trail, leading to yet another wider dirt road a little further out. Peter didn't know if they would ever see people again. He wondered if his mom was out there driving around on one of those lonely roads, looking for him, searching for telling signs of him and his father. Peter prayed that there would be people wherever they were going. He found himself praying all the time, really. As if his inability and fear at communicating with his dad had forced him to talk to God, or the universe, even the ether all around him. Something that had the capacity to give back to the boy.

"What you thinkin', boy?"

"Nothing."

"Awe, now, you gotta be thinkin' 'bout something.

There's gotta be something in that little head of yours. Somethin' spinnin' around in there, huh? Right?"

More confusion and wonder. Verlin made Peter feel filthy inside, dirty and worthless.

Peter had never really known how bad he was before hanging out with his dad. Peter's mom and grandparents had just let his misdeeds slide all of his short years on the planet. Verlin just had high standards, he had said. Relentless and merciless, nevertheless. Peter felt grateful for the temporary reprieve in justice. They were on their way to work, father and son, and Peter soon realized in the midst of his talking to the air around himself that he would take what he got, no matter how little or fleeting it might be.

After a succession of dirt road upon dirt road, with the occasional smattering of tin shacks and faded, clapboard buildings, they pulled onto a dirt driveway leading to the construction site of a big house. The placement of the house, out there in the middle of nowhere, seemed as arbitrary as a crop circle in Nebraska, kindling Peter's young imagination just like the latter might. The house stood tall in the beginning stages of its construction, wood scraps scattered about and the skeletal walls erect on the concrete slab in the wet heat of the late morning.

"Here we are, son."

Verlin said son and boy as if constantly reminding himself of who and what relation Peter had to himself. The sound of him saying those words made Peter feel strong inside in a way as if the irritation they caused were somehow fashioning some wicked brand of deadly weapon that he would eventually find the strength to wield.

"Come on, boy. Let's gitter done."

Peter's fingers had actually begun to feel a little better that day. The medical tape, turning a dark brown from the dirt and sweat, unraveled and curled at the ends of his fingers. He didn't want to bother his dad with the pesky request to change the dressing.

Peter would take care of it if and when he had the chance. He had cleaned his other hand, the punctured hand, with some spit and the edge of his t-shirt, and so he resigned himself to the fact that things would be worked out in due time in his own way and by whatever means possible.

Peter opened his door and jumped down onto the ground. Getting in and out of the van felt like an Olympic feat, being so short, yet Peter knew well enough that helping the old man would have its challenges too. The bum hand didn't help, but he had to get on.

Life didn't wait on the injured to mend or the sick to heal. Peter followed his dad up to the work site, where a large, pink-skinned guy with a flat-top stood up next to a wall, smiling as they approached.

"Cow Town, this is my boy, Peter."

"How you doin' big guy?" Cow Town said with a big, country smile. Sweat clung to the little spikes of his graying flat-top and beaded on his forehead, the hot Mississippi morning almost oppressive already.

"Good." Peter said, looking at the ground.

"What happened to your hand?"

"My dad smashed it in the door."

"Damn, Verlin, you gotta go beatin' on the kid?"

Cow Town laughed a big belly-laugh and looked down at Peter, tousling his hair. "Somebody better stop you 'fore you go and make a damned fool mess, Verlin."

"Yeah, Cow Town, kids these days," Verlin said, lighting a cigarette and turning to look down at Peter.

Peter thought, if you only knew, mister. But, then again, Verlin seemed to be feeling a little better that day, a little peppy, for whatever it was worth, and Peter decided that the past should simply stay put and that he would move on.

Peter had the inkling that people even liked his dad, for the most part. Cow Town even joked around with him, at the old man's expense, no less. Verlin couldn't be all that bad, and maybe he had just felt sick the night before, trying to shake some sort of obscure virus where a little mean fun was the only antidote.

"Pete here's gonna help us clean up," Verlin said.

"Good deal," Cow Town said, patting the boy's shoulder. "Come here Pete, I'll get you started."

No one had ever called Peter Pete before.

He kind of liked it, and he also liked the fact that his dad was the one to call him Pete. Almost like a nickname. Almost like they had already entered an enchanting unchartered territory of a blossoming new relationship that would shadow and blot out that sordid short past altogether. A pleasant turn of events. Father and son.

Cow Town led the way across the work site as Verlin went back to the van. Peter looked over at his dad, who leaned up against the van, intense in thought, and waved to him. His dad stood oblivious to Peter waving, smoking his cigarette, and popping a fresh beer.

After a while, once Cow Town had put Peter to work and talked a while with Verlin over by the van, Peter realized that he began to feel pretty good, lifting the 2x4's and sweating out in the sunny morning heat. They would stop for water breaks and Verlin for beer breaks, and then they would get back to work, chipping away at the daunting task of turning bits and pieces into something real that a person could live in, while Peter tossed the scraps and stacked the "keepers."

Verlin seemed to be especially happy that day.

Something about a good day's work.

A couple times throughout the day, he even horsed around with Peter, smacking the boy on the butt when he would bend over for a scrap piece of pipe, or dumping his bucket when there were just a few pieces in the bottom, taunting Peter into a little game of cat-and-mouse.

Peter liked the rough-housing and carousing in the sun because that's what boys do, dammit. Have fun. Besides, Peter's uncles back home constantly harassed him in that good way, and again, the familiarity of anything like home felt right and real, to the point of Peter almost feeling as if he were being initiated into some special brotherhood, where fathers and sons played together and worked together. That missing piece of the puzzle, the rite of initiation.

Hours into their work day, Peter came across a particularly large, messy pile of scrap boards, dusty copper pipes, and random construction debris. He negotiated the pile like a skilled mountain climber, happy to not have busted his butt thus far. Cow Town had given Peter a bigger bucket later in the day to pick up the scraps that he thought he could handle and told him to keep up the good work. Cow Town had also told Peter to straighten out the bigger boards, the good ones, and that the "help" would come around later and stack those keepers up for future projects.

Peter put a couple pieces of scrap wood in the bucket, stood up to wipe the sweat off of his forehead, and then took a step down the little pile to pick up a couple more pieces. He stumbled forward a step or two, beginning to feel a little faint.

Peter felt pretty agile still, despite his wobbly legs, having spent many an hour riding bikes and running around with the neighbor kids back home. Nevertheless, he stepped forward again and slipped, almost toppling onto his face amongst the boards and clutter. Stepping on that nail only felt more painful, knowing that he had almost escaped disaster altogether. Peter yelped, reluctantly looking down to see the large nail coming through the top of his foot, a dot of blood percolating through the dusty layer over his shoe and laces.

The pain shot through his foot and ankle as he dropped the bucket, shouting out at the same time. In what seemed like a split second and a slow moment simultaneously, the sharp pain in the top and bottom of his foot radiated out to a dull, thick sensation in his ankle and toes, and the boy had to sit down. Cow Town ran over to where Peter now sat crying, not wanting to move him, making the pain worse.

"You okay, Pete?"

"It hurts."

"I bet it does, buddy," he said. "You hold on now. That thing's gotta come out, okay?"

"No!"

"You just count to three, okay?"

"I..."

"Okay?"

Peter reluctantly started to count, "One...

"What happened, son?" Verlin said, coming up from behind Cow Town, sweating, as he lit another cigarette, bending down to look at Peter's foot.

"We're countin' to three, Verlin," Cow Town said.

"Go on, now. You can do it, buddy."

"One...two..."

"Come on, now."

"Three!"

And just like that, Cow Town had already pulled the board off, taken Peter's shoe and sock off, and started to gently apply a little pressure around the puncture wound.

"That's a big nail," Cow Town said and looked at Verlin. "You better take this boy to get a tetanus shot. He had one?"

"Hell, I don't know. His mama don't tell me shit."

Cow Town looked at Peter and smiled, and then back at Verlin and said, "Well you better go to town and see Dr. Bob. He'll fix'em up. You don't want your boy's yapper lockin' up on him, do ya?"

"Yeah, I guess you're right."

Verlin threw his cigarette down and picked Peter up off of the ground. He carried him over to the van, opened the door, and put him in. Peter's foot started to really feel sore, but he kept it to himself. His face and hands felt hot. He wanted to see his mom because she was better at easing discomfort than his dad seemed to be. The old man only made him nervous.

"I know it hurts, boy," Verlin said, getting in the driver's seat and shutting the door. Cow Town walked up to the driver's window and put a big hand on the ledge.

"Cow Town, I'll catch up with you later.

Tell your brother I'll be catching up with him when we get home."

"What you want with that sheister?" Cow Town said, handing Verlin the cigarette pack that he had thrown on the ground.

"Just tell him Verlin's gonna come see him," Verlin said, lighting another cigarette. "I need some advice. It's important. Got it?"

"I'll see what I can do for ya," Cow Town said, reaching into his pocket. "I'm gonna be in town off and on for some time now. We're buildin' down there too."

"We'll have to get together some time."

Cow Town rolled his eyes at Verlin as he held a wad of cash up for Verlin to see.

Cow Town peeled some bills off of the wad, handed Verlin a few bills, and then went around the other side of the van to give Peter a crisp twenty-dollar bill. Peter had never held a crisp twenty-dollar bill that he had earned himself before, feeling like a Rockefeller.

"Get that boy a shot, Verlin," he said and patted the side of the van.

And then Peter and his dad were back on the road, hopefully on their way to see Dr. Bob, Peter thought so that his yapper didn't lock up, as Cow Town had put it. Peter imagined not being able to move his jaw, not able to talk. Peter didn't think the old man would really mind.

"Why would my yapper lock up, dad?"

"Aw, shit, boy. He's crazier'n a damn coon. Don't you worry 'bout all that."

Peter stared out the window, trying not to worry about anything, which had become harder and harder the last couple days. He found himself thinking about bad things happening all around him all the time. As if the world really were on the brink of disaster, would indeed go up in flames any day. Rag-heads and nails and lockjaw and crazed hippies with guns.

They drove along in that old silence for a while, and then Verlin said, "Son, you can't go around telling people that I smashed your hand in the door. They'll think things, boy."

"It was an accident."

"I don't care, boy," he said and lit another cigarette. "You gotta listen to your old man. I been around the block a couple times. Ya know?"

"Yes, sir."

They went to the doctor, Peter got a shot, and then the nurse gave Peter a couple lime Popsicles. Peter stared at the new, sterile, white bandaging and shiny aluminum splints on his fingers and thought to himself that he had never had so many Popsicles in his life. Maybe vacation did have its perks. The doctor had pulled Verlin aside after he had finished giving Peter his shot and had replaced the bandaging on his fingers. The two grown men kept looking over at Peter with serious expressions, and then would go on to talk some more, and then the doctor left the room, only to give Peter his third Popsicle, 'for the road,' the funny doctor had told him.

The shiny metal splints with the soft padding inside felt a lot better on his healing fingers than the old, make-shift splints. More support the doctor had said so that Peter didn't bang them up and wiggle them too much. Peter told the friendly old doctor thank you, and so did Verlin, and then they were out the door.

"Are we going back to work?" Peter said, getting into the van.

"We gotta go, son," Verlin said and lit a cigarette, shutting his door. "I gotta be somewhere, boy."

"I didn't get to say bye to Cow Town."

"You can do that later," Verlin said. "That crazy sum bitch'll be around forever, buddy.

He has a way of just showin' up, ya know?"

Verlin pulled out onto the black-top road that ran by the doctor's office, giving that van all it had on the wide-open highway. The warm, moist wind whipped Peter's hair into a nappy frenzy. The wind felt amazing compared to being crammed into that little closet back in the trailer. He started to believe that they would have a good vacation after all, Popsicles and money, as if vacations by nature just got off to bad starts, perhaps.

Verlin stopped down the road, after only driving for a short time, to get some more beer and cigarettes, and got Peter some chips and soda, too. "We're rich, boy," Verlin said, laughing when he came out of the store, Peter following close behind, emulating the old man's hitch and swagger as best as he could.

Chapter 6

Verlin and Peter pulled up to an old gate made out of steel pipe. Out in Osage County, most of the ranchers made their gates and cattle guards from the scraps of the ubiquitous gas and oil pipeline: strong, lasting, and plentiful material, keeping the cattle in and the poachers out. Verlin eased the truck onto the cattle guard and Peter jumped out to get the gate.

"It's locked!"

Verlin got out and walked up next to Peter.

"That damned tight-ass. He afraid someone's gonna take his precious oil?" Verlin said. "Or his fuckin' cattle." Verlin spat through the cattle-guard beneath his feet. "Stand back, son." Peter stood back as Verlin pulled a pistol out of his back waistband, put a bullet in the chamber, and shot the lock off. The action didn't seem to be out of character one little bit, from what Peter remembered of his dad as a child.

Peter looked at the lock, and then at the gun in his dad's hand, and then back at the lock, just as the old man kicked the defunct lock off of its chain with his cowboy boot.

"That's how ya gitter done, son." Verlin pulled the chain off too and let it fall, clanging through the pipes of the cattle-guard and to the ground below.

He pushed the gate open with one big heave and said, "Get in, boy."

They got in the truck and pulled through the open gate. "We'll close it when we leave," Verlin said, gassing the truck a couple times, fish-tailing dirt and hay chaff up into the air behind them. A dirt trail with two tire tracks and a grass hump down the middle lead out into the vast, high plains. Plains that had been taken for granted as long as people had been around to take things for granted. The human eye is the only limiting factor to seeing to the end of the earth.

Out ahead of them, Peter saw a covey of quail nestled under a low-lying bush. Verlin stuck the .45 out the window and squeezed off a couple rounds. Good old dad. Yee haw! Adventure out in the great wide open, just like Peter and his friends driving around and drinking beer. His dad turned out to be just another carefree guy, just like him. They cut a couple more donuts, hauled ass over a high rise in the plain, and then slid in sideways next to a pond that rested down below the descending bluff. Verlin turned the truck off and killed his beer. Peter slammed his too.

"Let's do some shootin'," Verlin said. "Why don't you take that damned suit coat off, boy? I feel like your gonna try to sell me some fuckin' life insurance or something."

Peter brushed the chaff off of the front of his blazer, sweat, and itch under his collar. He looked over at his dad and shrugged as he scratched his neck and brushed at his sleeves. The old man really had a way with words, he thought.

"Come on, boy," Verlin said. "You got scabies or something? Let's go." Verlin got out of the truck and pulled the back of the bench seat forward to grab something from behind.

"Bet ya twenty dollars you can't out-shoot the old man," he said, walking down to the edge of the pond with his gun and a beer.

Peter obliged the old man by taking his suit jacket off and laying it gently on the truck seat next to himself. He loosened his tie as he watched Verlin at the water's edge. Peter rubbed his right hand in an attempt to soothe the phantom pain there. The pain keeping him in the present as the looming clouds from the west crept up on them like some rogue infantry. Verlin finished his beer and threw the empty can into the pond, and then shot at it a couple times. He turned to Peter, laughing wildly, his stance loose and flimsy with all of the beer and a little madness.

"Come on," Verlin said, laughing. "You ain't afraid of a little gun are you?"

"There's a storm rolling in."

"What, you the damned weather man now?" Verlin said, firing a couple more rounds at the bobbing can on the pond. He turned around toward Peter again, almost falling into the pond, as he came around a little too quickly.

"I've got a built-in barometer," Peter said, holding his hand up in the air.

Verlin stared at Peter's hand from where he stood as if he thought the boy's raised appendage was a personal challenge, a target.

Verlin opened and closed his eyes a couple times, like resting in between pot-shots at the can in the water.

"Aw, shit. You sure you ain't smokin' dope, boy? Come on, get your ass down here!"

Peter got out of the pick-up and walked down to the edge of the water, where Verlin stood refilling the magazine with cool bullets.

"Here," Verlin said, pulling the slide and handing Peter the gun. Peter took the gun from Verlin and looked at it. The pistol was a weathered Colt .45, model 1911, in pretty good shape and solid in the hand like a chunk of cool granite. "Safety's off, boy."

Peter aimed the gun at the can that had floated out to the center of the pond, pulled the trigger, and hit it, sending it rocking violently. He fired the gun two more times and hit the can once more, sending dancing circles through the water, out and away from where they stood at the bank. Verlin slammed his beer and went to the truck to get two more. He popped them both, came back, and gave one to Peter, who took a large pull and then emptied the clip, missing the can more than he hit it.

Verlin grabbed the gun from Peter as he lowered it, put another clip in, and emptied it himself. He didn't hit the can, but one time, the air thick with the smell of gun powder, ammonium nitrate, and freshly cut hay. Peter could tell that his dad felt a little frustrated at not hitting the can, and he patted him on the back. Verlin turned to Peter and nodded toward the pick-up. They walked over to the truck and leaned up against the bed.

Verlin took the magazine out of the gun and loaded it, now having three loaded magazines in total. Verlin put one back into the butt of the pistol and set the other two on the edge of the truck bed. Peter looked over and noticed that his dad had started crying.

"Dad."

"Your mom was a good woman. Fucked up, but good, son," he said. He set the loaded gun on the edge of the truck bed too.

"She didn't let me see you for a couple years. Then you came to visit me for a year and they took you back. Your fuckin' nosy uncles...who the fuck?...you know that?"

"I don't really remember any of that," Peter said, rubbing his sore hand, as he looked around them to see how much time they had left before the rain and wind and lightning came.

"I loved you. Your mom made me out to be the bad guy, you little fucker...your mom.

She always thought she was better than me. Better than my family. Her fuckin' big-time family, huh? She don't know shit." Verlin's countenance continued to darken as he became more self-conscious by the second, like a fragile schizophrenic at the onset of a psychotic episode.

"What are you talking about?" Peter said, trying to be as gentle as possible, despite his feelings on the topic.

"Boy, you aren't shit to me now!" Verlin shouted as if coming to life in some esoteric Santeria channeling ritual, and then he grabbed the gun off of the side of the truck bed, pulling the slide to put a bullet in the chamber. "I could fuckin' kill you right here! What do you think of that? Huh?

Are you scared? Right here!" Tears poured down his face as he took deep, labored gulps of air, trying his best to keep it together, to keep from totally losing touch with his fragile little world out there in the middle of nowhere. He let the gun down for a second and then raised it again, pushing the barrel hard into Peter's cheek. Peter slightly pulled away from the intense heat of the recently fired gun, eyes wild with adrenaline, as he stood there waiting for the storm to roll in and to die.

Then, as if some profound revelation had instantly overcome Verlin, he stared at Peter like he had just come back from another dimension, lowering the gun to his side. Verlin cried for a few moments more and then put the gun back to Peter's face, grabbing his collar and twisting hard so that Peter had trouble breathing.

When dealing with a sociopath in the middle of a psychotic episode, the worst thing to do is to act like something is amiss.

To show fear. Possibly where the Stockholm Syndrome begins coming into its own – the beginning of where the captive necessarily begins to identify with the captor for the purpose of survival only. Perhaps the benevolent arm of the collective unconscious is taking over for issues too big and complex for the average person to deal with on their own.

Peter tried to keep his eyes on the gun in his cheek.

He had had a couple guns pulled on him before, at a distance and short-range to be sure, yet never by his estranged biological father, and damn sure never having his face seared and smashed with the tip of a barrel. The moment felt crazy and common like reality TV. Almost like the unexpected was actually anticipated all along somehow, if only from the dark corners of the soul.

Standing there before his dad, the dead-beat he hadn't seen nor heard from in almost twenty years, who forced fear down his throat like an abusive cop, Peter couldn't help but feel like he had entered some ridiculous realm where things made even less sense than they already had on planet earth. A state where time slows to a pace of total control, however, where a person could choose their fate, and from where Peter had to work carefully so that the current situation didn't entirely deteriorate into a total, hopeless wreck…or death…for him or the old man.

Peter stood cautiously watching the dad he didn't really know, slumped over and sobbing at the side of the truck, one long moment, and then, all inebriation dissipating in the face of some deep, long-unknown reserve of compassion and empathy, as an enveloping wave of peace overcame him, he took a step toward his earthly father. Not a logical move, Peter thought once he had made that first step forward, granted, but it was all that he knew to do given the situation. Peter reached out and gave his dad the most ambitious hug that he could muster, lifting him up off of the ground a little bit. And that was that.

Verlin sobbed in Peter's arms like a broken child.

A grown, broken child whose whole existence had instantly and mercilessly become obsolete. Peter and Verlin hung on like that for a while, holding each other tightly, the front of Peter's shirt wetting with tears and sweat and drool. They held each other. They held each other to the point of Peter feeling a little uncomfortable, really, and not knowing what to do with his hands, not knowing what to say, if anything at all.

Peter had to finally let go when his arms started going to sleep on him, after an eternal few minutes. Verlin let go too, with his head down, and went around to the back of the truck to let down the tailgate, so that they could both take a seat.

Peter reached into the cooler to get a couple cold beers, handing one to Verlin, and then opened one of his own and took a long, hard drink. Peter lit a couple cigarettes from the pack that Verlin had set down when he plopped his butt on the tailgate himself. The two guys, father, and son didn't say a word, sipping their beers and smoking cigarettes, as the fields of closely-cropped hay stretched out in endless serpentine rows beyond the pond, where the riddled beer can had become stuck in the mud at the edge.

Swollen rain clouds wrapped in splinters of lightning were all about them now, as the wind churned up cool spittle that dusted them like mystic sea mist.

Chapter 7

Peter went to the front passenger door of the rumbling black Beamer, hesitatingly touching the door handle. Fr. Ligero sat behind the wheel, sunken into the smooth, black leather seat, playing with the buttons on the stereo receiver. Peter laid his cane at the edge of the seat and crouched down into the passenger side smiling, as he shut the door behind himself.

"Need a ride, mister?"

"Take me to Pony Town," Peter said, laughing now, looking straight ahead.

Fr. Ligero gave Peter a friendly little pat on the cheek and then grabbed his arm and shook it a little bit. "Can you find something on this radio? These damned things." Peter laughed at Father Ligero's frustration, thinking of how Grammie used to talk into the answering machine when the doorbell rang or how she answered the television remote when the phone rang. His mom would have been the same way by now, Peter thought, had she lived to see the day of his release.

Fr. Ligero punched the gas, firmly pushing Peter back into his seat. The engine growled as everything else outside passed quietly by. Peter threw his plastic bags into the back seat. He hadn't been in the front seat of a car in years. No handcuffs, no ankle bracelets.

"Everything go smoothly?"

"Sure did."

"I would hope so. They put me through the ringer. You're now my property while on parole."

"I don't scrub toilets anymore."

Fr. Ligero laughed and said, "Your dad knows that you're coming, but I must say that he was a bit startled that a priest called with the message."

"Ex-priest...with all due respect, your kindness."

Fr. Ligero let off of the gas once the speedometer hit 140 mph, bringing the car down to a modest 90 miles per hour, gliding over the barren Oklahoma highway like a silk scarf on a warm summer breeze.

"Here." Fr. Ligero reached into the console and pulled out a package, handing it to Peter.

"I thought you might like a good smoke on your first day of freedom."

Peter opened the brown paper package, which contained a plastic bag inside. He unfolded the plastic bag and opened it, pulling one of the dark brown sticks out, looking at it as if it were a lost artifact.

"Churchill?" Peter said.

Fr. Ligero winked at him.

Peter closed his eyes and ran the length of the cigar under his nose a couple times. He put the cigar back in the plastic bag, resealed it, and put that back in the brown paper bag.

"Those are special, Peter," Fr. Ligero said.

"My cousin rolls those down in Tampa.

These are only for special occasions."

Peter put the bag of cigars back in the console.

"Did my dad seem open to the whole thing?"

Fr. Ligero turned the stereo down and said, "Like I said, he wasn't too happy to hear from a priest."

"Did you tell him that you were an ex-communicated priest?"

"I don't think it's the station of *priesthood* that he has a problem with. At any rate, he was *open* to it, yes, but I'm sure it'll be interesting, to say the least."

"Did he mention my mom?"

"He said that he had heard he was the only family you had left, and that he didn't have a problem with you coming by to see him, if that's what you wanted to do."

"Aww, that's nice."

"Are you up to it?"

"I've been working up the nerve for the last year."

"This is your chance to put this all behind you.

You should honor your father, no matter how crazy he might be. That doesn't mean that you guys have to golf together."

"Smug bastard," Peter said, rolling the window down to catch the breeze in his hair. "I hate golf."

"You owe him an apology, Peter."

“Yeah. I honestly never thought this day would come.”

“You getting out?”

“Yeah...and me having to go see the old man again.”

Fr. Ligero kept his eyes on the road ahead. “Can’t the guy just die?” Peter said, sticking his right hand out the window, flying it through the air like an airplane. “There’s a storm coming in, Father. We better get to where we’re going before we get blown away.”

“There’s always a storm coming here it seems.”

Fr. Ligero pointed to the stereo, gesturing Peter to turn it back up as he punched the gas again, shooting them over the black strip of road, into the harrowing blue and purple horizon.

Chapter 8

The panel van blew a tire somewhere outside of Vicksburg. Peter remembered Vicksburg, Mississippi because the van had come to a shaky stop by an exit sign reading "Vicksburg," where some guys in old military uniforms stopped to ask if they needed any help.

Verlin got out of the van, went to the back tire and kicked it. Peter could hear him shout from behind the van as a camouflaged, crew-cab Dodge pulled up behind them. Two hearty guys lumbered out of each side of the truck and walked up to Verlin. One of the guys wore a gray uniform, the other a blue uniform. Peter stood up in his seat to see if they were there to help with the tire or to take them prisoner. He looked out into the field of live-oaks across the highway to see if any cowboys or Indians were coming up too. The two guys talked with Verlin for a minute or two and then they got back into their truck and pulled out.

Peter's stomach dropped when he saw the big guys ambling back to their truck to leave. He felt better about having someone else around, anyone, even if they might take him and his dad to some kind of work camp to labor under the hot sun for the rest of their lives. Carla, Cow Town or a random store clerk, for that matter, would have been a welcome change to that draining silence.

Verlin opened the doors to the back of the van. "Damned crazies," he said. "They gotta live a hundred years ago for fun." Scraping sounds came from the back of the van as Verlin drug the spare tire and tools across the floor board, throwing them onto the ground behind him. A widening ring of sweat dampened the collar of his shirt. "They as dim-witted as that fuckin' Roland Stacks asshole." Verlin slammed something in the back of the van as he said the preacher's last name. "The whole fuckin' planet's goin' crazy, boy. Ya know that?"

Peter nodded, and then bent down and grabbed the radio off of the floor.

Vicksburg hosts an annual Civil War re-enactment festival of sorts, where a bunch of people get together and rehash all of the atrocities of the Civil War, after which they can safely satisfied go back to their cable-television and drive-through meals without having to be gone but a long weekend. The two guys that pulled up in the camouflage truck had told Verlin that they were on their way to the Eat-n-Git down the road, and that they could give him a lift if he needed. Verlin told them that he had it under control, but thanks anyway, and for them to go ahead and have fun playing war, to which they huffed under their breath, shook their heads and went back to their truck.

"You need some help?" Peter said to his dad.

"You just stay in there. You could get run over. Hold still, I gotta jack the van up to change the tire, okay? Just hold real still, and we'll be done in a flash, alright?"

Peter thought that his dad could fix anything, whether it was a van, a motorcycle or some broken fingers. He tried to hold as still as he could when he felt the rear end of the van coming up off of the ground, save for a swipe or two of the forehead, that wet heat slathering itself all over his face. The van jerked a couple times and then it sat still. A moment later, it jerked a couple more times and then rested again.

Peter turned the transistor radio on and dialed it into the first station without static. A story about a missing girl, Ramona Whitcanuck, had traveled across the country since it first caught wind. Peter put the radio to his ear so that Verlin didn't hear him listening to that "damned trash," as the old man often referred to news of any sort. Nevertheless, any voice from the outside world felt good to Peter, kindred almost. Those voices in the radio made Peter feel connected to something bigger, more real and alive than riding around with his dad made him feel.

The newswoman said that Ramona Whitcanuck had been missing for five days, and that there were a couple leads into the case so far. The reward for finding the child was set at twenty-thousand dollars. Peter choked at the mention of twenty thousand dollars, such an unimaginable amount of money. The reporter said that the child's family in Arizona pleaded with the captor in a public announcement not to hurt their child and that they would understand, and not even press charges if she were returned safely.

The next story on the radio was about the Patty Hearst case. They played a clip from one of her tapes that she had sent in to the authorities claiming her allegiance to the Symbionese Liberation Army. Short and sweet. The woman on the radio told the audience that Hearst's father had distributed millions of dollars worth of food through his agency called People in Need, per Patty's captors' request to set things straight. Peter thought that the lady's dad must have really loved her. That's a lot of food. What did one thing have to do with the other? Peter pulled the radio away from his ear and looked at it.

Peter felt the van lowering back down to the ground, and heard his dad throwing the old tire and his tools into the back of the van again. Peter clicked the radio off, set it back on the floor and then turned to look at the tire. The rubber frayed around the rim like a tattered flag that had been wadded up and left for dead on the floor of the van. Verlin's face poured like a faucet, the sweat ring around his collar having spread all the way down to the top of his beer belly.

"Let's get outta here." Verlin shut the doors and climbed back in the driver's seat. "How's the hand, boy?"

"Pretty good. It only hurts at night."

"How's the foot?"

"Good."

"You hungry?"

"Sure."

After driving for another hour or so, Verlin pulled onto a dirt road that went down to a river below the highway. He said they could catch some dinner. Better food than the shit in the stores, anyway.

Verlin sat his fishing gear up like before. He said the water was black and dank enough down there that you could even catch some good catfish in the daylight, probably. Peter didn't want to fish or bait a hook, and his dad said, "Suit yourself," so Peter walked down the river's edge to see what he could find.

Peter walked a couple minutes, and then looked back to see if the van was still there. The fear of his dad leaving him out in the middle of nowhere felt kind of real to the boy. Verlin sat at the edge of the river, in front of the van, looking as content as an old dog lying in the sun on a Sunday afternoon, yet with beer and cigarette in hand, unlike any dog that Peter had ever seen. Peter continued walking down the edge of the river amongst the sand, rocks and weeds, skipping rocks as best he could with his left hand, allowing himself a little time away from the old man. Some breathing space, as his grandpa liked to call it, like all those hours spent down in the garage taking things apart and putting them back together again, just for the sake of doing so.

The undergrowth kept tripping Peter up, so he didn't think he could run away very fast, even if he wanted to. He couldn't see anywhere to run to, at any rate. Things had gotten better with his dad ever since the closet incident anyway, and Peter would do what he had to do to be happy, and to make his father happy, as well.

Peter had the uncanny ability to hedge his bets in taunting fate, so he just curbed the idea of fleeing for the time being, saving it for a later use perhaps, and continued down the river's edge until he came to an old barbed-wire fence that went out into the river, slowly dipping under the surface as it got further out toward the middle of the creeping, brown water. The current looked strong by the way long, defined V's surfaced on the river where the fence wire stuck out.

Peter shook the fence to see if anything would come up to the top, as a couple old milk jugs attached to the top wire of the fence popped up on the water and then quickly went back under. Peter shook the fence again, but the jugs didn't resurface. Peter shook the fence again, yet nothing again. The river reminded Peter of the creek by his grandparents' house, but bigger and wider and going somewhere even more exciting.

Peter and his friends would swim and catch crawdads in the creek behind his grandparents'. Peter's head began to feel thick and dull as he thought about his friends back home. He let go of the fence and walked a little further down the river. No one was anywhere to be seen, so he got on what seemed to be solid ground and unzipped his pants, so that he could take a pee in the water. Little splashes landed at the water's edge, bubbles floating away from Peter as soon as the little stream hit the murky shiny surface. After he finished peeing, he zipped up and sat down on the bank, watching the water pass before him. He just wanted to go home, somewhere different, another place altogether, just like that sleepy river.

When Peter snapped out of his trance, he decided that he should go back to where his dad sat fishing. He felt nervous and maybe even a little scared. He didn't want to be gone too long, worrying his dad into a frenzy. But then again, he liked the quiet for a change. His dad didn't stop yammering on and on.

Peter slowly got up from the bank and dusted himself off, realizing that he must've been sitting for a while, because his legs were stiff and one of his feet had fallen asleep. Peter looked a good deal up ahead of himself the whole way back to see if he could see the van. To see if his dad had stayed put. He tried to shake the pins and needles loose from his dead foot, as he trudged back on through the thick undergrowth.

By the time that Peter had almost gotten all the way back to the van, he noticed that his dad had already packed up all of the fishing gear and the two folding chairs, and was waiting in the driver's seat, smoking a cigarette, stroking his hair back. Peter didn't really know how long it could have been that he had been downriver, but it couldn't have been that long, he reasoned with himself. Peter could feel the thickness, the tension, in the air before he could actually even see his dad's eyes. And then Verlin moved suddenly, as if he were startled by Peter's footfalls in the weeds. The old man got out of the van once he saw Peter and came around to grab him by the arm.

"You little shit! Where the hell you been?! You scared the shit out of me, you know that?!" Verlin grabbed the back of Peter's head and started swatting at his butt in long hard strokes. Peter kicked and swatted like he'd fallen into a hornet's nest. Verlin just commenced to dragging the boy by his hair back to the van, with or without the little shit's cooperation. "Boy, you ain't too fuckin' smart, are you?"

"Stop it!"

"Don't back-talk me, ya little shit!" He swatted the back of Peter's head, then picked him up by the arm and the hair and tossed him over to the passenger seat from the driver's door. "You could'a got lost! Dammit!" Verlin got in after Peter, shut the door and started the van. "Take a nap. You'll eat later." Peter braced himself in his seat for whatever might come next, as Verlin continued shouting at him. "Dammit, boy! You can't do that! You can't take off like that!"

Verlin pulled into a gas station an hour or so down the road. The store seemed to be out in the middle of nowhere, but still a line of cars waited for gas. Verlin still fumed in the driver's seat, so Peter just kept his mouth shut. The cars ahead didn't lighten the old man's sour disposition any either. Peter felt like his dad might just get out of the van and start beating in the windshield of the nearest car at any moment.

"This shit's only gettin' worse, boy."

Peter figured that his dad must have been talking about the 'rag-heads' again. There were handmade signs scattered about the grounds of the gas station that said, 'Five Gallons Only,' and 'Pay Before You Pump,' and 'Slow Down.'

The last car ahead of them finished fueling, and then readied themselves to leave with chips and soda and ice. Peter noticed a boy in the back window of the light, metallic-blue Chevy Impala staring out at him as the car pulled away. Peter wondered how long the boy had been staring at him with that hungry and head-thumped glare. Verlin pulled up, turned the van off and got out.

Verlin yelled something unintelligible after a couple minutes of pumping gas and slapped the side of the van with an open hand. Peter could hear him putting the gas nozzle back onto the gas pump and muttering something angry to himself again. Peter thought that the 'rag-heads' must have really been up to something crazy this time.

Verlin went in to pay, but didn't come right back out. Peter thought that maybe the old man had met another pretty lady in the store. He figured he better just sit back and enjoy the day as best he could, not wanting to make Verlin's sour mood any worse than he already had. Peter sat trying to forget his thirst, and the fact that he wanted to go home, and that he was lonely and scared and tired and worried about his mom. He stared at the blue sky, hoping to see someone other than his father come out to the van to get in. Someone who smiled. Anyone familiar by some miracle.

Peter woke up when he heard the door to the van open. Verlin had a twelve-pack of Coors and a carton of Marlboros in one arm and a magazine and a bag of chips in the other. He tossed the bag of chips at Peter, hitting him in the face. Verlin laughed out loud.

"Klutz! Boy, your mama didn't teach you shit, did she?"

"Did you catch any fish?"

"Where the hell you been, Einstein?" Verlin said, shutting the door once he got in. "I couldn't fish 'cause of you, boy. You half scared the dog shit outta me. You know that?"

Peter sat up straight and started to open the bag of potato chips. "Can I look at your magazine?"

"This ain't for no shithead kid." Verlin leaned over to grab a beer. "This is an adult magazine, boy. I'll teach you about that soon. When you're ready, okay?"

"Yes, sir." Those were really the only safe words with Verlin, it seemed. Anything more or less than thinly-veiled, weak attempts at respect and interest could set his dad off like a damp box of explosives. Yes, sir. Peter opened his chips and started to eat dinner. Verlin popped his beer, lit another cigarette and started the van.

"Purrs like a kitten, don't she?"

Peter shook his head 'yes.' Verlin pulled out, and they were on their way.

Peter ate one, two, three chips, and then one handful after another. The salt and fat made him even more thirsty than he had previously been, but his hunger beat out his thirst, he realized, and so he continued to bite his tongue, so that he wouldn't send the old codger on yet another tirade about how Peter was ungrateful and a little bitch and too whiny and needed to grow up and shut the hell up, dammit!

After his blind junk food-stuffing spree, Peter looked into the empty chip bag, dusted with crumbs and satiated, asking if there was anything else to eat before he realized that he was speaking out loud. Verlin told him to sit tight and that they would catch some fish later on.

Peter thought that holding his tongue felt like holding a pee for a long time, a certain itch and crawl under the skin that left you feeling hot and a little crazy. He knew better than to disrupt Verlin's concentration on the road ahead, however. He remained silent, and continued to watch the road pass beneath them as he began to think about what the next day might bring. Anticipation like fond memories had its tonic effect. Peter felt sad all of a sudden. He almost started to cry, but knew he had to hold back those nasty little tears.

After what seemed to be two lifetimes and a couple hours, Peter just had to ask for a drink. He felt like the dryness in his throat would spread to his wind pipe and surely suffocate him if he didn't act quickly, if he didn't get something wet down soon. The back and forth, the desire and silence, and the waiting and fear finally gave way to Peter tapping Verlin on the shoulder, as the old man stared down the highway ahead like he had to go kill a man.

"Yeah, boy. What you need?"

"I'm thirsty, dad."

Verlin told him to get into the ice chest there and get him something to drink.

"There's only beer in here," Peter said, rummaging through the ice and cans.

"Go ahead, it won't kill ya. Real men drink beer."

Peter figured if his dad said so, it must be okay, so he grabbed a beer and tried to pop the top like his good ole daddy. Verlin saw Peter struggling a little too dramatically with one hand bandaged and tattered and the other not that strong or adept to begin with, so he bent over to help his son open his first beer.

"Thank you, sir."

"Drink up, boy."

Peter scrunched up his nose after he put the can to his lips. He looked over at his dad who squinted his eyes in a puff of cigarette smoke, casually taking a drink from his own beer can. Peter squinted his eyes just like his dad did and took a big swig of the cold beer.

"Gross, dad," Peter said. "This stuff tastes like wet bread. It stinks."

"Boy, you better not waste that beer," Verlin said. "I work hard for my money. You understand?"

Peter nodded 'yes,' that he did in fact understand some more good ole redneck logic.

Verlin reached over to Peter and pushed the bottom of the can up as he put it to his lips again. Peter's throat strained to get all of the beer down without choking, but inevitably, he got the juice down the shoot, and then a quick moment later it all came back up and out of the boy's mouth, splattering across the metal dashboard.

"Thatta boy."

Peter put the beer up to his lips again, not wanting to disappoint the old man, and then took another big swill, without his dad's help that time. Then another. And another. After a couple minutes, Verlin was grabbing Peter's empty can along with his and throwing them out the window, opening another beer and handing it to the boy. They drank one together.

"This one's better than the other one, dad," Peter said, wiping his mouth with the back of his hand, loose smile and shiny eyes. "It doesn't taste as strong as the other one."

Verlin laughed. Peter laughed too.

Peter felt light, airy and strong, without a care in the world, his vacation coming alive and dancing with color and sound and omnipresent electricity. The ride somehow seemed smoother to Peter, as if they floated on air, above the road. Unwittingly enough, Peter hadn't thought once about his next meal or where they were going or who they would meet or anything outside of that particular moment in the passenger seat. His stomach didn't hurt, and he felt good, dammit! He felt great! Hand, foot and all. Like a hero on holiday.

Peter had discovered a new potion of sorts, and could see himself drinking it every chance that he got. There would eventually come a time when he could have as much as he wanted, he thought. If he could only grow up and be done with childish things. He thought that his dad must have felt like a super-hero, as much beer as he drank. Peter looked over at the pack of Marlboro Reds on the floor next to the "adult magazine," and then looked up at his dad again.

Peter finished the last of his beer, before it had a chance to get hot.

"How do you feel?" Verlin said.

"Like I'm dreamin'."

"Good boy...good," Verlin said. "Makes you feel good, don't it?"

"Yes, sir."

Verlin took a double-take of Peter who sat slumped in the passenger seat next to him now. The old man may have noticed the more relaxed countenance about the boy, or that maybe Peter didn't fidget and mess with the bandaging on his hand the whole time, like some neurotic imp, but whatever the case may have been, Verlin smiled and seemingly noticed the boy sitting next to him for the first time since they had set out on their grand voyage across the country. Peter felt happy. Included.

Peter felt confident to speak freely to the old man with whatever crossed his mind, without the normal fear of saying the wrong thing, something that might land his ass in hot water again. Verlin talked more that day than he had the whole time put together. Like he and Peter had broken through to something real between them, something palpable that they could hold onto and stand on and toss around like chums. The old man talked about Louise, his girlfriend back home, Verlin's home, and his plans for all of them to be together some day, living happily-ever-after, like some tall tale. Peter thought that the idea seemed strange, considering that his mom and them were supposed to be on vacation together in the first place. He didn't ask questions though, not wanting to ruin the moment with stupid questions that might make his dad look at him with that uneasy sideways smirk that made Peter feel so small and stupid. So worthless.

"You need your daddy, boy," Verlin said in the midst of one of their dialogues.

Peter stared out the window and smiled. Yes I do, he thought. Yes. The day would soon be dark, at which point they would end up somewhere new and strange and temporary.

Peter woke up from the deepest, most gratifying sleep he had experienced in weeks, or so it seemed. His arms and legs felt thick and weak, as if they would wake up in a couple more days, leaving him to fend for himself, just a trunk of a boy. Verlin sat next to Peter, squeezing his arm tightly, trying to get his attention. Peter could feel the night around them like weight on the back, and rubbed his eyes to see that they were parked somewhere in the dark. He sat up straight and said, "Where are we?"

"Home."

"Home?" Peter said, sitting up a little more. "My head hurts, dad."

"You'll be alright, boy."

Peter sat up quickly, putting his hands over his eyes, hiding himself from his mom's baby-blue Volkswagon Beetle out in the driveway, until that last bursting second when he would remove his hands and surprise himself. The old, toothless neighbor's orange porch lamp would surely be glowing in the night, bugs clinging to the dingy glass.

All Peter could see, nevertheless, turned out to be more trees with Spanish moss, and those damp sidewalks that connected everything. Damp parking lots, damp roads, damp doorsteps in the murky night. Peter sat back in his seat and looked down at the floor. His potion had lost all its power, leaving him feeling out of place and lonely again, but even worse yet.

"Yeah, boy. We're home!" Verlin said, patting Peter on the leg. "Come on. Louise is waiting for us." The old man got out of the van and came around to open the door for Peter. "Alright, boy, jump down and let's go inside. You hungry?"

Peter shook his head 'yes' and jumped down, wincing when he landed on his newly punctured foot. He made sure to not get his fingers stuck in the door again, and wiggled them a bit to see that they were still there, feeling a little less pain and a little more stiffness in the process. The padding in the little metal splints had begun to stink. Peter sniffed his fingers just to smell that sweet and sour odor, both repulsive and attractive like pungent ethnic food.

"Son, quit sniffing your damned paws. You look like some kinda fuckin' perv, boy."

Peter thought the smell of that stink-bait was gross. His sweaty, flaky fingers just smelled a little like the sweet and sour pork that his mom used to buy at the Chinese place on Sundays.

They walked up to the front door and Verlin knocked. Peter looked up at him, wondering why he didn't just open the door with his key, but didn't ask.

"Hey guys," a woman said as she opened the door.

"Hey there," Verlin said and walked into the house, Peter close behind. The lady patted Verlin's arm as he passed. He went to the kitchen and got another beer out of the refrigerator and popped the top and threw the tab in the trash can.

"Can I have one?" Peter said.

Verlin and Louise laughed. Peter felt a little uneasy as the two adults stood there laughing, as if he were the butt of some inside joke. Peter looked around the apartment and then back up at his dad.

"That's beer, honey," Louise said. She pointed at Peter's hand from where she stood and said, "What happened?"

"It got smashed in the car door." He knew not to say that his dad did it.

"Oww," she said.

"I got a nail in my foot and hand, too."

"Damn, boy," Verlin said. "Don't go turning into no damned Stigmata on my ass. You'll be ridin' around with Roland Stacks before ya know it. Come on now. Get with the program."

Louise slapped Verlin on the arm a little playfully, and then moved away quickly, standing at a distance, like Peter and his dad were suddenly subjects in some sort of subversive social experiment. She smiled when she saw Peter looking at her intently. Peter thought that she had large breasts like the other lady. The nice lady that they spent the night with on the road. She had leaned over Peter, with her robe open, exposing her soft, tan chest, as her sweet smell made him feel fuzzy and nervous inside. Louise made him feel that way too, but in a cooler, more distant way.

"So, how was the trip?"

"Long." Verlin said.

"Did you two go fishin'?"

"I did. This knuckle-head didn't catch shit," Verlin said and threw his empty beer can in the trash, and grabbed another one from the fridge. "He'll get the bug, I guess."

Peter didn't want to get any bugs. He didn't like bugs really, but lady bugs and butterflies, and he didn't even know if those were really bugs or not.

"How are you?" Louise said to Peter, as Verlin came around her, smacking her hard on the butt. She bugged her eyes out at him.

"Good."

"You're bigger than I thought you'd be." She crossed her arms and bent over, getting uncomfortably close to him. "Are you hungry?"

"Yes ma'am."

"You have such good manners, Pete," she said. "Sit down here at the table and I'll get you something to eat."

Peter sat down and his dad patted him on the back on his way out the front door. Louise started grabbing Pyrex dishes and sandwich bags and Tupperware containers out of the fridge, putting them on the table in front of Peter. It looked like she expected a crowd by all of the food she put out, but he was used to that from being over at Grammie's house all the time. She would always put a feast out no matter if there were one or ten people over. Hospitality was her gift to anyone that came through her front door.

Peter thought that Louise seemed nice enough, but his dad and her seemed nervous, jumpy even, as if they had never talked to a kid before. Peter just sat in his chair watching Louise carefully, as she prepared the table. When she moved, her breasts jiggled in her t-shirt. Her really short jean shorts showed off her tan, muscular legs. His mom didn't wear shorts that short. Peter couldn't stop staring at her move through the kitchen, as if she were some kind of exotic jungle animal trapped in the kitchen. He perused her body, her face and hair, just waiting for her to jump across the room and devour him out of his seat.

"Have you been having fun?" she said, looking over her shoulder as she bent into the refrigerator.

Peter nodded that he had been having fun.

"You don't talk too much, do you, hon?"

"That's what my dad said."

"He talks all the time, Pete." She stood up and pointed the knife in her hand where Verlin had just been standing, like she was marking his spot. "We'll have to tell him to shut up if he keeps carryin' on like he does, okay hon? He's just a lot of hot air sometimes."

Peter laughed. He had never heard anyone talk about his dad like that before. Most people seemed to be really nice to him or kind of shy and quiet around him. She joked around about his dad, but then again, Peter thought that ribbing the old man would be off limits to him, disrespectful even, perhaps.

Louise made Peter a sandwich and put it on a plate with some chips and some spaghetti that she had warmed in a small Tupperware container. She could sure feed a guy like Grammie could, he thought.

Verlin walked through the door, arms full, dropping his cargo by the couch. "Damn, woman," he said. "You tryin' to fatten that little shit up?"

"You shouldn't call him names, Verlin."

"Shut the hell up," he said and went to the back of the apartment. Peter didn't know if his dad would come back to the kitchen raising hell or crying, swinging fists or dancing a jig for all the happy bastards he'd ever known. Peter sat quietly eating his food, almost crying that it tasted so good.

Peter could hear the shower running in the back room. He and Louise sat at the table eating, Peter his sandwich, her something that he had never seen before, that she got out of one of the Pyrex dishes. They didn't say too much to each other. Really, Peter just looked at her tinted glasses and those large, round breasts, not knowing why he felt the way he felt. She didn't seem to care that he could almost see right through her shirt, worn thin and tight as it were. She smelled good. She didn't smell like his mom, though, her smell making his throat feel thick and warm. Peter watched Louise chew her food, slowly. Her small mouth, her tan face.

Verlin came out of the back room wearing a pair of gym shorts and smoking a cigarette, his peeling shoulders and chest from sunburn, peppered with water droplets. He walked past them and got another beer out of the fridge. Peter thought about jokingly asking for another beer again, just to see what his dad and Louise would say, but just kept quiet, thinking that they might laugh at him again. Verlin didn't like stupidity.

"Boy, you need to take a shower after supper, okay?"

"I've never taken a shower."

"You damn sure smell like it, boy."

"Verlin!" Louise shouted, as if he had told them both to go to hell.

"Well, the boy smells like a dirty dog. He keeps smelling his fingers like a fuckin' nigger or somethin', ya know?"

"What's gotten into you?"

"You just heard him say he's never taken a shower."

"I take baths."

"You can help him if you want," Verlin said, bobbing and weaving like some hopped-up hick high school boy.

Peter didn't like making his dad crazy all the time. Louise seemed gentle with the old man's temper, as if she had been issued the missing owner's manual to the guy, the one that everyone else in his life had never been given. She could maybe keep a lid on things for the most part, when Peter got things stirred up.

Peter took the last bite of his spaghetti and pushed his plate toward the center of the table.

"Son, you need to wash your plate. There ain't no maids around here, like at home, alright?"

"We don't have a maid at home."

"Boy, you about as thick as a fuckin' horse dick, ya know that?"

"No, sir."

"Verlin," Louise said, feigning fatigue. "Sir?"

"The boy's got respect. You could learn a thing or two from the little shit, woman."

Louise got up and left the room. Peter could hear the water running again. He and his dad sat at the kitchen table, quiet.

"Do you have TV?" Peter finally said.

"Hell no. TV's for faggots, boy."

Peter didn't know for sure what a faggot was, but by the tone of his dad's voice, figured it wasn't something good, like a "rag-head," or a "hippie bitch," or a "fuckin' nigger." He stared at his father, realizing right then that the silence between them felt okay. Weird, but okay, and Peter didn't have satisfactory enough comments most of the time anyway, so he just kept his mouth shut yet again, giving the knot in the pit of his belly time to diffuse, to settle out of his system. If Peter had known the term "damage control," he would have given his task-at-hand a name, to be sure.

Peter ate some more potato chips right out of the bag. He looked over at his dad, who had started trimming his fingernails with a pocket knife that he had pulled from his tight jean-short pocket. He scraped under the nails with the tip of the knife and then went around the end of his finger, cutting the little white crescents off, and letting them fall to the table. After the old man did every finger, one-by-one, slowly and deliberately, letting each crescent fall to the table like flakes of ash, he pushed them into a little pile, and then looked up at Peter.

"Damn, boy. You're gonna have to get a job if you keep eatin' like that."

"Okay," Peter said.

Verlin laughed. That laugh felt real like rain to the boy. Peter smiled.

Louise came out from the back room and Verlin said, "You better let the water heat up before you run his bath. I just took a shower."

"So did I."

"More of a reason to let'er warm up."

"We didn't run that much water."

"You the fuckin' plumbin' expert now?"

"Verlin!"

"Well, shit. I don't need no damned punk kid and my old lady disputin' every damned thing I say."

"Thanks, Louise," Peter said. Louise's freshly shampooed hair smelled good.

"Call her mom," Verlin said.

"Verlin." Louise bugged her eyes out at Verlin, and then smiled at Peter. "You can call me Louise. That's okay, hon."

Louise walked over to Peter and gently patted him on the head. Her shoulders seemed to have fallen a little, softened some, and she smiled more when she addressed him. She had fed and talked to him, took a quick shower, and would soon run his bath water, as well. Peter liked the lady named Louise, as nervous as she might have been, she knew how to make a kid feel comfortable.

Verlin got up from the table when Louise sat down. He went over to the stereo in the corner and put a record on. Willie Nelson sang out into the room like a reluctant sigh. Peter had never heard Willie's raspy, romantic voice until that evening, the four of them in his new home. Willie talked about love and loss and crying in the rain.

Verlin went back to the table and said, "That's music, boy."

"Yeah," Peter said. He couldn't really argue, because he had only listened to what he heard being played around the house back home and in his uncle's cars. The Beatles, Edwin Starr, Mo-Town, Led Zeppelin.

"Verlin, can I go run his water now?"

"Go on, woman. Gitter done."

"I like rock-and-roll, Pete," she said and went to the bathroom to run his bath.

Chapter 9

Red-Headed Stranger played loudly on the stereo, under the booming deluge that came down from the swollen, purple-blue storm clouds. Willie Nelson sang out like a lone coyote might have at the sight of that ominous summer storm coming on like bad news. Peter felt the song from the inside out, his heartbeat and marrow murmuring...*the preachin's over, and the lesson's begun.*

The song felt like an old friend stopping by after years gone by.

Verlin opened what must have been about his third pack of cigarettes of the day. Peter had helped him quite a bit, just the same. Peter thought that he probably usually smoked a half pack a day, but he had drunk a lot of beer, and that usually bumped his intake up to about two packs. Between the two of them, they could keep a plantation and a pulmonary specialist thriving. Peter felt pretty good, though, hanging out with the old man, smoking and drinking and driving the now sopping wet country roads.

"Where we goin'?" Peter said.

"Town."

"No shit?"

Verlin looked over at Peter with a serious, off-guard look at first, and then smiled and said, "Chip off the old block, huh?" The old man gunned it when he pulled out onto the highway, fish-tailing wildly right before he passed a lone car. "Dumb ass," he said, looking in the rearview.

They barreled down that wide, sweeping highway on the high plains, wind and wet in their hair, and beer and cigarettes on their breath. Peter tossed his cigarette out the window and said, "We've been here before."

"You bet."

Peter only meant it as a partial jab, them rolling down the same highway they had traveled as Verlin had come to get Peter and his mother all those years ago, that vacation in Mississippi.

"Do you ever talk to my mom?"

Verlin turned down the stereo and shouted over the wind and roar of the 350. "Roll that window up! Your gonna get my shit all wet," he said, lighting another cigarette. Peter rolled the window up. "I called a couple times a few years ago, but she acted like I was up to something." A few years ago, Peter thought. "She said your step-dad didn't like me calling."

Peter knew better, because his step-dad didn't care about anything but his car, weight-lifting and porn magazines.

"Did you ever ask for me?"

"Your mom wouldn't let me talk to you." Another lie, Peter thought. His mom never said a bad word about his dad. She just let him know that they had their share of problems and that his dad had moved on, and that was that. His mom and Grammie were the two who actually encouraged him to reunite with his dad. "Anyway, I thought you should be the one to contact *me*," Verlin added.

"Oh."

"Boy, you sure talk a lot more than you did when you were just a little shit. Remember when you came to visit us in Mississippi?" Verlin quickly rolled down his window, rain splattering hard on his arm and the side of his balding head, and tossed his cigarette. He rolled the window up, and tossed the wet pack of cigarettes to Peter, telling him to get a couple more. Peter lit two cigarettes and handed his dad one.

Peter took a deep drag and said, "I used to be shy."

Verlin laughed, sitting forward in his seat to see better through the mess outside, the truck hydroplaning now and again.

They crossed the river bridge and slowed to make the turn near Grammie's house. The old brick streets were a little rough, as they had lost a brick or two over the last several decades. Those remaining simply stood as a sturdy reminder of the industriousness of Roosevelt and his WPA.

"When the hell are they gonna replace these shitty streets?" Verlin said.

"I like the brick streets."

"Well, you ain't gonna drive my truck down these damned things."

Verlin punched the gas, and the tires broke loose in the puddled streets, whining like a sick dog. Peter laughed at the irony, as he stared out the window through the prism of rivulets streaming down his window. Peter threw another cigarette out the window and tossed his latest empty beer can in the bed of the truck, and then rolled up again.

They pulled up in front of a familiar house. "You remember this place?" Verlin said.

"Not really."

"This is your grandma's old house. My friend lives here now."

Peter grabbed his suit jacket, smoothing his wet hair back, as they got out of the truck and walked up to the front door. Verlin let himself in, Peter following. A tall, skinny, blonde lady greeted them with a smile and a hug apiece, as if she had been waiting there for them all night. She didn't seem startled or caught off-guard. Two guys wet and drunk and reeking of cigarettes.

"Son, this is Carla, a friend of mine. You remember?"

Peter smiled as he sideways glanced at her lonely, green eyes. She smiled back. A pretty lady for her age, he thought. "I'm sorry, I don't remember."

"Remember our vacation? Mississippi?" Verlin said.

Carla turned and went to the kitchen, as if she had suddenly grown impatient with Peter's trying to recall her name. Peter could tell them yes, that he did remember her, and that it was so damned great to see her after all those years, but then he thought that surely the woman couldn't be that needy, could she? She couldn't have cared that deeply that Peter vindicate her presence, both past and present, with his memory of her from nearly twenty years before.

Carla walked back into the living room where father and son sat on the big, overstuffed couch, Verlin smoking another cigarette, flicking the ash into his hand.

"You got an ashtray, woman?"

"No smoking, Verlin," Carla said, pointing at a little carved bust on her entertainment cabinet.

"Is that Keith Richards?" Peter said.

"Yes it is," she said, sitting on the chair opposite them, looking bothered and a little distressed all of a sudden. "So, are you guys staying here, Verlin?"

Verlin laughed a little and elbowed Peter. Peter hated when people drugged him into their blatant jokes at other's expense. She asked a simple question, she deserved an answer for all Peter could tell.

"That's funny," Peter said to Carla.

"What's that, buster?" she said.

"The statue, the little bust of Keith Richards."

Carla looked at the figure on the entertainment cabinet and then aloofly said to Peter, "He's an ugly bastard, Peter. It reminds me of why I quit smoking Goddamned cigarettes, okay?"

"Sounds good," Peter said, forcing a smile, sitting up a little straighter, trying to put the lady at ease as best he could with good posture and attentiveness.

"Could he get a poke?" Verlin said.

Carla laughed out loud. Peter thought that the old man had said something about a little poke, the days drinking and smoking finally catching up with him. He didn't really feel too wasted anymore, however, a little foggy maybe, as his drunk had come all the way back around to a nearly stone sober state.

"Are you serious?" she said.

"He's my boy."

"Together?"

They carried on for a second as if Peter weren't even in the room. Another pet peeve, he thought. People talking about you while you're in the room, burned him about as much as someone asking you a point-blank question and then instantly becoming preoccupied with something else when you start to give the answer.

"What are you talkin' about?" Peter finally said.

"Do you want to have a little fun?" Verlin said, nudging Peter again, laughing.

Peter brushed him off, feeling like he should probably disinfect or something, really hating the fact that his dad was nudging him like a damned grade-schooler playing tricks on the little girls on the playground.

Carla got up out of the chair and headed back to her bedroom.

"Are you saying that you want me to sleep with your girlfriend?"

"Boy, you need to start growing up."

"I live with a girl. We have dogs and cats," Peter said. "I've been on my own since I was seventeen. I have aches and pains and heartburn, dammit! What the fuck are you talking about?"

"Don't you think she's good-looking?"

"That's not the point," Peter said. "Aren't you still married to Louise?"

"Son, you got a lot to learn."

Carla walked back into the room, where the guys still discussed whether or not Peter wanted to have sex with her. She had put on a sheer, oversized t-shirt and presumably nothing else on underneath. Peter had to admit, her legs looked good. She had a way about her that let you know *she* would be in control, carrying herself with a little more confidence than before, as if she just remembered what she was put on the earth to do. She moved over to the couch and sat between Peter and Verlin.

Peter did remember Carla, sure, finally, as reducing women down to lusty, physical attributes proved only too natural in a way. Peter couldn't deny the fact that he liked his women a little messed up in the head. More adventure. Like Perky, and like all of the others over the years, for that matter. Something desperate and slightly psychotic, which always helped to produce a feverish, sheer erotic passion once the clothes come off. Sex is like some ancient medium, channeling all of the confusion and regret and fear and desire into palpable physical pleasure. Peter tried to cover his erection, folding his hands over his lap, as he self-consciously darted his eyes around the living room.

Verlin got up from the couch and went into the kitchen, where Peter could hear a beer can opening, and then the back door creaking open. The screen door slammed closed. Peter looked over at Carla, putting his arms around her, as she leaned into him for a kiss, pressing her firm breasts against him, pulling him into her.

Chapter 10

The next morning, Peter actually woke up feeling rested. He hadn't slept that well in weeks. A five year-old boy doesn't usually think about getting enough sleep, let alone obsess about sleep, unless he isn't getting any. The sunlight came through the bedroom window where he lay on a makeshift bed of blankets and sheets. He stirred a little, his neck stiff from resting his head on a thick couch cushion. He could lay there as long as he needed to. He was on vacation.

As Peter thought about lying in bed for the rest of the day, the door to the room slowly crept open, and Louise's head popped through. "Would you like some breakfast, Pete?"

"Sure."

"Would you like to sleep some more?"

"Sure."

She brushed her silky, brown hair out of her eyes and said, "Your dad's still asleep. I'll wake you when he gets up, okay?"

He smiled as she closed the door.

What might've been an hour or so later, Peter awakened from a dream, sweating with mixed feelings. In the dream, his mom, her parents and her brothers all sat around a desk in a courtroom, trying to decide whether they would go to Disney Land or Disney World. Peter's uncle Lenny kept banging the judge's gavel every time the group got off track. The family cop. They would all start talking about Mickey Mouse or how California is better than Florida, and then sure enough, down slammed the gavel, right in the middle of the table, sending reverb through Peter's little arms like electricity. Life is short, Lenny would say, and then slam that damned thing to the table again. Nevertheless, the dream kept going round and round like that, until one last blow to the table with the gavel sent Peter's head popping up from his makeshift bed again.

The door to the bedroom eased open, and Louise craned her head into the doorway again. "Hi Pete," she said. "I have eggs and French toast if you're ready to eat." She paused for a second and then looked at him with what he felt was genuine thoughtfulness. She started to say something, paused and then added, "I tried to wake you before your dad left, but you just wouldn't budge, hon. You must've been real tired."

"Yeah."

Peter removed the sheet that covered him and got to his feet. Other than the sporadic sharp pains in his right hand, he felt good. Even his punctured foot felt a lot better. He felt clean, rested and ready to wreck some breakfast.

Peter padded out to the living room, where he heard the voice of an anchorman. The teaser for the afternoon news said something about the missing girl from Tucson. The guy on the television said that she had been missing for ten days now, and that her and her captor had possibly made it as far as Kansas City. Tune in this afternoon to hear more about the missing Ramona Whitcanuck, the man said.

"You better get in here, Peter," Louise said. "Your dad doesn't like television."

Peter clung to the periphery to hear what the anchor had to say about the hippie chick that went off with the crazy gang. Gas was at an all-time high. Fights were breaking out at gas stations in Chicago and L.A. Peter froze where he stood, his little mind firing every probability off like a mad chess player. If it wasn't crazy gangs and rag-heads, you were sure to meet your end at the dang gas station.

Louise moved quickly to the TV and shut it off. "Come on, now, hon. Your daddy don't want you watching that crap."

"Yes, ma'am."

A platter of French toast and sausage, and a bowl of scrambled eggs lay steaming on the kitchen table. Peter liked eggs, especially the dunky eggs. That's what he called over-easy eggs, because you can dunk your toast into the yolk and then scoop the white up with the soaked toast. His mom made dunky eggs. Scrambled eggs would suit him just fine, nevertheless.

"Sit down. You want some orange juice?"

"Sure."

Louise came back to the kitchen, where Peter had pulled a chair up to the table, and she poured him a glass of orange juice and told him to help himself to all the food he wanted.

"Where's dad?"

"He's at work."

"Where does he work?"

"For the government."

Peter's eyes got wide after Louise said "government." Peter's mom was just a nurse. He thought that his dad probably spied on bad guys, maybe vandals like the one's that put leaves in his motorcycle gas tank, and then had to give his full reports to the President each week. He was probably responsible for the safety of the whole country. His dad, the hero. Peter didn't know what the word "ironic" meant.

 Peter really just felt happy that he and his dad had finally made it home, to somewhere they could hopefully stay put for a while. He thought about the long ride, his dad being mean a couple times. No big deal, really. Not like that Ramona girl on the news. The news man said that they had possibly made it as far as Kansas City. Peter thought that he and his dad had gone a lot further than Kansas City. Ramona probably missed her mom too.

"We're gonna go see my mom and dad later," Louise said.

 "Okay," Peter said, looking at Louise, like a woman her age having parents was weird.

Louise sat down at the table, where Peter had piled his plate high with a little bit of everything. She scooped a serving-spoonful of eggs and grabbed a piece of French toast and a piece of sausage. He looked over at her plate and then back at his. She smiled at Peter.

"Can I call my mom?"

Louise looked at him like she'd heard something strange outside and then said, "You better wait 'til your dad gets home. He's got the number."

"I know the number," Peter said, beaming.

She smiled again, then patted his left hand. "I'm sure you do, but I don't know if the phone will dial long distance right now."

Peter felt a rush of air leave his lungs all of a sudden, as if all the available oxygen in the world had just been sucked up into a void beyond. The sweetness of the French toast turned bland, and the juice suddenly tasted like water. His breakfast didn't look nearly as good as it had only a moment earlier. He almost felt like a hostage, had he known what a hostage felt like.

"Okay," Peter said, somberly turning to his cooling food to take another bite.

Chapter 11

Peter and Verlin said their goodbyes to Carla, lingering, awkward kisses all the way around, and let themselves out the front door. On the drive over to Peter's mom's house, they stewed in their silence, both keeping their eyes glued to the windshield, rain still coming down outside, as it made contorted images in rivulets, under the diffuse, yellow glare of the street lights. Verlin pulled into the side driveway of his mom's house and turned the truck off.

After sitting silently a moment longer, they got out of the pick-up and made themselves a little camp in Peter's mom's garage, the rain pounding the earth all around them again. The guys talked about the past, making up their own future. Suspension of disbelief wasn't just about watching action movies, Peter thought, as he sat in his metal folding chair, wet with sex and rain, listening to his dad ramble on about anything he felt worthy of embellishment. The passing day had been like a story Peter had heard somewhere years before in passing. One of those stories you hear that makes you think, 'Better you than me.'

Verlin told Peter about how his mom had screwed him over all those years that he couldn't remember, and how all of her brothers worked together to keep him out of the picture forever. Peter's grandparents too. They were all in it together to spite his poor old dad.

"This right here's what I got my purple heart for, boy," Verlin said.

Peter leaned in closer to see the little scar on his dad's right index finger. "What?"

"Yeah." He popped open another beer that he'd grabbed from the cooler sitting between he and Peter. "They thought I took a shot. It was a beer can tab."

"Are you serious?"

"One of them old-style ones. The ones you pulled all the way off, ya know?" Verlin laughed at Peter, still bending over the old man's finger, shaking his head in feigned disbelief.

Sure, Peter thought, he wanted to believe almost anything the guy told him at that point. The old man giving him a custom '51 Chevy pick-up, the Army-issue, model 1911 Colt .45, and all the other bells and perks between. Peter stood up and walked to the edge of the garage to watch the rain for a second.

"Didn't you almost kill some preacher back in the day?" Peter said with his back still turned to his dad.

"Ah, shit, boy. I was just having some fun, ya know?"

"Do you want to spend the night here?"

"Hell no! Your mama don't want me to stay in her house," Verlin said. "Your step-daddy wouldn't like that too much, anyway. He'd probably get scared havin' a real man stay the night, huh?"

Peter turned around to look at his dad and said, "Why did you take a purple heart, if you didn't really get hurt in combat?"

"I thought it would be a good souvenir. They're cool fuckin' medals, man."

"When are you gonna fix your tire?"

"Damn boy, you sound like a fuckin' cop now. All you got is questions."

"I asked a lot of questions when I was a kid, didn't I?"

Verlin looked up at Peter with an expression of equal parts shock, frustration and constipation.

"You sit down for a little bit and rest. I'll change the tire," Peter said.

They blew a tire right up the street from the house. Verlin punched the gas coming onto Peter's mom's street and the truck got away from him in the pouring rain, for a split second, hopping up into someone's yard, only to come down back onto the street with a shredded tire. "Fuck it," Verlin had said, and punched the gas again, jerking the pick-up from side to side down the street, until they pulled into the side driveway.

"Okay?"

"Shit, boy, you can do it, then," Verlin said, chuckling to himself.

"I gotta take a leak."

"You need to tell that step-dad of yours to put a bathroom in out here."

"Yeah?"

"Shit, he probably can't do that though, huh?"

Peter didn't like his step-dad, at all really, but then he also didn't appreciate being manipulated by his dead-beat dad either. Peter stepped into the cool rain and went to the side of the garage where he unzipped his damp suit pants. He had left his jacket hanging on the doorknob of the garage to dry out a little. Peter zipped up and went back into the garage.

"Are you mad at me?" Verlin said, as Peter came back into the garage.

"Why?"

"Aww shit. That little deal at the pond earlier."

Peter thought about his answer for a second and then said, "I understand. Things have been hard for you."

Then, as quickly as the old man's odd demeanor of remorse had come, it vanished, and he said, "Shit boy, I just wanted to toughen you up a little." Verlin's eyes looked as if they could almost roll back into his red face. "You need a man around to teach you a thing or two. Ya know?"

Peter grabbed another beer from the cooler and opened it. Verlin stood up from his chair, stumbled a couple steps forward, and then went to the bed of the pick-up, where he moved some things around. The old man pulled a jack and a four-way out of the bed of the truck and sat them down next to the shredded tire. He reached back into the bed and started to lift the spare out. Peter came up beside him and patted him on the arm.

"Go sit down, dad. I'll take care of it," Peter said, pulling the full-sized tire out of the truck bed.

Peter could see himself in Verlin, or see Verlin in him rather, like a preview of life to come, if he didn't get his shit together. He realized, if only for a split second, that he had to quit lying to himself and accept his limitations, get away from Perky, go back to school maybe, get a real job at some point. Peter thought if nothing else came from the visit with his dad, he would at least be able to see what he didn't want to be.

Peter wanted to scream, but didn't, probably out of fear of pissing his dad off, or hurting his feelings, or waking people up, or simply realizing that it wouldn't do any good anyhow. That fire in the belly would still be there. His desire to tear the world down, to tear it all apart, so that it could possibly, one day be rebuilt into something more resembling hope would still be inside like a fever, that grind and itch. The same old fear, relentless and dull, like a guilty conscience, numbing from the inside out. Peter wanted nothing more to know his father one second, and then the next, all of the pain and longing and resentment made him clench his fists and hold his breath like a risky bet.

Verlin stood over Peter, watching his deliberate movements as Peter broke loose all of the lug nuts, and then went to put the bumper-jack under the shiny, chrome bumper. Peter jacked it up, took the lugs all the way off and replaced the brushed aluminum-alloy wheel and shredded tire with an old steel wheel that had a good tire on it.

"Boy, where'd you learn to change a tire?"

"On the side of the road somewhere," Peter said, putting lug nuts on, one by one. "I have my own business, you know?"

"That don't mean shit," Verlin said. "I know grown men that can barely wipe their own ass that run Fortune-500 companies."

Peter partially tightened all of the lug nuts with the four-way and said, "I believe it." And then he let the truck down on the jack.

"Your step-daddy teach you a thing or two?"

"My grandpa. My uncles," Peter said, tightening the last lug nut, really cranking down on the four-way for added emphasis.

"Aww, ain't that cute."

Peter got up from beside the truck and put the shredded tire and tools in the bed. Verlin watched him move in the drizzling rain, not saying a word, as if he had just realized that his son did in fact exist, moving and breathing right there in the summer rain like a hungry animal. Verlin put his arm out as Peter busied himself right outside the garage door picking up the little mess that he and his dad had made during their impromptu jam session. Verlin put his arm down and squinted at Peter when his gesture went unnoticed, not having anything clever to say. Peter walked back inside the garage and closed the ice chest and grabbed another cigarette from the pack sitting on one of the folding chairs.

He lit up and said, "Dad, I gotta crash. I have work tomorrow."

"Yeah, I better go." Verlin said, swaying, putting his hands in his pockets and then pulling them out to cross his arms. Peter feared that the old man would fall down, but decided he couldn't do anything for him right then, at any rate. Letting Verlin drive home drunk would be a guilty pleasure that Peter felt he could live with...but then again...he admitted to himself that he would feel a bit responsible if the old man ended up in a ditch dead somewhere on the way to God-knows-where.

"Where are you going?" Peter said.

"What do you care?"

Peter thought that he should say, 'Aw, ain't that cute,' but left it alone, unfortunately feeling nothing but pity for the old man.

Verlin clumsily packed up his ice chest and walked it over to his truck, straining to heave it over the edge into the bed. He put his crushed cigarette pack in his wet breast pocket, and then put out his hand to shake with Peter. "I'll call you in week or so, to see if you still wanna come down to visit. Okay?"

"Sounds good," Peter said, shaking his dad's hand, squeezing hard enough to register.

"Damn, boy. You gonna crush my paw."

Verlin pulled Peter by the hand, closer to himself, and gave him a big hug. Peter stood there, totally sober then, not wanting to let his dad see him starting to cry, not wanting to let go of the safety of close proximity, his face out of sight, yet feeling repulsed in a way, as if it all were a sham that would inevitably fade once the sun came up. The first form of affection Peter could ever remember from his dad, that hug. He held on tight, despite his mixed emotions, as if he might blow into the mist and rain if he let go too soon.

"Boy, come on, don't you go turnin' gay on me."

And just as quickly as Verlin surprised Peter with his affection, he squashed the moment like only Peter knew that Verlin could. Peter assumed that tender moments weren't too comfortable for guys who had never come to grips with their feelings, their past, and he let go of Verlin. Peter watched him stagger over to the truck, waving Peter's concern for his safety off like a pesky fly.

"You be careful," Peter said.

"I'm just goin' over to Aunt Bitty's house." Verlin started the truck and slowly backed out of the driveway, pulling out onto the street. "See ya, boy."

So much for feeling responsible for the old man.

Chapter 12

After the first night at his new home, Peter felt pretty confident that it could be a while before he saw his mom again. They had not spoken in weeks, and his dad didn't seem too concerned about making calling Peter's mom a top priority.

The move had been confusing to Peter. He thought that they were staying put in the apartment where they had first arrived in Mississippi, but were soon packing up and moving to a house out on the edge of town. He just wanted to stay somewhere, and to meet kids and to play outside, and to see his mom. He liked knowing what would happen next.

"Pete, when you get done eatin', you can take a shower, or bath, if you want to," Louise said, with a towel still around her body and another around her head. "Did you like your breakfast?"

"Yes, ma'am."

"I'm gonna get ready," she said. "We'll go to see my folks after a bit, okay?"

Peter had never been asked so many times if things were "okay" with him, or really been asked his opinion about much. She treated him like a little person, a little man, he thought. It felt weird at first, but he had to admit that it made him feel good, important in a way.

Peter finished his breakfast, went to the sink and washed his dishes, and then put them in the drying rack on the counter. He could smell the clean scent of shampoo and fresh skin lingering from where Louise had been standing. He decided that he too would just take a shower, just like the adults did. Peter was getting older, after all.

Louise came back into the kitchen and said, "I put a towel and washcloth on the toilet for you."

"Thank you."

"Do you know how to work the shower?" Peter hesitated for a moment, so she said, "Come on, I'll show you how it works."

They went into the bathroom where she told him to undress. He had never undressed in front of anyone but his mom and grandparents back home. He stood perfectly still for a moment until she said that she would leave the room and come back in after he had gotten in the shower and was behind the curtain.

He undressed and yelled 'okay' through the door, letting her know that she could come in. Peter could hear Louise creep through the door and come all the way into the bathroom. He felt a little nervous with her so near, him being naked and all. She moved the shower curtain over enough to turn the water on and said, "You just turn it on like you're running a bath, and then you just pull this little lever up, and the shower comes on." She pointed to the little lever above the faucet. "Go ahead."

Peter pulled the lever, and the cold water rained over him, making his skin seize like nails on a blackboard. Louise reached up and turned the shower head to where the water wasn't directly showering over him. She leaned halfway into the shower to adjust the water and then stared right at Peter.

"Hon, you just adjust the temperature just like a bath, okay?" She smiled at him and said, "My, my, your little weenie shriveled right up, didn't it?"

Peter put his hands over his crotch and looked down at the faucet.

"I bet you take after your daddy when the water's all hot and steamy, huh?"

Peter kept staring and the faucet, then hesitatingly said, "I don't know."

Louise quit smiling and then ducked out of the shower. She told Peter to take his time and wash up real good. Peter felt relieved at hearing the door close behind her.

The shower felt otherworldly good to Peter when he finally found the right temperature. Then slowly, as his body adjusted to the heat of the water, he turned the temperature up in slight increments, until he couldn't stand it any hotter.

Peter got out and toweled off in front of the mirror. He felt dirty even though he just got out of the shower. He thought about taking another one, but didn't want to make his dad mad with using too much water. He looked at his little five year-old body in the mirror and dropped his towel. His penis pointed out in front of him, bald and erect. Peter frowned in the mirror thinking about what Louise had said. He didn't know why he felt bad, but that something just didn't feel right. He thought about staying in the bathroom for the rest of the day, but then thought that his dad would get mad about that too, and come in with a beer and a belt and go to work on him, ruining another good start to a day. The days had become dull with a gray sameness that Peter didn't like. No kids, no playing really. Just him and Louise and his dad once in a while, when he wasn't out doing whatever he did.

After standing in front of the mirror for a few minutes, he went to the door and cracked it, looking out to see if anyone moved about. "Louise, could you bring me my clothes?"

"Do you have anything that's clean?"

"I don't think so."

Peter could hear her rummaging around in the other room, and then she lightly knocked on the door after he had already closed it. "Here you go, hon." Peter opened the door again and grabbed the clothes that she held through the little opening. "Do you need some help drying off?"

"It's okay," he said, feeling instantly nervous at the question, as if the woman would come in there with him anyway and yank on his dick just for the fun of it.

"We'll get you some new clothes today. Maybe after we go to mom's. Sound good?"

"Okay."

Peter got dressed and said the *Our Father* to himself. Grammie always said the rosary. The *Our Father*, yet another proof of his good parochial school upbringing. He said the prayer on automatic, like the blessing before his meals. He didn't really know what else *to* do. He couldn't teleport himself to another time and place, couldn't shape-shift, yet all he really wanted was to feel safe and normal and warm again. Everything had become so unpredictable, so unstable, with no reprieve from the fear inside, welling up like dirty water. And the fear had not been there before. It felt to Peter like it came out of the air like a cold or a stomach bug comes out of the air, and so he thought that hopefully it would soon leave just the same.

Chapter 13

Perky had really begun to drive Peter mad lately. He caught her messing around on him again, with some guy that she knew from high school back in the day, and told himself that he had to leave the crazy bitch once and for all. He didn't feel like he had any options, though, only feeling trapped in his convenient misery with nowhere to go or no power to change. Sure, he had a little money, but he had stashed that in a safe at Grammie's house for her eventual investment. She was good at that sort of thing. Peter had to get more money for now, he thought. Fast.

Perky's old man said that he seriously needed Peter's help in the family business. B and C-credit transactions for deadbeats and malingerers trying to vindicate their dismal lives with some crappy starter house, Peter's words. That was the family business, sub-prime mortgages, and Peter had begun to have his fill with that too, but didn't want to disappoint Perky's dad by saying that he was moving on to something better. There wasn't anything better, as far as Peter could tell.

Peter decided to call his dad. Verlin had told Peter to call him if he wanted to come down for a visit. That the boy could even come stay with him and his family for a couple weeks if he wanted to. Meet the family and see how he liked it in a smaller town, where people were simpler, where life happened a little slower. Verlin said that maybe Peter could get his life together, really get it together, and that a new place might just be the solution to all of his problems. Verlin was his dad after all. The boy needed his daddy.

Peter dialed the number, and Louise answered. He hadn't spoken with her since the end of his "vacation," some decade and a half earlier. She still spoke with that smoky voice, cool in her indifference.

"How have you been?" Peter said.

"Good," she said. "Some days are better than others, you know?"

Yeah, Peter did know, but he just wanted to cut the small-talk and get right to business. "Is Verlin there?"

"He's really excited about you coming to visit."

"Oh...good."

"He's outside with the girls right now. Let me go get him."

"Thanks."

Peter looked at the phone and thought about hanging up, but put the receiver back to his ear. A flash of an image of Verlin slamming beers and shooting his pistol in the back yard, with the little girls dancing, came and went. He thought about calling his mom to ask if he could just go stay there until he had the chance to regroup, thinking that he could make things work with his step-dad if absolutely necessary. Peter could get back in touch with his dad when he did something with his life, eventually. Something important and real.

Peter put the phone back to his ear.

"Hey there, boy."

Peter heard his dad's voice, feeling his heart beating in his chest, as he gripped the cold plastic of the telephone receiver up to his ear. The eerie beat of his pulse reverberated up his arm, to the point of hardly being able to hold onto the phone any longer, his ears thumping.

"You comin' down to see us?" Verlin said. Peter thought that amends from the old man would be nice. He thought that the previous visit had left him with some big questions about his father's intentions in general, and he really wanted to know that things could actually progress now that they had moved onto a new day.

"I was thinking about it."

"You got two sisters here that are pretty damned excited about meeting their big brother." Peter heard a cigarette being lit at the other end of the phone, and then an exhale a moment later. "You knew you had a couple sisters, didn't ya?"

"Yeah," Peter said, half-heartedly, as he faintly recollected some mention of half-sisters in the midst of their drinking spree together. Peter didn't actually know his dad and Louise were still together. Peter figured that his dad went psycho on her years ago, and that she probably bailed on him or killed herself. But then again, Peter did remember her living in a certain kind of hypnotized, subservient acceptance of his father. Not denial, per se, but in a brain-washed-minion sort of way, perhaps.

"They're really excited. Your sisters."

Peter didn't like the sound of "sisters." It had a cheap ring to it, as if his dad simply attempted to coax him with whatever ammo he might have at his disposal right then. Sisters, money, trucks and guns all began to sound like some not-so-clever marketing scheme to him.

"Yeah?"

"Do you think your mom could bring you down? Maybe we could all visit or somethin', ya know?"

Peter laughed into the phone.

"What's so funny, boy?"

"Are you serious?"

"Well, fuck it, if that's the way you wanna be. Forget I even said anything," Verlin said, almost sounding hurt.

Peter thought that he should just end the whole charade right there. The guy was too damned unstable. Peter swallowed his inflammatory comments and said, "Okay."

"Okay what?"

"Let's forget it."

An awkward silence percolated that Peter felt in his chest and arms.

"When do you want to come down?"

"Tomorrow."

"Damn, son. You don't mess around, do ya?" Verlin said. "You really want to see your old man. I like that, boy. I guess you got a little ambition after all. Just like the old man, huh?"

Peter thought that maybe his dad was a little retarded, affected in a way. Closer associations might not bring the renewal that he so desperately wished for. Grammie had always told Peter to check his motives. He knew that they were not pure in this current situation. He wanted saving. He felt like if he picked up with his dad where he had left off so many years ago, that he would somehow heal on the inside, and become whole and finally be able to move onto something great and honorable and in which he believed.

Peter got all of the details, told his dad that he would call him later that night and then they hung up. Peter went to the kitchen and got into the little stash tin that he and Perky had on the counter. Nothing was in the can but some old cookie crumbs and a couple dried-out rubber bands. Perky had come home earlier and left in a hurry without saying anything to Peter, who stood folding laundry in the utility room. She had most assuredly come to get her stash. He just wanted a little something to take the edge off, but then felt a little relief that he didn't have to go down that road.

Peter went to the living room and turned on the television. All of the mayhem surrounding the acquittal of the police officers responsible in the Rodney King beating had just blossomed into a violent, chaotic anarchy a couple of days earlier. Peter sat on the couch and watched the images of Reginald Denny being dragged from his commercial truck, beaten and bashed in the head with a brick, as some sort of medieval tit-for-tat, or so the thugs doing the deed perceived.

After the public acquittal of the corrupt cops, the fires began, the looting, the destruction of small businesses that generations had spent building. People seized the opportunity to steal as many electronics and shoes and appliances and diapers as they felt they deserved, because of the seemingly defunct system of justice in America. A steady diet of fear is what the American people got, and Peter wasn't immune to the manipulations himself, sitting there on his couch, taking it all in like some Draconian torture victim.

The fear that the end had come, that the riots would surely spread into his living room, up onto his couch and into his face felt real like the sunlight coming through the window. Fear had become like chronic pain in Peter's life, yet a bit nebulous or diffuse, like a permeating gas slowly filling a large room. It kept him grounded in a way he thought, however, perhaps the proverbial thorn in his side. Oh, how we love to put labels of utility on our self-destructive aberrations.

Peter went to the fridge, got a beer and went back to the couch. It was time to turn fear into entertainment. He shuffled some random bills and slips of paper and receipts around to see if Perky had left a roach behind that he could smoke. A cigarette cellophane was under a Sylvia Plath book that Perky had checked out from the library last year. Peter unfolded the cellophane, shaking out the three little blue pills into his palm. The television flashed from morbid scene to idyllic fantasy. Peter popped the blue pills, swigged his beer and threw his feet up on the coffee table.

The coffee table collapsed under the weight of his feet.

Peter jerked when the front door banged open. Perky and some guy Peter had never met were playing around like a couple special-needs school kids on a field trip to the Crayola factory.

"Oh...Pete...hey." Perky looked at him, obviously drunk or high, and then pointed at her friend and said, "This is...uh..."

"Jimmy," the guy said, grinning like he might have taken one too many blows to the head.

Peter stood up from the couch, calmly, and smoothed the front of his suit pants with his hands. Jimmy, all of a sudden, didn't look like he was having as good a time as when they first barged through the door, Perky still oblivious to the change in the mood.

Perky reached into her big hippy purse and threw Peter a sandwich bag full of pot. "Here," she said, laughing, as if she had just absolved herself of any need to apologize for disrespecting Peter in their own home.

Peter caught the bag, looked at the paltry indulgence, gave her his approval with a wink, and then went to the kitchen to put half of the pot in another sandwich bag. He walked back into the living room and tossed her bag of weed back to her.

"Hey!" she shouted as she looked at the smaller bag in her hand.

"Tell Neider I said thanks."

Neider supplied all of Perky's party-favors for the most part. Peter didn't ever question the long nights at Neider's house, choosing to trust her most of the time. "Have a good one, Jimmy," Peter said, grabbing his suit coat by the front door, and walked out.

"Neider gave me that coffee table!" Perky shouted from the front door.

Peter laid his suit jacket over the passenger seat of the car, after he opened the door to let all of the heat out, before he got in. He had been looking for a job all morning, one foot already out the door of Perky's father's business. Peter attempted to keep the spirits up, hence the pot he gladly took from Perky. He didn't want to fall back into counter-productive behavior, but he wanted to feel like crap even less, so he decided that a little more relief wouldn't necessarily kill him.

Peter got in the car, as a brand-new, black, seven-series BMW pulled up in front of their house. Peter thought that it might have been one of Neider's associates coming to collect money from Perky, maybe even shoot her and Peter both right there on the spot for the hell of it. The window of the black car rolled down, and Peter could see through the glare of his passenger window that Mr. Rando, Perky's dad, sat behind the wheel.

"Hey bud, I gotta couple sweet deals for you," Mr. Rando said, as he jumped out of his new car. Peter stared at the car as Mr. Rando came up to Peter's driver's-side window. "You got time to talk business?"

"I'm on the way down to my dad's. Perky's inside."

"Yeah?" Mr. Rando looked up the street and then back at Peter. "When will you be back in town?"

"I don't know."

"Shit, man. Who's gonna help with all these sweet deals?"

"Perky's inside."

Mr. Rando rolled his eyes and patted Peter on the arm.

Peter hesitated and then said, "I really hate doing this kind of work. I feel like it's always some sort of scam."

"Everybody's gotta have a house, my friend."

"I don't believe that shit," Peter said. "It can't last."

"Yeah, well, don't put all your eggs in one basket, if you know what I mean," Mr. Rando said, as he opened Peter's door. "Come on, kid. I'll give you a ride to your old man's."

"I'm going over to my mom's house."

"Whatever, sure. Come on."

"Nice car," Peter said.

"Thanks, man. Come on, let's go."

Peter rolled the windows up and locked the Honda. He went inside and threw the keys onto the scraps of a coffee table. He decided to roll a joint out of the bag that he had in his pocket, so he went to the kitchen and did his work. He could hear Perky and Jimmy fooling around in the bedroom. Peter laughed to himself when he thought about her inciting a suicide pact with her new friend and Sylvia. Perky reading that sad dribble out loud to the guy, his dick hard and ready, her beginning to cry as she closes her book. The same old, same old with new faces and bad timing.

Peter finished rolling his joint and threw the bag of pot on the coffee table as he let himself out. He didn't really want it anyway. He took the bag more to get under Perky's skin than for his benefit, anyway. She needed her medicine too.

Peter went outside and got into Mr. Rando's car. The wide, black leather seats folded around Peter like a cool glove. The cockpit of the Beamer felt like the future itself. Clean, refined and with no sharp edges to cut oneself on. Peter longed to live in that kind of luxury someday. To have a nice, pillowy buffer between him and all the danger and messy business of the world out there.

"How's the whole thing going with your old man?"

"He's pretty fucked up."

"Yeah, my old man was a crazy bastard too," Mr. Rando said, handing Peter a cigarette out of his pack. "He worked all the time, and drank when he was home. He liked smackin' us around a little for stress relief, I guess."

Mr. Rando pulled away from the curb, heading toward Peter's mom's house.

"I don't know how this is gonna turn out, but I'll just hope for the best."

"Be careful. Things can get out of hand real quick sometimes."

"Tell me about it."

Mr. Rando told Peter some more unsolicited stories about his childhood, his father, his coming up in the world. Peter nodded, yes and no, letting him do all of the talking. Mr. Rando liked to talk, like Perky. Peter liked Mr. Rando, however.

Mr. Rando pulled into the side driveway. "Just call me if you need anything. You hear?" Peter said that he would if he did.

Peter had to admit that he did feel somewhat comforted by the fact that Perky's dad did seem genuinely concerned about his well-being, yet that only confused matters worse. Keep the job, leave Perky, honor Mr. Rando? The dismal combination made Peter want to punch something.

"We'll talk when I get back," Peter said. "So, this is my mom's place."

"I've been here before with Perky."

Peter looked up and down the street, as if he had just forgotten where he was.

"I'll see you later, Pete. Like I said..."

"Yeah. I'll call you if I need anything, sir."

"Bye."

Peter got out of the car, noticing the solid, quiet thud of the car door closing, the quality obvious.

Lunch-time was coming to a close, so nobody would be home. Peter tried the back door, because his mom never locked it. The door was locked.

"Dammit."

Peter stood before the door for a moment, like doing so would magically unlock it as a breeze of good fortune quietly swung it open. He went around the house to try the side door. Locked. He went to the front door. Locked. He looked both ways down the street again, to see if his mom was coming home from running errands. No one to be seen. He decided he would just go to the park and chill out for a minute while he waited on his mom to get home.

"Hey!"

Peter jumped, and then turned to see his sister Ariel riding up on her bike. "Oh, hey there." He threw the cigarette he had been smoking on the ground and smashed it with his foot.

"Those things give you cancer."

Ariel had just turned fourteen.

"Yeah."

"I told mom she needs to quit or I'm going to go on a hunger-strike."

Peter laughed, relaxing a little bit realizing that he was there with his sister, and not some stranger that had caught him in the act of something devious. "How's that going?"

"I always get hungry right before bed," she said, and laid her bike down on the ground. "Have you ever tried to fast?"

"Hell, no."

"Figures."

"Aren't you supposed to be in school?" Peter said, lightly punching her in the arm.

"We're out for the summer, dummy."

"You should put your bike in the garage, so it doesn't get stolen."

Ariel looked at Peter as if she were trying to figure out his species, like he had just wandered out of some dense backwoods. "Did you and your dad party in there the other night?"

"I guess you could say that."

"He called yesterday," Ariel said and picked up her bike, wheeling it over to the side door of the garage. "Mom says that he's a little crazy."

"A little, I guess."

Peter looked at his sister, just realizing that she had become a young lady somewhere in the last couple years. He had spent too much time away from family. Family he knew and loved. He wondered if he had contributed in any way to her adult understanding and seeming intelligence. Probably not, he thought. She spoke with such confidence, clear-headed and concise.

"Do you think I could meet him?" she said.

"Who?"

"Your dad."

"Oh, yeah...I don't know if that would be such a good thing."

"Perhaps," she said. "But don't you think someday, maybe?"

"I'm going down there."

"Well?"

"We'll see."

"Okay," she said and punched Peter back in the arm, as he came over to help her open the door. "I love you."

"Likewise," he said and closed the garage door after she put her bike in.

"Do you want to come inside?"

"You have a key?"

"I've had to start locking up. There are druggies in the neighborhood these days," she said with a taunting smirk. "Mom doesn't get it."

Peter followed her inside. Once they got inside, he heard Grammie pulling into the driveway, and quickly getting out of the car. He went back to the door to let her in, but she had already pushed her way through.

"Hi Grammie," he said, as she let herself past him and into the dining room.

"Are you ready, Pete?" Grammie said, scanning the house, presumably to make sure things were tidy and orderly. Just as the air had thickened and congealed, Peter's mom walked into the dining room where everyone had formed into an awkward little cluster.

"I thought you weren't home, mom," Peter said.

"You know I work nights," Peter's mom said, rubbing her eyes and brushing her hair back with her hand. She looked at Grammie tiredly. "Hi, mom."

"Hello, honey," Grammie said, and then turned her attention back to Peter. "Pete, are you ready?"

"Hello, grandma," Ariel said.

"Hi, sweetie," Grammie said to Ariel. "I'm sorry, I have to run Peter down to his dad's. We've really got to go."

Peter looked at his mother and she smiled. "I called Grammie. I can't take you today. I have meetings today before work."

"Where's your car, Pete?" Ariel said. "Grandma has to take you to your dad's," she added mockingly.

"Perky needs it, ya little shit."

"Hey," Grammie said.

"Hold on, Grammie," Peter said and went to his old bedroom, got his bags that he had left a couple days earlier, knowing that he would make an escape from Perky sooner or later, and went back out to the dining room where he overheard Grammie doing her check-up on his mom. How's work? Are you getting enough to eat? Are you getting enough sleep? Is Jack (Peter's step-dad) working? Do you have enough money? Did you pay the phone bill? Is Pete drinking? Is he drinking too much?

"Let's go," Peter said. "Bye mom, I love you."

"I love you too. Be careful." She turned the stove off and walked over to the door to give Peter a hug. "I hope you and your dad can get some things straightened out. Be careful."

Peter hadn't told her about the events of the last meeting. He could save that for another day.

Peter and Grammie got into her new Chrysler and pulled out of the driveway.

"Are you nervous?" Grammie said after a long moment of silence, as they made their way out of town.

"A little."

"I think it's a good idea that you're getting to know your dad."

"He's a little crazy, I think," Peter said. He really wanted a cigarette, but his grandma didn't know he smoked, and he didn't want to blow his cover.

They drove down I-35 for at least an hour, Paul Harvey the only person speaking in the moving car. High plains of green and gold, peppered with oil rigs and cattle, glided in the periphery, as Peter contemplated all of the potential outcomes with the visit to his dad's.

"I always thought that you should make your own decisions regarding your dad, Peter," Grammie said.

"I appreciate that."

Grammie and Peter's grandpa had been his wise counsel for as long as he could remember. Their stability gave Peter hope in a lot of ways. He didn't ever question their motives, and trust had never been an issue.

Peter looked out at the truck-stops and pre-fab buildings beginning to crowd in on each other, on the north end of the city. The sweeping expanse of green and gold fields turned to drab buildings, more concrete and lonely bridges and overpasses. The silence in the car comforted Peter, sporadic murmurings from his grandmother, and the ride had gratefully become mellow and contemplative like an esoteric form of meditation. He needed some time to gather himself before they got to his dad's house.

Verlin lived thirty minutes west of "The City," what many Okies call Oklahoma City. Peter's mom had given Grammie the directions after she had agreed to give Peter a ride. Grammie never complained, she simply got things done as necessary, and that was that.

A couple hours had passed, and Peter and Grammie were pulling into Verlin's driveway. Peter closed his eyes and took a deep breath. Dad's house, he thought. It looked pretty nice, nestled in among all of the suburban sameness.

"Are you okay?" Grammie said. "You don't have to stay, you know? We can visit, and then go home, as easy as we came."

"Thanks. We'll see."

They both got out of the car. Peter got his bag out of the back seat, and he and Grammie walked to the front door where Peter rang the doorbell.

Louise answered the door.

"Hey there," she said in her cool voice, standing there in her big, dark glasses. Peter could never shake the feeling that Louise had something more to say, but never did. As if all of her statements were left incomplete, somehow lacking the main jest of what she meant to get across.

"Hello," Grammie said.

"Hi," Peter added.

Louise took a step back and gestured them to come in. "Verlin went to the store, he'll be back in a minute," she said. "Come in."

"Thank you."

"Would you guys like something to drink?"

"I would love an ice water," Grammie said.

Louise led the way out of the entry and said, "Pete?"

"I'll take a soda if you have one."

The three of them made it to the bright, white kitchen. Grammie and Peter sat down at the table. A young girl entered the kitchen and went to the sink. She stood at a distance, staring at Grammie and Peter, as if they had just passed through the walls into the kitchen.

"Hi there," Grammie said.

"Mary, this is your grandmother and brother."

Mary stood in place, hands folded in front of her like a servant awaiting her orders.

"You can call me Grammie."

Grammie nudged Peter in the arm and bugged her eyes out.

"Hi there, Mary," Peter said.

"You're my brother? I thought you'd be bigger. Are you coming to live here?"

"Pete's coming to visit, hon," Louise said.

"Yeah."

Louise handed Peter a can of Coke and Grammie a glass of ice water. They said their thanks, Mary still standing by expressionless. Peter began to squirm in his seat a little as he looked at Mary staring at him with that cold objectivity. He followed her eyes with his, as she scanned him over. Peter thought that the girl might have been "special" or some such thing, socially inept, at least.

"Nice to meet you, Peter," Mary said, and went back from where she came.

"She's really excited and nervous to me you, Pete," Louise said, sitting down at the table with Peter and Grammie.

"I can tell."

Peter couldn't help but think that every statement Louise made was some sort of co-dependent, placating manipulation, as if she had ulterior motives even now. A mafia wife comes to mind. Maybe just a gimp.

"Thanks for bringing Pete down here, Mrs. Dernovish. I know it's a long drive. Verlin just wanted to see if Pete could at least make it here on his own. He's gonna have to grow up someday."

"He should've had a father," Grammie said, and then stood up from her chair. "Thank you for the water, Mrs. McDash." Grammie looked at Peter, cool as spring grass and said, "Are you wanting to stay, Peter?"

"Sure."

"Mrs. Dernovish…"

"You all have a good time now," Grammie said. "I'll let myself out."

Louise got up from the table and followed her to the front door, where Peter could still hear them talking. The conversation didn't seem to be out of hand. It sounded like Grammie spoke in her sharp, direct tone and Louise simply bantered and groped, ending the conversation with over-enthusiastic good-byes and farewells.

Louise came back into the kitchen, visibly calmed. She could be whomever a person might want her to be, at any given moment.

"I hope I didn't make your grandma mad," she said.

"She's very passionate."

Louise laughed her husky, insecure laugh, as she sat down at the table, giving him a sideways glance. Peter heard the front door open. Louise got up from the table and scrambled over to the sink to tidy up a little pile of dishes that sat next to the sink. She turned and tightly smiled at Peter, saying, "I think your dad's here."

Verlin walked into the kitchen and put a twelve-pack of Coors and a carton of Marlboro Reds on the long kitchen counter. "You made it, son," he said, opening the twelve-pack and then holding a fresh beer out to Peter.

"Thanks."

"She didn't stop to talk. Was she in a hurry?" Verlin nodded in the general direction of the front door, from where Grammie had just left. "I don't even think she knew who I was."

Peter nodded, mid-drink of beer, that yes, she was in a hurry.

"Did you meet Mary?"

"She's nervous, Verlin." Louise said.

"What the hell are you talkin' about?" Verlin said, patting Peter on the back. "Come on, boy." Verlin grabbed a couple hard-packs of Reds and the twelve-pack and went to the back sliding-glass door. "Let's go have a smoke."

Peter threw his empty beer can in the trash by the door and followed his dad outside. Louise finished her task at the sink, and then disappeared to somewhere in the back of the house.

Chapter 14

What Peter remembered most about Mississippi back then was the smell of the pines. He also remembered the feeling of nearly being wet all the time. His dad hadn't been around much since their vacation had moved to the Magnolia State. Louise said that he had a lot of work to make up, since he had to go all the way to Oklahoma to pick up Peter. Whatever the case, Peter was excited about meeting her parents. Old people, like Grammie and his grandpa had an easy, gentle way about them, even if they weren't much into compromise.

Louise and Peter pulled up onto the drive, leading to the front of an expansive, white, ranch-style house. Magnolias and sweeping Kentucky Bluegrass spread out like a gentle sigh in its idyllic comfort. The place instantly put Peter at ease. It felt cooler somehow, more promising.

"Here we are," Louise said.

"This is your parents's house?"

"Nice, huh?"

"Yes, ma'am."

They got out of the car and walked up to the front door. Louise knocked. Back in Oklahoma, family never knocked. Everybody's home was open to others, no matter how occasional the visits might have been.

"You have to knock on your parents's door?"

"It's polite, Peter."

Peter looked up to Louise and nodded, watching the door.

An older lady opened the door and said, "Well, hello." She bent down, getting a closer look at Peter. "This must be Peter."

"Sure is," Louise said. "Say hi, Pete."

"Oh, you little dear, come in here," Louise's mom said, not giving the boy a chance. She bent to give Peter a hug. "You're so cute." She tousled his hair and stroked his arm lightly, getting a better look at him. "You can call me Pinkie, okay?"

Peter laughed and said, "Hi, Pinkie." He paused to let her love on him for another second. "That's a funny name."

Louise elbowed Peter and looked down on him with an awkward smile.

Pinkie looked up at Louise with hard eyes and said, "You bet, sweetie. Come on in here out of that heat. Louise, come on."

They went inside, as Pinkie shut the door behind them.

Peter didn't think that he had ever been in such a nice, big house before. Grammie's house was nice and always smelled good, but this house was like a southern mansion. Like a real gentleman's quarters might be, he thought.

"Come on you two, I have some lemonade and pie," Pinkie said. "You hungry Pete? Do you mind if I call you Pete, hon?"

People said 'hon' a lot in Mississippi. Peter nodded, sure, 'Pete' would be okay. He followed Louise and Pinkie to the kitchen. They passed large room after large room. Rugs and tables, clocks and pretty lamps. Peter thought that Louise's dad must work for the government too. Something important, where he made big decisions and people looked to him for all the right answers.

"Do you like Key-lime pie?" Pinkie said.

Peter stood in the middle of the big kitchen next to the maple chopping-block island, white enamel and smatterings of lace all around him. He smiled at Pinkie, her speaking volumes of comfort without all the empty assurances. That place almost felt like home to Peter.

"I don't know, ma'am."

"My lands, dear," she said and patted Peter on the head, busying herself with the preparation of the pie and drinks.

Louise had left the kitchen, to where Peter could hear her on the phone in the other room. She spoke evenly and seriously, as if the fate of their lives might just lay in her hands right then. She had become more serious like that overnight, as if she had suddenly realized that the responsibility of taking care of a child might somehow require a little more attention and time than what she had possibly learned from her morning talk shows. Maybe she worked for the government too, Peter thought, but quickly snapped out of his daze when Pinkie invited him to sit down at the big oak table, putting a glass of milk and Key-lime pie in front of him.

"Thank you," he said.

"What happened to your hand, hon?"

"I smashed it in the door."

"Well, I never. Are you okay now?"

"I went to the doctor and got some new metal fingers," Peter said, holding up his aluminum splinted fingers for Pinkie to see.

"Those are splints, hon."

"I have super powers now, ma'am."

"I'm sure you do."

Pinkie cut herself a piece of pie and poured another glass of milk. She put the plastic wrap back over the pie and put it and the glass quart of milk back in the refrigerator. She sat right across from Peter, where she continued to look at him as if he were a long-lost friend.

"So, how do you like Mississippi?"

"It's good," he said, taking another bite of the cool, tart pie.

Pinkie looked real serious all of a sudden. "How's your dad?"

"Good."

"Are you here for the summer, hon?"

Peter thought that old people sure asked a lot of questions. Peter shook his head that he didn't know. Pinkie continued to look at him with that same searching yet comforting look, almost like Grammie did. Strong, but loving. She glanced down at his plate, as he looked up at her and smiled.

"Another piece?"

"Yeah."

She got up from the table and said, "Excuse me, hon. I'll be right back to get you some more, okay?"

Pinkie went to the other room where Louise still talked low and even on the telephone. Peter could hear the two of them talking, Louise and her mom. Louise's voice raised a bit, still calm, but defensive, "Sure, mom. Whatever," she said.

Pinkie came back into the kitchen, cut Peter's pie and filled his milk glass again.

"Can I have some lemonade too?"

"You and Sewell will get along just fine, hon."

"Who's Sewell?"

"That's my husband. Louise's daddy." She put the slice of pie on Peter's plate and put the glass of lemonade in front of him. Pie, milk and lemonade. "Hon, you're gonna fly away after you eat all that sugar. But that's okay for right now, ya hear? You're on vacation, right?"

Peter laughed. He had never heard someone with such a strong accent in real life. She sounded like Foghorn Leghorn from Saturday cartoons. Pinkie seemed nice like Louise, but not withholding, if Peter would have known what withholding meant. Old people don't have secrets. They just seem to be who they are every time you see them.

"Do you want to stay here this afternoon?" Pinkie said. "You can meet Sewell. Maybe he'll take you down to the fields. You can see the horses." She took a bite of pie and chased it with some milk. "Do you like horses?"

"They're pretty."

"All the pretty horses, hon. You're just a little prince, aren't you?"

"I guess so."

After Louise left, and Peter and Pinkie finished their pie and drinks, she took him out to the barn to see the baby chicks. Peter pinched his nose off as they got right up close to the neat little chicken coop, that noxious stench feeling like it could almost burn the inside of his lungs.

"Stinks, don't it, hon?" Pinkie had said, gently patting him on the shoulder. She told him that they raised the chicks so that they would grow up and lay eggs to eat. The little, yellow babies had some time before they were ready to be let loose in the yard, where they could gorge themselves on scraps and bugs to their heart's delight.

She showed him the big magnolia tree, under which Louise used to play dolls and house. They smelled the low-hanging flowers, sweet like rich, butter-cream. Pinkie picked one of the big, white flowers and held it out gently so that Peter could get a good smell of it. "That smells good."

She nodded and smiled.

"Can you eat those?"

She laughed and said, "Sure smells like it, don't it?"

Peter looked at the flower a little more closely and then put it down to his side, walking away from the trunk of the tree. He stopped after a couple steps, staring at the metal stake sticking out of the ground.

"You like to play horseshoes?"

"Sure." Peter had played a couple times with Grammie's neighbor. He wasn't that good, but liked it just the same. He liked being outside and throwing things. Pinkie said a couple shoes were missing, and asked if he could help her find them.

Peter kicked at the thick grass, freeing a mushroom here and knocking the wispy tops off of dandelions there. He passed the edge of shade that the magnolia cast, and finally saw one of the rusty horseshoes laying in the grass all by itself. He bent to pick it up, but dropped it just as quick.

"It's hot!" Peter shouted over to where Pinkie stood bent over in the grass.

"Hold on, hon. I'll be there in a minute."

Peter bent over, took a deep breath, picked the shoe up and turned to try to hit the stake that stood to attention in the magnolia's wide shade. "Owww!" he shouted, as the rusty horseshoe left his hand, wobbling side to side, missing the stake by a couple feet.

"You okay?"

"Yeah."

Pinkie tossed a shoe that she found in the grass on her side of the tree. She missed. Peter tossed another one and missed again. Peter ran up to the stake and grabbed one of the shoes that had been laying there, ran back out to the edge of the shade, and threw his shoe at the same time that Pinkie had bent and thrown her own shoe from where she stood. They both hit the stake, Pinkie's catching the post and circling around it a couple times before it sent up a puff of dust where the grass had become worn. They both laughed at the same time.

Peter ran and fetched the shoes after another toss apiece, hanging the heavy steel over his forearm, as Pinkie still kicked around in the grass, out in the bright sun. Peter held the two horseshoes that were still a little hot in his hands, nevertheless, because they felt like they would burn right through his forearm if he hung them there with the others.

Pinkie and Peter steadily tossed one shoe after the other for an hour or so, trying to stay in the shade as best they could. "You're pretty good with them super fingers, buddy," Pinkie had told him, in an effort to keep him interested in the game for a little longer, hopefully until Sewell got home.

Peter inevitably began to feel restless after a while, nevertheless, yet didn't want to disappoint Pinkie by asking if they could quit playing horseshoes. Right about then, however, a green, four-door pick-up pulled onto the long, curved driveway, and came to a slow stop near the front of the house. Peter heard a horseshoe hit the stake, but kept his eyes on the pick-up in the driveway, wondering who would pop out of the driver's seat to greet them now.

A big man with a worn and dusty Western shirt stepped out onto the ground with a hard-working rigidity, smoking a cigar and smiling like a brand-new daddy. Pinkie patted Peter on the back and said, "Come on, hon, let's go meet my sweetheart."

The man walked toward them slowly, still smiling. "Where'd you find that little thing?" he said.

"Sewell, this is Pete," she said, leaning into the man for a kiss and a hug, once they closed the gap. "He's gonna spend the day with us. I thought maybe you could take him down to see the horses. Maybe show him the dog pens and the cattle too, if you want."

"Well sure, darlin'," he said, dusting off the front of his jeans and stomping his boots a couple times. "Where you from, Pete?"

"Oklahoma. I'm on vacation with my dad."

"You don't say?"

"Yeah, he's at work."

Sewell and Pinkie looked at each other as if they were having a staring match, faces blank for a quick second, but like adults, quickly smiling nervously when they saw Peter looking up at them. Peter turned to the road to watch the dust settle where Sewell had just pulled onto the driveway from. The dust clung to the moist air, waiting for an answer.

"You guys hungry?" Pinkie said.

"Hungry, Pete?" Sewell said.

Peter snapped out of his daze and said yes, that he was hungry, thinking that country people sure ate a lot of food. Pinkie took off for the house like she might have had a pie burning in the oven. Sewell and Peter followed her inside. Everyone filed into the big kitchen, washed in the big porcelain sink and sat down at the big oak table. Pinkie spread all of the dishes out in front of the boys, one by one. Roast with carrots and potatoes. Steamed cranberry beans and fresh fruit. There were a couple things Peter had never seen, but he knew it would all be good. All fresh from the garden, Pinkie had told Peter when they were out by the garden, her bending to show him the baby beans and melons.

"What happened to your fingers, Peter?" Sewell said.

Peter laughed and then sighed.

"I bet everybody asks you that, don't they, buddy?"

"Yes, sir," Peter said. "I smashed them in the car door." Peter held his hands up for Sewell to see.

"Them's nice little fingers you got now. Do they hurt?"

"I've got super powers now."

"Well, I'll be..."

Peter shook his head in the affirmative and smiled at Sewell. Pinkie put out even more food and a tall crystal pitcher of fresh lemonade, complete with freshly sliced lemons and crushed ice.

The pitcher of lemonade looked like a glimmering, silver tower in the middle of the table. The glass sweating with anticipation, as Pinkie finally sat down with them. Sewell grabbed a deck of worn cards from the center of the table and showed Peter a card trick that he said he had learned in the Army. Sewell was an Army Air Corpsman just like Peter's grandpa had been. They could've been on the same bomber for all he knew. Peter thought about them flying the not-so-friendly skies over occupied Europe, playing cards, Sewell smoking his big cigars and laughing, as his grandpa surely tinkering with someone's broken watch or gun, as the others intently looked on.

"Come on, now. The food's gonna get cold, hon."

"Where's Louise," Sewell said after he put the cards up, Pinkie looking impatient.

"She said she had some errands to run."

"Well, this little guy can stay for a while, can't he?"

"Of course he can."

Pinkie sounded serious right then, like Sewell was in trouble. Peter sat in his chair, plate loaded, digging into his home-cooked, country meal.

"Is the roast off of the farm?" Peter said.

"You bet," Sewell said. "I'll take you down to the pastures later. We'll look at the horses and cattle if you feel like it, buddy."

"Yeah," Peter said, chewing. He knew better than to talk with his mouth full, but he didn't want to be rude and not answer either.

Later that evening, Peter woke up to Louise tickling the bottoms of his feet that stuck out past the sheets. It had gotten late, so Pinkie had put him to bed in the spare bedroom. He nearly went to sleep in the bathtub earlier that night because he and Sewell had been so busy brushing the horses and putting out water for the grazing cattle.

"Oh hi," Peter said, rubbing sight into his eyes.

"Come on, hon," Louise said. "Your dad's out in the car waiting."

Pinkie stuck her head in the doorway. "Why don't you just let him stay the night?"

"Verlin wants him home, mom."

Pinkie sighed, going to the side of the bed where she began stroking Peter's hair gently. She bent to give him a kiss on the forehead, as Louise stood up straight, looking at her mom as if she had just forgotten who she was. Pinkie sat at the edge of the bed and whispered in his ear, "You're an angel, Pete. You come back real quick now, ya hear?"

Louise had left the room after her mom sat at the edge of the bed. A moment later she came back in, stroking her hair and glaring at Pinkie's backside like a nervous rush-hour driver.

"Where's Verlin?" Pinkie said, not turning to look at Louise.

"Out in the car." Louise clapped her hands quickly and said, "Pete, we gotta go! Come on!"

Pinkie stood up and said, "What's the big hurry?"

"Verlin doesn't like to wait."

Pinkie helped Peter out of the bed, helped him get his shoes back on, and walked both he and Louise to the front door. Verlin's silhouette could be seen from the front porch, looming behind the wheel of his car. Peter and Louise walked out to get in, as Pinkie waved goodbye to them from the front porch.

"Cool car!" Peter shouted, nearing the idling, blue Corvette.

"Ssshhh," Louise said, putting her finger over her mouth.

"Tell Grandpa Sewell bye," Peter said, turning back to Pinkie, who still stood on the front porch waving.

"Grandpa?" Louise said, pushing Peter into the car.

"I will, hon! You hurry back now! Sewell needs all the help he can get!" Pinkie shouted. She went back into the house.

Peter thought about working out on the ranch until he got married, and had his own money, and could buy his own big truck.

"Hey bud," Verlin said, pushing the passenger seat forward, so that Peter could get in behind it. "It's a sixty-three split-window." The familiar smell of beer and cigarettes greeted the boy into his other world. "You're gonna have to crawl in there. It's tight, but you'll fit, okay?"

Peter used to like building tents and snow forts, crawling into small, safe places, but recently had become a little claustrophobic after his dad had locked him in that dank closet out there in the middle of nowhere. Verlin said that it would toughen him up a little. Peter just felt a little more scared than usual, the news of nuclear bombs and gas shortages and kidnapings having just come into his world.

Peter got into the little space behind the passenger seat, taking short, shallow breaths for a moment, and then slowly began to adjust somewhat, when Louise started to put the seat back. Peter put his arm out to keep the seat from going all the way back. He couldn't get a full breath and his skin felt hot and tight. "Hey, hold on," he said.

Louise stood by the car for another moment and said, "Are you okay, hon? We gotta go. Your dad's gotta work in the mornin'."

"The government?" Peter said, tapping his dad on the shoulder, still holding the seat up with his other hand.

Verlin laughed and said, "Yeah boy. Real cops and robbers shit. Come on, let's go, woman! Get the fuck in the car, will ya?!"

Peter finally got a full breath, and slackened his arm so that Louise could put the seat back. She slowly got in and then shut her door. Peter pushed the back of the seat again, as he felt the car closing in around him yet again.

"Calm down, boy."

"I can't breathe." The air in the little cubby-hole hung heavier than the humid air outside had. Peter began to sweat, breathing shallow, rapid breaths again. "Can you roll down the windows?"

Louise rolled the window down, as they pulled out of the driveway. Peter imagined that Pinkie still stood in the door waving and blowing kisses like Grammie did. She was *his* angel, he thought. Grammie and Pinkie both. Pinkie said that he was an angel, but he knew that she was *his* angel.

"Did you have fun, boy?" Verlin said.

"I got to brush the horses. We watched the cows and drove around the farm. I like Grandpa Sewell."

"Grandpa?"

Peter could see Louise patting Verlin on the hand. He brushed her hand off of his and turned to look back at Peter in the little cubby-hole.

"Whoa, slow down there, big shot."

Peter looked up at his dad with a blank stare and even less to say. He didn't want to make his dad mad with any back talk, but he hated being made fun of like that. He knew when someone was talking down to him, and it made him want to break something, or to scream out loud for a change, really do some damage.

"Who the fuck do they think they are? They just take over my boy. Are they fuckin' retarded?"

"Verlin," she said.

"Don't fuckin' Verlin me."

"I like them, dad."

And just as quick as Peter had given his two cents, Verlin had elbowed the cooped-up boy in the face like a dog. It didn't hurt as much as getting hit in the nose, Peter thought, but it hurt just the same. It really hurt his feelings. He scrunched further back into the space behind the seats. Nothing like a blow to the head to take one's mind off of a little claustrophobia.

"You need to learn not to fuckin' talk when no one's talkin' to ya. Got it, shithead?"

"Yes, sir."

Peter tried to pull his body further back into the cubby-hole, as if his retraction would keep his dad from stopping the car and yanking him out of there, smacking him around, beating some damned sense into the boy, as the old man then tossed him into the nearest ravine, where Peter would surely be left for dead.

They drove silently for some time until Willie sang into the damp, pine-sweet air once again. That air and Willie's raspy voice had a way of making everything seem alright for the time being. Almost sickeningly nostalgic, if Peter could have put such words to the sensation of it all. Willie sang about the preacher and the lessons again. The air whipped Peter's hair, cooler and moister now, while the boy thought about the day to come, the hum of the road tickling his belly, calming him like a mother's lullaby. Slowly drifting...hoping...falling...to sleep.

Peter woke up to Louise gently shaking his arm. He rubbed his eyes and opened them to see her crying. His forehead felt sore where his dad had elbowed him. Louise had a deep, darkening red spot around her right eye.

"Are you okay?" Peter said.

"Come on, hon."

"What happened?"

"The door."

The darkening area around her eye seemed to get bigger the longer Peter lay in that little space behind the passenger seat, looking up at her. He wanted to make sense of it all, but felt as if it were all too big, too much for him to understand, just a kid and all.

"The door bumped into you?"

"I ran into the door," Louise said, sighing, and then reached into the back of the Corvette to help him out.

"Where's dad?"

"Work."

The night sky covered them like a big, black sheet-tent.

"Come on, hon."

Peter woke up the next morning to a little, black Cocker Spaniel pup licking his face. He pushed it away to keep it from licking the skin right off of his cheeks, as he climbed out of his little, make-shift bed, sitting up Indian-style. Verlin came into the bedroom and smiled from ear to ear, cigarette hanging in the corner of his mouth like a broken limb.

"Whattaya think, boy?" Verlin said.

Louise popped her head in behind Verlin and tip-toed around him to see the little creature bouncing and pouncing, jumping at Peter, licking and biting.

"He's so cute, Verlin," she said. "Well, she's so cute. Don't you think, Pete?"

Peter finally got a hold of the pup and held her up high in front of himself. She wiggled about, trying to bite his hand, and then started barking.

"Oh boy, she's a fighter," Verlin said.

"You be good, now," Peter said, jostling the pup, getting her really worked up. "You're my new best friend."

"Whattaya gonna name her?" Louise said.

"I don't know."

"Well, you better think of something, boy. She don't wanna be a nobody, do ya girl?"

Verlin bent to pet the little dog, and she snipped at his right hand. He stepped back and said, "Wow. She *is* a fighter." Verlin stood up straight again. "You gotta take care of this little shit, now. You hear?"

"Yes, sir. I'll feed her and take her out to pee and poop, and do everything. I promise."

"Yeah, yeah. I've heard that before," the old man said, and left the room.

"Gotta go pee? Come on, girl." Peter stood up, holding his new puppy in his arms tightly. She wriggled, tireless in her attempts at escape, not even realizing how good she had it right then. Peter and his new pup left the room to go outside.

Chapter 15

"So, ya little fucker," Verlin said. "It's about time you made it down here to visit the old man."

"Yeah," Peter said, looking down at his pant legs, brushing imaginary lint off of them. "Can I have a smoke?"

Verlin handed Peter one of the packs of cigarettes and his Zippo. He had a chummy proud expression of an out-of-practice politician stuck on his face, like he'd just given the boy the keys to the city.

"Did you mean what you said about the truck?" Peter said as nonchalantly as he could, not wanting to seem desperate. "Can you help me fix up an old truck of my own, like yours?"

"Hell yeah, son. You're my boy. Hell yeah," Verlin said, patting Peter on the leg, giving the boy his best good ole boy assurance, loud with slaps and guffaws.

Peter sucked a couple hard and long draws on his cigarette. He popped a beer and took three or four big gulps. Coors Original wasn't that bad. A good banquet beer, some would say, whatever the hell that meant. Peter lifted his can again, looking at the nice little picture in the center, silky water flowing, beer made from the best Colorado spring water available. Peter wanted to crawl right into that picture, be anywhere else, really, feeling like he had just come out of a coma, landing where he sat, without any say-so in the matter.

The silence between Peter and his dad felt expectant, wanting. Peter knew that they both had so much to say, so many questions, yet neither one of them knew where to begin, that great chasm of years, real like some nameless desert canyon. Peter realized that they couldn't possibly fill that space between them with just any small-talk or the red-neck yammering of the last visit.

Peter dropped his cigarette butt on the ground, startled from where the ember had begun to burn the webbing between his middle and index finger.

"Here, boy. Put your butts in the can."

Verlin handed Peter an old Folger's can as Peter bent to pick the butt up off of the ground. Peter threw the butt in the can, and stood up for a second to stretch out. A couple beers and a cigarette had taken the edge off a little bit. Peter felt pretty good about drinking with the old man on his back porch, swatting mosquitos in the evening heat.

"You shoot pool?" Verlin said.

"Sure." Peter said, his voice rising a little as the word came out of his mouth. He knew agreeing with his dad was the best thing to do, no matter what. Almost like dealing with a maniac who walks into your local bank with a bomb strapped to himself, as you're making a deposit. One minute you're signing the back of your check, and the next you're face down on the cool floor trying not to offend or frustrate the unstable character who holds the gun in your back. Playing it safe, but not too safe, is tricky business indeed.

"You ever been to the Stallion?"

Peter imagined that "The Stallion" was probably a dingy strip-club where burnt-out hags shook their stuff for the hayseeds out there in Pony Town. He didn't make a habit of hanging out in red-neck bars, or strip-clubs, for the most part.

"No. Sounds cool."

Verlin stood up from his lawn chair and went inside. Louise came outside and sat in the empty chair after a couple minutes. Good cop, bad cop, Peter thought. "Are you guys havin' a good time?" she said, settling in after an awkward minute.

"Oh...yeah...it's really cool to finally get to hang out with the old man."

"He's wanted this for a long time, Pete," she said. Rain or shine that woman spoke with the coolness of a clinical shrink. She did her job just right, feeling Peter out for anything that might give the old man some insight into his only son's life. Something to grab onto and work with. Louise jumped when Verlin said jump. "Your dad said that you guys want something to eat before you go to The Stallion. You like fried chicken?"

"Who doesn't like fried chicken?" Peter said, as his dad came back through the sliding door. Louise got up and went back inside. Verlin didn't even have to say a word, Louise being fully trained and all. Peter thought that it was kind of strange how they were never in the same area for more than a minute or two. They damn sure didn't touch or kiss, Verlin just not being the type, he thought.

"Drink up boy, and we'll go eat," Verlin said as he tossed another butt in the can. "She's going to KFC to get a bucket'a chicken. You like chicken?"

"Sure."

"You're alright, son."

"Where's The Stallion?" Peter said, and grabbed another beer from the carton.

"It's on the edge of Pony Town. I been goin' over there ever since I got the job at Freightliner. 'Bout fifteen years, son," Verlin said, lighting a cigarette and squinting through the smoke, as if he were trying to gauge how impressed the boy might be.

Verlin sold heavy equipment and tractor-trailers. "Louise don't like it, but she don't know shit." Verlin threw his empty beer can at Brownie, his brown Cocker Spaniel, who lounged in the shade by the chain-link fence. Brownie looked like she'd seen it coming, was used to it, and just lay there trying to stay cool, knowing the probability of the can hitting her was not too high, at any rate. Verlin grabbed another beer, popped the top and took a drink and said, "You're just like your old man. You gonna be alright."

Peter sure as hell hoped that he didn't turn out like the crusty bastard. Yet, on the other hand, he really wanted to get to know the guy, because Verlin was his father, the other half of his genes. Peter felt like he only knew half of himself, really. He felt like a machine with no owner's manual, running full-bore, toward an inevitable malfunction, breaking down, his moving parts no longer in motion. Verlin could be the missing link.

"That girlfriend of yours is a little firecracker."

"Yeah...she can be a lot to handle sometimes," Peter said, taking another contemplative drink of Coors. "We've had some issues over the last year or two. I guess we're working things out, though. I've thought about leaving her and doing something different, but, I'm afraid to leave her."

"What the hell does that mean?"

"It would hurt her too much."

"Shit boy, she can find another hard dick out there," Verlin said, killing another beer. "You ain't the best catch in the sea anyway. You know that?"

"Yeah? Really?"

"Boy, you need a man in your life. Not like a faggot or nothin', I mean your old man...me." Verlin poked his finger into his chest.

Peter laughed and then said, "Sounds like a good idea."

"You ain't got no damned self-esteem, 'cause you ain't had no old man to teach you shit. I'm here now. You talked about doin' somethin' different, and I'm already one step ahead of you. Understand?"

Peter laughed to himself, as Verlin busied himself getting another beer and opening the other pack of cigarettes. Verlin had said 'different' with only two syllables, like 'differnt.'

"Yeah," Peter said, as cryptic as the old man's message was.

"Shit boy. Does she give good head?"

"What?"

"Come on boy, give me the goods," Verlin said.

One thing was for sure, Peter thought. His old man could drink like him. Everybody else Peter drank with seemed to lack gusto. They'd get weirded out by the fact that he tossed 'em back like a coal miner on sick leave. Peter and his dad had one thing in common, and that was as good a place to start as any.

"Yeah," Peter finally said. "She's a real Hoover, if you know what I mean."

Peter felt like he had just further cheapened what little integrity they had going for them, within their relationship, he and his dad, not to mention the fact that talking with his dad about his girlfriend's bedroom performance creeped him out a little, in and of itself, but Peter felt willing to make some compromise to ease the awkwardness wherever he needed to. It was his dad after all.

Louise came out through the sliding door again, carefully, and quietly said that dinner was ready.

"That was quick," Peter said.

"The KFC's just down the street," she said, looking like she'd just pulled off a master illusion.

"She's too damn lazy to cook her own chicken."

Peter winked at Louise, as she forced an obligatory smile, turned and went back inside.

When Peter and his dad went inside, the girls were already at the table, sitting in front of their respective plates. Both Rachael and Mary each wore a pink dress. The contrast between Peter and his dad's conversation out on the patio, and the feeling of austerity and cleanliness inside felt jagged like gnarly metal.

"Hey there," Peter said to the girls.

"Hi," Rachael said. She reminded Peter of a puppy, jumping all over the first person to give her attention. Mary sat erect with her hands in her lap, looking straight ahead, as if someone had taken her batteries out and tossed them.

"Mary, say hi to your brother," Louise said.

"Hello...Peter?"

"That's it. And you're Mary. We met earlier, right?" She nodded yes, and then Peter pointed at Rachael, "And you're Rachael? My two new sisters. Glad to meet you both."

"Are you gonna live here?" Rachael said.

"Well..."

"Rachael, leave your damned brother alone," Verlin said from the kitchen sink, where he stood washing his hands. "We gotta lot to figure out before we go talkin' about livin' here and all that goddamn happy horse shit. Got it?" He dried his hands on the perfectly folded towel that hung on the oven handle. He yanked the towel off of the handle, neatly folded it again, and gently placed it back over the long handle. "Did you girls clean your room?"

"Yes, sir," they said in unison.

"Dad, can we say a prayer?" Rachael said. She seemed totally unaware of the awkward weight in the room. Peter felt like she was his only reprieve, his only hope for normalcy. Her and a little booze, maybe.

"What the hell you wanna do that shit for?" Verlin said.

"Go ahead," Peter said.

Verlin looked at Peter like he had just stolen his high school sweetheart. "Aww shit, boy. You're one of them fuckin' pussies?"

"It's okay, Rachael. I'll say a prayer with you." Peter and Rachael bowed their heads and closed their eyes, as she began.

"God, thank you for my new big brother, and thank you for fried chicken, and thank you for my big sister, and thank you for my mom and dad, and thank you for Brownie, and thank you..."

"Rachael! We ain't got all damned day!" Verlin shouted. He made his way to the table. "Food's gettin' cold. Come on, girl, that's good enough, ya hear?"

"Thank you for everything, God," Rachael concluded and opened her eyes, smiling.

"You're lucky I don't pop you a good one," Verlin said to Peter. "We got enough problems around here without a bunch of holy bullshit mumbo-jumbo flying around at the dinner table. This is where we eat, boy. This ain't no damned circus."

"Yeah?"

"Boy, you gotta loosen up," Verlin said, beginning to laugh, to show that he had in fact just made a joke.

Louise was the last one to sit at the table. Mary still had her hands crossed in her lap, staring straight ahead like a preparing mercenary. Rachael bopped in her chair like a little ball, as Verlin had already torn into a piece of chicken, mopping up mashed potatoes and gravy with the crispy skin.

"Go ahead girls," he said. "It's time to eat."

And just like that, Mary and Louise began to put food on their plates. Rachael brought light and air into the room, and when Peter caught himself getting nearly nauseous at how Mary and Louise acted around his dad, he concentrated on Rachael's smile, her ruddy cheeks, being grateful for another angel along the way.

"What grade are you in, Rachael?" Peter said.

"It's summer, Peter. We don't have school," Mary said.

Peter glanced at Mary to see her still sitting erect, and then looked back at Rachael and said, "Well, what grade will you be in this coming school year, Rachael?"

"I'm gonna be a first-grader," she said, clapping excitedly. Her plate looked like a many nameless young children. She had scattered the assorted menu items about her plate, giving the impression that she had eaten more than she really had. She smashed all of her green beans into oblivion, leaving them for dead. The dog sat under the table at Rachael's feet, licking her lips, almost up in the girl's lap at that point. "My mom's gonna take me shopping before school starts."

"Cool."

Mary flinched at the sound of her sister's voice right then. She stopped eating for a second and stared at her mom, feeling her out. More awkwardness. Louise put her plastic spork down on her paper plate and looked at Mary.

"You didn't get straight A's," Louise said. "We talked about this at the end of the school year. We had an agreement, remember?"

"We ain't gonna talk about this shit at the table," Verlin said, and the room fell silent again, except for Rachael shifting in her chair, as if she were going to blast off through the roof at any moment.

"Mom's gonna start giving me an allowance, too," Rachael added.

"What do you need money for?" Peter said.

"Colors, candy, dolls..."

"Come on, Rachael. You gotta keep on yappin' all the time?" Verlin said. "Hurry up and finish your dinner and go do some homework."

"It's summer!" she said.

"I don't need no damned weather report, just gitter fuckin' done, will ya?!"

Mary got up from the table and said, "Excuse me, sir," and left the room before Verlin had the chance to grant her permission. Peter thought the move quite bold.

"What the hell's wrong with that little shit?" Verlin said to Louise.

"Verlin," Louise said, finishing her last bite of biscuit, and stood up from the table.

"Hurry up, boy. We got some pool to shoot. We gotta meet a buddy of mine down there."

"Who are you meetin', Verlin?" Louise said, picking up Mary's full plate.

"Not that it's any of your damned business," he said with a mouthful of food. "But we're meeting Addie."

"Isn't he on duty tonight?"

"Since when did you write Addie's fuckin' work schedule?"

And that was the end of that matter. Verlin could be effective.

Peter and Verlin had another beer, while the girls and Louise cleaned the table, and seemingly tidied everything else in the house. Verlin had told them to quit being lazy fuckin' bitches and to get some work done around the house, before he had a heart-attack and went fuckin' ballistic, going to town on all their asses with a belt. Rachael had said that her dad couldn't 'bleepity-bleepity-bleep, if he had a heart-attack first,' to which Verlin yelled at Louise, and then led Peter back out to the back patio.

After they finished their last beer, Verlin said, "'Bout ready, boy?"

"Sure."

Verlin got up from the lawn chair, stumbled a little bit, and then threw another beer can at Brownie. He missed. She didn't budge.

"Are you okay?" Peter said.

"Does a dog have a dick?"

"She doesn't." Peter pointed his empty beer can at Brownie, and then he placed the empty can down next to the lawn chair where he sat.

Verlin lit another cigarette and belched. "Boy, you're a regular fuckin' comedian, ain't ya?"

"I try."

Peter felt pretty confident that he could kick his dad's ass at that point. Verlin looked drunk and out of control. Peter had had plenty of beer too, but his old man had gotten really hammered somewhere in between the first beer and right then, looking sloppy and tired and red all over.

Peter picked up a few random beer cans from the yard. He went inside and threw all of the cans in the garbage under the sink, when he overheard some whispering in the hallway. Verlin had gone inside, and he and Louise were taking care of whatever business they needed to take care of before he and Peter went down to The Stallion.

"What's up there, Sport?" Verlin said, coming out from the hallway.

"Waiting on you," Peter said.

Louise walked out from the hallway and stood a safe distance from the guys. She didn't have anything to say. She stood by in case Verlin needed anything, his faithful minion.

"Let's go, boy."

Verlin grabbed the keys to his truck and he and Peter went out through the kitchen to the garage, where his '51 Chevy pick-up awaited them. They got in and Verlin opened the garage door with the remote. The deep rumble of the modified 350 bounced against the inside walls of the garage when Verlin started the truck.

The set of shelves in front of the pick-up were nicely ordered with auto and cleaning supplies. Peter looked around the garage and noticed that everything was in perfect order, had a shine to it almost. Even the big garbage can in the corner looked like it had been spit-shined and polished that morning, the floor spotless. There were car parts still in boxes, with receipts taped to them, all lined up on top of a shiny, red and black shop toolbox.

Verlin punched the accelerator once, let it idle down and backed the truck out of the garage and out onto the street. The sun blazed hot in the early evening over the repetitious suburban neighborhood. Every house looked exactly the same, all of them painted in muted, drab colors.

"How do you know which house is yours?" Peter said.

Verlin responded by putting the truck into drive and pushing the gas pedal to the floor, tires spinning all the way down the block, past the stop sign and out into the main street heading out of Pony Town.

"How ya like them fuckin' apples?" Verlin shouted over the groaning engine noise.

Peter sat back in the passenger seat, tense from the sudden speed. Verlin saw Peter looking at the speedometer and laughed out loud over the wind and road noise, Fleetwood Mac on the stereo.

"Ya scared, boy?"

The question felt like an ancient one, as if Verlin had been born to ask that taunting question over and over at random points in Peter's life, like some sort of dark sentinel testing the mere fiber of the young man.

"No."

"She runs good, don't she?"

Peter shook his head up and down in the affirmative, as he looked straight down the road ahead. Then, as if they were idling down the road, Verlin pushed the gas pedal all the way to the floor, pinning Peter to his seat furthermore. Nowhere to go, but forward or the grave, Peter thought. Verlin let off the gas and slammed on the brakes, sending them into a long, slow-motion side-sliding stop in the middle of the old blacktop road.

"Wanna drive?"

"Sure," Peter said, still looking forward through the windshield, smoke roiling all around them like fog, a golden field in the haze ahead. The guys switched sides. Peter slowly put the truck into gear, easing from the middle of the road over to the right side.

"Go on, give 'er hell," Verlin said. "She's an automatic, so just punch 'er if ya wanna break 'em loose!"

Peter pushed the gas pedal all the way to the floor and the truck engine screamed in harmony with the squealing tires. The pick-up quickly spun out of control, so Peter let off the gas until he could straighten it out. Verlin pointed out the way ahead, and sure enough, Peter could see the sign from the road, a little distance away. The Silver Stallion, the sign read, brazen pony and all, right there outside of Pony Town, like some kind of consolation oasis on the horizon.

"Turn here," Verlin said. Peter turned at the street before the saloon, and then Verlin told him to make his next right. "We all park here in the back, boy. Don't want no pesky old ladies finding us and comin' in here and bitchin' and raisin' hell, ya know?"

"Makes sense."

The lot behind The Stallion was full of pick-ups and a beat up Camaro or two. Peter thought that his life had become such a dismal farce, going to places like he had passed so many times over the years, living in Oklahoma. There he was, just another burnt out good ole boy, drowning sorrows at the edge of another old blacktop highway, out the middle of nowhere.

Peter and his dad walked in through the back door, down a little hall and into the saloon by the pool tables. Peter couldn't see anything, his pupils still pin holes from the bright sun outside. The bar was dark and dank with the staleness of cigarette smoke and spilled beer. Country music played low on the jukebox. Willie and Waylon were the only country Peter knew, and he thought that he hadn't been missing much, by the sound of the twangy whining he heard in the dark room.

"Wanna beer?" Verlin said.

"Does a dog have a dick?"

"Boy, you better watch it."

Peter sat at a little table and watched as his old man walked over to the bar and started talking to the young bartender. He talked with his hands for a second and then pointed over to Peter. The girl's nervous smile softened when she looked over to see Peter sitting there, him giving a little nod and smiling back. Verlin got her attention by slapping the bar. The girl's smile tightened again. That same feigned, forced smile of the girls back at the house, placating the unpredictability of someone they had learned to live with.

"I'm dyin' of thirst over here, pal," Peter shouted over to Verlin.

Verlin grabbed the beers from the bar and walked over to Peter. Peter waved over to the bartender. She smiled again, but her friendliness was cut short by some burly farm-hand that bullied his way into view. She didn't smile anymore, as the dude looked over at Peter and then back at her.

"That shit stain's not supposed to be here," Verlin said. "Did he give you a dirty look?"

"No." Peter didn't want his old man to get stupid. He knew that his dad probably sat there packing heat in his waistband, and the chick obviously had a guy friend who might give him a good fight anyway.

"Where in the hell is that pecker-head?" Verlin said.

"Who's that?"

"Addie," Verlin said. "His name's Adolf. Ain't that funny?"

"I guess if he's crazy and has a little moustache."

"Fuckin' Nazi."

Peter slammed his beer and tipped the empty glass in front of his dad.

"I'll get a pitcher," Verlin said, and walked back over to the girl. The girl's nervous smile softened a little bit when Verlin ordered the pitcher. She gave him an extra glass.

Verlin walked over to Peter and set the extra glass down on the table in front of him. The big oaf over by the bartender looked like he was choking on some steak, his face turning red as he contorted a little bit on his stool. The bartender threw her bar towel at the big guy and then stormed back to the little kitchen. The guy stood there looking dumber than he had just a moment earlier.

Another big oaf, who wore a flat-top and an LAPD t-shirt, walked right up to Peter and Verlin. Peter thought that the big boy at the bar must have had some back up. Peter thought about kicking the guy in the balls and getting the hell out of there as fast as he could.

"Addie!" Verlin shouted over the music that had been suddenly turned up for the evening crowd. The lights a little dimmer.

"Hey, fucker." Addie grabbed the empty glass and helped himself to the pitcher. "Where's Carly Jo?"

"Her man pissed her off, I guess," Verlin said. "She threw her towel at 'em and went in the back."

"I told that fucker to stay away from here."

Addie walked over to the bar and stood next to the big guy that could have been Addie's brother for all Peter knew. Addie leaned into the old boy like he had a rumor to spread. That's when Peter noticed that the back of Addie's shirt said, "We treat you like a KING," the last word emphasized in bold lettering.

"How ya like that shirt?" Verlin said, elbowing Peter in the side. "Get it?"

Peter did get it, indeed. He'd been obsessing over the news in Los Angeles ever since the whole sordid affair began the previous year with the beating of Rodney King – the acquittal, the riots, the fear of it surely soon coming to a neighborhood near him.

The bartender hadn't come out from the back yet. Her friend left after Addie went over and talked to him. Addie lumbered back over to their table, his cropped hair and cop moustache.

"This your new boyfriend?" Addie said.

"My boy."

"How's it going," Peter said, and put out his hand to shake.

"You're a pretty boy, son."

"You're pretty damn ugly," Peter said and took his hand back.

Verlin busted out laughing, punching Addie in the arm.

"You got a cigarette?" Peter asked his dad.

Verlin gave him a smoke and Peter slipped off to the toilet. His stomach felt queasy. Perky had given him an ulcer earlier in the month, and sometimes just moving around helped a little bit, like a baby with colic. The drinking and cigarettes would probably have to go eventually, but Peter figured that he could deal with that later, after he got the business of dealing with his dad out of the way. Choose your battles is what Grammie would have said.

Peter went into the men's room and looked into the bathroom mirror. He always did that when he got drunk. He didn't really look into the mirror out of disbelief or disgust of himself, because he loved himself when he was drunk. It was the only time he felt one-hundred percent, really, when all of his unspoken plans and dreams became reality, if only for a second or two, until inevitably he would go back out to the party, continuing to maintain the ruse as best he could. Inebriation, that powerful friend and subtle foe.

Peter did his business and went back out into the saloon. The bartender had made it back to the bar. She smiled at Peter as he walked over to Verlin and Addie, who were racking a game of pool. Peter grabbed his empty glass off the table, poured another beer and walked over to the bar to talk to the young lady.

"What you smilin' at?" she said.

"Am I smiling?"

"Gitcha some, boy!" Peter heard his dad shout from behind him, he and Addie punching each other like a couple drunk frat boys.

Chapter 16

Fr. Ligero signed the ticket and gave the little metal clipboard back to the highway patrolman. He thanked the officer profusely for giving him a break and for not charging him with reckless driving. The officer told him that he was lucky to be a man of the cloth and that he better slow down, because the next cop might not be as understanding.

"Nice car, by the way," the officer said. "For a Nazi, I guess," and he went back to his cruiser, laughing to himself. Fr. Ligero had looked bothered by the comment, obviously, to which Peter told him the cop was probably making reference to the fact that he drove a German car and not an American car. That could be a serious point of contention out there in the sticks of Oklahoma, even if the reference might have been a little off. An old boy's gotta buy American.

Fr. Ligero took a couple of the cigars out of the plastic bag that lay in the console and cut them both. He handed one to Peter and lit his own.

"Most of the Bavarians weren't Nazis, Peter. Bavarian Motor Works. They were agrarians, like the good people of the Heartland here, the bread basket. People shouldn't use that term so loosely."

"Okies don't know any better," Peter said. "How long have you smoked cigars?"

"My dad was a Cuban Creole."

"Yeah?"

"He made money in tobacco, but then moved to the U.S. right before Fidel's revolution. I was a buncher when I was a kid. Dad didn't let us roll when we were kids, though. He said that was a man's job. One had to pay their dues, you know? Like sushi chefs, or Jesuit priests."

Peter felt pretty intimate with paying dues.

The officer pulled out from behind them and turned to go the opposite direction. Fr. Ligero looked in his rearview for a minute and then pulled out onto the road once he and Peter had gotten their cigars lit. They drove in silence for a while and then Fr. Ligero said, "Maybe that's why the church doesn't want priests to drive sports cars. They can't afford the tickets."

"I thought you were supposed to take a vow of poverty, anyway."

"Well..."

Fr. Ligero had been excommunicated for his involvement with a young woman with whom he had fallen in love. He didn't consider it God's will that he stay abstinent for the rest of his life, yet most of his colleagues and superiors simply labeled him an incorrigible rebel, a heretic at best. A priest is an educated person, despite his loyalty, or lack thereof, to the Roman Catholic Church, Fr. Ligero often told Peter. "Why not just become an Anglican priest," many had asked, to which he always said that he thought he could be more useful as a layman. He would focus on his love for the imprisoned, the sick and the widowed, true religion, as Jesus himself put it. And, that is how he became acquainted with Peter.

Grammie had attended a Catholic conference in Kansas City a couple years after Peter went to prison. Fr. Ligero was giving a speech on the importance of living out the Gospel more intentionally, and Grammie knew right then and there that her attendance of the conference was definitely a divine appointment, so she marched herself right up to the podium after his speech and suggested that he have coffee with her afterward, to which he laughed and said, sure, he would love to.

"What do you think?" Fr. Ligero said to Peter.

"Pretty good. I haven't had a cigarette in years."

"These aren't cigarettes."

Fr. Ligero cracked both windows so the smoke could escape. Peter nudged Fr. Ligero in the arm and bugged his eyes out, looking at the speedometer.

"Yeah, yeah," the ex-priest said, quickly changing the subject. "Cigar tobacco is far superior to cigarette tobacco. A totally different monster, altogether. The production much more involved, and cigar-rolling...cigar-rolling is an art and an honor. The trade is passed down generation to generation."

"Did you ever learn to roll cigars?"

"Sure."

"So you paid your dues?"

"My dad owned the factory," Fr. Ligero said, rolling his window down to roll the ash off of the end of his cigar on the side mirror. He rolled the window back up to where it was slightly cracked. "My dad was all over the place. His right-hand man would grab me when dad was busy somewhere around the plantation and show me how to roll. I learned a lot of things from that man that my dad couldn't teach me, Peter."

"Kind of a mentor?"

"Mentors are necessary to manhood, Peter."

"Yeah..." Peter looked out his window, puffing on his cigar.

"It's never too late, you know?"

"Are you offering to be my mentor?"

"Some might say that I am already. Don't you think?"

Peter continued to stare out the window, the fields passing by like the details of a dream. Everything appeared so vivid, electric and surreal one moment, only to slip back into the great unknown like frothy waves being absorbed back into the vast nameless ocean. The days had turned into weeks, into months, into years.

"You're out now, my friend. Now we just have to get your mind out. You have to leave that place behind, those years spent in solitude behind. Nothing happens in this world by mistake. Look at Nelson Mandela. He was imprisoned for a longer time than you, on trumped-up charges to boot, and came out of there to change the world forever. To change South Africa for the better, at least. He made his mark."

Peter thought it ingratiating at best how his friend compared his situation to Nelson Mandela's, as if they were even in the same league. "Yeah, I remember reading about him before I even went to prison." Peter said, flicking the ash off of his cigar. "You should've been a shrink."

"I went to school long enough to be a shrink, a doctor and a lawyer," Fr. Ligero said. "The Jesuits are crazy about education."

"And I've just wasted this life so far. I gave my best years to the Department of Corrections."

"This life is but a drop in the bucket."

"I've heard that before."

"There comes a time when we all have to live for something or someone other than ourselves."

Peter looked at Fr. Ligero as if he didn't understand.

"You can start by forgiving your father, Peter."

Chapter 17

Peter barely slept the night before, his new puppy alternately bouncing about the make-shift bed on the floor, and then sporadically whimpering in a soft little ball right up against Peter's head.

Peter didn't realize the smell in the room until he rubbed his eyes and sat up on the balled-up blankets that he had kicked off somewhere in the middle of the night. The puppy still didn't have a name. She barked at Peter when she noticed that he had suddenly become conscious, almost as if she were protesting the sub-par sanitary arrangements herself. Peter rolled off of his hobo pallet of blankets and sheets and saw the culprit pile of dog poop in the corner of the room. He thought it was interesting that she pooped so neatly, right in the corner of the room. How considerate, he thought, almost flattered by the attempt of his new friend to be as discreet as she could, and then he suddenly realized that if his dad came into the room on his rounds and saw the feces, there would surely be hell to pay.

Peter walked out into the hall of his new house and tip-toed down to the bathroom to get some toilet paper. Nobody seemed to be awake, and so he thought that he could get in and out of the bathroom, clean up and be in the clear before anybody was any the wiser.

The puppy started to bark and whine as Peter made it about halfway down the hall. She started to scratch at the door, barking more loudly. Oh, man, be quiet, Peter thought, the puppy's noise causing him to have to pee even more than he did before. He didn't want his dad and Louise to see the mess in the corner of the room, right there on the clean carpet, so he picked up his pace and snatched a long sheet of toilet paper and hurried back to his room to pick up the crap.

Once Peter got back into the room, he held his breath and bent to pick up the little brown pile. The stool felt warm to the touch and very soft, almost too soft to pick up in one pile without it pushing through the toilet paper and onto his hand. Peter diligently worked at rendering his pet's waste, yet smudged it into the carpet even deeper than it had been. He told his puppy to be quiet and left the room again, going back to the bathroom to get a wet washcloth and some more toilet paper and maybe some soap.

He made it to the bathroom and lifted the seat to go pee, throwing the soiled toilet paper in under his yellow stream. Aahh, relief. Not only did it feel good to relieve himself, but his puppy had quit yapping and whining, so he had time to finish and make it back to the bedroom to clean up the rest of her mess before anybody had a chance to see it. Peter flushed, got some more toilet paper for his mess, and then tip-toed his way back to the bedroom.

Peter opened the door, bracing himself for the onslaught of love and affection from his puppy. Verlin stood in the middle of the room, holding Peter's new puppy by the nape of the neck, looking down at his feet and then back up to Peter, as the puppy wriggled in an attempt to free itself. The puppy had pooped and peed on the floor, right the middle of the carpet this time, and the old man had come in to find it fresh and stinking warm.

Verlin straddled the accident, actually, and there would be no way to stealthily clean up this mess with him hovering over it like some icy gargoyle. Peter looked over into the corner to see the smudged pile, the pile he was in the process of cleaning up, darkening the carpet like a tiny little cloud above might.

"Dad."

"I thought you were gonna take care of your dog."

"I..."

"You said that you were gonna feed her and take her out to go to the bathroom and all of that happy shit, remember?" Verlin said. "There's shit and piss on the fuckin' carpet. Is that taking care of your fuckin' dog? I don't think so! Your dog's in trouble now. You hear me, boy?! Fuckin' trouble, ya little shithead!"

"I was asleep, sir."

"You think 'sir's' gonna get your little, stupid ass out of this jam, boy?"

"I..."

"Shut the fuck up ya little, ungrateful fucker!" And just like that, Verlin threw the puppy against the wall and said, "Next time it's your ass, boy. You better shape up!" And then he left the room without further ado.

Peter's fear melted into horror, flopping back into fear and then sadness and then rage, all in less than a second, rendering him motionless. He got his bearings, however, and quickly moved to the edge of the room where the devastated puppy bawled like a beaten child, scrunched up against the wall. Peter tried to pick her up from where she cowered, but she just didn't trust him, and even tried to bite him in a futile attempt at self-defense. Peter pulled his hand back, wanting to help his friend, but at the same time not wanting to scare her further. He slowly reached for her, softly consoling her, a near whisper under his breath, but she wouldn't have it. She barked at Peter again. Her barks turned to little yelps then, as she scooted herself tighter up against the wall of the bedroom.

"Don't let her die, God," Peter managed to pray between sobs. "I'm sorry for letting her poop on the floor. I won't let it happen again. She's my only friend and I love her and I want her to be happy and love me. Thank you, God." Her yelps slowly turned to whining, as Peter continued to try to get back her trust.

After a while, the puppy finally let Peter pick her up and hold her to himself. He didn't want his new best friend to feel so much pain, to hurt so much. They would suffer together, he and his new friend. Peter made his way to the corner of the soiled room and sat up with her in his arms, softly hugging her, talking to her quietly.

"Simone," Peter said. "That's your new name. I won't let dad do that to you again. We're gonna stick together. Don't you worry." He lightly stroked her black fur as gently as he could, her breathing slowly returning to normal, her curling up tighter on herself just the same.

Peter and Simone awakened, sitting up in the corner of the bedroom, her still nuzzled in his arms. Peter lifted his head, wincing at the stab of pain in his right shoulder and neck, as he became more conscious. He moved his head side to side, trying to work out the kink. Peter then noticed that the room didn't stink as bad as it had earlier, and that the piles of poop and wet spots on the carpet had been cleaned up.

Peter guarded Simone as the door slowly crept open. Louise came through the door as if some slumbering monster might lay on the other side, waiting to devour anything or anyone who dared encroach on its space.

"Oh...hey...are you guys doin' okay?" she said.

"Yes."

Peter began to wonder if she really liked him. She called him "hon" and gave him food, and more than likely was the one who cleaned up the dog crap and the wet spots, but at the same time, she didn't ever come to the rescue when Verlin began acting like a monster.

"Can I go to Pinkie's house?"

"Well, hon, I'll have to check and see if they have time."

They said that he was welcome anytime, Peter thought. "Please?" he said.

"We'll see." Louise started to leave the room and then turned to say, "Your dad's at work."

Peter named his dog after Grammie's old neighbor, Simone Ravich. He really didn't know the old lady all that well, just having heard interesting stories about the reclusive woman at his grandma's kitchen table, whenever she had happened to have seen the old woman out hobbling around in her flower beds.

Grammie told Peter that Mrs. Ravich had driven an ambulance in Miami, during WWII, while her husband gunned down Japanese from the rear end of a B-17 Bomber. When she wasn't hauling the sick and maimed around the tropical city, she handed out cartons of stolen cigarettes out of the back of her ambulance to street people near the beach. These were all stories passed on to Grammie back when Grammie and Mrs. Ravich played cards together, mind you. Peter almost thought they were Grammie's own stories, only disguised as the neighbor's so that Grammie could preserve her grandmotherly ruse to the world. If Peter would have known what intuitive meant, he might have said that he had had a hunch.

Another lifetime ago, Simone also worked the apple orchards in Maine, crushed grapes in Palermo, rolled cigars in Cuba, and then went on to raise ten surly red-heads when she decided to settle down in Oklahoma. Grammie had nine kids, his mom included, Peter always thought, when Grammie came to that part of the story. Peter imagined that Oklahoma was as good as any place when you had seen it all. The wide-open spaces to run and jump around in are good for the soul. Life is slower and simple and less pretentious.

Peter knew that his little dog would surely see the world and have her own adventures, and the name seemed fitting for a black dog with a penchant for getting into trouble. Peter sat back down on the make-shift bed and put Simone on the floor. She went right over to the corner where she had relieved herself earlier, so he quickly jumped up and scooped her in his arms and opened his bedroom door to take her outside to go potty.

Peter walked as quietly through the house as possible. The hallway ran the length of the house, creaky hard-wood floors in the dim light, and so he had to be careful not to wake Louise, who had been sleeping a lot the last couple days. Peter really didn't mind the fact that she slept a lot, because he and Simone could keep each other company most of the time. Without Louise around, the day seemed a little brighter even. Peter and her had gotten off to a good start, sure, but she seemed to quickly lose interest in who he was and whether or not things were "okay" with him any longer.

The woman appeared to be slowly disappearing right in front of him. Not physically disappearing, but as if her personality were being zapped from her by some unseen force beneath the earth, draining her of energy, of her ability to engage with the world and smile. The whole house felt eerie, which only stoked Peter's motivation to take things outside every chance that he got.

Peter continued creeping slowly until he made it to the back door. Once outside, Simone ran to the edge of the yard, relieved herself, as if she had been holding it for days, and ran back over to Peter, who stood by the back door looking around the yard and up at the sky and every which way, like it was the first time he had ever been outside of a house before. Peter looked down as Simone started to pounce on his feet, taking little nips at his toes, as she barked for him to play.

Peter had never seen anybody next door until that day, when he noticed a man in his back yard watering the flowers, like Grammie used to do back home.

The man next door waved. Peter waved back.

"What's your name?" the man said over the chain-link fence.

Fear slapped Peter out of his bucolic haze. He knew that he probably shouldn't be talking to the guy, even if he did live next door. There were crazy people out there, Verlin had told him on many occasions. Crazy fuckin' bastards everywhere, to put it in Verlin's exact parlance. Peter picked Simone up and stared at an old live oak at the edge of the yard, the man now in Peter's periphery. Peter felt guilty. Not for any particular reason, really, other than the fact that Peter didn't think his dad would like him talking to anyone he didn't know, anyone to whom Verlin hadn't personally introduced the boy. Strangers out there in the fringe.

Peter continued to stand frozen stiff at the edge of the yard. The guy waved again, and said something that Peter couldn't make out. He suddenly felt nauseous, perhaps from the thought of going back inside the house, under that black cloud. Nevertheless, something felt even more remiss about remaining outside, as if he were being watched very closely, and at any moment would be grabbed by some deranged creep and taken into an even more dank and dismal dump. Maybe the neighbor was the bad guy. Everyone could be the bad guy. There was no telling who had heinous thoughts of homicide and torture wrapped up in their mad and sweaty heads, out there in that great and dangerous world.

Peter squeezed Simone tighter and then quickly waved to the man who continued watering his flowers nonchalantly, at that point oblivious to Peter's reciprocation. The man kept watering his flowers, engrossed by their dependence on his love and water, so Peter ran into the house and closed the door behind himself, as if he had just evaded a rabid Doberman. He looked out the window in the door to make sure the guy hadn't just been feigning indifference to the boy so that he could catch him off guard.

Peter turned around to see Louise pouring herself a glass of milk at the kitchen counter. He stood up against the back door, holding his dog, watching Louise, quiet like he had just spotted a bear in the woods. Half-shaken and not really paying attention, Simone wriggled her way out of his arms and ran off into the other room. He unintentionally held his breath, staring at the woman who seemed so overly preoccupied with pouring milk into a glass. He shouldn't have let Simone act so recklessly. Simone ran back into the kitchen and started nipping at Peter's toes again. He scooped the puppy up and held her more tightly, petting her maybe a little too hard, as she tried to bite his hand.

"Oh...hi hon," Louise finally said, looking at the frisky Cocker Spaniel in the boy's arms and then back up to her glass of milk that had begun to overflow onto the counter and down to the floor where it puddled beneath her. Simone busted out of Peter's embrace again and ran over to the puddle of milk and began lapping it up. "Do you want something for lunch?"

Peter looked at the clock. It read 4:35 pm.

"Sure," he said. Peter had not eaten in a couple days and would take whatever he could.

Simone continued to voraciously lap up the spilled milk on the floor, happy as a tick on a dog.

"Did you name your dog?"

"Simone."

"Oh...hon...that's nice," she said, slowly. "Do you want some lunch?"

"Yes, ma'am."

Peter sat down at the table, as Louise shuffled over to the pantry in her browned, fuzzy pink house slippers. Peter looked down at the bandaging on his hand to compare shades of brown. Louise rummaged through the pantry for something to fix for Peter, humming all the while she stood there. The tune sounded familiar to Peter, even though he really couldn't put a finger on it.

Willie Nelson? Fleetwood Mac? The notes were jumbled and monotonous to Peter, who patiently waited, studying the peculiar woman responsible for taking care of him.

"Is dad still at work?"

"Yes."

"Does he work all of the time?"

Louise momentarily stopped her search and deeply sighed, her back still to Peter. He stared at her, as if he expected her to turn on him, fangs protruding, with a crazed look in her eyes, as she lunged for him in an attempt to rip out his throat with her bare hands and teeth. However, she just continued to stand there silently for another moment, laboriously breathing, in and out, like she had just run to the kitchen in a mad sprint. Peter thought that maybe she forgot what she was doing.

Louise stomped her dirty house slipper to the floor, and then slammed the pantry door with enough force so that one of the hinges ripped loose from the framing, causing the door to hang to the side crookedly.

"Your dad works hard, Pete!" she screamed, beginning to cry. "Hard, hard, hard! Dammit!" And then she ran out of the room, banging all the way down to her bedroom where she went in and slammed the door behind herself.

"I know, ma'am. I'm sorry," Peter said to himself, looking down at Simone who was putting the finishing touches on the floor where the milk had been, leaving a shiny, clean circle.

Peter could hear the door to Louise and his dad's bedroom open, and then heard those soiled slippers padding down the hallway, to the living room, where he heard the ambient hum of the television come to life, and then someone's voice. He braced himself for the next inevitable outburst, as he got up and picked Simone up off of the floor. Her belly was taught with milk.

Louise made her way back to the kitchen and over to the dangling door. "How did that happen," she said, staring at the faulty cabinet door. She turned to Peter, smiling, and said, "Don't let her pee." She grabbed the gallon jug that she had poured the milk from, and put it back in the refrigerator. "Your dad is at work."

Louise got a butter knife out of the sink, and then some bread and sliced ham out of the refrigerator, and went to work making Peter's lunch. Peter watched the whole painful process of Louise assembling the sandwich, as if he were on the other side of a thick glass watching some primitive species with nerve-deadened hands attempting to disassemble an improvised explosive device. He felt anxious in his seat, wanting to get up and help her do what seemed to be a simple task, but one that she did with the slowest and most clumsy lack of precision he had ever seen. He didn't want to break whatever little concentration and dexterity that the woman had, however, and kept to himself, watching, waiting patiently for his reward.

Peter heard some dramatic intro music in the living room, and so he crept out there to see what the five o'clock news had to say. The polished and pomped anchorwoman smiled and told Mississippi that the top story of the day was that police were still looking for Patricia Hearst and her band of Symbionese Liberation Army members. Sympathizers. Brain-washing. Stockholm Syndrome. Too bad. Oh, so sad. The woman went on for some time, not making any sense to Peter.

The anchor repeatedly told her audience that the robbery at the Hibernia Bank in San Francisco had happened two weeks ago to the day. It was April 29, 1974. Peter couldn't have imagined in a million years that he would be on his couch eighteen years later, watching the latest dramas of the Rodney King riots in Los Angeles unfold on his own television.

Peter wanted to see if the lady would talk about the missing girl, Ramona what's-her-name? He tip-toed over to see if Louise had finished her sandwich-building adventure. She continued to stand at the counter, oblivious to Peter and his news interests. Peter went back in front of the television and leaned up against one of the brown living room chairs, petting Simone, holding her just right. The woman on the television said that America was still recovering from the results of the fuel embargo that had been lifted almost a month and a half ago. Ripple effects. Austerity. She said something about lasting financial impact. Peter wondered if that's why things had become so tense around the house. The fuel what? Peter thought the word sounded funny and real important at the same time. Embargo.

Peter walked back over to the kitchen doorway and looked in. Louise now stood motionless. He thought that maybe he should go poke her to make sure that she hadn't expired standing up. He walked back in front of the television. Gas. Economy. Gold. Past impeachment. Peter sat Simone down and then sat down himself, waiting for the story on the girl. He quickly got up, however, not wanting his dad to come in the front door and catch him watching news like the naughty little boy that he was. Peter grabbed Simone and went to the kitchen.

Louise finally finished the sandwich, and then put it on a dirty plate that she pulled from the sink. "You eat your dinner. It's about time to go to bed," she said, placing the dirty plate and disheveled sandwich in front of Peter, who had taken a seat at the table. He stared at the sandwich for a moment and then picked it up to take a bite. He looked up at Louise, who stood there hovering, as if she were assessing whether or not he was actually a real boy and not some apparition that had come to haunt her in the middle of her day. Her robe came open at the top, exposing her breasts to Peter, who tried to keep his attention on his messy sandwich, taking quick bite after quick bite, while he had the chance, but who wanted to stare at those swollen masses on her body, that thick sensation in his throat again, even more. Lust and hunger fought it out, as Peter tried to keep it together. Louise finally pulled her robe closed after she looked down at herself when she noticed Peter staring.

Louise padded out of the kitchen again and down the hall. The sound of the closing bedroom door gave Peter immense relief. Again. He wanted more time alone with his dog. But that naked body almost made him feel as if the awkwardness of being around Louise were worth it. He couldn't get the image of her bronze chest, those dark, aureola silver dollars, those nipples, out of his mind. He wanted to feel them, caress them forever, and perhaps even suckle there for comfort for as long as she would let him. That euphoric, yet nauseating sensation all over his body. Dry throat and fluttery belly. He felt crazy and sane at the same time, all fear being driven out by this new, rogue experience.

Peter finished his sandwich, looking at the empty plate. He started to feel guilty about not being more appreciative of his dad and Louise's attempts at making his stay comfortable. Peter didn't feel right about seeing his dad's girlfriend's naked body, but he thought it was something that he would just have to get used to. She was an adult, after all. Peter had felt uncomfortable when she talked about his penis in the bathtub that time too, but she was an adult, and adults knew better than to do things that weren't right. Right and wrong, right and wrong. Those shiny breasts, the sweat, her smell. Sun-spots. Short shorts. Tan legs.

Peter put his plate over on the counter. He grabbed a dirty glass from the sink and filled it up with water to wash his lunch down. He took the dish rag that hung over the faucet and wiped up Louise's mess of milk that she had left, sure that he would probably get the blame if he didn't take care of the problem. She had also left the glass of milk that she had poured in the first place, and so Peter put that in the refrigerator so that it didn't spoil. Simone sat on her haunches, alternately watching Peter and then chewing on the dining table leg. Peter put his glass back on the counter and went over to pick her up. 5:35 pm, the clock on the wall read.

Peter started to go to his room, but thought that he should probably wash the dishes first, not wanting any undue trouble. The house lay dark and still, but for Peter scrubbing.

Peter woke up what seemed to be much later, but really couldn't tell because of the absence of a working clock. Simone sat on her butt, waiting for Peter expectantly, when he opened his eyes.

"Hi, girl."

She wagged her tail furiously and jumped up on his head, licking him all over the face and hands, the onslaught of love overwhelming.

The house still felt dark and silent. Peter couldn't hear anyone moving around outside his bedroom door. Dad sure put in long hours on vacation, Peter thought. Simone looked at Peter with a cocked head, and then pounced again. He pushed her off and lay back down.

Peter began to think of his mom. She always sang to him when she put him to bed. His friends in the neighborhood had made fun of him for having a mother that still sang him to sleep, but he didn't care. He loved being loved, and felt no shame in being the object of maternal affection. He wanted to see his friends, though. Even if they did make fun of him. He missed home. He missed the familiar sounds of his mom cleaning the house on Saturdays, Marvin Gaye on the stereo. His grandparents would never expect him to stay inside so much, let alone sit crammed in a little room with no view and no fresh air. Peter could see his grandpa out in the garage "messing," as he liked to say.

Something seemed really wrong about going to bed in the summer when it was still light outside. He hated having to go to bed before dark at the beginning of the school year back home, too, but then his mom would sing to him and he felt better, despite the sound of the other neighborhood kids outside playing in the streets. He was on vacation and still had to go to bed early. No school and no singing, either. Peter began to wonder if he would ever be able to leave the house again, Verlin home less and less, Louise gone despite her presence, that ghost in dingy slippers, with those swollen breasts, and God knows what else underneath that robe. Peter felt cold and nauseous thinking about the whole thing. He shivered a little bit and Simone sat up and barked at him as if she didn't approve of his self-pity.

Simone had again relieved herself in the corner of the room. Peter couldn't really tell if the place stunk or not, because he had been cooped up in it for days, becoming one with the smell and dim light around him, like some obscure fungus. The cheap, brown carpet and plain, white walls had become his universe. He imagined that his father would come back into the room a totally changed man. Peter's idea of change fluctuated between his father becoming otherworldly kind and gentle, to the idea of the man fully developing into the monster that he was well on his way to becoming. Peter thought about that ham sandwich. Those breasts. That spilled milk. He would crawl on all fours and lick that milk up off of the floor right then if he had the chance...and sure...he would share with his friend Simone too.

He started crying as he began praying to the God that he had often heard of in school. Weekly masses and daily classes about this powerful deity that could do anything left him feeling only half-awake. He had heard at school that God would punish him if he were bad, but that God loved him immeasurably, as well, and that he could do anything, yet it seemed that all of his teachers and the other kids left all those beliefs at the door when they left school for the day.

Peter felt confused about the reality of the whole thing, God as it were, yet his mind gravitated to that place out of nowhere else safe to go. Grammie always told Peter that God would always be there when everybody else let him down. Mom had disappeared. Grammie was nowhere to be found. Peter said the "Our Father" out of habit, one more time, drifting back to sleep again, the only reprieve.

When Peter awakened later in the early morning or late evening, he thought he heard someone on the other side of the door tinkering with something, fixing something maybe. My door? Something in the hallway.

"Dad!"

Peter realized that the room smelled like a filthy dog kennel upon awakening, as if his senses had been heightened by the rest, and then instantly fired once he opened his eyes. He felt like he might vomit. Simone didn't look too happy either. Peter sat up on his pallet of sheets and that old, itchy blanket that Louise had given him a couple days earlier, waving Simone over to himself.

"Dad!"

Someone started beating on the door really hard, to the point of it nearly buckling in. Peter reached out and grabbed Simone as she began to whimper, and then he scooted his back to the wall behind them, holding her tightly.

There were several piles of poop, and probably wet spots all over the floor. Peter could hear his dad and Louise talking in the hallway, and so he yelled again. Then, as if his voice somehow had the power to make people instantly go mad, Peter heard a slap, then a weak squeal and a thud. Verlin started shouting obscenities at Louise, or so Peter thought it sounded somewhat like his dad. Then the sound of shattering glass echoed from the living room, and the screaming abruptly ended. The banging on Peter's bedroom door started again, growing louder and louder still, like an insane bull had been let loose in the house just to see what might happen.

Louise's small, battered voice called out in little yelps from down the hall. Verlin screamed something unintelligible as he pounded his way to the living room.

Crashing sounds came from down the hallway, the other way now. Verlin started screaming at the top of his lungs again, and Peter felt pretty sure that it was in fact Verlin doing the shouting this time. Peter pictured his dad going totally ape nuts, trashing the whole house, almost foaming at the mouth, as he writhed in wicked torment, due to some ancient demonic possession.

Peter had never seen that kind of rage before, but the rage came...and that's when the nightmares started. Very unpleasant nightmares with that little, pernicious demon of his own, in the corner of his room, from that night on. Relentless and shameful.

Now I lay me down to sleep,

I pray the Lord my soul to keep;

If I should die before I wake,

I pray the Lord my soul to take...

Both Peter's mom and Grammie had said that prayer to him every night before bed. He couldn't remember a night of missing it, ever. The morbidity of the whole thing didn't seem strange at the time. Anyone can die in their sleep, right? Now, more than ever, death felt near to Peter – real like plastic cups and birthday cake.

Peter said, *Now I Lay Me Down to Sleep* a few times, and then *The Our Father* a dozen or so times, trying to coax his eyes into drooping off into the world of unconsciousness. A good Catholic boy knows those prayers, plus the *Hail Mary,* and he thought that if there was any chance of getting out of there alive, that praying might just be the ticket. Peter had never really had a tangible use for God, to be honest, but fear has a way of squeezing a heavenly request out of the most atheistic and stoic of folks, some might say.

Since the vacation with his dad had started, Peter hadn't had to go to church once, which he didn't mind, because he hated church. Boring old people who reeked of ointments and bad breath. But then again, Peter would take church over vacation any day, now that he had the chance to explore them more closely in his ripe old age of five.

Peter finally fell asleep, as he let his thoughts separate from all the questions and concerns, his mind slowing to a dull hum.

When Peter awakened, he noticed that the house had fallen quiet again, his room dark again, and Simone cuddled next to him, trying to stay warm in the cold, air-conditioned room again. The bare ceiling light in Peter's bedroom had gone out somewhere between his dad's last explosion and nightfall. So, when the sun totally disappeared at the end of the day, that meant bedtime to he and Simone for sure. Peter didn't feel too afraid of the dark, however, knowing that he would eventually get little splashes of light through the cloudy window in his bedroom from the neighbor's motion light next door.

Peter tried to open the window the day before, to see if he could climb out, but it had been sealed shut. Peter didn't want to break it, because he knew that would make his dad really angry. Moreover, he realized too that there was nowhere to go anyway. Anywhere he went, his father would find him. There were crazy people everywhere. Robbers. Sympathizers. Rag-heads. Slimy creatures of the night waiting around every corner. The old man would surely lumber up to whomever had swooped Peter off the street, at any rate, and woo them with his wit and charm, only to drag him back to the dark recesses of Peter's new home the second they were out of sight. Seclusion.

In the recent past, Peter's only foreseeable escape had been sleep. He said his prayers again. Until that night, unconsciousness had been his second-best friend, next to Simone. Peter opened his eyes, and there he was. Peter had never met him before, but the creature seemed to know everything about Peter. The thing sat cross-legged, so proud and confident of himself and his capacity to evoke fear. Peter closed his eyes and opened them again, hoping to wake up. A priest had told Peter that when you're in the middle of a nightmare, to just realize it is a nightmare and you will wake up. Lucidity, he said, is a very powerful tool for living a full life. Whatever the hell that means, Peter thought, as he remembered the encounter.

Peter told himself it was only a dream, opened his eyes, yet there the creature sat, laughing loudly.

"You're a bad little boy, aren't you?" the creature said.

"Yes," Peter said. He knew that he hadn't taken care of Simone as well as he should have. Also, Peter made his dad mad all the time, causing him to be stressed out, and on their long-awaited vacation for fuck sake, as Verlin had put it so aptly.

"You know you're gonna die, right?"

"I don't wanna die. I'll be better, I promise."

The creature's laughter filled the room, and when it did, his color changed from dark brown to red. Peter expected the thing to burst into flames or something fantastic like that, but he just sat there in the upper corner of the bedroom, laughing, taunting Peter to further tears. The only thing consistent about the little guy seemed to be his yellow eyes and snickering laugh, because his demeanor otherwise changed along with his skin color. Peter could feel the life sap out of himself, as that damned fear spread like a virus within his chest and upper arms.

"You want to go to sleep, but you are mine now," the demon said. "You have ruined your father, and he cannot love you anymore. Jesus hates you. You're a fucking waste of space. Look at you lying in shit and piss like some kind of fucking pig," the creature said, beginning to laugh again. "Why don't you take care of the little puppy that mommy and daddy gave you? Huh, little piggy? Are you too fucking stupid? Huh? What do you have to say for yourself, loser?"

"She's not my mommy!"

"Watch your mouth, faggot!" His color changed from brown to red again. "I'm your only friend now, nobody loves you. Do you think your mommy wants you? Where is she? You're a fucking loser, boy. You know that? Son? Boy? What are you gonna do? Nothing! Boy! Son! Huh?!"

Peter couldn't speak. The demon in the upper corner of his room maintained total control. He spoke and Peter listened, having no defense, the weight of the creature's words too heavy to bare, battering Peter motionless. Peter cried and the little monster laughed, until the morning came, when Peter awakened.

"Dad!"

Verlin stood expressionless, with his arms crossed. He looked at Peter and then held a set of keys out in front of him, taking in all of the urine spots and feces piles in the room. Save for the animal waste and Peter's little make-shift bed, there was nothing else in the room, except the burned-out ceiling light that dangled like a forgotten question.

"What the fuck are you doin' in here?" Verlin said.

"I couldn't get out, sir."

"I give you a dog and you just let it shit and piss all over the fuckin' place in our new house." Verlin stepped into the room carefully, dodging the piles of crap on the floor.

Simone started barking at Verlin. He laughed at the dog as Peter held her by the little red collar that he had found by the door to his room, where someone had slipped it under.

Peter could see that there was a padlock latch on the outside of the door. Verlin saw Peter looking at the door, and shook his head "no" to Peter, who looked up at him with a hopeful expression. Then, as if he had come up with a solution to Peter's behavior issues like a magic trick, Verlin pulled his other hand out from behind his back, the one that didn't have the keys in it, and threw a Master Lock at Peter. It hit him in the knee, and it hurt like hell, but Peter knew better than to cry. Tears pissed the old man off.

Peter rubbed his knee with one hand and pulled Simone tighter to his side with the other. She continued to bark at the madman now in the room. Peter had taken off his finger splints and put them under his pallet of blanket. The shock that his dad hadn't noticed the missing braces made him blink and tick for a second. The old man seemed to have greater justice and lessons in store.

"She's a little killer, ain't she?" Verlin said, and then as quickly as he spoke the words, he hovered right above Peter, ripped the dog out of his hands, and set her on the floor behind him. "Did you think I wanted to hurt your little faggot doggie? Huh? Answer me, ya little shit! Huh?!"

Simone crept to the edge of the room.

"You wouldn't do that, sir."

Verlin grabbed the back of Peter's head by the hair, and smacked it against the wall behind him a few times. The next thing Peter knew, his face slid into one of the piles of shit next to his bed. His dad brought him up for a little air, and then pushed his face down hard and twisted it into another pile of shit, and then another. Peter couldn't breathe, so he couldn't really scream, but knew in the same half-second that his shouting and pleas would be a waste of energy, would go unanswered, at any rate.

"You little shithead!" Verlin let Peter up for air, as he breathed rancid beer and cigarettes into Peter's face, and then started laughing. "Get it?! Little shithead! Pretty fuckin' funny, huh?!"

"Yes, sir," Peter said, spitting shit out of his mouth. "That is funny, sir."

"You think you're so fuckin' smart, don't ya?"

"No, sir."

"What'd you say? You disagreein' with me, boy?"

Verlin slammed Peter's face into another pile of shit, and held him down into it, so that Peter could taste the acrid scat oozing into his mouth, coating his teeth and tongue, as his stomach turned and released, puke all over the already soiled carpet.

"You fuckin' little asshole!" Verlin allowed Peter to raise his head once again to get some air. "You puke all over my house! You let your dog shit all over my house, and then you puke all over my house?! You fuckin' waste of life! I should kill you! Kill you..!" He bent and stopped to breathe, and then lifted his head wildly. "Kill you!"

Verlin commenced to pound and kick the walls, putting massive gashes and dents throughout the room. Peter scooted back to the wall behind him, as Simone curled and whined in the opposite corner, not having the heart to cross over to Peter for protection. And then after Peter thought that Verlin would surely be tired from his mindless destruction, Verlin turned on him and grabbed the back of his head by the hair again.

One might not think that eating shit could ever become tolerable, but to Peter, honestly, it was a matter of perspective. Faced with death or humiliation, most people would take the latter. Peter braced himself for the first second or two and then just let his body go slack, as Verlin dragged Peter's face from one pile to the next, and to the next, and again, until the old man had smeared Peter's face in every pile of stinking dog shit in the room, the only limiting factor seeming to be the old man's lack of endurance. Too many cigarettes and too many beers might have just saved someone's life that day, Peter had thought later in his life. It wasn't as if Peter enjoyed it, per se, but just that he realized that if he had fought much more, his father, his one and only, would have killed him right there on the spot. Despite the dismal potential for his future, Peter wanted to live, and so he made up his mind to do so by relenting.

After Verlin finished smearing all of the shit into the carpet with Peter's face, some piles repeatedly so, Peter couldn't help but cry. He let the tears pour through like a sieve percolating through a mud plain. Peter lay prostrate on the floor, crushed under the immense weight of his father's hatred for him. Peter could feel the man standing over him, breathing heavy, and then he heard Verlin's Zippo open, a cigarette being lit, and then the definitive close of the lighter...and smoke filled the room.

Simone nipped at Verlin's heels while he stood over Peter, looking down proudly, as if he had finally satisfied some twisted sense of archaic justice. Verlin's simple presence had begun to make Peter's bones ache from the inside out like gamma rays. Peter could feel his imminent death, even if he felt that he had chosen life by letting his father have his way that particular day. The little monster might be right, Peter thought, I am a waste of life.

"You need to clean your room, son. Okay, buddy?" Verlin said, sounding real chummy now, and then he turned to leave the room.

"Yes, sir." Peter pressed his face against his pallet of blankets that had become a ball of filth in the corner of the room.

Simone began barking at Verlin again. He kicked her out of the way, she yelped and then ran back to Peter, and Verlin left the room. Peter took her into his arms and cried for mercy, to God, to himself, to the earth and sky and universe. To whatever and whomever might be able to affect real change. The door closed and Peter could hear the sound of the lock being put back through the latch on the door.

"You be good in there now, okay?" Verlin said, patting the outside of the door, and then walked away down the hall.

"I love you, Simone," Peter said, closing his eyes.

Chapter 18

Pinkie wiped her forehead with the sleeve of her t-shirt. She knelt in the dirt in front of the umpteenth Azalea that she had planted that day. Powder-pink, fuschia, white and whatever other color the nursery had in stock. She took her gardening gloves off and sat them down with her tools.

Pinkie stood up as Sewell pulled up into the yard in his big truck. He got out and walked over to her with a sullen look.

"Where you 'magine that boy's been?" he said.

"I worry about him."

"Verlin don't seem right, sometimes, does he?"

"Hon, I think you should call Louise," Pinkie said. "Make sure she's alright."

"I called. She don't ever answer."

Sewell took Pinkie by the hand, and they walked over to a couple of chairs that rested under the shade of the big Magnolia. Sewell took his beaten straw hat off when they sat down and beat it against his leg.

"I love you," Pinkie said.

"I love you too."

They looked out into the pasture across the road, both contemplative, looking again for all those answers that tend to float around out in open spaces. Sewell pulled out a pouch of Red Man and pinched a clump to put in his mouth. He held the pouch out to Pinkie.

"You better get that outta my face if you wanna keep it," she said and then slapped him on the arm.

"Hell, I don't even know where they're livin' these days," Sewell said.

"Verlin seems to move a lot. He isn't from here."

"That's for sure," Sewell said and spat on the ground. "Seems like a big-city shyster, if you ask me. I don't think he's ever told the truth about nothin'." Sewell stared off into the distance again. Pinkie sat pensively, then looked over at Sewell's profile. "Sorry, hon, I just don't trust the old boy."

"I know."

"I'll call Cow Town. See if he knows anything."

"What's Cow Town got to do with that man?"

"He tossed a little work to Verlin some time back. Helps him out sometimes, ya know?"

Pinkie shook her head, staring out at the road.

Despite their concern for the boy, they continued to bask in the silence, almost like the world outside their own didn't even exist any longer. Sewell chewed his tobacco, and Pinkie brushed off her pant legs gently. Pinkie and Sewell held hands, saying a silent prayer to Peter. They would do what they could to help the boy out, granted they got the chance to see him again. Their only child raised, with no grandchildren to speak of, and they had all the time in the world to offer a young man if they got the chance.

Pinkie's legs began to get tingly from sitting too long, and she said, "You hungry?"

"You bet."

Pinkie went inside and got Sewell a glass of ice water and brought it out to him. He smiled and told her he'd help if she needed it. She said she didn't and went back inside to fix a late lunch.

Pinkie had all of the fixings on the table when the phone rang. She went over to the little table against the wall near the doorway where the phone rested and picked up the receiver.

"Hello."

Nobody said anything on the other end. She could hear the live air through the phone, though, like someone had called, gotten cold feet and clammed up on second thought. She didn't know anybody like that, shy and all, she thought. She didn't think too much of it and hung the phone up. A moment later, the phone rang again. Pinkie stepped a little quicker this time and got it on the first ring.

"Hello."

"Mama," a still, small voice said from the other end.

"Louise?"

"Mama, we're gonna go outta town for a couple of days," she said. "Do you think Peter could stay with you guys?"

"Well..."

"Mama...is that okay?"

Pinkie let out a sigh of relief, still not wanting to seem too eager, and slowly said, "Yes, it is."

Pinkie held the phone to her ear, mustering patience, waiting for Louise to say something else. Pinkie felt anxious whenever Louise called and sounded so spaced-out, like the girl had more to say but couldn't as if someone were standing over her, telling her what to say or not to say, like an amateur criminal couple pining for a ransom.

Pinkie felt as if she needed to train Louise upright again, maybe start from scratch, as if she were dealing with some kind of child gone invalid all of a sudden, but Pinkie felt too far away, dreaming as she may, and the realization sat in her gut, that she too was powerless and helpless to do anything but wait for the woman to come around.

"Are you okay, hon?"

"I'll see you in a couple of days, mama."

"Are you sure you're okay?"

"I love you."

And the phone went dead.

"Dammit to hell!"

Pinkie slammed the receiver into the cradle so hard that the rotary dial fell off the front of the Seventies mustard-yellow phone. She stood over the phone as if waiting for it to complain so that she could smack it one more time for good measure.

Sewell ran into the kitchen, hat in hand.

"You okay?"

"That damn girl!" Pinkie said, crying. "She doesn't care about anybody but herself."

"Louise?" Sewell pulled Pinkie into his arms as she cried into his chest. "It's okay, babe. Don't worry about her. She's a strong woman. She's your daughter."

"That's what scares me."

"Oh, come on," he said, giving her what comfort he could. "You married me, didn't you?"

Pinkie laughed.

"Huh?"

"Is that supposed to make me feel better?"

"Hey."

Pinkie pulled away from Sewell, smiling despite her tears, "You know I love you."

"I know," he said, stroking her hair lightly. "Was she okay?"

"She always sounds like a zombie when I talk to her on the phone. She said that she was bringing Peter over in a couple of days. She's so damn secretive anymore."

"Peter comin's an answered prayer."

"Yeah, it is, hon," she said. "I just want Louise to be okay too. She worships that man, and he ain't no damn good."

"She's gotta live her life. We gotta let her."

"I'm just afraid she's gonna kill herself or something."

"Oh, come on. She's your daughter. She's too damn proud to go and do some damned fool thing like that."

"Yeah?"

"You know it."

Sewell walked Pinkie over to the kitchen table and pulled out the chair for her. He got all of the sandwich fixings off the counter and put them in front of her. He poured a glass of cold lemonade out of the fridge for her and poured himself another glass of water.

"Take it easy. Okay?"

"Thanks, hon," Pinkie said and began breaking up iceberg lettuce from the head on the table. "If you say so."

Chapter 19

Peter and his dad closed the Stallion down that night. Peter went home with the bartender, and they got to know each other a little better. She said that she didn't usually take guys home on the first night and that she didn't want him to think she was a slut or anything. Why would I think something like that, Peter had said. She said he might take it the wrong way, her taking him home after serving him a few beers and then having sex with him and her roommate into the wee hours.

That was as good as things got for Peter. Random sex partners, girlfriend at home, her doing the same thing. He really didn't see anything wrong with it, per se. As a matter of fact, it seemed like the only things that he could feel anymore were reckless indulgences. No love, really, just ravenous conquests that might never end if he were indeed left to his own devices, or vices, that is.

In the back of Peter's mind, for some reason, he thought the reunion between him and his dad would somehow magically mend all of the nasty ragged ends of his fragile psyche like a new baby, or an impulsive marriage might complete some other lost soul. Like the mere relationship, just the energy and intent between them would send a soothing ripple throughout his life, putting all things emotional and otherwise into their destined and right places, that paradigm shift that he felt that he so desperately needed.

"Hey, you," the bartender said as Peter jerked a little to her voice. He had been staring at the ceiling from where he lay in the young lady's plush bed. "You're still here." She nervously laughed out loud.

"Yeah."

The soft, black sheets draped across her back, waist-high, partially covering what Peter had covered so thoroughly the night before. The young lady rolled over into Peter, her breasts tan and firm, as she put her smooth leg over his. Peter stroked her dark brown hair, drinking her body in, as the fleeting intoxication of it all evaporated just as quickly as it had come with each passing stroke. Peter could never get enough. He began to feel ill all of a sudden.

"That was an interesting night," she said, tickling his chest with her fingertips.

"Yeah."

"Where's Renee?"

"She was gone when I woke up," Peter said.

The girl turned a little more, her breasts pressed hard against Peter's body now, so hard that he all of a sudden wanted to eat her up, his hunger soul-deep.

"Do you like me?"

What kind of question was that, Peter thought. They had sex, did some drugs, had more sex, and threw the little gorgeous naughty roomie in the mix for good measure. Verlin would have been proud. Did he like her? Of course, he did, indeed. He might even say that he loved her. He loved how she moved and took charge amid their mutual gropings and ravenous lust for each other's flesh and heat. The open, supple warmth of her body pressed firmly against his was a very real reminder of their mutual desire. The feel of her sent a charge through his head and belly. Oh, yes, he thought. I do, I do.

"Yeah," he finally said.

"Is that all you can say?"

What did she want, a damned dissertation on the past evening? A comparison-contrast analysis? Did she really want Peter to tell her that she was that special one, that she had instantly filled his empty life with promise and passion and meaning? Peter began to get a little bothered by the whole exchange. Booze and drugs have a way of smoothing the little interpersonal burrs of becoming sexually acquainted with someone you had just met a couple of hours earlier, and he felt that there were possibly a couple of developmental steps missed in the previous night's courtship that even alcohol and cocaine couldn't replace.

"I've gotta go see my dad."

She laughed again. "Are you serious?"

"Yeah, that dude I was with last night."

"He's your dad?"

"Verlin?"

"Yeah. He's tried to get into my pants since the first day I started at the Stallion."

Maybe he should've ordered a different kind of beer, Peter thought. "You know him?"

"Not really," she said. Peter still didn't know her name. "He's always in there with Addie, my uncle. They're good friends, but Addie doesn't talk about him too much. They're weird like that."

"I don't know him too much either," Peter said. "Addie's your uncle?"

"Yeah," she said, looking down at the sheets.

"Interesting guy."

She stopped tickling Peter's chest, which didn't bother him too much because he thought he would get sick if they had to sit there carrying on like that for too much longer. To be honest, hat subtle, repetitious tickling had begun to feel like some variation of Chinese Water Torture. She was very accommodating and attractive and gentle, sure, but it didn't seem to be working for him anymore, waking up sober, having to deal with so much need for intimacy like that.

Despite his feelings, though, they had sex twice more. Being inside of her, calming the twitch in his gut, feeling their bodies becoming one, felt more intoxicating, easier really, than having a more awkward conversation. She was very physical, and he needed a good morning workout, after all. All the talk in the world wouldn't lead to anything real anyway, he thought. Afterwards, she said she wanted Peter to call. He said that he would. He thought he even might if he ever went back to visit his dad.

Peter went to the bathroom, washed up and put his wrinkled suit back on. They exchanged a smattering of obligatory words, and Peter let himself out after he kissed her one last time, patting her on that perfect, round butt of hers. Peter walked in the direction where he thought he had seen a convenience store the night before.

Peter spent his last few dollars on an orange juice and a pack of Camel Lights at the *Chug-n-Scram* convenience store. The dingy digital display on the bank down the street already read eighty-seven degrees, and then 9:13 am, back and forth, the only thing moving in Pony Town on a Saturday morning.

Peter sat on the curb waiting for his dad to pull up as if the *Chug-n-Scram* were the default rendezvous for those separated by a night of heavy drinking in Pony Town. Peter called Louise, and she said that Verlin hadn't come home, and then she asked where Peter was. He told her that he had stayed with a friend. She asked no further questions, having been quite well trained to not be too inquisitive. Peter then told her where he was and to tell Verlin and Addie to come to get him if she heard from them. He could have asked her for a ride, but her face made him feel sick to his stomach. He didn't want to feel any worse than he already felt, and she sounded tired; God bless her little heart.

"You sure you don't need a ride, hon?" Louise said.

"Yeah. I'm just talking to a friend up here."

"Well, you sure make friends fast."

"I guess so."

"Okay...well, I'll tell Verlin where you are if he comes in," she said. "You call me if you need a ride, okay?"

"Alright," he said and hung up the phone.

Sitting on the curb in a convenience store parking lot, having spoken with Louise and smoking his millionth cigarette, Peter thought he couldn't have possibly felt crappier. That moment, however, was the first time that he realized he still had some pretty deep resentment toward the woman. Sitting on a curb in the morning sun, sweating, his childhood, a lifetime ago.

For all intent and purpose, he still felt like a child, sitting on that curb, feeling sorry for himself. Nevertheless, Peter felt like he had played the victim card for all it was worth. That childhood when Louise had stood by watching as his only father systematically broke him in two, chopped up what little morale he had, and then left him for dead at the side of the road. Peter resented his step-mom more than he did his dad, who, by all reason, was the one who should've faced the brunt of his confusion and hatred.

When it really came down to a point, Peter realized that he had never quite learned to respect any women, and perhaps Louise made a more sensible target to him, seeing how she didn't carry a gun and piss fire like the old man. She was used to the abuse anyway, he thought.

"Fuck it," Peter said out loud to himself.

A truckload of Mexicans pulled up in front of the store and barreled out—four in the front and six in the back. The old three-quarter ton's engine finally sputtered to a stop when the last one of the guys jumped from the truck bed and went inside the store. The guys looked like they had already put a day's work in, dirty and sweaty and full of life. The clock down the street read 9:24.

Peter hadn't had a real job in years. He went from one shady deal to the next, hands clean but conscience a bit murky. Here, these guys were, fresh across the border and already working in his country, buying old work trucks, cold soda, hot microwave sandwiches and beef jerky. Peter sat on the curb in his wrinkled suit, like a sitting-duck, as if chance or God or some unimaginable circumstance would just sweep him up and away– take care of everything, once and for all.

The Mexicans came out of the store more excited than when they had gone in. The driver of the truck looked over at Peter and nodded.

"Hola," Peter said.

"Buena dia," the man said.

"Tienes trabajo para mi?"

A couple of the other guys laughed out loud.

"No, 'migo." He pointed at all of the guys, and they laughed again.

Peter didn't know if they laughed at the irony of a white dude in a suit asking them for a job when there were so many of them to keep busy, or if they were simply happy to be alive and grateful to be able to work, eat and live.

"Gracia 'migo," Peter said and waved to the others.

"Adios," the leader said, tipping his hat.

They all got back in, the driver fired up that big V-8, and they were off to finish whatever job they had taken a break from.

Peter watched the truck go down the road, the American Dream at its finest. Those guys would probably work for a quarter of an American's wage, spend ten times less, and send more money back to Mexico than the average American spends on home and family altogether. How does that work?

Down the road, the Mexican truck swerved to avoid hitting an oncoming pick-up as they were almost out of sight. The big 4x4 that almost hit the Mexicans grew larger in its approach, nearing where Peter sat on the curb in front of the store. It almost looked like they intentionally tried to hit the truck full of workers, and the next thing Peter knew, the 4x4 bared down on him, ripping through the parking lot, where it screeched to a stop directly in front of him. Peter could feel the heat from the engine on his face, the smell of burning rubber and brakes all around.

Addie and Verlin nearly fell out of either side of the truck. Peter stood up and watched them as they came around to the front where Peter stood now.

"Hey, boy!" Verlin said as if Peter were deaf.

"Hey, guys."

"You get you some booger last night?" Addie said.

"Yeah, boy. Ya gitcha some?"

Peter looked down at the ground and kicked at the black-top, thought about the question for a second, then mustered up some redneck bravado, and said, "Hell yeah! I gotter done, all night long!"

Verlin and Addie yelped and hollered like they were at the State Championship Rodeo, and all hopped up on meth and whiskey. Addie punched Peter in the right arm, his congratulations, and Verlin punched him in the left, by golly.

"Be right back, son," Verlin said, going into the store.

He and Addie swayed into the store and out of sight. Peter thought it strange that Addie would be congratulating him on gittin' er done with his niece, but then again, Peter just felt good that Addie didn't get jealous at the competition, really.

Peter walked around the side of the truck to check it out. The shiny pearl-white finish gleamed with emblazoned bright blue flames slithering down the sides. The tires were almost as tall as Peter himself. If he crouched down a little, he probably could have walked right under the truck. Peter tried to wrap his mind around the amount of money that had been wasted on that thing. He could've bought five Hondas like the one that he and Perky had for as much money as Addie had spent on that beast.

Verlin and Addie came out of the store, both smoking, Verlin with a case of Coors Original under his arm. "Come on, boy! We're goin' fishin'!"

Memories.

Peter hesitated for a second and then fell in, ready to experience whatever may come. Addie got in and fired up the pick-up. The music blared out of the windows, which Peter hadn't even noticed when they had pulled up. That loud, new-country crap had to be the worst music in the world. That or Top-40, for sure. Nevertheless, Peter got in, and then Verlin. The old man popped a round of beers for the three of them, and they were off.

Chapter 20

After an hour or so, Verlin came back into the bedroom smiling. Not the kind of smile suggesting Peter's stupidity or unworthiness, but a real smile, genuine perhaps. He had a black garbage bag in one hand and a washcloth and dustpan in the other.

"Here," Verlin said, tossing the bag at Peter. "Go ahead and clean up, and Louise will show you how to get all the stains and smell out of the carpet the right way. Okay?" He sat the dustpan down neatly by the door jamb.

"Yes, sir."

"Hey! Brighten up, boy. You're gonna be okay. You just gotta take care of yourself and your room, okay?"

"Yes, sir."

"Clean your damned face off, will ya?" Verlin said and tossed the wet washcloth at Peter. "You look like some kind of fuckin' freak, man."

Peter tried to conjure up a fake smile to make the old man happy, but it felt altogether impossible at the moment. Peter didn't trust him anymore, and all he had to do at that point was to survive, he told himself. Verlin told him earlier in the week that if Peter felt like making stories up and telling people that his daddy was mean to him, he wouldn't be responsible for what happened to Peter. Your choice, boy, he had said. Peter didn't really know what that meant but didn't really want to find out, either. Peter's lessons were well underway, and he could tell Mr. Roland Stacks and Willie Nelson a thing or two himself for sure. Yes, sir.

Verlin left the room after investing in his son another nugget or two of priceless advice, smiling as if he'd just won the Nobel Prize for fatherhood, not missing a beat.

Peter picked the garbage bag up and went to work on the poop remnants after he wiped his face off with the washcloth. The piles of feces had been smashed into the carpet pretty good by his face, so there were slim pickings as far as neat little piles. Simone helped him by attacking the garbage sack whenever he put it to the floor, working on the next smeared pile.

"Stop it, Simone. Come on!"

She bit at Peter's heels, excited to be alive. He picked her up and took her across the room to get her out of the way, but she followed him right back to where he knelt next to the trash bag, back to her antics, barking at and biting the trash bag with all the vigor of a whirling dervish.

"Simone!" Peter screamed.

She darted over to the corner and cowered. Peter jerked at her reaction, feeling as if he had unforgivably betrayed her and somehow abused her beyond reconciliation, out of sheer animal determinism. He stopped cleaning and slowly moved over to the corner to pick her up, petting her softly. "It's okay, baby. You're okay. Come on, now. I'm sorry. I am. Come on, honey." Peter didn't want to scare the only friend he had left. He and Simone were a team, and he wanted to keep her happy and safe.

After some time, with Simone tearing at the garbage bag as if it were the most stimulating game ever, Peter had gotten all of the poop up off the floor that he could. The bag became tattered, but the crap was in there, nonetheless. Peter did the best he could with what he had. He had tried to rub the smears out of the carpet with the damp washcloth at first, but to no avail, as it had already become filthy from his wiping the shit off of his face. The thing had even become a bit dry, with a light crust forming at the edges, to the point of the semi-dried scat chipping and flaking back onto the floor, only making more work for himself. He needed a pail of soapy water so that he could wash the rag out as needed. Dad told him to wait for Louise so that she could show him how to clean up the "right way."

Peter waited.

Simone pooped again, and Peter cleaned it up because he still had the tattered garbage bag in his tired hands. He worked fast, not wanting the old man to see the new pile. Peter's learning curve for damage control proved to be steep and short.

He waited for Louise.

Peter thought long and hard about how he should have kept his room clean, with no way to let Simone out or with no supplies with which he could clean. The confusion of it all made him feel crazy, sick almost as if he were trying to put a jig-saw puzzle together, swearing all the pieces were there but missing the last one, pulling his hair out in frustration. There had to have been a way to get the job done, or Verlin wouldn't have been that mad. The old man had high standards, but then again, he hadn't even given Peter any newspaper, nor a scoop, not even a trash can, or anything, really. Peter just wanted to make his dad happy. Growing up can be hard.

Peter sat in the little room, random brown stains and all, the situation festering in his mind, irritatingly so, like a piece of corn between the teeth, after an otherwise satisfying meal. He thought long and hard about what his dad had done, what Simone had done, yet had no answers, and then started brewing on the fact that Simone, after all, was the one who got him into the trouble in the first place. No dog, no poop, he thought, and he stood up and kicked the wall. Simone cowered into the corner again, peeing on herself with nervousness. Peter caught himself, turning red, and then looked up to see out of the dingy window above, trying to divert his attention away from his puppy.

The flash of anger toward Simone passed quickly, yet it scared Peter to feel and see her that way, as a detriment, his enemy even. He looked at her in her fluffy innocence one second, and the next saw her as a liability to his survival, a little black creature of misfortune sitting there pining for his doting affection. His only friend? What the hell was he thinking? Like hearing second-hand that someone you love dearly has been smearing your name all over the place. The disbelief turns to distrust, then back to disbelief, leaving you unable to trust your own thoughts. Peter went back to his pallet of blankets, sat down and called Simone over, despite his ambivalence.

After who knows how long, Peter heard the lock and latch open from the outside of the door. Louise poked her head through the widening crack in the door and said, "Hello."

"Hi."

The old man proved predictable in his psychosis, Peter thought, as where Louise could be a friend one moment and the betrayer the next. Peter didn't know if he was getting nice, helpful, caring Louise or if he was getting the indifferent sentinel to blind malevolence. She came into the room playing the good cop, the friend. Peter sat in the corner on top of his pallet of dirty blankets.

Louise slowly walked across the room. She had finally gotten out of her nightgown and dingy slippers, no longer looking like a ghetto chick on her way to the convenience store to buy pork rinds and a lottery ticket. She had even put on some clothes that didn't showcase her large, happy breasts. Peter smelled her perfume wafting through the air, pleasant compared to the raunch of the piss and shit to which he had so recently grown accustomed.

However, the deep, blue-purple bruises around Louise's eyes and mouth weren't too attractive. She had caked a thick layer of makeup over the blemishes to hide them, which only made the bruises look worse like she had some kind of jungle fungus growing over her wounds, eating its way through her flesh. She continued to move slowly across the room as if Peter were next in line to punch on her for a bit. She forced a smile and said, "Would you like me to help you finish cleaning?"

"Yes, ma'am."

"Here." She held out her hand for Simone. "Let's put the dog out so that she can go to the bathroom while we clean up, okay?"

Peter didn't really want Simone out of his sight for too long, not knowing where she might end up, yet he relinquished so that they could get things done quickly. An image, a flash, of Simone's maimed and disfigured body came and went.

"Is my dad here?"

"He's at work, hon."

Louise almost seemed normal again to Peter. Nevertheless, Peter knew that nothing would ever be the same. Nausea loomed, and the fear felt like it had surely taken up permanent residence. He stared at the carpet, wishing he could vanish for good, evaporating into another world where it all made sense to him. Peter wanted to see Louise's mom and dad, Pinkie and Sewell. He felt safe with them.

"What happened to your face?" Peter said to Louise.

She looked away, then bent to pick up the garbage bag in the corner of the room.

"Louise."

She busied herself with the garbage bag in one hand and Simone in the other, feigning utter absorption into her little task at hand. Peter thought that maybe she was going deaf, that maybe she had been around loud machinery all night, that had eventually gone haywire or something, hence the bruises, and that she just couldn't hear him. He spoke louder to get her attention.

`"Quiet!" she snapped. She looked weary with jitters. She calmed down pretty

quickly, however, as she had just regained consciousness from some kind of hypnotic trance, and then she said, "I fell down the stairs."

"What stairs?" Peter said.

"At my mom's house."

Peter didn't say anything more. He just watched her leave the bedroom and come back without Simone. Peter didn't want to bug her about Simone because he didn't want to upset her again, but he didn't want his dog, his only friend, to disappear, either. If Peter knew what conundrum meant, he might have used it to describe his worry and reluctant compliance.

Louise helped Peter take his little pallet out of the room, and then she got a pail of hot, sudsy water and a scrub pad and a sponge. They diligently scrubbed side by side while Fleetwood Mac played in the background. They didn't speak to each other, really, but only communicated silently, in their collective goal to finish the room before Verlin got home to inspect their handiwork. Not knowing when the old man might show up, they worked fast and steady like Asian fishmongers during the holidays.

After they made the last rinses and dabbed up what they could with the sponge, Louise went to the other room to get a fan. She returned to Peter's room and plugged the fan into the socket by the door. Peter closed his eyes and leaned back against the wall as the air blew on his sweaty little body. He sat there with his eyes closed, thinking about the last time he had eaten, denying the hunger in his belly, the air feeling like it could almost blow right through his skinny little arms and chest, the sensation of the blowing air skittering on the surface of his skin. Peter felt a warm sensation go down his neck and arms, to his back and then between his legs. He looked down at his pants, soon realizing that he had pissed himself.

"Shit!" he shouted and stood up quickly.

"You better not talk like that around your father," Louise said, then standing in the

doorway.

Peter looked down at his pants again and back at Louise, who was still hanging around for reasons Peter couldn't determine.

"Can I use the bathroom, ma'am?"

After what looked like a moment of deep thought, she walked over to Peter and sat down. He noticed that her face was very puffy under the black and blue patches of oily skin, which gleamed under the patchy layers of the reckless make-up job. She looked sick. Peter wanted to help her but quickly realized that he could do nothing for her. She and Verlin had their own way of dealing with life. Peter only wanted to go back home. No more vacation for him.

"Can I change my pants?"

Peter heard the front door opening. Louise jumped to her feet and was out of the bedroom in one failed swoop. Peter could hear the latch and lock go back on the outside of his door and then silence. The sound of shouting and splintering furniture would be next, he knew. The blood would rush to his dad's head, and the old man couldn't help but fix what he saw that needed immediate fixing, dammit! Peter sat in the corner of his bedroom– clean room, no bed, no dog, pissed pants. He had even gotten rid of the finger splints that he had stashed and the dirty bandaging from his foot puncture that the doctor had put on him.

Peter could hear footsteps coming down the hallway and then the sound of the latch and the lock clunked again outside the door.

Verlin poked his head into the room. "Hey there, son. Wanna go to the park?"

"Yeah," Peter said, not wanting to hesitate and make Verlin think that maybe he didn't want to go out for a day of family fun. "Should I make my bed first?"

"You bet, boy," Verlin said and turned to the empty hall. "Louise! Where's the boy's bed stuff?"

"In the washer," she said from the other room.

"She's washin', okay. Come on, let's go," Verlin said, just like 'oh boy' and 'by-golly.'

Peter followed his dad to the kitchen, trying to conceal his pissed pants, not wanting to go back into his room as punishment for ruining a perfectly good pair of jeans. Peter waited on Verlin as he looked out the back-door window. Verlin turned to Peter and grimaced but didn't say anything. Verlin continued to stand at the window and then pulled a cigarette out and lit it. Peter shifted his weight from one foot to the other, feeling a little burn in his pants, the old man stared out the window, taking deep drags off his cigarette. Peter didn't want to break Verlin's concentration, so he kept his hands in his dirty pants pockets and continued to wait.

"Okay," Verlin finally said, opening the door and blowing a thick plume of smoke outside. "Go out there and get Simone. Hurry, alright?"

"Yes, sir."

"Good boy." Verlin patted Peter on the butt as he went through the doorway. Simone ran up to the young boy like an old lover. Peter scooped her up off of the ground and went back inside.

"Are your pants wet, boy?"

"No, sir."

Verlin pulled Peter close to himself and lifted him to get a better look at his jeans. "The fuck if they ain't. You been jerkin' off, boy?"

Peter looked at Verlin with an expression of confusion.

"Aw shit, boy. Nevermind. That shit can air out at the park. Whattaya think?"

"Yes, sir."

"You're alright, boy. I tell you what."

Verlin turned the radio on that sat on the counter while he and Peter waited for Louise. Verlin said she had to hole up in the bathroom to get her ugly ass pretty. Peter tried to force another awkward smile but still couldn't get his face to comply. Verlin yelled at her a couple of times to get her ass in gear, in good spirits, granted but quickly fell silent for a moment when he heard that voice on the radio again. Roland Stacks. Fuckin' preachin', as the old man liked to say.

"That asshole don't know nothin', boy! I got an inklin' to go find that rat-bastard and shut him up for good! You know that, boy?"

Peter stared at his dad as if the crazy man might just march right out the front door, with .45 in hand to find the radio evangelist himself. Peter couldn't smile or nod or whistle *zippity-do-da* if his life depended on it.

"That damned woman's gotta take her damned sweet time primping and doctoring herself, don't she, boy?"

Peter nodded 'yes,' that she, in fact, did need to do that.

The three of them, and Simone, of course, pulled up to the park about twenty minutes after Verlin had finally gotten the whole posse loaded up into the panel van. He drove the panel van because he had to go to work later that night, he had said. The panel van, what Verlin had told Peter's mom was his new motor home, is what he used for work, Louise had said. Peter imagined that the truck was the best in undercover vehicles. It didn't look like anything special, a little run-down in fact, but that was the whole point, right?

Peter noticed Sewell and Pinkie sitting at a picnic table in the shade about a hundred feet away when Verlin pulled the van up to the edge of the expanse, green park. Peter burst out through one of the van's back doors and bolted across the lush, green grass, straight over to where the older couple waited under the horizontal boughs of antique live oak. They both got up and started walking in his direction.

"Angel," Pinkie said, wrapping Peter up in her firm, tanned arms once he got close enough for her to grab. Sewell grabbed Simone from Peter, from where he stood behind Pinkie, stroking the dog despite its trying to wriggle free. Peter kept his arms clamped around Pinkie's neck like a buoy in raging waters. She didn't let go or slacken her arms in the slightest, either, until Peter finally loosened his grip a little, and then she held him out at arm's length, like a mama bear might.

"Hon, you look sick," she said, looking Peter up and down like a school nurse. "You need some good cookin', don't you?" She put Peter back down on the ground.

Peter shook his head 'yes' and then looked up at Sewell, who continued to unconsciously pet Simone. It seemed like he didn't even notice the boy standing beneath him as he stared out in the direction of the van, where Louise and Verlin were still sitting safely inside.

"Sewell!" Pinkie said.

"Oh...Come here, buddy." Sewell handed Simone to Pinkie and bent down to pick Peter up. "Give me a hug."

Peter jumped into Sewell's arms, clamping his arms around him too. Sewell smelled like chewing tobacco and dust and motor oil. Progress. Just like Grandpa back home. Peter squeezed him as hard as he could, dangling from the sturdy man's grip until his arms ran out of juice and he had to loosen up. That sweet and rustic smell of homemade Peter think of grandpa tinkering in the garage again, as he and Peter had on so many Saturday mornings.

"Dang, boy. You're gonna break my ribs," Sewell said.

Peter let go all of the ways, looking at Sewell startled, but then realized that he was only joking. Peter had become tender to the mention of violence, breaking bones, and killing. He was a little jumpy when he heard the words 'boy' and 'son' in the exclamatory sense, yet quickly realized that he would have to loosen up a little bit if he was going to hang out with a jokester like Sewell.

Sewell lifted Peter up to look him over, kind of like Pinkie had done, and then he put him back down to the ground. Pinkie handed Simone back to Peter and started walking out to the van.

"You gonna stay with us for a few days, okay?" Sewell said.

"Yes, sir."

Pinkie and Louise stood next to the van in the bright sun, talking. Verlin didn't get out, the motor still running, cigarette smoke wafting from the driver's side window. The ladies looked like they had something really important to talk about. Peter stroked Simone's fur over and over, looking out at the van. He looked up at Sewell as he looked out toward the van. Louise and Pinkie started yelling at each other, waving arms and getting closer to each other. Peter didn't realize it, but Simone was trying to bite his hand, trying to get loose, because he had suddenly begun petting her too hard, groping her. She finally wriggled free and fell to the ground, quickly getting her bearings before running off.

"Simone!"

She ran full-speed in a couple of large, sweeping circles around the massive oak tree as if it were a new game to which only she had the rules. She stopped all of a sudden and then sniffed the ground and then darted over to pee right next to the trunk of the tree like she had just remembered the reason she had wriggled free in the first place. Pinkie had begun to speak to Louise a little more calmly now, Louise stroking her hair back, over and over. Peter didn't want anything to happen to Pinkie.

"Pete, you stay right here, okay," Sewell said and walked out toward the van. Peter just let Simone do her thing. He didn't feel good about Sewell walking out to the van with everyone yelling. Then Verlin yelled out Louise's name, and she got into the van like a well-trained dog. No questions asked, no hesitation. Sewell started running toward Pinkie, and the van pulled out. No goodbye, no see ya. Sewell slowed to a walk yet quickly closed the space between him and Pinkie.

Peter watched them talk for a minute, and then they hugged. He thought they must be best friends, just like his grandparents seemed to be like he and Simone were. The love the couple shared felt real like he imagined that people were supposed to act toward each other all of the time.

The ride back to the house passed like an aching dream. Pinkie said they would eat lunch and then that Peter could help Sewell out in the fields. The mood felt somber, however, something not right, even though Peter was well on his way to bucolic Mississippi at its best. Pinkie and Sewell looked well and fit. Peter didn't care if he ever saw his dad again. The silence, however, like the silence he felt with his dad most of the time, nothing to say, no common ground or levity, made him ache with apocalyptic dread for but a moment. Peter hoped that they weren't mad at him for being so dirty or not taking care of his dog properly. He felt really confused and a little bit scared, to be honest.

"Where's your mom?" Pinkie finally said.

"She's in Oklahoma."

Sewell looked at Pinkie and then back at Peter, where he sat in the big back seat of their car.

Peter suddenly felt the fear prickle up under his skin even more because he didn't want to get into more trouble, and he started to squirm a little bit, just like Simone did when she got anxious.

"It's okay, buddy; we just wanted to know if you would like to call your mom." Sewell sat up tall and looked at Peter in the rearview. "Do you?"

"Yes, sir!"

"Have you been hurt?" Pinkie said.

"No, ma'am," Peter said, looking down at his puppy. He started to fidget with Simone's collar as he continued to look down at her with an intense concentration like it was the first time he had ever seen a dog, that maybe he had just realized that there was one of those foreign creatures in his lap even. He knew that if he said that his dad had been stressed and had punished him, the old man would have to punish him some more. Verlin had said so himself, in a weird sort of way. He said that if Peter made up lies about his dad, he wouldn't be responsible for what happened to the boy. Peter looked out the back window, stroking the little, black dog over and over.

Peter suddenly wondered if Sewell and Pinkie were just prying him for information. That maybe they just worked the angles for his dad to see if Peter could remain loyal. They planned to kill him and throw him into the woods, like what probably happened to that girl from Tucson. Ramona Whitcanuck. The newsman said they may have made it as far as Kansas City.

"Pete," Pinkie said, turning to Peter. "Are you okay, hon?"

"Yes, ma'am."

"Are you sure?"

"Can we watch the news tonight?"

"What's a boy your age want with the news?" Sewell said.

"Hey, mister, if the boy wants to get educated, let him, okay?" Pinkie said, slapping Sewell's arm.

Sewell shrugged his shoulders, staring straight ahead, continuing to drive the big car.

They pulled into the long circular driveway, and Sewell turned off the engine. He and Pinkie just sat there like they didn't know what to do next as if their arms went numb even, and their bodies had become paralyzed.

Sewell turned to Peter and said, "Pete, you look really scared. We're here to help. We're your friends, okay?"

Peter shook his head 'yes,' but had a real hard time making eye contact with Sewell right then. Peter said a quick prayer in his head, with his eyes closed, and then opened up and stared at the floor before he could acknowledge his burly friend again.

"Okay," Peter finally said.

They got out of the car and went into the house. It smelled like Grammie's house inside, sweet and savory, like every day was a holiday. Pinkie went to the hallway and came out with a towel and washcloth. She handed them to Peter and told him he could use their shower if he wanted, the one in their bedroom. Peter followed Pinkie back to their room, where she led him into the bathroom and turned on the light.

"Do you need help, hon?" she said.

"No, ma'am," he said, looking down at his feet as if he were a little embarrassed by the question.

She bent to turn the water on, adjusted it and then waited for the temperature to get just right before she turned the lever to activate the showerhead.

"You let me know if you need anything, any help, okay?" she said and let herself out of the bathroom.

Peter shut the door all the way as she left the room. There was no lock on the door. Peter didn't want either one of them to come in while he showered. He didn't like when people he didn't know watched him in the shower, especially when they had something to say about his little penis, which felt really weird.

Peter got out of the shower and looked into the mirror, dark circles under his eyes. He stared at the eyes staring back at him, humorless, tired and rattled. Maybe if he stared long enough into his own eyes, he could figure out what in the world to do next with himself. Really, all he wanted to do was call his mom. Pinkie and Sewell said that he could call her, too. No real mystery. Peter rubbed his face, thinking that he looked like the Indian man at the dry-cleaners back home. The place always smelled spicy and sweet. Peter imagined that he had become a street merchant in Mumbai, like in a book that his mom had read to him back home. Dark circles, dark eyes, selling junk to unsuspecting dimwits from the West, in the loud clamor of somewhere different and wild.

Peter put on a t-shirt that Pinkie had put on the edge of the sink when he had been in the shower, and he wrapped the towel around his lower part and went out into the kitchen where he could hear Sewell and Pinkie laughing. Peter poked his head around the corner to see if he could hear what they talked about. He thought for a second that maybe one of them had peeked into the shower while he wasn't paying attention and that they had just had a good laugh at his expense—no lock on the door. Then, just as quickly as the thought had come, it left, and Peter had an instantaneous feeling that Pinkie and Sewell were indeed his friends, there to help him, and just laughing because they were happy people, and that was what happy people do.

"Feel better?" Sewell said, catching Peter off-guard as he came around the corner.

"Yes, sir."

"You hungry?"

"Yes, sir." Peter went into the kitchen and sat down at the table.

"I'm washing your pants, Peter," Pinkie said.

"Thank you."

"But now we eat," Sewell said. Keep that towel wrapped up, for now, ya hear?"

And just like that, the food came like a flood. Pinkie had made ham sandwiches with mayonnaise and fresh Vidalia onions, a big side of macaroni and cheese and then some apple sauce and a couple of slices of toast. Peter had only been in the shower for a few minutes, and all that food and more just appeared on the table like a miracle. Oh, yes.

Peter noticed a chocolate-cream pie on the counter, his favorite. Pinkie pulled out some red Jello and some whipped cream and sat that on the table with everything else.

"Now, if you need more to eat, just let me know, okay?" Pinkie said and patted Peter on the back, laughing.

Peter couldn't imagine ever needing to eat again, with all that food. Sewell sat across from him, putting applesauce on his cottage cheese.

"Eeww," Peter said, pointing at Sewell's plate.

"You ever tried it?"

"No way. That's gross."

Sewell handed Peter the jar of applesauce and the container of cottage cheese and nodded for him to take a little of each. Peter put a dollop of each on the edge of his plate so that it didn't touch anything else and sat there looking at it for a second.

"Go ahead. It'll make you stronger'n a bull, buddy."

Not even holding his nose, Peter took a little bird's bite of each, one right after the other. He had a look of disgust on his face before the food even went into his mouth. Peter dramatically chewed for a second, just like he might have if he had put a whole bagel into his mouth at once. Peter's bitter face suddenly melted away after a couple more seconds of histrionics.

"Whattaya think?"

"It's pretty..."

"Good, huh?"

"It's good," Peter said. "Yeah."

Pinkie busied herself at the sink while the men ate like kings after a conquest.

"Sit down, hon," Sewell said to Louise.

"I'm not hungry. I got things to do," she said, washing and rinsing and drying all at the same time. "We gotta get you some clothes, hon." Pinkie didn't turn around but kept steady at her task.

She seemed kind of nervous and full of energy. Peter figured she did house chores to calm down, just like his mom did when she felt upset. Peter could always tell when his mom was really mad because she would rearrange all of the furniture in the house, not once, but several times, and then she would clean every crack and crevice of the place. Waxing, polishing, window-cleaning and the whole bit. The woman would get downright sweaty with industriousness; she would.

Peter looked out the window, chewing his food, glad to be alive and eating well.

"After dinner, hon, we thought you could call your mom if you wanted to," Pinkie said, her back still to Peter and Sewell.

Peter had started on his second sandwich, his second serving of applesauce and cottage cheese, and his second serving of macaroni and cheese. He didn't really know what to say about calling his mom, though. Verlin and Louise said that it wasn't possible to call his mom and that Peter's mom didn't want to talk to him, anyway, even if he could. Peter didn't want Verlin and Louise to find out that he had called for fear that it might hurt their feelings. He would get in big trouble if he called her after they had said not to, no matter the reason. Verlin told Peter not to defy his authority. Simple fucking instructions, Verlin had said.

"Well, what do you think?" Pinkie said, turning to the guys, drying one of the plates with a dishtowel.

"I don't know."

"Don't you wanna talk to your mama?" Sewell said.

"Yes, sir, but I don't think she wants to talk to me."

Pinkie put the dish on the counter and walked over to the table. She put her hand on Peter's hand and Sewell's shoulder at the same time. "Hon, your mama, is worried sick about you if you haven't talked to her this whole time," she said.

"Really?"

"I've talked to her, hon."

Peter turned to look at Pinkie. She looked as serious as a judge. He believed her, just like he believed when his dad said that his mom didn't want to talk to him. Peter looked at Sewell and then at Pinkie. He felt confused again. They had asked where his mom was earlier. He wanted things to not be so hard to figure out as they used to be. Pinkie kept gently stroking Peter's hand, trying to calm his nerves.

"Finish up, Pete, and we'll get you on the phone, okay?" Sewell said.

Sewell finished his lunch and grabbed the chocolate-cream pie off of the counter. He cut himself a slice and then looked at Peter and his plate, raising his eyebrows.

"Yes, sir."

He waited until Peter took the last bite of his sandwich, and then he put a nice, big wedge of chocolate pie right in the middle of his plate. Pinkie handed the whipped cream to Peter and smiled. Peter got a big dollop and plopped it on top of the pie.

"Get enough?" Pinkie said, picking up the container and holding it out.

Peter looked at the pie, then looked at the container of whipped cream. "I think so," he said but then got another scoop, just to be sure.

Pinkie put the whipped cream back in the refrigerator and turned on the radio on the counter. She turned it to a program where a man spoke with a familiar voice.

"Hey!" Peter said.

"Hey!" Pinkie said.

"I know who this is," Peter said after he swallowed his bite as if his proclamation just couldn't wait any longer.

"Roland Stacks?" Sewell said.

"My dad said that he has stacks and stacks of money. That's why he talks all the time so that people will give him money."

Sewell rolled his eyes at Pinkie and then patted Peter on the hand.

"I see," Pinkie said.

Chapter 21

The wind blowing through the windows felt good on Peter's face, almost relieving his nausea and anxiousness altogether, if only for seconds at a time. Peter wanted to get somewhere with the old man. They had wasted too much time talking about nothing and feeling each other out.

"I talked to Carly Jo this morning!" Addie yelled over the stereo, wind and engine noise, looking over at Peter. Peter pushed the 'volume down' button and said, "What?"

"I talked to Carly Jo!"

Something about red necks and shouting: maybe too many power tools and stock-car races, Peter thought. "Carly Jo?"

"Boy, you got you some pussy and don't even know its name?" Verlin said.

"Oh...Carly Jo...yeah. How is she?"

"Boy, you must be some kinda weirdo!" Addie shouted over the stereo that had already been turned down. "She don't think too much is weird! She said you something weird, though!"

"Thanks."

"Don't you worry 'bout all that, boy. Your daddy and I will straighten you out. Just hang with the winners, okay?"

Peter wondered where those winners might be. He turned the music back up and looked out the window at those endless plains, unrolling past many more tomorrows. Peter resigned himself to the fact that he should go ahead and get good and wasted since his dad and the big cop were already in that state of mind and that there wouldn't be any chance to talk about serious matters, at any rate, and that it didn't even really matter at that point, as the whole thing almost seemed irreconcilable, to say the least, if he even wanted reconciliation, that is. Can't beat 'em, join 'em, as they say.

After several beers and a horrible stint of pop-country, Addie pulled his truck up in front of a building with a weathered wooden sign reading, "POLICE." The sign looked as if someone had taken an old barn door and made a sign out of it as a last resort.

"What the hell are we doing here?" Peter said.

"I gotta check-in, boy."

"Oh yeah." Peter had forgotten that Addie, or Adolf, was one of the area's finest. A cop of all things. One of only three cops in town to make things even more interesting. Peter imagined that most of the cops in towns like Pony Town were derelict, drunk Nazis. *We treat you like a KING*, his shirt read, only now a little tarnished with beer spills and a spatter or two of the chili dogs they had for midnight snacks.

Peter imagined Addie had a drawer full of the white t-shirts at home, maybe in his old Army foot-locker, clean and neatly folded for each day of the week, some with more appropriate witticisms for various other occasions.

Verlin and Peter sat in the truck.

"I gotta proposition for you, boy," Verlin said after Addie had gone into the building.

"Oh yeah?"

"I typed it up when you told me you were comin' down to visit. I think I can help you straighten your life out."

Peter looked over at his dad with a surprised look on his face. Peter slammed his beer and nodded for another. Verlin slammed his beer and got two more.

"What do you think needs straightening out?"

"Boy, you can't be a sheister your whole life."

Peter opened his beer and took a drink. The warming, cheap beer suddenly tasted the like. He looked out the window, not knowing what to say to such a direct claim, and then turned to his dad.

"I make a living," Peter said. "I'm not looking to start over. We just got some things to sort out, don't you think? You and I?"

"Boy, if this is about the other day, I told you I was sorry."

"You've never said sorry about anything."

"Don't you smart-mouth me. I ain't gonna stand for no smart-mouthed little shit."

"I'm not a kid anymore. You can't treat me like your daughters. I'm not Louise."

Verlin coughed up a little beer, looking at Peter like he might just want to smash his partially emptied beer can into the boy's ungrateful fucking head…but he didn't…yet maybe only because of fatigue and drunkenness. Addie stuck his head out of the door of the building and waved to Verlin and Peter to come inside.

"We'll talk when we get home," Verlin said and got out of the truck. "Are you comin'?"

Peter started to get out behind his dad. He wanted to believe that the old man had good intentions, but realized, on the other hand, that good intention wasn't good enough. He watched Verlin lumber out of the jacked-up pick-up, almost falling to the ground because of the distance between the floorboard and the ground.

Addie stuck his head out of the door and waved again, looking like he'd just found a bag of large bills.

"Hold on, ya fat fuck," Verlin said, finally stumbling out onto the ground. "Hold on."

Peter got out of the truck behind Verlin. He hadn't realized how sad his father really looked until right then. Verlin had a paunch of a gut, his head balding, and his face looked weathered and weary. Too much drinking and smoking, too much anger and resentment, over too much a span of time. The old man didn't seem capable of admitting that he was just a human who made mistakes like the rest and that that was okay. Peter watched him amble toward the door, his .45 sticking out of his waistband at the lower back as if they were in the middle of some covert black-op out in the middle of some stinking backwater. The sad bastard couldn't even leave the house for a night of pool and beer without his gun, Peter thought.

Verlin and Peter walked into the building, where echoing shouts came from the back somewhere. The voice sounded like it came from a cell or some other empty, bare-walled room or hallway. Peter and Verlin followed the noise and then heard Addie's voice firing off in short, tense shots. They came to a room where Addie and the other guy stood by the cell bars.

"Come on, ya little nigger, go ahead, I dare ya," Addie said, laughing between words that appeared to take more effort than he had energy. "Hey, guys!" Addie's face poured with sweat as he looked over his shoulder at Verlin and Peter. "Wanna poke?"

A young black man stood cuffed to the bars in the crappy little holding cell. Fast-food scraps, napkins, and random trash were scattered about the cell as if a rag-tag bunch of frat boys and raccoons had been holed up in there for a couple of days. The black man's mouth and nose were bleeding, nothing but watery fear in his eyes. Peter didn't know what Addie meant by a "poke." Forcibly sodomize the guy? Beat the shit out of him? Maybe both?

The prisoner didn't bother saying anything to anyone. They were all whitey as far as he was probably concerned. Anything that came out of his mouth would be turned against him like a bat in the hands of a methed-out sadist. The terror in the man's eyes turned to defeat as he first perused

Peter, and then Addie again, and then Verlin. His face slackened yet a little more with the acknowledgment of each of the guys standing there, judge, jury, and executioner.

Peter didn't know what to say. Sure, he had seen violence. His dad was beating his mother, minor league hockey in New England, merciless schoolyard fights, but this...well, he had never seen. Peter knew cruelty existed, sure, but at the hands of supposed law enforcement? Naivete, some might say.

"What'd the little coon do?" Verlin said.

"He beat up some old man."

Verlin walked into the cell with the black man, who began to cower. Not a good choice of emotional expression in front of a sociopath, Peter thought. That fine line between being scared enough yet emotionless enough was the key in a situation like that. Peter had had his crash course in nut-case mediation as a young boy and wished that he could reach out and give that little guy some valuable advice. The pricey inexperience of the young black man felt awkward and painful in Peter's powerlessness.

Verlin spat on the floor in front of the prisoner. The good-ole-boy goofiness seemed to have disappeared somewhere between the truck and the holding cell. The old man appeared to be all business at that point. Addie had gone outside the cell to sit down behind a little desk. He reclined in the swivel chair as if he were watching some vaudeville act, with a warm beer sitting on the desk in front of him, a creaking seat, and a sweaty face.

"You wanna little sip?" Verlin said to the prisoner, holding his beer out to the guy.

The prisoner stared at the ground as if he were trying to make it ripple by telekinesis.

"Nigger! You wanna fuckin' drink?! Huh...jungle bunny?!" Verlin emphasized each of his words by quickly poking his chest out at the man as he shouted.

The man still didn't say anything. Peter stood speechless, beer in hand, looking over at Addie as he sat in his creaky chair, smoking a cigarette and going through letters on top of his desk. Then, just as quickly as an Oklahoma storm rolls in, Verlin smashed his beer can on the prisoner's face, sending him to the ground with a sharp yelp and a spray of warm beer all over the cell. The prisoner didn't fall all the way to the ground because his hands were cuffed to the bars behind him. He dangled from one of the strap-iron cross members that hold the vertical bars in place. He groaned in front of Verlin and Peter like a contorted puppet on an unlikely stage in someone's basement.

"What's wrong, little nigger bitch?" Addie said, looking up from his desk indifferently.

"I don't think he likes Coors," Verlin said, laughing.

Addie laughed out loud, tossed the papers in his hand across the desk, and then got up and went into the cell with the prisoner and his friend. Peter wanted to help the man but figured his dad and Addie would just kill him too if he did anything to stop their morning fun. But then Peter figured again, God as his witness, that if he never did another worthwhile thing in his whole pointless life from then on, not doing something about that situation right then would surely solidify his rank as the biggest cowardly lump of shit in the world.

"What the hell are you guys doin'?" Peter finally spoke up.

"Boy, you better shut your faggot mouth," Verlin said, and then as if punctuating his point, he kicked the already prostrate man in the ribs as he continued to dangle there on the cell bars. Verlin kept his eyes on Peter the whole time.

"You really are sad," Peter said.

And then, as if he wanted to further Peter's point, Verlin bent down and punched the guy in the face with all the strength his drunk, the worn body could muster...and then again. He must've hit him six or seven times in the face as Peter stood by, hypnotized at first and then struggling to break loose, as Addie had gone back behind him, holding him back by his arms.

"Verlin, come on, buddy, I better help this little nigger boy up...come on. He don't look too good."

Verlin stood up straight and turned to leave the cell, patting Peter on the back as Addie let go of his arms. Peter shrugged his dad and the beefy cop off of himself. Addie uncuffed the man, and he fell to the floor of the cell, a crumpled, bloody mess.

"Come on, little nigger," Addie said in a sarcastic tone. "Here you go, buddy."

The man stood up as straight as he could, wincing and not wanting to look at Addie. Addie pushed him in the direction of the other cell across the hall. Conveniently enough, there seemed to be one cell to beat on prisoners and one to hold them captive, keeping clean-up to a tidy, organized minimum.

Peter watched Addie, and the man leave the beating cell, and that's when he noticed that Addie had a black-jack or billy club hanging off of his belt on his side. Peter hoped that Addie had a little more compassion and mercy than to wail on the guy right after he'd just mustered enough strength to get up and walk, to follow directions.

Peter went up front to try to find Verlin and then heard the screaming again. He ran back to the cell, but too late to do anything. The black man lay in the middle of the floor writhing, holding his right knee. Peter stared at Addie standing over the man on the floor. Peter started to get nauseous again.

"He tried to escape," Addie said. "I can't have no crazy nigger out there runnin' around and beatin' on people."

"Where's my dad?"

"Hell, if I know."

Peter walked back outside and got into the truck. It felt twenty degrees hotter than it had when they went into the jailhouse only minutes earlier. Peter leaned his head back on the seat and closed his eyes.

Chapter 22

Peter ran an envelope containing an old letter from his mom through his hands. The letter had been a follow-up from her, after she had told Peter a little more about his father, from what she could remember from Peter's early childhood. Peter had kept the letter throughout his stay in prison, and now he held onto it as the only remaining connection to his mother left on earth.

Peter stared at the rivulets of water cascading down the passenger-side window of the BMW. Fr. Ligero, oblivious to anything but the road, hypnotized by the swishing of the windshield wipers, the rain, barreled down the black-top highway as if life's culminating mission were unfolding right before them.

After Verlin had visited Peter that first time, back when he was twenty-three, the first time they had seen each other since Peter and his father's "vacation," Peter had gone back over to his mom's house the next day and told her about everything that his dad had told him that painful, strange night in the garage, amidst the summer deluge. The old man's side of the story, so to speak, and why he had never come around, and what made him want to see Peter again after so many years had already passed. Peter and his mom had never really talked about his dad before that day at the dining-room table.

Peter's mom wanted to give Verlin the benefit of the doubt, she had said, and not mentioning his name or her perspective on their life together seemed the best way to do that.

"So, you've had some time to get to know your dad?" she had said.

"Yeah," Peter said, reaching for her Camel Lights on the small dining room table.

"Did you guys have fun?"

"I guess you could say that."

Peter had to give it to his mom for dealing with such sensitive issues with such delicate grace. Years of dealing with the criminally insane teaches a person to choose words wisely, battles even more wisely, Peter assumed.

Peter's mom had worked her whole career for the Oklahoma Department of Corrections as a psychiatric counselor in the Mental Health Division. Coincidental, some might say, but Peter thought that her occupation simply chose her out of her own personal need, a natural progression of sorts, as she herself had survived the short few years of marriage to Verlin and then just had to go back to humanity to help solve the mystery of the fractured mind. Maybe even deep down inside, she thought that she could prevent Peter from becoming like his father, and her choice of vocation had simply grown out of her life, her past pain and experience, and she felt that somehow she would be able to curb his genetic potential for becoming a sociopath himself.

Peter opened the letter and unfolded it. He took a deep breath as if beginning a meditation.

Peter,

Hello sweetheart. I'm sorry I had to run off to work when you came over the last time I saw you. I would have stayed forever, holding you tight, if I could have known things would end up the way they have. I apologize for laughing when you asked about our vacation with your dad when you were young. I didn't mean to be evasive or insensitive. The question simply shocked me more than anything else. It just threw me a little, honey. I couldn't really get into that before I went to work, and it kills me, and I feel like a failure altogether for not giving you the answers right then. I almost feel like I should have told you about your "vacation" and that that somehow would have created a different course for you right then. Maybe you wouldn't have even gone back to see your father if you had known his capacity for cruelty and his propensity for delusion. I wanted you to make your own decisions, and you did, and I am so sorry. I love you.

I want to now tell you, before Ariel and I come to visit, about how your trip with your dad all those years ago began. I'm sorry it has to come like this, but I feel like you need to know now that maybe somehow, this information can assuage some of the guilt you might feel for accidentally killing your stepmother. Not really a justification, but maybe just some insight into why you made the choices you did.

Your father called me out of the blue, about a year after our divorce, and said that he had just bought a new motor home and that he wanted to work some things out and take us on a picnic. The three of us. Our little family. He said that he missed his family. Your dad could be very charming when he wanted to be. He is a smart guy too.

As usual, he showed up a couple of hours late. His motor home was a van. I should have known—a fairly new van but no motor home. I wanted to give him a chance. He's your father. He asked me to give him another chance and that he was sorry for all the hurt he had caused us. He didn't have any food or anything for a picnic in the van, but I thought that maybe we would stop somewhere out in the Osage and get some supplies. Or, maybe we would go fishing and just cook that over a fire. Your dad really liked fishing.

There weren't even any seats in the back of the van, just an old motorcycle and a bunch of tools and gas cans and junk. We went anyway, as I said, the benefit of the doubt. We left town after we had talked for a while. I went against my better judgment by going, but I wanted him to be able to see you. I tried to call Grammie to tell her that we were going on a picnic with Verlin, but I didn't get through. I remember being glad that she didn't answer, however, because I knew she'd just tell me I was crazy for going anywhere with your dad. She'd bailed me out a million times with him. She and Daddy told me not to talk to him without a cop or attorney present. They didn't trust him at all.

I started getting worried when we went past the lake. I asked him where we were going, and he told me he had a special place he wanted to take us. I told myself that it was true, that he did have a special place in mind, that everything was okay, and that we'd be fine. I tried my best not to act scared at that point. Your dad gets flared up when he sees that you're afraid. It makes him mad to see that people are afraid of him, and it's easy to get scared when that happens, too.

He kept driving further out on the old highway, way past the lake. That's when I really started to worry. You were totally oblivious, excited to be on a trip with your mom and dad. I tried to be happy about that, but the fear of your dad's potential capabilities was too great.

He pulled the van off the highway and went down a little dirt road that trailed behind some trees, out by my friend Mary's house. You know Mary, right? I knew something wasn't right, but I knew I couldn't act scared still. I thought he was going to kill us or kill me and take you. I couldn't do anything, though, so I just smiled and kept my mouth shut.

He reached under the seat, and I just knew he was pulling his gun. He never went anywhere without that old gun his crazy father had given him. He reached around, back and forth, as I just held my breath, as if I could have a different outcome by denying myself the next breath.

I was able to breathe again when I saw that he pulled a little box out from under the seat. I kept my eyes on the package, praying inside. He saw me looking at him, and then he looked back at you and then smiled at me. His hands worked slowly, deliberately at the box. He pulled a brand-new, battery-operated transistor radio out of the box and then held it up for me to see. He smiled again and said, 'What's wrong, honey? It's just a radio. Don't you like music?' He really gets off on messing with people's heads. I should have at least told you that.

He took the back off of the radio and put the cover on his leg. I sat there, still a little nervous, but also thinking that maybe we were going to have a picnic, after all, a talk at least, seeing how we didn't have any food or drinks to speak of. He pulled a nine-volt battery out of the breast pocket of his shirt and put it in the back of the radio. He turned the radio on, and then he turned it up slowly, the static getting louder and louder as he just sat there for a minute with the static up loud, like he was trying to discern secret messages from the midst of that eerie white noise. He closed his eyes and put his head back on his seat.

After a minute or so, he finally turned it to the local rock-n-roll station and tossed it to you. You were so excited. You'd never got to play with a new radio like that. I had never bought anything like that before. I could have cried to see you so happy. You were just a sweet little boy. Innocent.

He told you to turn it up while he and I got all of the stuff out for the picnic. So, we got out of the van and left you in there with the new radio. You always loved music. 'We'll be back,' I said loudly over the radio. You just bobbed your head to the music, oblivious to anything other than whatever song played on the radio, smiling the whole time. I was so happy for you and sad at the same time, for reasons I couldn't even explain at the time.

I walked around to the back of the van where your dad was rummaging around between the open doors and waited for him to hand me something. I couldn't see you because of the motorcycle and junk in the way, but I could hear that radio playing. I knew you were there, that you were close enough for me to grab if I needed to.

I know it sounds funny, but I didn't ever want to leave you with your dad out of my sight. That was a big step in trust for me, just going around the back of the van like that without you in my arms, even if he was back there with me. You were out of my sight, and Verlin was near, but I still felt nervous.

Then, just like a cruel practical joke, the next thing I know, I was standing in front of your dad dumbfounded, looking down the barrel of a shotgun. I was scared to death. I stood still, looking at the ground, silent, praying to God in my head as he nudged me with the end of the barrel. He'd pulled a gun on me many times before and had threatened to kill me even more, but that was something that I could never get used to—staring down a gun's barrel. He told me to look at him as he continued to nudge me with the shotgun. I didn't want to look at him almost as much as I didn't want to die. I stood there for a painful second or two, and then slowly, I looked up at his face.

'You're gonna take a little walk into the woods, okay?' he said. He enjoyed wielding power over me. He always did. I couldn't contain the fear any longer and started to cry. I knew he'd kill me if I gave him any chance to do so if he knew he could get away with it. 'What are you gonna do with Pete?' I said. He told me that he was going to take you and that I couldn't do a fucking thing about it. He told me that I was gonna fuck you up and that he was there to get what I had stolen from him. He felt justified. I didn't argue with him; I just wanted you to be okay. Praying inside, crying on the outside now, him smiling, I knew the only thing I could do was to let him take you. I didn't want to die, and when I played it over in my mind, I knew he wouldn't kill you. He did love you; he just had so much torment inside.

I walked off and let him take you. I didn't know what else to do. I pictured you bobbing your head to the music, sitting on the floor of the van, as he pulled out of the woods, leaving me behind. I fell to the ground, crushed under the weight of what was happening. I couldn't believe it. I really thought the worst of our relationship was behind us.

After about five minutes of bawling my eyes out, I got up off of the ground, dusted myself off, and told myself that I had to pull it together. I had to do something. I walked out of the woods and out onto the highway. The day was already warm as I took one blind step after the other, going back home without you, not knowing what to say to Grammie and Daddy.No one was on the highway that day. No ranchers, no truckers. Nobody is driving by on a weekday afternoon. I just kept walking and crying. I hated myself for being such a coward, but then again, I knew there was nothing I could do, really, so I just kept walking and crying.

Again, I'm sorry to have to deliver the answer to your question this way, but I thought that maybe you would like to know all of this before our next visit so that we didn't use all of our time talking about this only. I am going to do everything that I can to get you out of there. I don't know how right now, but I'm working on it. Your Uncle Lenny has hired further counsel, and he seems to think there is some way to get things done, to at least get your sentence reduced. I don't know. I'm sorry.

Ariel and I are coming down to see you in two weeks. I'll pray for your peace in there. Just know that your mother and your sister love you and support you, and will always be here for you. I love you.

Please write to let me know if there is anything that I can bring to you. Books, magazines, money (if you can use it in there), or anything else that you might want or need. Ariel said that she's writing you a letter too. I wish I could just come in and get you out right now. We're working on that.

Write me back as soon as you can.

Love,

Mom.

Peter's mom and sister Ariel died in a car accident on the way to their first visit with him in prison. The visit that his mom mentioned in her letter. That last conversation with his mother, the day he left with Grammie to go see his dad, could have been only the day before; it felt so fresh in Peter's mind. He folded the letter and put it in the envelope. He turned the envelope over in his hand, perusing the faded ink and yellowing paper. The clinging, melancholy nostalgia faintly ached in his bones. He turned the letter over and over in his hand as if the mere motion could bring his mom back to life. He missed her so much. The best woman he had ever known.

Peter thought about the evening when he opened the letter in jail before he had been sentenced. That lone letter from his mother was like a beacon of hope from the outside world. He had torn it open with excitement, read it slowly, and then again. He wanted to bash his head against the bars of his cell, bludgeoning himself into oblivion afterward. Nevertheless, he read it again and again, wanting to believe that the joke would be up soon and that his imminent release from prison was right around the corner. Assuaged guilt. Fuck that old bastard. His step-mom was dead. Louise. The old man could feel some pain now, perhaps, he had thought. Peter remembers hating himself for feeling justified in his unconscious revenge, if for only a moment.

Peter pulled one of the plastic bags from the back seat and put the old letter back into it. Fr. Ligero stared down the hood of the black BMW as they barreled down the highway on the way to Pony Town, rain still pouring, new possibilities all around them.

"What was that?" Fr. Ligero said.

"A letter from my mom."

"I'm sorry, Peter."

"Yeah, well, I guess we all die."

"This life..." Fr. Ligero began to say but stopped.

Peter looked over at Fr. Ligero and sighed. Death seems so final. There's nothing you can do about that vacuum that is created by someone's passing. No fix. No reprieve. The mourner faces his own mortality, trying to make sense of the loss, placating oneself into believing in eternal life, and forever, with loved ones that are in heaven and all that.

"This life isn't it, right?"

"We live by faith, which leads to hope. No one wants to be in despair, my friend."

"Okay."

Peter continued to stare out at the wet day, his hour of freedom surreal so far. His fear was still there after all those years, under the skin like some creeping death. He had to face his dad once-and-for-all. There could be no rest without that meeting.

Chapter 23

Peter finished his slab of pie and heap of whipped cream.

Sewell pulled a little piece of paper out of his shirt pocket and put on his reading glasses. Peter watched him carefully from where he sat, anticipating every move and gesture.

"Okay, buddy. Let's call your mama. Whattaya think?"

Peter jumped up from his chair as if it were spring-loaded. He scrambled over to where Sewell stood by the rotary phone, waiting to dial the number for Peter.

"Hold still, now," Sewell said as Peter bounced from one foot to the other.

"I'm gonna call my mom," Peter said to Pinkie, who came back into the kitchen to get something. Sewell began dialing the number, Peter already with the receiver to his ear, shuffling feet.

"You can talk as long as you want, okay?"

"Yes, sir."

And finally, as if Peter had been waiting for weeks for the President to okay his phone call, the phone began to ring on the other end. And it rang. And again. With no answer after all that energy and excitement.

Sewell looked at Peter, obviously broken-hearted at the boy's misfortune. Nobody answered the phone. His mother wasn't home. Peter thought that maybe his mother didn't want to talk to him after all. Maybe his dad wasn't lying. Maybe he wouldn't even talk to his mom again, as long as he lived, the pathetic little shit.

Sewell grabbed the receiver and hung it up. "We'll try her later, okay? I promise."

"Okay," Peter said, hanging his head, slowly shuffling over to where his empty plate sat on the table.

After Pinkie had a chance to talk to Peter about his mom, Sewell and he went out to do the rounds on the farm. They left Simone in the house with Pinkie because Sewell said that she would chase the cows, and he couldn't have that. Peter asked Sewell if they could go brush the horses after they fed the cows. Peter loved the shiny horses, their powerful legs and chest, swishing their wispy tails in the wind, seemingly indifferent to the world of humans and all of their strange ways of doing things.

After they had done all of the feeding and watering, Sewell and Peter went to see the horses. They looked up from where they stood next to each other, eating grass when they heard the truck pull up—the *whish* of their tails in the air like assertive whispers. The horses looked at them cautiously, as if Peter and Sewell might jump the fence and try to grapple them down to the ground. Sewell quickly put them at ease with a bucketful of feed that he brought from the truck so that they could get close enough to pet them. He grabbed a handful and told Peter to go ahead and grab some.

"This is where I come when I'm having a hard day," Sewell said.

"You have hard days?"

"Sure."

Peter stared at the horse's mouths as they stuck their head over the top wire of the barbed-wire fence. Their lips stretched out like fleshy pink hands to grab the feed out of Sewell's hand.

"You wanna try?" Sewell said.

Peter looked at the horse and then at Sewell, almost startled. He held the bucket out to Peter, who reluctantly grabbed another handful.

"Now, you just put the feed in the palm of your hand and hold your hand out flat as a board, okay. They just scoop it right off of there. Got it, buddy?"

Peter stuck his hand out over the fence, nervous and a little shaky, as some of the sweet grain fell off of the side of his hand.

"Calm down now, and just put your hand out flat...there you go...flatter...good."

And the bigger of the two, the Appaloosa, lapped up the feed with her thin, unfurling lips in a couple of funny little lip-stretching movements. Peter wanted to pull his hand back, but he didn't. He held out his other hand, a little bit sweaty now, with bits of grain stuck to it. The same horse made light work of the next nibble.

"Good job, buddy," Sewell said and held out the bucket for Peter. "Here. Give her another handful. That's the one you're gonna ride. You wanna make'em as comfortable and trusting of you as you can."

Peter looked up at Sewell as if he had told the boy to jump off a bridge.

"She likes you, don't you think?"

"Are they nicer if they trust you?"

"They aren't as ornery, that's for dang sure."

The Appaloosa put its head down so that Peter could pet its smooth, flat nose and jaw.

"You wanna ride?" Sewell said.

"I never have."

"No better time to learn. Come on; I'll show you how to saddle'em up."

Sewell put the feed bucket back in the truck after he gave the smaller of the two horses a handful of feed. They walked over to the barn, and Sewell grabbed two ropes, handing Peter one, and then they went out to get the horses. Sewell showed Peter how to put the rope around the Arabian's neck and how to cinch it up so that it didn't come loose. He took the rope that he had handed to Peter and looped it around the Appaloosa's neck, talking the whole time, giving calm instructions as he went. They walked the horses over to the barn, where Sewell hitched them to the barn door, one after the other.

Peter followed Sewell into the barn to watch his every move. He wanted to learn everything he could, just like he did by following his grandpa around the garage back home. Peter felt happy and important watching both of the old guys working in their respective sanctuaries of a sort. The quiet confidence the older gentlemen exuded as they performed their tasks at hand felt eternal, like the breath of life itself. Calm and peaceful, yet productive.

"Pete, you think you can lift one of these," Sewell said, holding out a saddle in front of himself, both arms outstretched with a little strain.

Peter stepped over by him and grabbed the saddle by the horn and by the back of the seat, just like Sewell had grabbed it. The weight of the hard leather fell to the ground, puffing dust into Peter's eyes when the man let go. Peter kicked the saddle and then decided that he didn't want to let that thing get the best of him. He took a deep breath, shook his arms out a little bit, and then gave it all that he had, half lifting, half dragging that thing across the dirt barn floor, if for only a second or two.

"Damn, boy. You're stronger'n a bull."

Peter dropped the saddle and looked up at Sewell, not knowing what he had done wrong. There was that word 'boy' again, sharp like a blade on the forearm. The visceral fear of the curse word and one of his father's pet names felt like a punch in the gut. His dad called him 'boy,' and he didn't like the sound of it from anyone. Peter didn't want to make Sewell mad all the time like he did his dad.

"Hey, hey, Pete. You're alright. Don't you worry; you're doing just fine, okay?" Sewell went over to where Peter stood next to the saddle on the ground and put his hand on the young boy's shoulder, lightly rubbing it. "Okay?"

"Yes, sir."

"Pete, I ain't mad; you're just a strong little cuss, that's all. You surprised me...you're doing good. Come on, buddy."

After a second, Sewell pulled off a thick blanket that he had hung over the door and laid it over the Appaloosa's back. He picked Peter's saddle up and heaved it onto the blanket, all in one big swing of the arms. He pulled the padded leather strap that dangled from the other side of the saddle under the horse's belly and through the buckle on his side of the saddle. He put his knee into the side of the horse, pulling the strap tight against the old mare's ribs. He made a loop with the leather strap below the buckle and pulled it into a tight, flat knot.

"Look here, Pete," he pointed to the horse's side in the sunlight. "See them spots? That's how you know she's a real Appaloosa. They call that the Leopard Complex. See?" he moved his hand back and forth over the horse's dark brown coat.

Then, all of a sudden, like a magic trick, the spots jumped out at Peter after he let his eyes totally lose focus for a second. "I see 'em, I see 'em!" Peter said, pointing at the dark rings beneath the surface of the horse's coat.

"They'll get a little darker as she gets older."

Sewell tied the back strap at the base of the horse's belly, making another flat knot. He saddled the other horse, talking and showing Peter the steps along the way. It was a lot of work just getting the horses ready to ride, Peter thought, but it was okay just the same because Peter liked being with Sewell out there doing guy things together, getting to know each other. He liked the way Sewell talked to him like a little man, how he explained things to him as if he were worth all of the time and instruction. It made Peter feel good. Sewell reminded Peter of his Uncle Lenny when it came to that kind of respect.

Once they got the horses ready, they led them up next to the house. Sewell took Peter inside and gave him a pair of jeans that someone had left behind. Peter got dressed, and they went back outside.

Sewell told Peter that he could ride the horse with the spots because she wasn't as surly as the wild, gray horse. The gray horse was an Arabian stud, he told Peter, slapping it on the butt. The Arabian snorted and kicked at the dirt, whinnying and cocking up his tail like a Spaniard's plume. That cocky horse looked as if he could fly off at any second, like Pegasus into the wind, leaving behind the messy world below for someone else to deal with.

Sewell lifted Peter up onto the other horse. He let a little yelp out because it hurt where Sewell grabbed his arm. Peter got his butt square in the saddle and then tried to touch the stirrups with his feet.

"You hurt?" Sewell said from on the ground.

"My arm's just a little sore."

"Let me see, Pete."

Peter started to lift his sleeve up as Sewell reached up and helped him push it all the way up to his shoulder.

"Ouch, buddy. You gotta bruise from hell on that arm."

"What?"

Then Peter remembered his dad grabbing him by the arm, squeezing it hard, and holding his face down in all those piles of crap on the bedroom floor. Peter couldn't get up because Verlin had him gripped by the arm and the back of the neck. Peter couldn't remember his arm hurting then, the stench and misery of the whole thing, but it felt really sore sitting on that horse, after the fact, with Sewell examining him like a country doctor.

"Did your dad do this?"

"I don't think so."

"What do you..." And then Sewell stopped short of what he was about to say, just standing there for a minute, looking at Peter. "You wanna ride?"

"Yes, sir."

Sewell looked like he wanted to say something else but didn't. His face got a little red, almost like he'd been holding his breath, but he wasn't, and then he looked Peter up and down again from where he stood below. He noticed Peter struggling to reach the stirrups.

"Oh, pardner, let me get those for you."

Sewell grabbed Peter's foot and a stirrup and tugged and twisted until the stirrup was high enough for Peter to slip his foot into it. He went to the other side and did the same thing.

Peter looked down at Sewell as he looked up. Sewell's face had pretty much gone back to his normal brown shade from days in the sun. Sewell smiled and then patted Peter on the leg. Sewell got on his horse, and they were finally off into the moist Mississippi evening. Two cowboys heading into the sunset.

Chapter 24

Peter opened his eyes to Verlin and Addie, stumbling out of the jailhouse. Peter didn't really know how long he had been asleep, feeling a little rested now. He hurried to sit up straight before they got in with him.

"Hey, little fucker, what you doin' out here?" Verlin said.

"Well..."

"You missed the rest of the fun, boy," Addie said. "You could learn a thing or two from how we gitter done out here in the real world."

Peter tried to keep the thoughts, the images elicited from that comment, from entering his head, but all the booze and pills and stress had left him a little weak in constitution. Given the opportunity, people tend to gravitate toward the lowest form of existence, he thought. Peter sat up in the truck seat and put his sunglasses on. "Do you think we could go home, dad?"

"Louise's probably bitchin' by now, I guess," Verlin said.

Addie slapped Verlin on the back. "Damn, Verlin. You pussy-whipped, is ya?"

All of a sudden, Peter felt nauseous again, looking at Addie and his sweaty, flat-topped head that pissed out that whiney, redneck voice, tight strings of saliva stretching between his lips when he spoke. Peter's stomach soured with each word that came out of the guy's mouth; it was all that he could do to keep his irritable stomach from sending its contents back up and out all over the inside of the truck. Peter could smell Addie's bad breath from where he sat.

Peter looked down at his hands to distract himself from the seemingly inevitable purge. He closed his eyes to summon whatever pleasant thoughts he could, and then, slowly, he picked his head up to tell the guys to get moving. They both laughed as they were getting in on either side of him, and that's when Peter noticed the growing sweat rings on the armpits of Addie's infamous LAPD t-shirt, steamy in their yellow tint. Peter couldn't keep it down any longer.

"What the hell are you doin', boy?!" Addie said.

Peter just let all of that beer and convenience store food come up and out, all over Addie's truck seat right next to where he sat. Peter knew that he couldn't hold it down, couldn't control it, so he just let 'er rip, as the old man would have said.

Addie jumped back out of the truck as if it were full of bees, and he was deathly allergic.

"Get the fuck outta there, boy!" Verlin shouted.

Peter could feel his dad tugging at him from the collar of his shirt, but Peter's body was rigid with regurgitation, and there wasn't a bull in town that could have pulled him out of that truck right then. Peter braced himself inside the truck, still puking, as Verlin continued to pull at the collar of his ripping dress shirt. After Peter dry-heaved several more times, after his stomach had emptied of all that vile sourness, he raised his head and loosened his bracing arms and legs from the door frame of the pick-up.

"Sorry, Addie," Peter said, strings of spittle dangling from his wet mouth.

"You're sorrier'n hell, boy!" Addie said. Peter couldn't tell the difference between a statement and an exclamation coming from Addie. The only volume the guy knew was 'way up'. "You gotta wipe that shit out!"

"I feel better now." Peter lumbered down to the ground.

"Come on, Addie," Verlin said. "We'll clean 'er up."

Addie went over to Peter's side of the truck to inspect the mess. He shook his head and then went to the bed of the truck. He returned with a towel in his hands and threw it at Peter. "Clean that shit up, boy. I gotta take you two shit heads home before you go and do anymore damned fool shit to my truck."

So, Peter went about wiping up all the vomit as best he could, moving the acrid globules around like a kid rearranging unwanted veggies on their dinner plate. Addie went inside and came out with a bucket of water and a sponge, and a couple more dry towels. He pushed Verlin out of the way, who stood hovering over Peter pushing the vomit around with the old towel, and he tossed one of the other clean towels at Peter.

"Here ya little shit," Addie said, taking the soiled towel from Peter and throwing it on the ground behind him. "Use some hot soapy water to get in there and scrub. I'll get you some rinse water. Come on, boy, don't let that shit soak in, ya hear?"

Peter shook his head, suddenly beginning to laugh hysterically, uncontrollably.

"Real funny there, ya fuckin' numb-nuts!" Addie said.

At that, Peter laughed even harder, despite the fact that the cop and his father liked to beat up defenseless people. Peter probably wasn't defenseless enough, though, having fought his way all the way through life.

Addie went inside to get the bucket of rinse water.

Peter kept his mouth shut when he came back out to deliver the other bucket and kept his focus on the task at hand, not wanting to provoke them to exact their colorful brand of justice on him. He wanted to get home and lie down.

While Peter scrubbed with the hot, soapy water and rinsed and wiped and rinsed and wiped, Verlin and Addie just stood by watching him like a NASCAR race on Saturday afternoon, dully enthralled, waiting for the next turn of the track. Peter made light work of the clean-up, considering the sheer volume of the mess, and he felt light and strong from having vomited up all of that poison in his system. He couldn't help but think of cleaning up all that dog feces back when he was just a little boy, Verlin standing by – always the inspector, always the big man.

Peter felt like turning around and beating his father senseless with whatever blunt object he might have at hand. Taking the old man's gun and shooting him if he resisted. He and Addie. Maybe even take the truck for a joyride down to Mexico. Peter was a coward, though. Hadn't he proved that to himself and the guys in the jail cell already, that scrawny black man taking the scourge of hatred from Addie and Verlin?

Peter dumped the buckets onto the ground behind himself and then threw them to Addie, who had sat in a folding chair in the shade, where he still sweated profusely through his tiny, pudgy pink face. Peter stepped down out of the high-rise truck and hung the towels over the side of the bed. Addie aligned all of his mass and energy to get himself up and out of his chair. He bent over and grabbed the buckets by the handles and then grabbed the towels off of the truck bed, along with the one on the ground, and then put them all in the buckets. He made some comments under his breath and put the buckets inside the side door of the jailhouse.

"Let's go," Addie said after he locked up and came back to the truck, and they were finally off.

Conceding to the innermost feeling that his dad had to have some redeeming qualities, Peter continued to look past all of the quirks and the racism, the anger and the lying, to see the hurt young man who had never accomplished what it was that he thought he should have accomplished with his seemingly pointless life. Verlin didn't have an honest or remorseful bone in his body. Peter wanted so much to see his dad in himself, but all that he could come up with were the obsessive-compulsive traits that made most people around him nervous and scared. Peter tried to accept his heritage but couldn't. He simply wanted to cut out all of the sinew and gristle and muscle off of his bones, to extricate the blood and nerves and vessels that had come from his father, obliterating that working-class, red neck curse once and for all before it was too late, and he was simply stuck being the person he never wanted to be.

When Addie had dropped them off at Verlin's house, he said that they were meant for each other, Peter and Verlin. Despite his disgust at the situation at the jailhouse, Peter had to admit that the comment made him feel good in a way. He and his dad were supposed to be meant for each other, in a filial sort of way, and it felt right to finally be there with him, sorting things out, kind of. Father and son, making the most of a bad situation. Peter knew that once the details were worked out, he could be a whole person, knowing more about the man who had contributed to half of who he was, genetically speaking, at least.

Louise and the girls were gone when Peter and his dad went into the house.

"Those bitches are probably spending all of my money at the mall," Verlin said, crumpling up a little piece of paper that sat on the kitchen counter. "Them girls need to do more shit around the house."

"I need to take a shower," Peter said and went back to the bathroom.

"We need to talk, boy," Verlin said as Peter walked down the hall.

"Yeah. In a minute, okay?"

The bathroom felt like a doctor's office waiting room, antiseptic in its cleanliness and order. All of the magazines, some of which were *Hot Rod, Better Homes and Gardens,* and *Highlights*, were all dust-free and systematically fanned out in the brass magazine bin, which rested between the brass plunger and the toilet itself. Peter remembered the girls getting into trouble for leaving water spots on the mirror shortly after he had first arrived. Peter made sure to be careful not to mess anything up, so he slowly undressed and gingerly got into the shower. He thought of the time that Louise had tutored him on taking a shower. She had commented on his dick, and he remembered feeling weird as hell and dirty and ashamed. She didn't look too bad for an old lady, Peter thought, turning the hot water up a little.

Peter took his shower and then went back out into the kitchen. He could hear the water running from the master bedroom, where Verlin must have been showering. The fresh smell of shampoo wafted down the hallway, making Peter feel a little more human, not so dirty, and confused about his crappier new existence. He sighed like a worn-out housewife, feeling a little relief in his stomach and the back of his neck, almost calm...and then he thought about the bathroom...that maybe he should go double-check to see if he had left it the way he found it.

Peter padded his way back to the bathroom and turned on the light. Steam still thinly clung near the ceiling, and Peter could see freshwater spots on the mirror. The hand towel barely hung on the brass ring by the sink.

Peter grabbed the towel and started to wipe the mirror off. Looking into the mirror, he almost felt that if he just stared long enough, the fear and dinginess would simply disappear right before him, as if perhaps he hadn't looked deeply enough at himself, scathingly enough into himself all the times before, as if he had looked into the mirror and right past himself all those years. Peter wiped away the drops from the mirror, continuing to stare at himself, nearly putting himself into a trance when his dad appeared in his field of vision from behind.

"What the fuck are you doin', boy?"

"Cleaning the mirror," Peter said, looking down at the sink.

"Shit, boy." Verlin stepped into the bathroom with Peter and stared at him in the mirror. "You ain't on drugs, is ya?"

"No."

Peter finished wiping the mirror and neatly folded the towel, and then neatly hung it on the brass towel ring. Verlin walked away down the hall, whistling *Whiskey River* to himself. That song is forever etched into Peter's mind from all those years ago. He had a fleeting image of himself floating down a river of whiskey, laughing like a schoolboy, drunk as a sailor, but quickly snapped out of it when he noticed a little puddle of water at the edge of the sink. No more floating for you, bud, he thought, almost guiltily. Peter looked around the bathroom to make sure that he had flushed the toilet, wiped and closed the shower door, and smoothed out the rugs. Everything looked as if he had never been there. He felt free to leave.

Peter went back to the kitchen to see what his dad wanted to talk about.

"Here." Verlin handed him three typed pages.

The first page had the date and a cordial greeting to Peter's mother.

The letter read:

Enclosed is a list of stipulations that I have set forth for Pete to live at my home to get him on his feet and to make responsible decisions for himself.

I realize that these, I guess you could call them rules or standards of behavior, are very strict and may even seem a little harsh, but I want to see him succeed and prove to himself and others that he can make it on his own and that he doesn't need anyone else interfering in his life counter to his best interests. I simply feel that during this time period, he does not need everyone else's problems while he is trying to get a job, save money, and think about where he will be in six months to a year.

After talking with him last weekend, I will tell you this; he would be making the biggest mistake of his life if he were to go into the military or college right now, considering how he just quits when things get a little tough or don't go his way. I'm willing to take the chance that he will hate me for being so tough on him so that he will succeed rather than he will like me and fail. I'm hoping that you will support me in this. I feel that this is the best thing for him at this juncture.

Just to give you an idea of what my intentions are during this period:

1. Expenses- None other than personal items and clothes.

2. Financial- $4.50 x 40 = $180 - 35% tax = $117 net per week - 4/5 savings 1/5 personal – $93.60 savings per week x 26 weeks = $2,433.60 total savings.

3. Evaluations- to help him chart his own progress to let him determine what areas he needs to improve in for making sound decisions and that success, no matter how small or large is an accomplishment to be proud of no matter what others may think.

4. Outside influence- he has to know himself and deal with his own problems before he can help anyone else with theirs. As you noticed, I allowed him a 15-minute paid phone call with you because I feel you can be an influence on his success. I hope this will be the decision he makes, but it will be his choice and no one else's. As far as the birthday, Thanksgiving, and Christmas portion of the rules, this was put into place because of his low self-esteem and the ability of others to influence him in non-positive ways; just like the recovering drug addict or alcoholic, it only takes one time, and you're back to where you started. I just feel if he gives it the full six months, he will be mentally tough enough to make his own decisions (right or wrong) without interference from others. If at the end of the six months if he is doing well, then he will have the option to stay another six months, but at the same time, should ANY rule be broken, no matter how insignificant anyone thinks it is, he will be moved out of my home IMMEDIATELY because that will be a decision he made by breaking those rules and not me.

As I said, I know this all sounds harsh and cold, but I'm sure you'll agree with me that something has to be done that makes him responsible for himself as well as for others. The military was not an option because of the lack of self-discipline and responsibility on his part. College was not an option because the first time he and his girlfriend had an argument, or some problem between you and your new husband arose, he apparently threw his hands in the air and gave up on himself to worry about others and their problems right away. This way, HE does it, or nobody will do it, and by earning his own money, having a job, and accepting responsibility, he may someday be ready to go to college with a realistic goal for his future.

He's our son, and I know you only want the best for him; that's why I'm sure you will support me and help convince him to do this for himself. I am here to make sure that he has the support necessary to meet all of the above standards of living for a man today in this world.

Always,

Verlin

P.S. – If you have any questions, call me collect any afternoon before Friday because Peter must make his decision by 8 pm Friday.

{See next page}

I have enclosed a list of the rules which Peter will have to abide by if he chooses to live in my home. These rules are not negotiable, nor are they in any way to be modified by me, Peter, or anyone else for that matter.

RULES

1. No outside influence or interference.

Your mom, Perky, relatives (all of them), or anyone from your hometown or

bars or dancing clubs.

2. If you accept my terms, you have a place to live for at least six (6) months. If for any reason, you change your mind or don't like the rules, you cannot come back to life. EVER.

3. You will find a job within two (2) months. If you do not find a job in that time period (2 months), THE DEAL IS OFF, and you must immediately EVACUATE THE PREMISES.

4. You do not quit your job for ANY reason other than going to a better job. If you get fired FOR ANY REASON, you are to EVACUATE THE PREMISES IMMEDIATELY!

5. You can drink a couple of (2) beers at home per day only. NO DRUGS or HARD LIQUOR or INHALANTS or CRACK cocaine. If you come home and have been drinking or taking drugs, YOU ARE GONE!

6. Month to Month Evaluation of your Progress.

(i.e., Savings, EMOTIONAL STABILITY, Your Job, Attitude, General Behavior).

7. Paydays- Bring check home. 4/5 of income goes directly into a savings account (No checking). 1/5 of income is kept by yourself for personal use.

8. No lies about your job, where you've been, what you were doing, who you were with, your sexual orientation (if gay, even a little gay, YOU ARE GONE!), or any of your expenses. If I catch you in a lie or become privy to a lie on your part, you are to IMMEDIATELY EVACUATE THE PREMISES!!

9. Curfew- 10 pm 7 nights a week.

No exceptions unless you have employment that requires you to be later than this posted curfew.

10. Phone calls- One (1) Person, your choosing, once a week - other than work or new friends (upon my inspection and subsequent approval). I'll pay for a 15-minute call on Saturday or Sunday for you to call your mom if that's who you choose to call. Any person other than your mom is at your expense, and the call will be monitored randomly at my discretion.

11. Since your birthday, Thanksgiving, and Christmas fall within the six-month period, you will be expected to spend them with us. (I will explain if needed). Call Friday before 8 pm if further explanation is needed.

<u>If you break ANY of the above rules, YOU ARE GONE!</u>

Any changes in the above rules must be mutually agreed to, yet change is strongly discouraged for fear of manipulation by Peter in the details of this proposed agreement. Thank you for your time.

Wow...eleven rules. Nice odd number, Peter thought. At first, the thought of such a letter, including rules, didn't really seem too strange to Peter, considering the source. It didn't even make him mad, for the most part. Honestly, he thought that maybe his dad just missed that week in elementary school when they covered punctuation and run-on sentences. Peter felt like he should correct the damned thing and return it to the crazy old man with a grade, red ink and all, but he felt pretty sure that his dad would miss any humor in the gesture and decided to let it go.

Peter looked at the garbage can in the corner of the kitchen, holding the letter tighter still. Verlin had disappeared after he threw the letter down on the table for Peter to read and lit himself a cigarette. Peter assumed he went back to his room to sharpen a knife or load one of his guns for some peace of mind. Peter got a little antsy thinking about the letter, thinking that he and his dad's relationship amounted to the contents of that letter– that the whole thing came down to his dad's fragile ego and shitty pride. That crappy, cheap list of rules. Why couldn't the old man just fucking apologize for being a mean-spirited douche-bag all those years ago? Hell, he had shown his ass the first day of the meeting again, after nearly a small lifetime.

Peter felt angry...and sad...and lost as he dangled out there in space on planet earth, feeling disconnected from his own father and life and everything else.

Verlin would show up out of the smoke and mist and fix his boy, by golly, once and for all. That's all he had to do, Verlin probably figured, as he thought about the outcome long and hard, coming to his solution by some twisted good intention that felt as cheap and fragile to Peter as Chinese plastic ware.

Peter went to the fridge to get a beer. He grabbed an open pack of cigarettes that lay on the table and took everything out to the patio. Peter read the last couple of lines of the letter again. *If you break ANY of the rules, YOU ARE GONE!*

Just like the delusional captain, nudging his unwitting soldiers into the enemy fire– the guy would destroy everything for the sake of his pride. Peter sat looking at the letter when Louise came out to the patio to check upon him. Good cop right on cue.

"Hey," she said, standing over Peter.

"What's goin' on?" Peter kept his eyes on the letter in his hand.

"Just playing *Pixie Quest*," she said, staring out into the yard as if she saw an apparition. "I just need a break. I can't get anywhere today. *The Oodles* keep getting my *Pixie Dust*. They stole my *Chalice of Light*, and now I can't get into the *Booty Room*."

Peter looked up from the letter, a torrent inside but smooth like glassy waters on the surface. He held his eyes on her because she looked like she had something else to say. He didn't want to break her train of thought, so he kept his mouth shut, despite his mounting desire to knock her over the head with the chair he sat in, slapping her back down to planet earth.

As Peter sat quietly waiting for her to speak, to no avail, he realized who she reminded him of. His uncle Lenny's friend, Tobias. Tobias used to smell like oils and spices from fantastic, exotic places, and she wore opulently ornate sequin skirts and vintage corsets and braziers. Her skirts swept the ground like Ms. Pacman's fringe, traveling through her Byzantine maze to eat ghosts and fruit. Tobias never really said much either, like Louise, mostly laughing all the time. More intriguingly yet, Tobias did this thing where she would always say, "Weeeeee," whenever she got excited. As if she were perpetually on a roller-coaster ride. A psychic roller-coaster, man.

"Hey, Tobias," Lenny would say when he and Peter went over to her house to give her a ride to the store. Tobias always needed a ride to the store to get incense or brownie batter, and every time Lenny and Peter walked into the living room, she would invariably say, "Weeeee," at first sight of them – their presence triggering some obscure, buried pleasure-center in her brain. Over and over again, all of her answers were the same until *everyone* had started laughing. A gift, actually, some might say.

No matter the situation, Tobias said, "Weeeee." Death in the family, "Weeeee." Won a new Camaro convertible, "Weeeee." Her pet's severed head, at the hand of a pedophile meth-head, "Weeeee." Peter wanted to take her on a real roller-coaster ride to see what she would say. "Four score and seven years," he imagined her pontificating in the middle of the first gut-twisting barrel roll.

"Your dad loves you, man," Louise said after some time, bringing Peter back to the present moment. She stood next to him as if she had just been issued her body and didn't quite know what to do with it.

Peter looked up at Louise, not wanting to laugh out loud at the absurdity of his life. "Damn...hey...sit down," Peter said after he waited a couple more seconds to see if she had anything more to add.

"Are you okay?"

"Where's my dad?"

"He's getting ready for work. He told me to tell you that he'd be back and that you guys could talk about the letter then."

"He went to work?"

"He works a lot."

"Yeah." Real cops and robbers shit, Peter remembered his old man saying.

Peter relaxed in his chair, resigned to the fact that there wouldn't be any good conversation the rest of the evening. All that Louise could ever talk about was her stupid game and Verlin's intentions. Neither one of them was worth their weight in dirt, as far as Peter was concerned. Peter stared at Louise for a second and then said, "How long have you two been married?"

"Almost twenty years."

"So you got married right after dad kidnaped me?"

"Peter."

"Come on, really? Did you guys ever get charged?"

"Peter."

"Is that all you can say?" He stood up, laughing angrily like he just might lose it, and then he suddenly sat back down. "You let that fucker treat me like a dog. You know that?"

Louise turned and went back inside. Peter stood up, fists clenched at his side, and then sat back down again. He didn't really know what to do with himself, his hands, his body, as he shifted in the lawn chair, feeling like it would crumble any minute, sending him to the ground, through the ground, down into hell below. He ached all over and wanted to break something, to release that Neanderthal urge to be violent.

Louise came back out to the patio with a couple of glasses of iced tea. She handed one to Peter. Peter lit another cigarette and slammed his beer after he put his iced tea between his legs.

"Louise, do you smoke weed?"

"Oh my God," she said, covering her mouth. "Your father would kill me if he knew I had smoked marijuana. He doesn't like drugs."

Peter smiled, holding the letter his father had given him out for Louise to look at. She sat in her chair, mouth covered, as he continued to hold the papers out for her. Peter wanted to fold them up into a little paper hat and put it neatly on her head and then take her inside to put her in the corner so that she could think about how ridiculous she was for living Verlin's lie with him. Her histrionics made Peter want to slap her face, but then he figured that his dad probably did enough of that for the both of them. The old man proved quite proficient in dishing out pain and abuse.

"There, go take a time-out and wait for your master to come home, okay?" Peter imagined himself saying, her wearing her little paper hat, mouth covered in disbelief, as she stood in the corner wondering how she got there, like a toy car with low batteries.

Peter put the letter on his lap for a second and then quickly got up to go back inside to see if the girls were around. Mary stood at the kitchen counter, making herself a sandwich.

"Hey, Mary," Peter said.

"Oh...hello...Pete?" she said, like they had met in passing in some parallel universe light-years ago. Maybe when she still wore diapers.

"That's it," Peter said. "You got it, girl."

"Are you moving in with us?"

"I'm leaving this evening," Peter said, surprising himself as much as his new half-sister. Peter didn't realize how tightly he held the letter in his hand, standing there with Mary, but caught himself nonetheless when he noticed her staring at the shaking papers at his side. He loosened his grip a little too much, and the papers careened to the floor, back and forth, like large, square feathers.

Peter thought about striking up a conversation about Rainbow Brite, and maybe even the Care Bears because he had seen Mary and her sister's posters on the walls in their room. Peter was surprised that Verlin allowed anything to be hung on the walls, just in case the house went up for sale after the girls graduated college. Peter looked at Mary softly, with the compassion that one might bestow on a severely crippled child. He didn't mean to be sentimental, but he felt for the girl. Her *and* her sister. Peter didn't think Mary had ever had anyone gaze upon her with a genuine look of concern because she said, "Are you okay, Pete?"

"Yeah," he said, and then he picked the pages of the letter up off of the floor. "Where's Rachael?"

"She's at gymnastics."

Great...sports. Peter could talk about sports with Mary, perhaps the way into those frigid waters without serious injury.

"Are you a gymnast?"

"Do I look like a gymnast?" Mary said, taking a bite of her plain ham and American cheese sandwich.

"Do you mean, do I think you're short?"

"I know I'm tall, Pete."

"You sure are." Then all of a sudden, Peter got paranoid that his little half-sister might think that he was trying to flirt with her and freak out. He didn't want her to go grab the Glock from under her Strawberry Shortcake pillows. Verlin probably had the girls gun-trained by the time they were potty-trained. Peter imagined Mary sitting on her Little Tykes potty, sippy cup in one hand, a Smith and Wesson .357 in the other. Peter did a double-take to make sure that he was still talking to a young girl. She couldn't have been more than nine or ten, but she made him feel small and insignificant. She had to wield payback somewhere for all of the abuse she had probably already endured.

"Mary, you take care, now. I'm gonna go take a nap, okay?"

She shook her head in the affirmative as Peter took his letter and went to lay on the couch.

Peter forgot that he had already called Perky to pick him up. He had left a message earlier during his payphone frenzy, searching for a ride home from the convenience store, when his dad and Addie had showed up in his big, redneck truck.

Peter opened his eyes to Mary standing over him with a spatula in her hand. "Is it already time for breakfast," he said, still half asleep.

"You've only been asleep for thirty minutes," she said, turning to go back to the kitchen. Peter wondered how long she'd been standing over him with that spatula. She could have injected him with sodium Pentothal for all he knew, preparing him for her sick, silent experiments. She came right back into the living room, just as silently as she had walked out.

"You have a friend here to visit," she said, staring at Peter as if he were some obsolete tool lying around the house.

"Oh, shit," Peter said and jumped up off of the couch. He didn't really think that Louise and Perky needed to spend any time together. They were both sad enough without some further bleak, apocalyptic synergy taking place. Throw Mary in the mix, and a suicide pact would soon be drafted.

"Dad doesn't really like visitors, and he might come home at any time."

"Yeah, well, I'm gonna take a ride, okay?"

Peter fluffed the pillows once more and then went back to the spare room where he had put his bag. He still couldn't figure out why he had to sleep on the couch when they had a spare room in the house, two spare rooms, actually. He got his bag and then went to the spotless bathroom to search through all of the pill bottles that he had seen earlier. Some antibiotics, no thanks. Some non-codeine cough syrup, a waste of time. Some glycerin pills, pointless. And then, yes...some Vicodin. That would do. Peter put all of the other bottles back into the cabinet and opened the large bottle of pain pills. He took a small handful and then tapped a few more into his palm when he realized that he probably wouldn't go back to visit for a while. "What the hell," he said to himself and took the whole bottle. He noticed a bottle of Demerol that he had missed and grabbed that too. It was full. Peter turned around and noticed Mary standing in the doorway.

"Gotta headache."

"Your friend is in the living room," she said and then paddled back down to the kitchen.

Peter left the bathroom and went to Louise's computer room to say goodbye. She sat in her straight-back chair, typing away on the keyboard. The screen looked no more complex than Asteroids did on his Atari as a kid. Two-dimensional, green lines and dots, up against the black abyss of the computer screen. Louise floated in her chair, engrossed in her game, so Peter decided to make it quick.

"Louise, tell dad that I said goodbye, okay?"

"Does he know you're leaving?"

Peter thought about telling her yes but then told her the truth. She eked out a smile and stood up from her chair. Peter bent to give her a hug, looking over her shoulder. The black screen with the tiny two-dimensional stick figures buzzing behind her, calling her into its world.

As he patiently stood there hugging his step-mom, who he didn't really know, Peter thought that he had never felt an emptier, less electrical embrace in his life. He wanted to push her away, to get her invisible soul ties off and out of himself, so that he could be free of all the disease again, but then realized that the hug would probably be the most affection she ever got for the rest of her life, except Rachael maybe, and he continued to hold on, squeezing a little harder yet to conclude their farewell.

"Alright. You take care, now. You hear, hon?" she said and turned back to her computer screen, sitting down as if her time in the real world had expired.

Peter walked out into the living room, where Perky and Mary sat across from each other in matching chairs. He wanted to get a picture but dreaded the whole ordeal of trying to find a camera and waiting and all of that, so he grabbed Perky's hand and headed for the front door.

"Good to meet you, Mary," Perky said, and they were gone.

Once they got outside, Peter told Perky to get lost. He had picked up the keys to his dad's truck when he noticed them on the counter. He decided that he would get his old truck one way or the other.

"Why did I come and get you?" she said.

"Here," Peter said, tossing her the two bottles of pills. "Go have some fun, will ya?"

Perky looked at the bottles and smiled. "Thanks."

Chapter 25

Sewell and Peter got back to the barn after dark. Sewell had to go to the house to turn the outdoor lights on so that they could see what they were doing, putting saddles and blankets and bridles away. He came back outside, handing Peter a tall glass of lemonade.

"I 'bout got into trouble with the old lady," Sewell said. Peter thought that it was funny that a man Sewell's age could actually get into trouble too. Peter knew all about getting into trouble. Peter patted Sewell on the lower back, as high up as he could reach. If the boy could have articulated the fact that he felt a bond with Sewell through their collective mischief, he would have.

Peter helped Sewell unbuckle the belly straps holding the saddles on. Sewell heaved both of the saddles off, one by one, then the blankets, and then hung them all back on the wall next to the others. The loose end of the bridle reins stayed tied to the barn door so that the horses wouldn't wander off. Sewell got two brushes from the workbench and handed one over to Peter.

"Just like this, Peter." Sewell showed Peter how to make long, firm strokes with the brush. "You brush as high as you can go, and I'll get the rest. Sound good?"

Peter shook his head and got to work.

"Start high and brush down, just like this." Sewell demonstrated again how to stroke the shiny horses' coats.

They both brushed with smooth, intentional movements, Sewell high and Peter low, as the ponies stood there relishing their post-ride grooming, like a couple of equine royalty. Peter looked over at Sewell, who brushed the damp hair where the saddle had been. Peter started brushing the damp hair where the belly strap had been attached. The wet hair smoothed out like wet sand. Peter looked lost in his meditation, in the simplicity of it all, back and forth, chest, legs and belly with that course brush.

Sewell went to the workbench and grabbed another brush, a coarser, longer bristled brush, and began brushing the mane and tail of the surly Arabian. The horse snorted and whinnied, shaking its head and long neck as it hooved at the dirt near the barn door. That stud could've gone on two more rides for the same duration, at twice the intensity.

"You sure are a good helper," Sewell said, "how long you plan on stayin' here in Mississippi?"

"I don't know." Peter handed his brush to Sewell when he had gotten all of the horses that he could reach. Sewell pointed over to the workbench where the brushes went. Peter walked over and put his brush with the others. He opened a drawer, pulled out a pair of hoof trimmers, looked at them as if they were some Medieval torture device, and then put them back in the drawer. He perused all of the tools and hammers and gadgets that hung above the workbench. Some of the tools were neat and orderly, while there was that smattering of bits and pieces that lay spread randomly over the workbench, just like grandpa's garage back home. Peter started to feel homesick all of a sudden.

Sewell watched the boy taking his silent inventory. But for a moment, all of his tools took on newness and novelty, as he now saw the collection through the curiosity and wonder of the young man's careful eyes. Tools that had become simply extensions of the older man's hands themselves had momentarily become things to be discovered, explored for the first time.

"I sure like havin' you out here, Peter."

Peter smiled at Sewell, feeling good about his usefulness. Everyone wants to be useful at some point in their life – even if they are boys.

Peter imagined that he had talked to his mom earlier in the day after eating pie. She said that she and uncle Lenny were coming to get him, that he should just sit tight, and that everything would be okay. She asked Peter if he was having fun, and he told her that he really liked Pinkie and Sewell. She asked about Verlin, and Peter told her that he was fine too. She didn't ask too many questions, but Peter imagined that she would have cried on the other end of the phone, her missing him, her wanting to be there with him as soon as humanly possible. He thought that perhaps she should have come on vacation with them if she were going to be so sad. She shouldn't have gone back home without saying goodbye to Peter and his dad. Adults were weird like that, though. They didn't make any sense sometimes.

"Come on, Pete. Let's get this show on the road. Pinkie's gonna kill us if we don't get our tails inside soon."

Sewell and Peter led the horses back out to the pasture and closed the gate behind them. Sewell reached over the fence and took both bridles off, and handed one to Peter. "Go on and hang yours up, Pete," Sewell said, turning to go back up to the barn.

Peter ran ahead of Sewell and went straight to the empty hook next to the blankets and saddles, tossing his looped bridle up and onto the curved end of the hook that stuck out of the wall. "Good job, cowboy!" Sewell came up from behind Peter and hung his bridle on the hook next to Peter's. "You gonna be a horseman, after all, I tell ya."

Once they were back inside the house and Sewell turned off the outside lights, Peter asked if he could have another piece of the pie. Pinkie cut him a bigger piece than she had the first time. Grammie would have never let him eat pie that late in the evening, not to mention after he had already had a piece earlier in the day. Peter, Pinkie and Sewell sat around the table, not saying a word for several minutes, Peter and Sewell eating their pie, Pinkie doodling on a napkin with a Magic Marker.

When Peter and Sewell finished, Pinkie got up and took their plates and put them in the sink. She went to the living room and turned on the television. Peter heard a man's voice coming from the living room.

"Hon, you're gonna make yourself sick," Pinkie said, looking at Peter's plate as she returned to the kitchen. "The news is on."

Sewell bugged his eyes out at Pinkie. "We need to get him washed up," Sewell said after an awkward moment of silence.

Sewell walked Peter down to the bathroom and got a washcloth from under the sink. He wet the cloth and methodically wiped Peter's face and hands with it, rinsed the cloth and did it again. "There, buddy. You could'a grown potatoes outta them ears." Peter could see little new potatoes poking their way out of his ears, and then he thought of Mr. Potato Head, him and his big nose, eyes missing from being tossed around the house one too many times. "That'll hold you over until I can get your bath water run, okay?"

Peter was anxious to get out to the living room to see the evening news. He didn't get to stay up that late too often and felt excited like a teen standing outside his first rock concert might.

"Okay. Go out there and watch TV for a minute while I run your bath," Sewell said.

Peter walked into the living room, where Pinkie sat in her favorite recliner. Peter walked over to her as she put out her hand for him to hold. He sat down next to her chair on the carpet, still holding her hand. A guy in a really cheap suit shouted from the screen, telling all of his viewers to buy a car at his dealership because they had the lowest prices in Mississippi. The annoying guy went away, and the evening news came back on.

The top story was a continuation of the same story that Peter had been following his whole vacation, about the abducted young girl, Ramona Whitcanuck. She had been missing for months now, according to the newsman's account. The last known location was Akron, Ohio. The authorities said that one of the two suspects in the case had received money from a Western Union in Akron. The girl may or may not be in the custody of the man in question. Peter stared at the television, his face awash with kinetic blue hues. The award in the case had been raised from twenty thousand dollars to one-hundred and twenty thousand dollars. The girl's family's church, with the help of concerned family and friends, had raised the money for the ransom. Any information leading to the arrest of the perpetrator, and the safe recovery of the girl, would be rewarded by the sum in total.

"That's horrible, hon," Pinkie said.

"Her mom probably misses her, don't you think?" Peter said.

"She's dyin', I'm sure."

Peter thought about how much he missed his mom, how she had cried when he imagined that he had talked to her on the phone. He looked up to see Pinkie staring at him as if he were wounded.

"Come on, buddy," Sewell said, walking into the living room. Peter got up from beside Pinkie and gave her a quick kiss on the cheek. She smiled at him and blew him a kiss as he walked out of the room with Sewell.

Sewell closed the door behind Peter once he was in the bathroom.

"Holler, if ya need me, okay?"

"Yes, sir."

Peter undressed, putting his clothes over in the corner in a neat little pile, and then he slowly slipped into the hot bathwater.

Peter splashed in the bath for a little while, and then he drained some water out of the tub and turned on the hot water to fill it again nearly to the top. He lay back in hot water, staring at the ceiling, thinking about Ramona Whitcanuck. She had traveled across the country, probably with some dirty, old man that snatched her off the street on her way home from the park. Peter didn't really know about sex but would have shuddered at the idea of how that could play a part in a kidnaper's intent. Peter wondered if she was having fun, if she was happy, or if she had been hurt. He wanted to meet Ramona Whitcanuck and maybe tell her that his summer wasn't going all that hot either. There was Sewell and Pinkie, but he always had to go back to his dad's house at some point, and you never knew what would happen in that place.

Peter held his breath, pinched his nose off, and put his head under the water. He counted as high as he could before he came back up for air.

He heard Sewell's voice outside the door.

"What?" Peter shouted with ears full of water.

"Come on, buddy. Go ahead and finish up, okay? Let's get you to bed," Sewell said through the door.

Peter splashed a little water over his chest and neck. "You can come in," he said.

Sewell went into the bathroom, handing Peter an old flannel shirt for him to wear like a gown. "Pinkie's gonna wash your stuff for you, okay?"

"Thank you."

Peter got out of the tub, pulling the drain plug up. Sewell helped Peter get dried off and then led him down the hall to the spare room. Pinkie and Sewell had fixed him up in a nice room with a Queen-sized bed and a little TV. Sewell sat on the edge of the bed and asked him what he wanted to read before he turned the lights out. Peter pointed at the Richard Scarry book sitting on top of the bookcase. He knew where the book was because Sewell had read the same book to him last time. Peter liked the portly little characters in the Scarry books. Their expressions were bright and curious, almost mystically contemplative in their combined innocent mischief. The cars and buildings were puffy too. Peter liked the fire trucks and race cars, the speed boats and airplanes.

Peter lay there meditating on Sewell's comforting voice and earthy-sweet smell, forever reminding him of grandpa back home. The low rumble of the air-conditioner and the turning of pages harmonized with Sewell's voice as Peter drifted slowly off to sleep.

That night, the little devil up in the corner of his room didn't come to visit. Instead of the demon and his taunting, Peter dreamt that he sat in a stadium munching popcorn and Milk-Duds with his mom. They basked in the bright stadium lights at an evening baseball game, yelling at the batter to hurry up and hit the ball in between mouths full of junk food. Peter couldn't tell who was playing, but it could've been the Kansas City Royals, seeing how he had been to their ballpark before. The place seemed familiar in the way things seem familiar only in dreams, a slight resemblance to somewhere you've been in the past, but misplaced, in another time perhaps, or altogether twisted into some queer melange from an alternate universe.

Everyone shouted at the batter to do something, to hit the ball. The crowd got louder each time the batter scratched to get his footing, stepping out of the batter's box, stalling the pitcher as he held out his hand toward the mound. Not only were Peter, his mom and all the people in the stands yelling at the guy, but all of his teammates were yelling too. The guys in the dugout clung to the fence like crazed chimpanzees, seething to bust out and charge the plate to get themselves some monkey meat. The whole stadium, in fact, echoed with cheer, as if that one hit dictated the fate of the universe, right then and there, batter at home plate, scratching like a kid in new sneakers. Peter thought that the opposite team shouting at the batter to hit the ball was kind of weird, too – all of the players in position on the playing field, rooting for the guy at the plate.

Peter began jumping up and down in his seat, sweaty with excitement, as the outfield got louder still. The crowd, the players, the coaches. Then, all of a sudden, like a minor, dissonant note resonating throughout a quiet room, the game spontaneously turned hostile. The whole ballpark turned bad. No more fun and games.

It all started with one guy who decided it would be a good idea to smash his ballpark frank into another guy's face. The victim had a delayed reaction to the assault, wiping his face clear of smashed meat and smeared mustard, looking at his hands, and taking a deep, shaky breath. The guy with hotdog and condiment all over his face then commenced tossing the offender over the seats in front of where they were standing, sending the guy tumbling down several rows and crashing into some other folks. Those in the falling guy's path didn't really appreciate getting trod upon and thus got up and started making their case known to the others around them as they groped to get up to the man who had thrown the other down on them. A punch here, a little biting and scratching there, and the next thing you know, fights were breaking out all over the park in little pockets, spreading quickly to form one large mass of madness, people pouring their beers on the people in front of them, and kids kicking old ladies in the shins. A downright ugly affair, to say the least.

The announcers even got nasty in what they said, too, talking about "scumbag" this and "worthless shithead" that, the batter still down on the field, looking around himself like a deaf kid at a tremendous fireworks display, wondering if he were somehow responsible, or if he should do something at least.

Out of the blue, the stadium fell silent, with remnant echoes resonating to utter stillness. Peter looked around at the seeming still life of the whole place, feeling really out of place now, and he took a deep breath to get his bearings. He felt the weight of a stare on his right side and looked over to see a crazy fan running right toward him like he had anything to do with anything. A crazy woman. The hysterical woman got right upon him, and then she started throwing money at Peter, screaming at him to shut up, to just shut the hell up, by God!

Peter stood speechless, he and the batter down on the field holding his bat, watching the frozen crowd surround them like water, closing in, and that lady throwing money at Peter, screaming insanities, as if the end of the world had surely come.

Peter's mom was nowhere to be found in the midst of the chaos, and so he started to cry. The crazy lady saw him crying and then started yelling, "I hate you! You don't understand!" over and over, in slow motion, louder still with each blurt from her frothy mouth, until the umpire finally came up from behind the batter, from all the way down on the field and up into the stands, and grabbed the disgruntled woman, wrestling her to the seats below, as they finally ended up on the concrete at the edge of the baseball diamond, smashed together like that hotdog had been smashed in the unwitting fan's face.

Peter could see the lady's eyes down below; the umpire passed out underneath her. He tried with all his might to not look her into those eyes, but that hideous glare simply rendered him impotent, and he just had to give in. Those black eyes, drowning him, his life draining out of him, slowly, and then, just like that, Peter quickly sat up in bed, sweat thick around the collar of the flannel shirt that Sewell had given him.

Peter could still hear the shouting. For a second, he thought that he had somehow ended up back at his dad's house because he could hear Louise yelling in the other room, "I hate you...shut up...you don't understand!" which was scary in and of itself, because he had never heard her yell at his dad like that before. Peter imagined the old man riddling her with bullet holes once she had her histrionic say, shutting the bitch up for good.

The door burst open, light flooding into the room like an obnoxious visitor, and Louise cut through the glare and straddled Peter before he could get out from under the covers. His first instinct was to thrash about, to kick and scream, hoping that he could jar her off of himself and send her to the floor. She was just too heavy. He looked over to the doorway, waiting for his dad to come through with a gun or a bat or a knife to get her off of Peter, killing the lady all over again. Sewell and Pinkie appeared in the old man's place instead.

Still struggling to catch his breath, Peter continued to push Louise, trying to get her off. He felt safer knowing that Sewell and Pinkie were nearby, but that didn't change the fact that his lungs were crushed under the weight of his dad's crazy girlfriend.

"Pinkie," Peter tried to yell as Sewell went over to the bedside slowly like he wanted to see what would happen before he leant a hand. Peter stared at Sewell with expectant, scared eyes, wanting him to swoop down on the situation and take charge. Peter didn't want to not trust Sewell and Pinkie, but he did feel a little betrayed by the fact that Sewell just stood by while Louise went ballistic.

"She isn't gonna save you, little fucker!" Louise shouted. "You guys ain't..." and then Sewell slapped Louise's face like he had that surly Arabian's ass out there in the pasture.

"Mama!" Louise yelled, a writhing mess on the floor next to the bed, screaming and thrashing like a cat on fire.

"Louise, calm down; that boy's not goin' nowhere with you," Sewell said. "You better go on and clean up. I'll tell your boyfriend that you won't be home tonight. You hear?"

"I hate you guys!" Louise shouted and stormed out of the room like a young, spoiled child."Go on, now," Pinkie said, seemingly not too impressed with Louise's display. "Pete's had enough for tonight."

It made Peter feel scared and bad and confused all at the same time that the three of them talked about him like he wasn't even in the room. He sat on the bed perfectly still, waiting for his dad to come into the room and open fire with his Army issue.45, no questions asked. Peter covered himself with the blankets, just knowing that they would all soon be dead, bullet holes and torn flesh, as the blood and breath of life dissipated like mist in a fierce gust. "God, help us, please," Peter said to himself in a whisper.

Peter's prayers had gotten very concise, very to the point, on that vacation. He didn't know what else to do when in the face of such paralyzing fear like that. He just wanted the quiet, the calm of Pinkie and Sewell's house, or even his grandparents' house back home. The quiet came and went. Only the nightmares lasted, and that's exactly what lay in wait as Peter eventually drifted back off to sleep, after all of the madness had momentarily subsided, after his *second* Richard Scarry session of the night had ended.

There he sat, sure as the sun rising, as Peter slipped into that world where dreams live full time.

Peter's little demon seemed, for all intent and purpose, a harmless little figure, like a creature from a Disney cartoon, yet he had the uncanny ability to emotionally drain his subject like hours of water-boarding might. The monster's mocking smirk and malicious glare didn't help his overall unpleasant disposition, either. Peter opened his eyes as if just awakening, and there he sat Indian-style, up in the corner of the room, waiting, sneering.

"Boy, you really did it, didn't you?"

"Go away!" Peter shouted, hoping that it would awaken Sewell and Louise.

"There's nobody to help you, little shit," he said. "Now you're a little fucker, too. Mommy didn't seem to be too happy with Petey, did she? She didn't even answer the phone, ya shithead."

Peter didn't want to say anything because he knew that the demon, appropriately named Meany by Peter, would simply turn his words on him like a vicious whip gone awry. Peter couldn't move his body, only able to sit in bed staring up at the creature in the corner. His "flesh" turns from brown to red and red to brown again. The tormenter. The accuser. This creature's mission was to drive Peter stark-raving mad, it seemed. Peter had to take the beating, as his uncle Lenny used to say, the elder's reference to dealing with unpleasant situations.

Peter told the monster to go away and to leave him alone, which only gave the creature the desire to ridicule and torment Peter even more aggressively. Peter had come to the point of no reprieve, neither in life nor dreams and wanted to peel his skin off right there and die. He lived in a state of consistent, sporadic fear, knowing that anything good would soon turn for the worst wouldn't last. If he woke up, he would just be in the midst of his pointless life again. If he fell asleep, he would have to contend with Meany and his torment and ridicule. Peter began crying again, a bad choice in Meany's company. Meany had a way of kicking a man when he was already down and bleeding.

"What's wrong, little buddy?"

"Go to hell!" Peter said, with what little force he could muster, his throat sore and weak. The room seemed to absorb any sound that came out of Peter's mouth, channeling it to some random dimension where only the bones of the dead might have jangled in response. Peter had the urge to bolt out of the room and run away from everything but instantly knew the attempt would be futile, given the opportunity.

Peter had tried to push the bedcovers off of himself with all of the strength that he could summon, yet couldn't even budge the light blanket and sheet to save his life. He could feel everything around him, sure, but he had no power to push or pull, lift or move. He could feel life in his limbs and muscles but not enough energy to put them into motion. Paralyzed but fully feeling. Like trying to run but not being able to move in dreams.

"Are you ready to die? Huh? Don't you think you've caused enough pain for your father and mother? Not to mention your dear old grammie and grandpa back home? They don't want your sniveling little ass, you know? You drain everyone around you with your stupid, incessant questions. Are you retarded, little shit? Huh? Is that why you ask so many questions? Huh? Do you like that? Huh? Are you gonna cry? Huh? Come on, little shit. I can see you're mad. Do something! Are you mad? Huh? Pussy! Huh? Huh? Come on, do something, you powerless little waste of breath! What's wrong, pussy? Huh?"

Meany's crescendo left Peter twisted further into a powerless lump on the bed,

broken. He cried even more than before, knowing there would be no escape. Peter closed his eyes.

"Open up and look at me," Meany said. "Come on, you know I'm your only friend. You can do it. Come on, little shit. Come on, buddy. Boy, son…little fucker…Hey!"

"Jesus!" Peter shouted all of a sudden, and the dream ended. He lay awake in Sewell and Pinkie's spare room, breathless as if he had just run across the whole state of Mississippi by himself in the wet heat of summer.

Sewell had left a nightlight on for Peter near the dresser so that he could see in case he had to get up and go to the bathroom. Pinkie told him to get some rest and that he would spend the night again. Peter was very happy about that. On the other hand, however, he knew that he would have to leave soon and that he would have to go back to his dad and Louise's to stay. The thought made him nauseous and restless, and tired all over again.

Peter had yelled at Jesus. Those short prayers had become shorter yet. He could have said "help," one syllable less, even more concise, but wasn't too sure that that would have worked quite as well. Peter thought that it must have been something about the name of Jesus that ended the torment. No, he told himself. Well, maybe. Only in your head, he thought. At that point, Peter didn't know why it really mattered. The dream had ended with one word, like a brief mantra plopping him down into another dimension, into greener pastures, so to speak.

Peter sat up in the bed and looked at the doorway. Meany wasn't above the door anymore. He had moved from corner to corner the last few times that he had come to visit, but he seemed most comfortable by the door. In case he had to leave quickly, Peter thought.

Peter sat up in bed saying, "Our Father," not knowing what else to do. He thought that if he could keep his mind off of his dad and Meany that he could have some rest in his head for a little while longer because, honestly, he thought that either his head or heart would burst from all of the internal pressure he had been feeling lately. He didn't know if a five-year-old was supposed to feel like that or not. He imagined it must have been how old men in stressful jobs with spoiled children must have felt. Peter felt old.

Peter looked sick; someone had said at the store the other day. Peter overheard Pinkie and her friend talking when the lady looked over at Peter, and he heard the word "sick" in there somewhere, the dire look of concern on the old busy-body's face. Pinkie told him to not mind that old curmudgeon, a funny word he remembered thinking, and that she was always talking about someone being sick or dying or something. *His-tri-on-ic* is what she called the lady. Peter imagined the old lady in front of a class teaching about the Civil War, telling stories of bloody soldiers in battle, like those guys that helped him and his dad on the side of the road in Vicksburg.

Peter spun on his butt, surprised by the regained ability to move his body wherever he chose. He put his feet on the floor and contemplated going out into the hall and down to the bathroom. He hoped that Louise wasn't around, that she was somewhere where he didn't have to see her. "You little fucker!" she had said.

Peter's only hope was Sewell and Pinkie, and he had to stay there until his mom came and got him. They said that they had talked to her. Maybe they could take him home if his mom and grandparents even wanted him anymore. Many had said that they didn't want Peter, that he only caused problems. No, it wasn't true. Or was it? Things were getting too difficult for Peter to sort out, to deal with. He almost felt like he was in the dream again, rendered powerless to move, powerless to make any decisions, if only for a second.

"Hey there," Pinkie said, opening the door, him sitting on the edge of the bed. "Where's Simone?"

Pinkie went over and sat down next to Peter. She stroked his moist hair and kissed him on the forehead, just like Grammie used to do. The pressure lifted right out of his head and chest, as she stroked him lightly. Peter started crying.

"Louise took her home."

Peter looked up from his lap, startled.

"She'll be okay, sugar, okay?" she said. "You're sweatin' bad, hon. Did you have a bad dream?"

Peter said yes, as she pulled his head into her chest. Her fresh smell and strong arms folded around him gently, filling him up with peace like cool water. Peter's cries turned to sobs, and so Pinkie just held him tighter still. He wanted to tell her about Meany, but the demon said that he would skin Peter alive and feed him to ravenous dogs if he ever told anyone about their "friendship." Peter didn't think being skinned alive would feel too good and decided to keep quiet. He thought he had figured out a way to end his relationship with Meany anyway, to end the dreams as soon as they came.

"I talked to your mom again," Pinkie said. "She can't talk to you right now, but she wants you to know that she loves you very much, and she's gonna see you soon, okay?"

Peter said okay. He couldn't imagine why in the world she couldn't talk to him right then. He thought that maybe his dad was right, that his mom didn't want to talk to him, and that his life with his dad was as good as it would ever get. Peter started feeling a sour stomach again, thinking about everything. Why did he have to make his dad so mad all the time? Peter had to learn to be a better son to his father if they were going to make it.

"Hey there, buddy," Sewell said, coming into the bedroom, sitting down on the bed's edge next to Peter and Pinkie. "You up for some more Richard Scarry?"

Peter didn't really feel like Richard Scarry, he said. He looked down at the floor, holding his eyes there, as Sewell and Pinkie sat by him, lightly tracing their fingers on his back.

"You okay, buddy?"

Peter felt sad inside because he knew that he would have to leave again soon, his dad with more lessons, Louise there in the wings waiting for her orders. "Yeah," Peter finally said. Sewell and Pinkie continued to caress Peter until his eyes got heavy again, and he lay back on the bed, having cooled off a little. Sewell got up and left the room. Pinkie sang *Let Me Call You Sweetheart* to Peter, over and over, until he fell asleep again. This time deeply and without nightmares.

The next morning Peter woke up with his dad standing over him, the dim light casting faint shadows on the carpet below. The demon hadn't come to visit Peter in his sleep. Then, all of a sudden, there he was, standing over Peter in a different form altogether, nudging Peter's warm feet under the blanket with the end of his shoe. Peter tried to fake-sleep his way through Verlin rustling him awake, nudging him, but the old man proved persistent, mechanically tapping at the arch of Peter's blanketed foot with his Nike.

"Get up, boy," Verlin said. "We gotta go."

Peter imagined that he was a monster himself, an unstoppable oaf of a beast, savagely running over his dad with no feeling or hesitation, never looking back. The anger Peter felt almost convinced him that he could physically take his father on for the first time. That he could actually resist Verlin by force, knocking the old man over the head with the nearest blunt, heavy object, and that victory over the matter would finally be his, leaving him to stay with Sewell and Pinkie forever if he so chose – or go back to Oklahoma.

Deep down inside, Peter really knew that his mom probably wouldn't make it down to Mississippi. She had finally gotten rid of him, and why would she come all the way to get someone she had so laboriously had to work to get rid of.

"Come on, boy. We ain't got all day."

Simone jumped on the bed and started licking Peter's face. He pushed her down to the floor, trying to get the stench of her oily fur away from his nostrils. Pinkie said Simone had rustled up a skunk and got doused from head to toe while Peter and Sewell were out riding horses. The smell was so strong that it almost smelled good, like the confusion between hot and cold water when you first turn the faucet on and quickly put your hand under the stream, like gasoline smells good. Simone barked at Peter and jumped back on the bed, ready to play. Peter asked Verlin if she was coming too.

"You think we'd leave your good old dog here, boy?"

Sewell came into the bedroom and turned on the ceiling light. Verlin stuck a smile onto his face and said, "Thanks for watching Pete, Sewell. We needed some time to get things straightened out."

"I hope you figured out a thing or two. Pinkie and I are gettin' tired of seein' our little girl with marks on her face. Do you hear? That boy's a good boy, too." He went over and patted Peter's arm, standing between him and Verlin. Peter didn't like the way that they looked at each other. He didn't want his dad to do anything mean to Sewell but then figured that Sewell could take care of himself just fine. He had a way of letting someone talk themselves silly while he patiently waited with that sober look on his face that said, "Hello, nice to meet you, don't fuck with me, or you'll get smacked."

"Let's go, boy," Verlin said, breaking eye contact with Sewell and turning to Peter. "We'll see you later, Sewell...come on, get your dog, son."

Peter snatched Simone off of the floor, holding his breath, as she wriggled like a big, hairy night-crawler.

The ride back to the house seemed a lot longer than the previous trips between Verlin's house and Pinkie's. Peter couldn't stop thinking about Pinkie crying as he and his dad left the living room of the big, cozy country house. She told Verlin to bring Peter back whenever he wanted. She didn't ask any harsh questions or try to set Verlin straight; she just hugged Peter and granted a weak smile to his dad. She seemed to have a tough acceptance toward things running their course. Peter felt worried and comforted at the same time about that, not really knowing where the whole thing with his dad would end up. Peter left Sewell and Pinkie behind out of trust, hoping that he would get to go back to their house. He didn't really understand why he couldn't just stay there until his mom came to get him. Verlin and Louise were always busy, and the three of them never did anything fun together, anyway.

Verlin dug around in between the seats of the van, found the transistor radio and turned it on. In between boring, old songs, the newsman announced that the missing girl's body had been found. Peter leaned down toward the speaker to hear the story a little better.

The authorities in Birmingham were thrown at first, having found a little boy, after searching virtually from coast to coast for a young girl. Nevertheless, they soon realized that the little boy was actually a little girl with a shaved head and boy's clothes on. The kidnapper had disguised her as a boy and had probably made it a little further because of the fact. Her crumpled baseball cap was found in the floorboard of a stolen Chevy pick-up that turned up in a ditch at the edge of Birmingham. Peter wondered if Birmingham was next to Akron because the night before, the newsman said the kidnapper had last been thought to be in Akron, Ohio.

In and around the stolen Chevy pick-up that the authorities found outside of town, there was no sign of the kidnapper, no foreign fingerprints, no telling fibres or hair, only the little baseball cap with the young girl's blood on it lying in the midst of trash and dust scattered about the cab. Ramona Whitcanuck's body had turned up in clothes drier at Willie Joe's Laundro-Mat in Birmingham. The police had no leads, not even a sniff, and they had said that they were counting on the ears and eyes of the good people of Birmingham for anything tangible so that they could bring the kidnapper to justice.

Peter had never seen a dead person before. The boys down the street from Grammie's house had killed Mr. Thompson's cat and cut its eyes out, but that was a cat. He remembers getting sick and scared and sad all at the same time. Seeing that shell of a creature lying prostrate in the gutter as those malevolent little tykes went to work on the neighbor's cat.

Thinking of the dead girl's body only made Peter feel sick too, and he wondered why in the world someone would want to harm a little girl and kill her, having to hide for the rest of their life. Adults made less sense to him each day. They seemed to do messed up things because they were too afraid to ask someone how to do the right thing, like an old man refusing to pull over to ask for directions to his destination, except a lot worse, he thought. Maybe most people just had dads like his. Verlin didn't like questions, and Peter had begun to learn it was just easier not to ask any.

Chapter 26

Peter and Fr. Ligero pulled into Pony Town and went to the only place Peter knew other than the Silver Stallion and his dad's house, although he didn't think that he could find his dad's house on a bet.

Fr. Ligero pulled the car up to the curb out front and put it in park. He left the engine running to keep the air conditioner on, keeping the sweat at bay for the time being. Peter looked out the passenger-side window, noticing the same ridiculous sign standing out front, weathered by the years, in disrepair, and faded like a pair of old jeans: Tote and Chug, it read. As good a name as any for a convenience store, Peter thought. The same convenience store that he had walked to after leaving that chick's house, the one whose name he couldn't remember the morning after they had slept together. Addie's niece.

Peter couldn't tell if the place was even open. It looked as desolate inside as it did outside, from what he could tell, trying to discern the slightest movement through the dingy glass. Grass grew out of the cracks of the ashy, oil-stained black top parking lot, the black BMW the only thing in the near vicinity that appeared useful and in working condition. Everything looked worn thin and abandoned.

"Are you going inside, Peter?"

"No life here."

"Did you know someone who worked here?"

Peter kept staring out the window and then said, "I came here to use the payphone after a one-night stand with a bartender and her roommate. I came here the day I got arrested."

Peter felt as if he were just awakening out of a dream. He knew that he had been there before, yet he felt that maybe he hadn't, as if he had been inhabited by some other person or some other thing, some ancient manifestation, or perhaps that he had simply mentally strung together a grab-bag of non-sequitur impressions from his adolescence or childhood altogether, and had just come to the first place where they could park the car and stretch their legs, waste a little time before having to face his dad.

Peter started to get nervous about meeting up with the old man. He felt a mix of melancholy and edginess and light-headedness. He realized that he could simply leave that place and go somewhere else, maybe revisit the opportunity to reunite with his dad at a later time. The warming, dusty gusts of wind rocked the car like a small boat in the water. Peter felt safe inside the car.

"Did I ever tell you why my dad was able to keep me for so long?"

"Something about the courts?"

"The court in Mississippi didn't recognize the interstate-kidnapping charges."

"How did your mom get you back?"

"Her and my uncle Lenny kidnapped me back."

Peter rolled down the window to check the temperature outside. Most of the clouds from earlier in the morning had cleared. He rolled the window back up against the encroaching rising heat.

"I guess they had told my mom that she could have an hour of unsupervised time with me and then reneged…twice before…when my mom had gone all the way out to Mississippi to see me."

Fr. Ligero watched Peter intently.

"I guess my mom finally worked something out on the sly with Louise's parents...Pinkie, I think her name was. And I can't even remember the old man's name. They were good people."

"You've mentioned them before."

"Sewell. That's it. Sewell. That was Louise's dad's name."

"They were instrumental in getting you back home, right?"

"Yeah. I think they pretty much saved my ass. I really thought that I was dead."

"Did they take you to your mom?"

"I didn't even know what was going on," Peter said. "I was at the parade, watching the floats, up on my tip-toes one second, and then the next moment, Louise's dad, Sewell, was swooping me up and carrying me down the sidewalk a couple of steps faster than the parade itself had been moving along."

"Do you remember the occasion for the parade?"

"The parade had been held in honor of this preacher that my dad hated...Roland..."

"Stacks?" Fr. Ligero said.

"Yes, sir. That's it."

"He was a pretty big voice of the Protestant church in the seventies. He laid some serious groundwork for healing prayer and inner-city outreach. He's got quite the legacy. Forgotten for the most part by society-at-large, but quite the legacy, nonetheless."

"My mom and uncle had set up a meeting point, had planned for Louise's parents to get me and bring me to the rendezvous, at which time I would then go back to Oklahoma with them."

The two men sat in the cool, leather seats of the air-conditioned car, looking out at the gusts of wind bending the tall weeds from the cracks in the parking lot, meditative amongst the silent motion outside the vehicle.

They both jumped, almost banging heads when a lady loudly tapped on the passenger-side window with her fist full of cheap rings. They hadn't heard or felt her nearing the car, and then, just like that, like an apparition in the fog, she popped into sight, rapping the window with all of that gaudy carnival jewelry like some lost swap-meet vendor in the whipping wind. She looked like she had been up for a few weeks shooting up crank in a dingy trailer somewhere. Her aquamarine eyeshadow smeared up around her eyes, clumps of black mascara in her scraggly, fake lashes. Peter caught himself staring into those bottomless, spastic eyes, Manson Family eyes, like death had come to snatch him up for good. The woman's eyes had no iris showing, her dilated pupils, black discs spilling out from the abyss. Peter wanted to roll the window down a crack and throw a five at her and tell her to go eat something, but he pulled himself together instead and put down the window to see if she was okay.

"You lost?!" she said as if he and his friend were across the parking lot. His hair stiffly blew over her face and then back again.

"Not really," Peter said. He wanted to roll the window right back up into her face but kept his eyes on her, window down. The dribble around her mouth had turned a crusty white, flaking onto her dingy little breast-exposing blouse. She started rubbing her breasts right there in front of Peter, licking her nasty mouth with her swollen tongue.

"You smoke crack?" she said.

Peter wanted to say, "Hey, crazy bitch, do I look like I smoke crack?" but all he could muster was, "no, ma'am, I'm sorry."

"Don't be sorry, mister," she said, "crack ain't no good no how."

"Would you like something to eat?" Fr. Ligero leaned over Peter to say, making eye contact with the lady. He had the uncanny ability to see through someone's off-putting exterior and right into their heart, to see that they were just another human in need of love. Thank God for that, Peter thought. The man had come to visit him when nobody else would, so many years ago.

The woman smiled the most forced, awkward smile that Peter had ever seen, as if she had some archaic painful machinery pulling up at the corners of her mouth when he realized who the woman was. He hadn't seen this person but once in his lifetime, yet he could not have forgotten that smile, no matter how contorted and tortured it might have become. Addie's niece stood there, in a detached expectancy…shaking a little bit and bobbing her head to an inaudible beat, as Peter took in the moment that had just become an expanse of twenty years, an ocean of time, speechless.

"No, thank you, sir," she said after she and Peter had finished their chance encounter outside of time. The wind continued rocking the car, blowing the lady's dry, fragile hair like trampled straw.

Peter still couldn't remember her name, thinking that her life had taken a turn for the worst since the last time he had seen her. She had been very strong and sexy back then. Having sex with the customers without having ever met them before didn't seem that bad compared to what the woman had become. But then again, she had spent all of those years outside of prison bars, free to do what she chose with her life.

Peter felt overcome with a sense of gratitude for having been locked up, for having been spared his own devices, if only for a quick moment. He felt that he possibly could have ended up hanging out in a convenience store parking lot, spun out on methamphetamine, had he not been taken out of his life and put into a whole new environment against his will.

"Do you need a ride somewhere," Peter said.

"I work here," she said, "I can't leave the store." she fidgeted with her red vinyl belt, adorned with cheap, thin metal studs. It looked like it had a hole or two added sometime after she had bought it, accommodating her ever-growing pleated, acid-washed jeans around her shrinking body. She caught Peter staring at her jeans and said, "Why…do you wanna get high?"

"I'm okay. You're open?"

"Sure, baby."

"The store?"

She rolled her eyes. "Yeah, come on in, hon," she said and turned to go inside.

The way the girl said 'hon' reminded Peter of Pinkie all of a sudden, like all of his years, had somehow been fit into this moment, the illusion of space and time falling apart altogether. He couldn't really picture Pinkie's face in his mind anymore, nevertheless, but he did remember her being his angel in a scary time. He had trusted her, just like he trusted Fr. Ligero right then. Things were simpler as a child…or were they? People tend to romanticize the past, good or bad. Everybody does it to some degree.

Too many years in prison left Peter with overwhelming agoraphobia that he couldn't seem to shake. The sensation hit him when he realized that he had to get out of the car to get inside the store. The outside world had somehow become scarier than life inside prison.

The Oklahoma City Bombing. The World Trade Center. Tornadoes and earthquakes. The World Trade Center. The economy. Religious zealots. Republicans. Democrats. Derivatives. Satanists. The United Nations. Russia. 9/11. Massacres. School shootings. North Korea. Night-club shootings. Robots. Nuclear War. China. Global Warming. Climate Change. Neural implants. Terrorism. Regime Change. Alienation of the family. Gender neutrality. Falling and stagnant wages. The conquest of Mars. Space wars. And on and on it went.

If the terrorists and bankers and weather and earth didn't kill you, God surely would, if he even exists, he thought some things never change, and then he suddenly caught himself clenching his fists white and holding his breath, face red and so he opened the door as an outright affront to the fear itself, and he stepped out of the car to battle the wind to go inside the store.

He wanted to ask the convenience store clerk if she remembered him but thought that it would be better left alone. She might call her uncle Addie and have him come arrest Peter on some trumped-up charges, maybe beat on him for a little late-morning fun, if the guy was still alive, that is. He had probably choked to death on a rack of ribs by then, at any rate.

Peter got scared when he suddenly remembered that he had made an anonymous call to the Oklahoma State Bureau of Investigation reporting Addie after he had stolen his dad's pills and pick-up. Peter had just mentioned that they might want to look into one Deputy Addie (Peter didn't have a last name but naively figured there weren't too many Addies or Adolfs in a town like Pony Town) and told them that he had overheard some talk in a bar of Deputy Addie's potential involvement in beating prisoners of minority persuasion there in the Pony Town City Jail. Peter had felt at the time that he had almost redeemed himself for being such a worthless coward in the jailhouse that summer day when he witnessed the beating.

Peter stood on the other side of the convenience store counter as Addie's niece rifled through all of the cigarette packs behind the counter, stocking one or two packs and then ducking under the counter to grab a couple more cartons for the shelves. It looked like she'd already stocked the cigarettes, but that didn't keep her from pushing all the packs in, trying to make more room.

"Do I know you?" Peter said.

She stopped pushing and pulling all of the cigarette packs and looked down at the ground.

She looked up at Peter and then over at Fr. Ligero, who busied himself with a copy of Guns and Ammo over at the magazine rack, and then she looked back down at the floor like there was something moving under her feet.

"Carly Jo?" Peter said, having finally remembered her name.

"You ain't from one of them talk shows, is you?"

Peter smiled at the question, thinking it was funny how he remembered her name after all those years when he couldn't remember it the next day after they had slept together.

"I'm just visiting."

"I ain't into no weird shit, mister."

It was her for sure, Peter thought. His throat felt fuzzy with lust as he reminisced that night so many years ago. It had been so long since he had been with a woman. Peter stared at her staring at him and then looked down at his feet, feeling something other than lust right then, however. Maybe pity, maybe shame. Carly Jo looked scared, possibly waiting for Peter to not be so damned cryptic. Everything is a conspiracy with a meth-head, a tweaker.

"I'm a friend of your uncle's."

"Bobby Ray?" she said, eyes bouncing all over the place.

"Addie."

Her face went blank, and she almost looked as if she were calm for a second, not fidgeting or jostling behind the counter anymore, with a couple of packs of cigarettes in each hand. "Addie...Addie ain't alive no more," she said.

"Oh, man." Peter felt like a heel after the words came out of his mouth. The girl's uncle dies, and all he could come up with is, 'Oh, man.' He stepped back from the counter and said, "Could I get a pack of Camel Lights," just like that, not knowing what else to say. He hadn't bought a pack of cigarettes since before he went to jail. He didn't even buy any on the inside. Had plenty of opportunities but felt like he should quit, knowing that the food in there would be bad enough for him.

Carly Jo brightened up like he had just complimented her on her hair and said, "Sure, hon," and grabbed the pack from the freshly stocked bin, grabbing another carton from under the counter and putting a new pack in the bin where she had taken his pack from. She handed him the pack of cigarettes and smiled.

"Thank you. I'm sorry to hear about your uncle."

"He was a good man."

Peter wondered if they were talking about the same Addie. He had never been able to shake the cruelty that Addie and his dad had dished out to that young black kid. Verlin and Addie had worked that guy over. More hate in a hateful world. What made the memory the most unpleasant, however, was that Peter stood by and let the whole thing happen, without stepping in, maybe putting his own neck on the line. He just sat there and watched as the two red necks treated that man worse than some rabid dog. Just one more thing to feel guilty about all his life.

"I hadn't seen him in years," Peter said.

"You wanna go have a smoke?" Carly Jo said.

"Sure."

They went outside into the now dusty gusts of wind, leaving Fr. Ligero in the store with his magazine. He had said that he needed a little break from driving and for Peter to take his time talking to his old friend.

Peter looked out into the field across the road. There was a single, solitary cow standing alone in the vast, browning field. The bank down the street looked as abandoned as the convenience store looked.

Peter thought of Cow Town, the man that his dad had done some work for in Mississippi, and how he had made him feel like a little man. He had been one of the few people who had been normal or nice to him that year that Verlin had taken him to Mississippi. The guy was from

Hereford, Texas, home of one of the largest feed lots in the world. What a claim to fame. Peter laughed out loud, and Carly Jo looked over at him as if he might be laughing at her.

"I was just thinking of a guy," he said.

"Funny guy?"

"Yeah."

Carly Jo seemed to be calming down a little bit as she lit her second cigarette before Peter had even finished his first. The taste was horrible. He had taken the first nasty drag and then just decided to hold onto it so that Carly Jo didn't ask him if he wanted another one. He wanted her to be as comfortable as possible.

Peter and Carly Jo discussed the merit and quality of microwave chimichangas in comparison to microwave burritos and how they both liked the chimichangas better yet would both eat the burritos if they happened to be in a pinch. Carly Jo told him that she wished the New Coke would come out again because it was so good compared to Coke Classic. Peter said that New Coke just tasted like a crappy version of Pepsi and that he was glad when they came out with the original recipe again.

They talked about nothing and everything, but that made Peter feel good, nonetheless relieving the weight of uncertainty and anticipation that continued getting heavier as he prepared to see his dad again. The conversation felt real between him and Carly Jo as if ulterior motives had become something of the past. No agenda, just two people connecting on the most basic levels, being there for each other, despite their sordid histories.

"You ever thought about kickin' the crack habit?" Peter said.

"Ever day, hon," she said. "Are you some kinda preacher? I don't like church, mister."

Peter had been a talk-show host and a preacher in a matter of minutes. He laughed out loud again when he realized why she thought he might have been a talk-show host earlier, her life being the drama it was. He could damn sure relate.

"What you laughin' about?"

"Do you want to go get something to eat?"

"Damn, howdy! All that talk about chimichangas got you hungry, don't it?"

Peter smiled.

"I guess I can leave a note on the door. We don't see nobody anyway."

Carly Jo went inside, where Peter could see that Fr. Ligero had started talking to her. She laughed at whatever he had to say, standing there with a cigarette hanging out of her mouth. Her uneasy stance in the late-morning light felt refreshing, even if she did seem a little down on her luck. Fr. Ligero put his magazine back in the rack and pointed at another one that rested on a lower shelf. Carly Jo laughed like he told her he could fly, a little uneasy, with a sideways grin. They looked out at Peter, who stood outside staring at them, and then they went out to join him.

"What you lookin' at, mister?" Fr. Ligero said.

"You could make friends in a morgue," Peter said.

"My other uncle owns this shit hole anyway. He ain't no good. I'll be damned if I'm gonna pass up some good company and a free meal," Carly Jo said, locking the door.

She left a note on the glass of the front door, and then they all piled into the BMW and headed out for the best little diner in town, according to Carly Jo. The place was aptly named "The Best Diner," named of course after the owner Mikey Best, she had said, who happened to be an old family friend of Carly Jo's parents.

On the way to the diner, Carly Jo told the guys about herself; the years have passed by way of one roughneck after the next. She got a job dancing in a strip club shortly after she quit The Silver Stallion, and that's when she got into meth, she said. She had become something of a legend in those parts with the work she did "on the pole," she kept saying over and over. The best years of her life had long gone by; she added as if she were reminiscing over an illustrious life of leisure and travel.

Carly Jo told Peter that she wanted to be a veterinarian when she was a little girl. Peter felt sad all of a sudden, considering the jagged remains of so many people's shattered dreams. It was never too late, sure, but then again, no one gives an old burn-out the sort of latitude they might give a bright-eyed kid, wet behind the ears, which is just getting their grip on life.

Peter patted Carly Jo's shoulder and told her that he could relate to having wasted so much time. He told her about his stint in prison and all of the days that were exactly the same. No exit, and no freedom of expression, locked in a concrete compound with the hopeless and degenerate society. You don't have any rights when you're a prisoner, he told her. But then again, he committed the crime and didn't go down blazing. Life is simply a series of choices.

They passed the old police station where she said that her uncle Addie had worked before, the building as run-down and sad as the fields with their abandoned oil pumps and sickly livestock. She told them that Pony Town dried up after all the oil was gone, but Peter never remembered it as anything but dead. The oil had just moved a little over to the west, where the drilling had become a new boom.

Fr. Ligero pulled up to the old diner and parked the car right in front. They went inside. The waitress at the front counter, who had the same uneasy, weathered look, grinned at Carly Jo and told the three of them to sit anywhere they liked. Carly Jo picked a booth by the window where they could see the BMW. She said that they probably wanted to keep an eye on it, so no damned crank heads didn't steal it. That had been happening a lot lately; she informed Peter and his friend.

"It's insured, sweety," Fr. Ligero said.

Carly Jo laughed her nervous laugh and told the waitress to bring some coffee over to the table. She lit a cigarette, looking at Fr. Ligero to make sure he didn't mind.

"You should try a cigar some time," he said.

Carly Jo laughed again, easing into the shroud of smoke in front of her. "Man, howdy. Them thing's too damn big and strong for me."

"You ever try one?"

"They ain't got no fancy cee-gars like them around these parts, sir."

Peter ordered for himself and told Carly Jo to get whatever she wanted, which she did, in abundance. Fr. Ligero ordered too. The three of them got more acquainted with each other, talking about where they came from and what they wanted, and where they were going.

Everybody was laughing and talking when the food came.

"Hey! I had sex with you, didn't I?" Carly Jo said suddenly as the waitress put everybody's plates in front of them, rolling her eyes and then walking off.

Peter spit his coffee on the table in front of himself, Carly Jo busting out laughing. Fr. Ligero blushed a little and said, "I guess you guys do know each other then, huh?"

"You and your roommate," Peter said.

"Those were the good ole days," Carly Jo said, already spastically stubbing out her cigarette. She lit another, drawing hard on the filter, the creases deepening around her mouth.

Peter felt a little uncomfortable talking about his former sex acts with her, even if she and Fr. Ligero were open-minded. That had been his first and only menage a trois, and it had left a lasting impression, to say the least. Peter had thought about her time and again, not enough though, he thought, to get in touch with her again somehow from prison.

"I've never been happier than I am now," Peter said and pushed the ashtray closer to her. "Whatever happened to your roommate?"

"Meth killed her."

Peter stopped chewing his food and swallowed. "I'm sorry."

"That's how shit goes around here, hon."

She exuded a kind of wisdom that country folk do as if the harshness of country life quickly ages the soul like it ages the skin and the eyes. Her pain had been a forging process, nevertheless, and there she sat, giving her heart to Peter and his mystical friend as if that moment at the table with their greasy breakfasts had become the culminating point of their collective lives. She seemed fearless like she'd never told a lie in her life, eating breakfast and smoking her cigarettes without a care in the world.

Fr. Ligero sat gazing out the diner window, noticing an old beat-up car pulling in next to the BMW. Carly Jo got up from the table, dismissed herself with a nervous smile, and walked out to meet the guy. The drug dealer had come to hook her up, Peter thought, as she touched the burly old man's hand resting on the edge of his open window. She walked back to the rear of the car, where she fidgeted with something and then pounded on the edge of the trunk, quickly releasing it up. She reached into the cavernous space and pulled out an old wheelchair that looked like it had been donated by the VA hospital sometime shortly after WWII.

Carly Jo wrangled open the wheelchair with the skill of a magician and wheeled it over to the side of the car where the old, fat guy loaded up. He didn't roll up the windows or lock his doors, seemingly not too worried about the crank heads.

Carly Jo wheeled the guy inside and to the edge of the table where they sat.

"Lookie here, Petey," Carly Jo said. Peter looked scared for a second like maybe his dad had popped in on him unannounced, wheeling up in a wheelchair, fat and bald and grayed over by a hard life lived. "Here's your buddy."

"Who the fuck is this little faggot?" the man said.

"Addie?" Peter said as Fr. Ligero stood up to greet the man.

"Who the hell are you, boy?" Addie said, indifferently shaking the old man's hand as he kept his eyes on Peter.

"I thought you said you were friends, Petey."

Peter looked at Carly Jo, bugging his eyes out. "I guess I've changed a lot over the years. You said..."

"Yeah, yeah," she said.

"You said he was dead."

Peter stared at Addie, not sure if the guy was going to jump out of his chair and strangle him or just fall over and die.

"He tells me to tell everybody that. He don't like surprise visits no more."

"You know my dad," Peter finally said to Addie, pushing his plate away and lighting a cigarette of his own.

Addie's face lit up like a baby's. He nudged Carly Jo's hand off of his shoulder and wheeled himself a few more inches, right up to the edge of the table. The waitress came by the table and rolled her eyes when she passed Addie, dumping their ashtray into another one that she carried on top of a short stack of other ashtrays. Peter smiled at her, and she smiled back to him a little uneasily, blushing. Addie sat up straight in his wheelchair, and that's when Peter noticed that he had on a POW t-shirt, and sure enough, that the wheelchair had white stenciled letters spelling out VA HCS on both of the vinyl sides under the arm rests.

"Are you Verlin's boy?"

"Yes, sir," Peter said, feeling a little respect for the old bastard, despite his memories.

"Boy, I know you called the police on me," he said with a pissed-off look. He tried to scoot the battered wheelchair a little closer to Peter, to the point where Peter could feel and smell his steamy, sour breath, but the thing was already bumping the table. Just the sound of his labored breathing made Peter put his cigarette out in the ashtray. Peter readjusted himself in his chair, looking at Fr. Ligero, who leisurely ate his food, as if he were on the veranda in Italy enjoying his summer vacation, basking in the morning sunlight.

The room felt as if it had quickly narrowed down to just Peter and Addie, staring at each other, waiting for the first to say the next word. Addie slammed his fist on the table, flipping the ashtray over, sending the lone, smoldering butt to the floor. Fr. Ligero looked at Addie for a second and then took another bite of his waffle. Peter stood up fast, coming out from behind the table.

"Hell boy, that shit don't matter!" Addie said, a tide of red slowly creeping up his neck and face, like a baby building steam for an eternal, gut-wrenching scream. Peter couldn't move but stood there, half in fear for his life and half-crippled by curiosity. Then, right before Peter witnessed what he thought would be the paraplegic's imminent cardiac arrest, Addie released a guttural laugh that tumbled into uncontrollable laughter, sending the old codger into a fit of phlegm-riddled coughing that appeared to be a whole new level of pain for the old man. Addie gagged on his own air a couple of times and then began laughing again. Laughter, coughing, and then laughter and coughing simultaneously sent his wheelchair rattling underneath himself.

Peter sat back down on the bench, not knowing what to do with his out-of-place self, feeling light-headed, but then finally said, "I thought you were dead, man."

Addie held out his right index finger like he wanted Peter to wait for a second while he got his breath again. Carly Jo had left the three of them together, disappearing to the back of the restaurant. Peter continued waiting for him to get his breath, looking at the pack of cigarettes as Addie reached for them. Fr. Ligero nudged Peter and nodded for him to push the pack toward Addie.

"Go ahead, sir," Peter said.

"Dammit, boy, call me Addie," he said. "I ain't got no damned suit on, do I?"

"Alright, alright."

"You see what them little niggers did to me. Hell boy, you sending me to the clink wasn't shit compared to them coons bumrushin' my ass. You done me some good, though. I'll tell you that right now." Addie looked at Peter like an eager student, as if the young man had all the answers to all of the big questions all of a sudden. Peter smiled at him, wondering if his dad looked as beat up and tired as Addie.

"You seen your daddy?"

"That's what I came to town for."

"Shit, boy." Addie nodded in the direction where Carly Jo had walked. He nudged Peter's hand resting on the table and winked at him.

"She's real nice, Addie, but I'm on a mission from God, you know?"

"That ain't..." Addie stopped mid-sentence, closed his eyes, and then said, "That's alright, boy. You done good, I guess. You seen your daddy? Oh yeah, right. You came here to see him. Shit boy, he's all ate up these days. He don't talk to nobody no more. He quit drinkin' and got all stupid in the head. I'll tell you what..." He went on and on, but Peter couldn't help but think that Addie had nicely skipped over the fact that his dad's wife had been killed. My dad quit drinking?

Peter imagined his dad as some kind of Southern Baptist tee-total maniac but couldn't see him shifting that far to the right. He imagined him as some kind of hippy Buddhist too, but then again, that would be even more ridiculously impossible for man for a man like Verlin McDash. Peter wanted to see his dad for himself, thinking that there might still be a chance for something real to happen between them, once and for all. It's never too late, as the saying goes.

Carly Jo walked back up to the table, "You guys catchin' up, is ya?" she said, smiling, and then scooted in next to her uncle like a shy high school date.

"Yeah," Peter said.

"This is Verlin's boy," Addie said.

"Yeah, I know, Addie. We done talked all about that."

"You think we oughta take the old boy to see his crazy, old daddy?"

"Aww, I don't know about all that. I ain't seen that pervert in a million years," Carly Jo said and then looked over at Peter sheepishly. "Shit, Petey. I don't mean nothin' by that. Your daddy's alright, I guess. He just got all weird after his old lady got kilt."

Peter looked down at the table and then over to Fr. Ligero, who was now eating a piece of apple pie.

"For breakfast?" Peter said.

"Apples are good for the digestive system," Fr. Ligero said, smiling at Addie.

Addie leaned forward in his wheelchair again, giving Peter a scrutinizing eye, just like the old cop he was.

"This your bun-buddy, Pete?" Addie said, nudging Peter again.

Fr. Ligero winked at Addie and kept on eating his pie.

Chapter 27

Peter and his dad pulled into the driveway of a house he had never been to before. The panel van sat parked in the street out in front.

"Where are we, dad?"

"Our new house, boy."

Peter thought that they had just moved to their new house but didn't feel like that was the time to have a debate on living arrangements with the old man. The house sat on a hill overlooking a field across the street. Peter thought that the front yard would be a good place to sled if they ever got snow in Mississippi. He didn't know where Mississippi was, only that it had four s's and two p's. His cousin had taught him that back home as they raced, spelling the word out to see how fast they could say it without messing up. M-I-S-S-I-S-S-I-P-P-I. Peter looked over at his dad as he lit another cigarette.

Peter let Simone out of the car, and she followed Verlin inside the house. Peter got out of the car and went inside after Verlin had already closed the door behind himself. The house was dark and cool. Shadowy boxes and a smattering of furniture lay scattered about the living room. Peter looked around for Louise but figured she had gone to bed or that she was combing her hair or staring into space somewhere in a dark back room. Peter called Simone.

"She's in the backyard," Verlin said from the other room.

Peter made his way around a pile of clothes and a couple of old end-tables to get out of the back door. Simone jumped up on his legs as soon as he came outside.

"Hey, girl!"

He bent down to pet her. Near her right back leg, he could feel a little wet, bald spot. He picked her up to look at the spot a little more closely. It was a moonless night, so Peter put her up closer to his face, where he could see that a patch of fur was missing. The missing patch of fur had left a puffy, bloody spot in its place.

Verlin came outside and stood over where Peter held Simone.

"She must've got into a fight with a cat or something," Verlin said, puffing on a cigarette, "you gonna be able to keep an eye on that little shithead now, though. I'll be out in the morning to feed you guys." Verlin turned to go inside.

"Dad!"

"We had to move 'cause you and your fuckin' dog shit all over the fuckin' place, boy."

"I cleaned it up, sir."

Verlin opened the door and went inside.

Peter stood up and banged on the closed door. He could see the light on inside, and his stomach dropped. He began to cry, holding Simone next to his chest. She wriggled out of his arms and ran to the middle of the yard to pee. Peter banged on the door some more but knew that he better watch himself, lest he ends up in another heap of trouble, his dad having to come out and "talk" to him.

Chapter 28

Peter could see Mary running down the street in the rearview, despite all of the smoke from the spinning tires. He told Perky not to wait up for him. He felt like going for a ride.

Peter came to a stop at the corner to see if Mary would actually run all the way to the end of the block. He stuck his head out of the window and yelled at her to hurry up. He could see her running faster. Clearly, the smoke had dissipated into the summer sky over gentle streaks of pink and magenta.

Peter opened a fresh pack of Marlboro Reds that he got from the carton on his dad's fridge as he waited for his half-sister to come up from behind. He brushed at a piece of lint on his suit jacket and tapped a cigarette out of the cigarette pack, and lit up. He smiled to himself as the truck lighter popped out of the little socket. The truck was fully functional, sure enough, he thought. Mary finally made it to the side of the pick-up, gulping air, trying to catch her breath, laboring to say, "Does my dad know you're taking his truck?"

"No."

Mary didn't say anything right away, staring at Peter. She wiped the sweat from her forehead with a nicely folded, embroidered handkerchief that she had pulled from the breast pocket of her frilly blouse. Her breathing slowed a little bit, and she said, "He's gonna be mad."

"I'm counting on it, Mary," Peter said, blowing smoke over her head. "Tell him to call me if he needs his vehicle back, okay?"

Mary stood perfectly still, not saying a word, and then slowly and slyly smiled at Peter. He could swear that the blouse she was wearing could have come from Grammie's closet. The girl was trying a little too hard to look older than she was, perpetually playing house in her grandma's old hand-me-downs, it seemed. Peter stared at her, wanting to be able to say something hopeful to her, to give her something to hold onto for future use, but could only watch as she mechanically turned from the pick-up and started walking back to the house from where she had come.

"Bye, Mary. Good luck."

Mary stuck a hand up in the air, not even turning around, as Peter put the truck back into gear and jammed the gas pedal to the floor, sending up another blue cloud of smoke into the unseemly still air. He must've gone a couple of blocks spinning the tires, fish-tailing from side to side, running down into the ditch a couple of times, only to pop back up onto the blacktop as the road unfolded before the speeding truck, pockmarked here and there, badly enough to swallow a wheel or two. The old man could fix anything, he had said, and Peter felt confident in his dad's abilities if anything were to go wrong with the old Chevy.

The early evening heat swirled inside the cab like a convection oven as Peter sped faster down the old highway. The ragweed and hayfields slightly bowed out in the distance, the calm of seconds earlier giving way to the breeze or the next storm.

Peter tossed his cigarette out the window and then rolled it up so that he could light another one. He brushed the ashes from his freshly pressed suit and shirt. Louise had gotten them cleaned and pressed for him while he had slept most of the day away. Same-day service, she had told him proudly, as if she had just installed an in-house fusion reactor. He felt grateful, nevertheless. She could surprise a guy every now and then. She said that she didn't want him to get it messed up, but he really knew that the suit made her nervous, as if the sight of nice clothes somehow indicated that she had broken with her dear working-class roots. She probably didn't want some yahoo in her house, making her feel dumpier than she already felt.

Peter rolled the window down and kept looking in his rearview to see if he had a tail yet. Really though, Mary didn't seem too hurried to rat Peter out. She almost gave her silent seal of approval, actually. She probably realized that Peter had gotten something that their dad really cared about. Neither one of them, Peter or Mary, had ever been able to get his attention. Now, with that damned, old pick-up, Peter held his daddy's heart in his hands, and that might have been the only thing in the world that the guy would have died for in the end. Peter felt entitled, justified, just like the way a terrorist might feel justified to blow some shit up. There really was no logic to him taking his dad's truck, risking his life, his well-being, but then again, sometimes it takes a radical act to shake things up enough so that the long-postponed reconstruction can take place.

The pick-up handled surprisingly well for such an old vehicle. Verlin said that he had replaced the original suspension with a new, beefy racing suspension, along with a racing transmission and a lower-geared rear end, hence the get-up-and-go. The only thing original was the body, pretty much the steel underneath the paint, according to Verlin, and that too had been sanded and welded and bent back into perfection...

Peter could see The Silver Stallion up ahead and decided that he would stop by to have a drink and maybe even a little visit with his friend Carly Jo. He pulled into the Stallion's back lot and went inside to see what the locals were up to.

"Didn't make'er in today," the crusty, old man behind the bar said after Peter had asked if Carly Jo was working.

"Could I get a shot of Crown?" Peter said.

The old man looked Peter up and down as if he had just called him a dirty old bastard. The bartender stroked his greasy hair back and continued to stare at Peter for a minute longer, almost like it was the first time he had seen someone of the human race walk into the bar. Peter returned the old man's empty gaze while he waited for some proof of life. The guy finally said 'okay' and served up the whiskey and told Peter '2.50.' Peter laid three singles on the bar, took his shot, and turned to leave. He didn't want to wait around to see the old coot fall over dead, with his tobacco-stained fingers and teeth. Peter continued out the door, back out to the pick-up, and got in and started it up, revving the engine just to hear the tinny resonance of the pipes bounce off of the wooden fence surrounding the parking lot. Peter didn't recognize the other two cars in the 'private' parking lot there behind The Stallion. He imagined that the owner of one of the cars was probably passed out in a bathroom stall inside the bar. Peter lit another cigarette and took off his suit jacket. He carefully laid it down on the seat next to him and backed the truck out of the space. He put the truck in 'drive' and pushed the accelerator down to the floor, spraying rock all around the parking lot like a frenzied hail storm.

The truck shook to a stop, the front end poking out of the gate, where Peter could see the only cop car in Pony Town pulling into a driveway down the street a little bit. It could have been Addie, or perhaps just one of his flunkies, and he realized that he had to maintain cover so that he didn't raise any unwanted suspicion. He stayed put for a moment longer until the cop car had fully pulled out of sight.

Perky had given Peter the directions to the new apartment the day before. She had moved while he was visiting his dad, on very short notice, actually, because she had a falling out with Neider. He had come into the house and wrecked it pretty good, just because he was a crazy asshole, according to Perky. "Yeah? Okay," Peter had said to her. He didn't believe anything she said anymore. Stolen drugs, stolen money. *Who knows and who cares what she did to piss the guy off this time,* Peter thought. He just bided his time with Perky, at any rate, as he planned to make his escape soon, leaving her to do whatever she felt like doing with whomever.

Peter made his way out to the interstate leading to the city, merged onto the outside lane, and blended in with all of the evening highway traffic. He felt comfortable, a certain level of anonymity, as he became a small part of a larger mass making its way back to cool homes and expectant wives and children and pets.

Chapter 29

Peter's fists throbbed from beating on the concrete patio all night long. He had tossed the lone lawn chair out into the grass and kicked over the rusty, old barbecue, somewhere in the middle of his fit, out of frustration. He wanted to go inside and clean up and get something to eat but didn't dare to beat on the door for fear of getting his ass kicked again and perhaps being cast to the backyard for the remainder of his crappy vacation with his dad. Verlin told Peter that he would be out to feed him and Simone in the morning, and Peter knew that as far as his dad was concerned, there would be no negotiation on the matter, no questions, and damned sure no sniveling.

Peter sat up against the house, nudging Simone awake. She lay there by his side, oblivious to Peter's anxiousness. Her eyes rolled around in her head, still puffy with sleep, as she readjusted herself next to his small, warm pant leg. Peter rubbed the sorer of the two hands, the one that hadn't even had time to fully heal from being smashed in his dad's van door, crying to himself, strands of spittle dangling from his mouth like stringy tentacles, as he stared out into the yard. It didn't even look like there were neighbors around there. No one he could run to even if he had chosen to do so.

Peter didn't want to end up like Ramona Whitcanuck. That little girl whose vacation ended with her lifeless, limp body being found in a clothes dryer in Birmingham. Alabama is where Birmingham is, Verlin had told him. You bet your sweet ass, boy. Right up the road, he had said.

Peter kept seeing Ramona Whitcanuck's bloody hat crumpled on the dirty floorboard of that old truck that the police had found. He imagined that the truck was just like his dad's panel van. Hole in the dash where the radio should have been, down to the dusty smell inside and all of the random junk scattered about in the back. The fact that she was right up the road, that she could have come through Mississippi, and that he could have even seen her and the man who kidnapped her somewhere made him almost miss her, even if they had never met. He still felt nostalgic and melancholy, like going to someone's funeral whom you didn't know, mourning the loss of someone who had left such a hole in the lives of so many, pictures of the deceased with surviving family members displayed.

Peter thought that maybe he had seen Ramona and her captor at a Denny's perhaps. A gas station on the side of a desolate highway, out in the middle of nowhere. He felt bad for the girl, just like he felt scared for himself. He couldn't do anything about his situation, though, and the fact that he was young and powerless settled into his bones, warm like blood. Peter knew the fear was there for good and that he had nowhere to go and no way to separate himself from this dismal fate.

Peter looked around the yard, making sure there were no houses next door, on either side, anywhere near, really. Verlin said that they had to move because Peter let his new dog crap all over the house. Peter knew better. He had cleaned the place up really well. Louise had even helped him do so, and when they were done, she said that the job was great. Verlin had inspected the room, even, and given his seal of approval for a job well done.

Peter swam inside his own head, not really knowing if he was dreaming or awake. The little demon in the corner of the room, the dreams of falling and floating, only to wake to Pinky and Sewell's embrace or to the weight of his father's stare and presence, blurred together in his mind like some cruel concoction.

"Hey, ya little shit," Verlin said, coming out onto the patio in nothing but his white briefs and a beer. "Did you sleep okay? Feels pretty good to sleep out in the great outdoors, don't it?"

Peter stared at his sore hands, pulling Simone a little closer to his side. He wanted to tell the old man to go fuck himself, to go find some deep, dark hole and to go into it and die, please but knew that a response like that would only be met with a swift kick in the face or maybe worse, depending on how the old man felt right then. Peter continued to stare down at his hands, feeling the weight of Verlin's disapproving glare like a thick layer of warm grit covering himself.

"Well, boy? You turn dumb or somethin'?"

"No, sir."

Verlin tossed his empty beer can out into the yard and lit a cigarette that he pulled from behind his ear, and then told Peter to go inside. Peter slowly got up from the concrete patio, looked down at Simone, and then looked up at his dad.

"Leave that little bitch out here, boy, okay?"

"She's not a bitch," Peter said, bending to the dog.

"Boy, you better watch that fuckin' mouth. Ya hear? I don't need no smart-mouth kid talking shit to me! Ya hear? I'm your daddy. I work hard."

Peter wanted to tell his dad that not everybody was deaf like him, that he didn't have to shout all the time but didn't. He instead kept his mouth shut, left the dog outside to fend for herself, and he went into the house before the old man had a chance to change his mind.

Once inside, Peter's eyes had to adjust to the lack of light. The air smelled musty and spicy like his uncle Lenny's house used to smell when Peter would pop in and catch him by surprise, people scrambling off of the couch and to the back room for the remainder of their visit.

Verlin came in behind Peter and shut the door, leaving Simone in the backyard by herself. The room fell pitch-black once the heavy door closed all the way. Peter's eyes had just adjusted to the dimness all around him. He thought he saw flashes of red and bright blue somewhere ahead of himself but quickly realized his eyes were just playing tricks on him. He stopped mid-step so that he didn't fall over a box or a random tool box or a stack of papers or a chair. He didn't want to break something and get into trouble.

"Hey there, Peter," Louise said from somewhere in the dark. Peter remained standing still in the middle of the kitchen or living room or wherever he was, not knowing the layout of the place yet. He hadn't even really been in the house yet. He could have been dreaming again, for all he knew, and wondered if the demon would show his ugly face; it had been a while since the last time. Right as the thought came, though, shards of light entered his eyes like so much dust all around him. He stood frozen, taking in the harsh light. Peter blinked a couple of times and then saw Louise sitting upright on the pull-out bed, smiling, her hand trailing down from the light switch on the wall behind her. Peter covered his eyes as a childish reflex to her naked body.

"Come here, honey," she said, nothing on her body but sweat or water, shiny gooseflesh in the obscene light.

Peter looked around the room for his dad but didn't see him walking around in his tight, white underwear. Tighty-whities, his friends at school, called them. Peter didn't notice the smell in the room any longer, now bombarded with sensations from under his own skin, like electricity and nausea fighting it out.

Sure, Peter had seen the naked women in the magazines that the boys down the street from grammie's had, but he had never seen a naked lady in real life. A grown woman exposing herself so comfortably, right before his young, inexperienced eyes, like something a person might do every day. Peter remembered accidentally walking in on his mom when she was dressing in her bedroom that one time. That was different, though. His mom had covered herself with the quickness of a Chinese grappler, her face flushed with embarrassment and nervousness, as she ushered him out of the room, slamming the door behind him. "You knock next time, dammit!" she had hollered.

Louise sat there in the buck, stroking her long, dark hair away from her rosy, shiny face.

"Peter," Louise said, patting the mattress and uncrossing her legs.

Peter's eyes couldn't look at that wily mound of hair between her tanned legs. Her bush looked like a lost pet, all nuzzled in there, covering her private parts for the winter months ahead. Louise had never seemed so happy to see him before, he thought, and he definitely didn't want to ruin a good thing, no matter how strange her wet, naked body made him feel.

Peter began to move toward Louise, holding his eyes down as best he could, not wanting to stare at her too much, but at the same time, not wanting to make her think that he didn't like her anymore, that he was better than her in some way. Louise's flush face and slender neck spilled into her full, round breasts, all then bunching together, falling down into her slender waist, only to continue flowing downward into those smooth, round hips again, and into those legs, eventual and long and smooth.

"Come on, buddy. Don't be shy."

I'm not your buddy, Peter thought, but then said, "You're naked, ma'am."

Louise laughed as if Peter had just uttered a sly pick-up line that she had never heard before. She put out her arms, waving him in. He moved to the edge of the mattress and stood there very stiffly, still looking down at the floor. Verlin walked into the living room and over next to Peter. Peter looked up at his dad, him standing there now, smiling.

"Ever seen titties like that, boy?"

"No, sir."

"Go ahead, boy, touch 'em. They feel real nice. Lot bigger'n your mama's, huh?"

Peter stood at the edge of the mattress, not wanting to look up at Louise anymore, his throat itchy and dry. His stomach felt sour and sore like he might throw up right then, the inside of his head thick like corn syrup but then again, that body, her naughty smile made him feel scared and powerful and something foreign, but good and then he had the overwhelming urge to just bite her breasts, to eat her up, something uncontrollable inside expanding like wildfire.

"Come here, hon," she said, pulling Peter into her pale, swollen tits. "I always wanted my own baby."

Louise's erect nipples buried themselves into Peter's cheek as he squirmed, trying to get comfortable. He wanted to bite her but, at the same time, couldn't help but drink in her warm embrace right then. Even the moistness of her skin. Her sweet and musty smell. That soft skin. He fell into her grasp, not having received a hug from her or his dad since the first day he had been with them. He thought of Ramona Whitcanuck again, and then he could see the little demon up in the corner of his room, laughing, and then he could see himself falling into the black all around him. Falling forever...

Peter lay in Louise's arms, not knowing what to do with his hands. Her body felt smooth and calm, yet warm and electric. He rested his head in the crook of her neck, keeping his eyes shut, trying to hide his erect penis and the fact that he had wet himself, and the subsequent euphoria of wetting himself, which felt like nothing before, the sensation amazing and dangerous and other-worldly. The pee didn't even wet the outside of his pants. It felt thick and slick inside his underwear.

Peter just wanted to keep falling into that abyss surrounding him, warm and weightless, until he came to a place of comfort, a place that felt right, not so confusing. Not a place of torment, but a place of peace. He suddenly saw his mom's face in the darkness behind closed eyes, and she began to smile at him. She was saying something, but he couldn't really make it out. I'll...we'll...don't worry, baby...I... as the impressions came in waves, like the static on the little transistor radio.

"Boy, you better save me some of that," Verlin said, pulling Peter out of his trance and away from the warm nestled spot of Louise's neck.

Peter turned around to see that his dad was totally naked now, just like Louise. Peter stared at his dad's swollen penis. He thought it looked like some vulgar tool used for some archaic form of torture. He wished that he had a knife to whack it off right then and there. Peter felt repulsed and curious at the same time, looking at his dad's dick, just like he felt about Louise's breasts and that smooth swath of skin between that huge bush and her belly button. That flat, tan belly. Peter felt compelled to grab the old man's penis and bite it or try to break it off even. Verlin bent over next to Peter and grabbed the transistor radio from under the mattress, and held it out to him.

"Here, boy. Go over and listen to the radio in the chair," Verlin said. "We gotta go to bed, okay?"

Peter walked over to the chair opposite the pull-out sofa and turned the radio on. He could see his dad crawl under the sheets with Louise, and so he tried to keep his eyes on the little window on the face of the radio but kept looking up once and again to see if his dad and Louise were really going to sleep. He turned the dial back and forth as if he could work up a station by some strange friction alone, and then, lo and behold; he was finally able to somewhat make out the melody to a rock song that he knew his mom liked. What was it? He had heard it a million times if he had heard it once before, the song being pretty new but already played out on the radio.

Dreamboat Annie. That was it. The song was by the band Heart. Yeah! Peter touched the dial lightly again, not turning it, hoping to not lose the song that he had finally found under all of the static. His eyes began to grow heavy as he sat in the cool of the living room of their new house, yet another layover on the journey with his father. Peter felt comfortable, a remnant of his mom's song playing underneath a dirge of white noise. His eyes were still heavier and heavier, him soothingly slipping into a deep sleep like a fading whisper.

He felt like he had maybe been asleep all night long when Peter heard the moaning, slowly opening his eyes. The almost melodic drone of the feminine howl reminded him of the woman whose house he and his dad had stopped at on the way to Mississippi. That relentless crescendo, the heightened intensity, only to end in a warm blanket of silence somewhere out of his sight.

Louise hadn't gotten quiet yet, however. Peter looked over to the pull-out couch where Louise was bouncing up and down on Verlin's lap, facing away from his dad, her breasts jumping like lively babies out in front of her. Her face was contorted and sweaty, and Peter couldn't help but think that she must have been racked with unbearable pain. He watched her go up and down on his dad like a rodeo queen, moaning like a feral cat trapped in a hot bathroom. Peter couldn't take his eyes off of her no matter how much he tried. Those lively breasts. Those muscular thighs looked like they could squeeze water from granite. Her throbbing body, bouncing on top of the old man like a frantic dervish, would forever be burned into his mind. Her naked body was like a devastating car wreck, the sight tumultuous in the heart yet totally irresistible to the eyes.

And then, just like that, the crescendo came to an uncomfortable shriek, and both Verlin and Louise, as if on cue, released the most heinous groans like Peter had never in his life heard before. As the groans mounted, both of their bodies instantly went stiff like a live, bare electrical wire had been slung over them, and then Louise collapsed on top of his dad, and they both lay there like they were dead, and that was that.

After a couple of minutes passed, Peter stared to make sure that they were both still alive. Verlin said, "Hey boy," pushing Louise off of him. She shook her hair out like a wild, coke-crazed stripper and started laughing.

"Peter," she said, pushing herself up onto her knees, laughing hysterically now on the bed. Peter didn't know what was so funny, because he felt really sick now. His head pulsed with a raw energy that could've cut through steel. If he hadn't known any better, he would have thought that the crazy bitch was laughing at him, at the look of terror that must have been on his face. Verlin was already snoring on top of the blankets. Peter stared at Louise as if he could hypnotize her into submission so that she would leave him alone, but to no avail. "Come here, buddy," she said to Peter, waving him over to her.

Peter walked over to the makeshift bed where his dad was fast asleep, that annoying saw of snoring getting louder still. Louise cupped her breasts and then coughed as if she were giving herself some kind of medical exam. She had a sweet, musty smell about her. Peter stared at her body like a burning pillar and then turned and ran out the front door.

Peter walked to the side of the house and called Simone, who ran up to the fence. He climbed the hurricane fence and jumped over. He grabbed his puppy and went to the corner of the yard for another day outside in the great outdoors, as his dad had put it. Honestly, Peter liked it better outside and decided that another night spent out of the house would be better than staying inside, where he only felt weird and scared and dirty.

Chapter 30

Fr. Ligero had met plenty of crazy bastards in his day, but rednecks were a special breed that he could never really figure out, never felt too safe around. That's saying a lot, seeing how his first pastoral position had been in a Mafia church in Kansas City, Missouri, many years before. That particular church had become a dirty-money laundry for the most part by the time he had taken his post, and he was promptly told that there were appropriate concessions that had to be made in a position like his. The confessions that his better judgment told him to report, but which nicely fell into the 'concessions' category, were difficult at first. Just like killing a man, one of his parishioners had told him once. After the first one, it gets easier, ya know? The second and third, and so forth, don't haunt you as that first one does. It's that first one that you're constantly trying to forget by killing others like maybe you could appease the devil someday, some way, if you only kill enough people to burn that first one from your consciousness, ya know?

Fr. Ligero had his parish to protect, per orders of the bishop. After all, most of the characters who performed their weekly catharses, their familiar voices behind that obscure screen, despite their attempts to disguise themselves, were simply protecting the working-class schleps who couldn't get a fair shake from the tax-paid police in rough times. Fr. Ligero had his doubts, sure, but he felt called to do the work of the Church more than he felt the need to make waves.

Rednecks were scarier to Fr. Ligero than the cock-eyed river boat captain and all of his mangled mates that he used to drink with in Mississippi, back when he'd taken a job for the Church in an attempt to save souls along the Gulf Coast.

Fr. Ligero had been to South America, ministering to the Sandinistas, the middle-East, against his better judgment, and he had been excommunicated, de-clothed, and left out for the world to devour, yet rednecks as a people-group held the title for unpredictable and outright dangerous in his eyes.

That old boy Addie had a dangerous recklessness about him for sure, as if he had nothing to lose and would do anything that he wanted to do, no matter the cost to him or others, seemingly oblivious to consequence altogether. Fr. Ligero felt like running into Addie might not have been such a bad thing, however, and that maybe the old cop could warm them up for what they might potentially have in store meeting with Peter's dad.

"So, Addie," Fr. Ligero said, "what is it you do these days? Not being a cop anymore?"

"This your boyfriend, Pete?"

"Just a friend."

Fr. Ligero looked over to Peter and winked at him, continuing to talk to Addie. "I got in touch with your old friend, Verlin, the other day, and I told him that we would be coming by for a visit in the near future. Is there anything that would ensure a better visit between him and Peter?"

"He ain't no faggot if that's what ya mean."

"No, Addie, that's not it. Verlin's just been a little violent in the past with Peter, and I don't want my friend here to get hurt."

"What about your sweet little ass?" Addie pointed at Peter.

Fr. Ligero smiled over to Carly Jo, who rubbed her uncle's arm lightly as a lover might do. Their strange affection really wasn't any of his business, though, because he had come to Pony Town to help Peter out, not necessarily to oust incest from Oklahoma altogether. Fr. Ligero realized that they had come this far and that the hard part lay ahead of them still, and Peter needed him. He had become a mentor to Peter for all intent and purpose. He had a responsibility to Peter, and he didn't plan on dropping the ball in the young man's time of need. Sometimes helping friends means risking one's life, he had once told Peter.

"Addie, I appreciate your good humor and all, but we really need to get this fucking thing going, okay?" Peter looked at Fr. Ligero as if the old man had started loudly singing Gaelic fight songs out of the clear blue. Carly Jo quit spinning her hair around her finger, holding Addie's upper arm tight now. "If you could help us," he continued, "we'd be mighty obliged, okay?"

"Sure. Anything, old boy," Addie said, brushing Carly Jo's hand away from his arm, "all you gots to do is ask, okay?"

"I'm asking."

"Let me call Verlin and tell him that we'll all be over after a while. How's that sound? Good?"

"Right as rain," Fr. Ligero said, taking his cap off, as Carly Jo wheeled Addie over by the restrooms, where he pulled his phone out to make a call.

"In a hurry, Father?" Peter said.

"Come on, Peter."

Peter stared at his friend as if he had been switched with someone else when Peter wasn't looking. "What's up?"

Fr. Ligero didn't know what to say to the kid, not really a kid anymore, about his dad, about the potential danger of dealing with a sociopath, but he did know that God had been in control his whole life and that he, Father Remy Ligero, was right where he was supposed to be at that very particular time and place. He hadn't maintained a relationship with Peter in vain. Peter had a lot to learn about many things, sure, but first things would have to be dealt with first.

Fr. Ligero had his father's blessing yet still chose to make bad decisions after bad decisions in his more formative years. He honored his father and had still traveled down one dead end after another. Instincts were there for a reason, he had told Peter once at one of their visits, and Peter had had his fair share of hunches, but then again, he had lost control. Passion had overcome him. He chose a life in prison by way of his unbridled rage. Isolation and separation, in a very real sense. Not like the sequestered mystics of a cloister but by the paradox of being imprisoned against his will due to his strong, reckless will.

Fr. Ligero looked at Peter, who kept his eyes on the two over by the restroom. He wanted to reach right inside of Peter and touch those places of hurt, smooth them out once and for all, but he knew that he couldn't and that they were on the right path to get the healing, nevertheless. Fr. Ligero looked over at Addie and Carly Jo, who were now walking back to the booth.

"What's the story?" Fr. Ligero said.

"He's goin' campin'," Addie said.

"I thought he was about dead."

"He said we're all welcome if we wanna go on out there."

Carly Jo scrunched in by Peter and Fr. Ligero, smiling. "You wanna go campin' boys?" she said.

"I just want to get this over with," Peter said. "Is that all the guy has ever done? Camping? Fishing?"

Fr. Ligero elbowed Peter. They all sat there now, Verlin going camping and the gang not knowing what to do next, like a bunch of high school girls on Friday night. Fr. Ligero excused himself from the table and went out to the BMW to fetch one of his cigars. After he lit up, he pounded on the window of the diner, right next to the booth where the others sat, and laughed when they all jumped in their seats, trying to lighten the mood. Peter had spent an uncomfortably large part of his life in prison contemplating the day when he would be reunited with his father, and now he couldn't even make a simple decision.

"Don't you worry, son," Addie said, nodding to Peter, who thumbed through his wallet to pay the tab, "they owe me one." Addie put a dollar bill on the table and closed his wallet.

Peter got up from the table, with Carly Jo and Addie behind him, and they all went outside to join Fr. Ligero.

Addie rolled his wheelchair up next to the BMW. "Nice car," he said. Fr. Ligero puffed a couple of times on his big cigar, letting the smoke roll from his mouth. "What does a little faggot have a car like this for?"

"It's my car," Fr. Ligero said, holding out his cigar in front of him to peruse the gold band. "I did some good in the stock market, and Peter donated some money while he was in prison. He said that he always wanted to drive an M5, so I got it for the both of us, really."

Fr. Ligero realized that Addie didn't mean anything by calling people 'faggots' and 'pussies' and the like. Actually, that's how the old dog showed affection for people. He hid his wavering love for others behind vulgarities that put most people off because he was just too damned insecure about being sweet to people for fear that they would be sweet and intimate with him in return. Charming, really, Fr. Ligero had told Peter at the table when Addie and Carly Jo had gone to use the phone.

"Well, you cock-knockers wanna go campin'?"

"Sounds good, dick face," Fr. Ligero said back to Addie. Carly Jo and Peter looked over at Addie with big eyes as if he might burst into some ridiculous tirade but could only laugh out loud when the dirty old bastard in the wheelchair busted out laughing himself. He gets me, the look on Addie's face said. That old man gets me. Everybody had a good laugh, bending over and knee-slapping and hootin' and a hollerin', and then they loaded up into the two cars, ready to go, and they were on their way, Addie and Fr. Ligero in Addie's beat-up Chevy, Peter and Carly Jo in the Beamer.

Chapter 31

Peter spent the majority of the next day beating on the doors, beating on the windows, and beating on the house itself. He had relieved himself outside just like Simone, several times over, yet felt a bit less than a dog for having to urinate and defecate in the grass where he should have been playing. He felt dirty squatting among the dandelions and the dying grass. He pooped and peed outside, he'd say to Simone, just like a dog, and thought that maybe he should get his food in a bowl right next to Simone, too, if he were so lucky. Maybe they could share a bowl of dog food even. Cut down on costs for the old man.

Peter thought about the neighbor at the old house. He wished that there was someone around that he could talk to now. Nevertheless, Peter wouldn't have really felt safe going to anyone's house for help. His dad had warned him.

Peter continued to walk around the house, one lap after the next, jumping the fence on the one side and through the gate on the other. He climbed up onto the air-conditioning unit now and again, trying to see whether his dad and Louise were moving about inside, whether they were still alive. Exercising maybe, he thought of having sex, or whatever it was that they did all day in there by themselves.

Peter got down from the air-conditioning unit when it would come on, blowing hot air into his pants and up all around him like a furnace from beneath the surface of the earth. The moist, hot air was denser and viler than the already muggy Mississippi summer air, taking his breath away, making him gag on his own breath like some eccentric, nervous might.

Peter went back and forth between the front and the back yard, hoping someone would come outside and let him in. He thought that maybe Sewell and Pinkie would come by to see the new house. Sure, that's what parents do. They go by to see their kid's new places and help them with minor repairs or preparations, or maybe even a little painting here and there, helping to make sure the move goes smoothly and that there's plenty to eat and drink while they work.

Sewell told Peter that his mother was coming to get him soon and soon couldn't come quick enough, as far as Peter was concerned. Peter walked around the side of the house with Simone at his side for what seemed to be the thousandth time. "Are you hungry, girl?" he said, her following him, as peppy as can be, no worries whatsoever. Peter felt hungry and tired. It had definitely been a couple of days since he had eaten, and he just wanted to get clean and eat and feed his dog and go home.

Verlin's panel van sat perched high in the driveway over the street below. The virginal, white van against the encapsulated gray sky above all seemed so bland and lifeless to Peter. He walked across the brown grass to see if the keys were in the ignition. No such luck. He looked up at the dense, gray sky, feeling like it had abandoned him too. The bleak color, no sun, no blue, felt like an ominous warning from God that Peter should begin to prepare for his imminent end, that he really had done it this time, and that there was nothing anyone could do for him any longer. Peter would surely be cast to the edges of humanity to be alone and hungry, him and his dog to brave death alone. The days had begun to feel as dismal as the nights to Peter, the light of day having no power to inspire him, to keep him hopeful.

Peter stood in the front yard waiting for lightning to strike him or for some altered reality to come over him, forever changing his where and when. He had done that a lot in his youth, not really thinking that his thoughts were any more macabre than the next kid's. He just wanted sublimation, disintegration, things like that, but didn't even really know what words like that meant. If he could only escape from his helpless human form to some nebulous, non-feeling vapor and float away into eternal, ethereal bliss...Ahhh, yes...

Peter walked over to the side of the van, opened the door, and got into the driver's seat. He had always wanted to drive but had never been given a chance, only being five or six years old. Nevertheless, he got in the seat and started moving the wheel as if he had just begun some great expedition into the unknown, or maybe even La Carrera Panamericana, the bulky van scaring up chickens and dirty Mestizo kids, hauling ass down one of what used to be Mexico's finest highways. The big steering wheel turned a little bit each way with every tug of Peter's scrawny arms. His hand felt okay, a little sore, but okay, and his little sojourn into the imaginary race picked him up and carried him through the gray and dreary day into a fantastical escape that had no concern for the weather and his hunger.

As Peter had been driving away into the colorful land of Mexico, Simone had run off without him. What could have been five minutes or an hour had gone by before Peter noticed that Simone had gone somewhere out of sight. Not only that, but Peter hadn't realized that his days had actually turned to weeks and then to months, and he had changed, aged a little, and he felt different, rather weary in a way that had no place in the heart of a child.

"Simone!" he shouted through the window he had just laboriously rolled down. He looked over the yard and peeped around the driver's seat and through the back windows to see if she ran out into the street below but couldn't see down that far. "Simone!" he called again and then stood still in the seat for a moment to listen for her rustling on the brown grass near the van. Nowhere to be seen or heard. Peter stood up in the driver's seat on his tip-toes and looked around one more time. "Simone!"

Peter sat down in the seat and started to steer the van again, grabbing the shifter on the column to put the truck in gear so that he could 'go find' his dog. His dog. Simone wasn't a puppy any longer, he just realized, as if he had just awakened from a coma. Peter stood up in the seat again, driving like a mad delivery driver looking for that elusive address, when he realized that the van had actually begun to move backward. The van was really moving! Not just in Pretend Land. And the next thing that Peter realized was that the van had picked up speed, rolling down the steep driveway and out into the street, right out from under his fluttering belly like a yanked table cloth. Fear splashed over Peter like cold water. He was play-driving one second, and the next, he could feel the van roll right out from under him, down the hill, crashing over the curb on the other side of the street, where it came to a rest, mangling the chain-link fence surrounding the lot opposite the house.

Peter sat still in his seat for a moment, hoping not to hear Simone screaming in pain from under the wheels of the van. Then the real fear came over him like a rash now. He knew that his dad would really kill him for such unforgivable transgression. He knew that his dad had every right in the book of fathering, if there were such a thing, to literally beat, flog and skin the boy alive. Peter had definitely crossed the shifting line his father had laid before him. He had destroyed property, and because of that, there would definitely and rightly be no mercy.

Peter looked up at the house on the hill, waiting for his dad to come out, running down the hill to jerk the boy from the van like a ragged doll that needed to be burnt. Peter began to cry at the thought of his sure punishment to come. It would be over now. Where was his mom? Why did he have to be such a rotten kid? Would death really hurt, or would he just go to another dream, like all of his dreams, like his life, floating by and through him like so much of his reality these days? Oh...lucidity...in space and time.

Eventually, Verlin came out of the front door, lumbering down the driveway in his short jean shorts and no t-shirt. Peter felt uncomfortable at the grin on his dad's face and the way he didn't even seem to be bothered by the sight of the van sitting there perched up on the curb, tangled in a chain-link fence. The tumult of the whole thing made Peter want to throw up. He knew his dad would be angrier than a sober coal miner, but then seeing his dad smiling scared him even more than the anticipated response of rage.

"Hey, boy," Verlin said. "You goin' somewhere?"

"No, sir."

"You ain't gotta be so damned serious all the time, ya know? You gotta have fun on vacation, ya know?"

"Yes, sir."

Verlin walked up to Peter's side of the van and rested his arms on the window ledge.

"Where's that rodent of yours?"

"I can't find her."

Verlin opened the door and told Peter to step out of the van. Peter wanted to run but knew that he couldn't outrun his dad, so he just got out of the van and started walking back up the hill to the house.

"Where you goin' boy?"

"Inside."

Verlin held up the keys to the van and then got in the driver's seat. Peter stood on the edge of the yard, hoping that his dad would just let him go inside and that he would leave so that Peter could get a shower and something to eat.

"You wanna go for a ride?"

"I'm hungry."

Verlin mocked Peter, like a schoolyard bully might, as Peter just stood there waiting for whatever judgment the old man felt necessary to dole out. Verlin started the van. Peter could hear him pushing the clutch in and putting the thing into first gear. Peter couldn't even reach the pedals, but he was able to get that thing to roll down the hill. He smiled for a second while his dad was messing with something under his seat.

"Boy, you're lucky you didn't kill anyone, you know that?"

"Yes, sir."

Verlin laughed and then said, "Son, you look like you seen a ghost. Why don't you go in there and get cleaned up, okay? Shit, boy, you look like a damned spook or something. It ain't that bad, son. Shit, I ain't gonna beat you or nothin'." Verlin produced a pack of cigarettes from somewhere out of sight and lit up. Peter didn't think anything could fit in those shorts other than the man that had already occupied them. The old man with girl's shorts on and greasy hair made Peter laugh inside for another quick second. Verlin drove down the street as Peter walked up to the house.

Peter went inside, the house dark and cool as usual. Everything was still in disorder as if the place had been left abandoned by some refugees who had just moved in. He felt strange being in the house alone with Louise since the last time that he saw her; she was naked and sweaty and acting really weird. He looked around to see if she was lurking in the shadows somewhere in the corner of a room. He softly called for Simone but didn't see her anywhere. Didn't hear her paws pattering near him on the kitchen floor. Peter went to the back door, cracked it, and looked outside for his dog, but didn't see her anywhere. His dog. Simone had gotten bigger all of a sudden. Was it all of a sudden?

Peter decided that he better get in the shower and then get something to eat before his dad got back and kicked him outside again. No, I better get food; first, he thought. The shower could wait.

Peter went to the fridge and pulled out a couple of containers that looked like they might have something good in them. The first container he opened had some meat and potatoes in it, but they looked a little green. He put his nose to the container, pulling his head back quickly from the sharp, sour smell. He put the lid back on the container, put it back, and pulled another Tupperware dish out, along with a package of bologna, or 'dog meat', as his grandpa called it, and put them on the counter. Peter looked at the bologna, thinking of Simone. He didn't want his dog used for lunch meat.

The other Tupperware container had chicken-fried steak and some green beans in it. He grabbed a piece of meat, devouring it in one, two, three, four bites. He grabbed the other piece of meat, doing the same, and then the cold, mushy green beans before he had a chance to really chew any of it up. He got back into the fridge and grabbed a pack of cheese slices and the mayonnaise from the door. Peter quickly put a double bologna and cheese sandwich with mayonnaise together. He threw the empty Tupperware into the sink, put the bread and fixings away, and went to the bathroom to start his water.

Peter had just turned the water on when he heard the commotion out in the living room. He turned the water off for a minute to make sure that the noise wasn't from an intruder or someone there to hurt them. He could hear his dad's voice rumbling low like the motor of his van. Peter thought that he had heard Louise out there too, but couldn't be sure, because their voices were low and muffled. Peter put his ear to the door but still couldn't hear clearly. He took another bite of his sandwich and then turned to turn on the water again.

"Hey, boy," Verlin said, opening the door on Peter; no knock, nothing.

"What?"

Verlin stepped into the bathroom and shut the door behind him. Peter stood next to the bathtub, the water running really hot now, and looked up at Verlin with a mouthful of sandwich, his belly already barking from eating the meat and green beans too quickly.

"What? What? Is that how you talk to your old man? Huh?" Verlin said, mocking Peter again. "You need to clean that mess up out there in the kitchen." He put a cigarette in his mouth. Peter stared at his dad's tight shorts as if they were going to disintegrate right there on the spot. He could see the outline of Verlin's pack of cigarettes in his pocket, under the faded, frizzy denim. The old man stood right in front of Peter with his bulging crotch in his face like an obscene animal. Peter really felt dirty and hot now. He moved back toward the bathtub a half step, almost falling in.

"Whoa, there, little fella. You better watch out," Verlin said and left the bathroom.

That the old man let him have his sandwich in the bathroom really surprised Peter. Verlin told him to clean up the kitchen yet didn't say anything about getting his ass back outside where he belonged. Peter thought that maybe things were finally changing for the better. He would take whatever grace and clemency he could get. Maybe the old man just had to warm up for a few months before the fun could really begin.

All along, however, in the commotion from out in the living room, and his dad's bursting into the bathroom, Peter had forgotten to plug the bathtub, letting the water run right down the drain the whole time. He decided to take a shower after all. He locked the bathroom door, undressed, and got into the shower.

The water didn't feel as hot as it had when his dad had come in, so he turned the hot up almost to full blast. He got wet, put shampoo in his hair, and then started to scrub his head, the water getting a little cooler yet. Peter turned the hot all the way up and then hurried to get soaped up and rinsed before the water got too cold. He started to rinse, the water cooling even more, and hurried yet a little more, running his hands over his body, rinsing off as quickly as he could, racing to beat the cold water surely to come, driving him out of the shower even before his dad had the chance to. Peter hustled and got done just as the water felt like it couldn't get any colder. He got out of the shower and dried off.

Peter could hear someone trying to get in and could see the doorknob jiggle a little bit. "Boy, you better unlock the damned door before I kick it in." Peter stepped to it, unlocking the door, towel wrapped around himself, trying to warm up from the cold shower. Verlin let himself in and said, "You better hurry up, boy. We need to talk." Verlin left the bathroom but left the door wide open.

"Hey, Peter," Louise said, walking by in her nightgown.

Peter hoped that she wouldn't come into the bathroom while he was undressed. He didn't feel safe around her anymore. He really didn't feel safe around either one of them, but she really creeped him out because he never knew which person he would be getting with Louise. Sometimes it was the really creepy, eerily friendly, naked, and sleazy Louise, and other times it was just the absent-minded and aloof Louise as if she had become some kind of stoned, fleshy robot that had no mind of her own. She had the ability to suck the life from a person either way, without even having to resort to violence or by playing the kind of head games that his dad continuously played.

Peter hurried to get dressed, wiped the sink and mirror, and hung his towel up to dry. He looked into the mirror to see if he recognized himself any longer. Peter had gotten skinnier than he had ever been, and the circles around his eyes had gotten larger yet. His hair was getting long. He felt old. He looked like he had aged maybe three or four years. He feigned a smile, thinking of himself as a little girl with golden locks. He stuck his tongue out and held it there and then scraped the surface by pulling it back into his mouth hard against the front of his top teeth. A thick line ran the length of his tongue where his missing front tooth didn't scrape the surface. He got another drink of water from the faucet, as much as he could gulp down without it coming back up, took a couple of breaths, and gulped a couple more swallows down before he shut the water off. Simone is getting so big. She's my friend.

"Come on, boy!" Verlin yelled from the other room.

Peter went out to the living room, surprised to see the curtains drawn and the smell of grilled cheese throughout the house. The light in the house felt good to him as if the darkness all around had fled for good, yet the contrast seemed awkward in a disconcerting way. Verlin and Louise had even moved a couple of things into place and out of the way in the living room. The living room almost seemed lived in now.

The clouds had broken outside, and the sun had begun to pour into the house. Good food, light, and fresh air made Peter think of home. He walked over to the kitchen table where Verlin sat smoking a cigarette, leisurely turning the pages of a newspaper. The familiar rustle of newspaper pages gave Peter a further sense of comfort, of home, thinking of his grandpa on Sunday mornings after church. Curls of smoke clung to the rays of light beaming through the window, spilling over the floor and up Louise's legs, where she stood at the stove.

"Sit down, boy," Verlin said.

Peter sat down at the table, looking over at Louise, who still had her back turned to him. She was dressed but didn't have much to say to either Peter or Verlin, the sizzle of the grilled-cheese sandwiches in the skillet the only sound coming from where she stood.

"Here."

Verlin handed Peter what appeared to be a package, a little bundle, wrapped up in some of the newspaper that Verlin must have already read. Peter slowly began to pull the package apart by pulling the corner of the newspaper so that the whole thing unraveled, the loose end getting bigger and bigger. Once the paper had been unraveled, Peter stared at the lump of gray slime in the center of the newspaper page. The little blob in the center of the page looked like a smut that grows on ears of corn. The gray, putty-like blob smelled sharp and pungent.

"What is it?"

Louise turned from the stove, looked at Verlin, and held out the breakfast pan. Verlin shook his head 'no.'

"That's what killed your dog, boy."

Peter looked up at his dad with the eyes of an old widow. The life and love and passion for living had gone like the wind on a dark night. Verlin looked at Peter as if he were going to say, 'I told you so,' but kept his mouth closed around his cigarette for a second longer, puffing, giving Louise the go-ahead to serve him his late breakfast.

"Simone?"

"She ran off and got into some poison, boy."

Peter didn't cry, get up from the table, or do anything that would give the old man the satisfaction of knowing that he had shown Peter who was boss yet again. Peter felt pretty sure that his father had killed the dog. That locking him outside wasn't punishment enough, that they, Peter and Simone, were incorrigible and deserved the most stringent discipline. Peter sat still in his chair, staring at the little gray blob in the center of the newspaper, waiting for that lightning, waiting for that angel.

Louise finally walked over to the table, sliding one of the grilled-cheese sandwiches off of her spatula onto Verlin's plate. She looked at Peter and went back to the stove to get the other sandwich she had just prepared. She shuffled back over to the table, dragging her feet, seemingly numb to everything that went on in the kitchen, and slid the other sandwich onto Verlin's plate.

"Thanks, babe," he said. "Can you put Peter out?"

Louise walked over to the back door and opened it for Peter. Peter looked at his dad for some recognition, for a glance at least, but then just folded the newspaper up around the lump of smut or poison or whatever it was and walked out the back door as if he were going off to his sure slaughter.

"Boy, you better think about what happened, okay?" Verlin said, Louise, closing the door behind Peter.

Peter walked over to the edge of the yard and kicked the chain-link fence, sending a reverb down the length of the yard. He sat down next to the fence and unfolded the newspaper, staring at the gray blob inside again, as if he could figure out its origin and substance by staring at it endlessly into the night and that somehow that knowledge would lead him back in time to where he could thwart fate perhaps, create a new outcome. He had never seen anything like it before, but he knew it wasn't natural, and he further knew it was something that his dad had given the dog to kill it. Why? Peter didn't understand. His best friend had died. Simone didn't hurt anyone. She was a cute puppy. She had become a dog. How long had they been friends? Sewell and Pinkie were gone too, and now Simone. Peter wanted to hurt his dad. He wanted to make him suffer and scream and cry like no one had ever made him do before.

Peter's stomach felt hot inside as if it would burn right through his shirt, sending the meager contents and steaming bile all over the ground where he sat. He threw the paper with the lump inside over the fence and then fell to his knees and started pounding the ground before him, crying, as he shouted unintelligible grunts like a drunk indigent. He carried on like that for a minute or so before he got tired and then decided to lay on the ground to try to go to sleep.

Peter stared up at the fluffy clouds that were pinned against the thin, blue covering of the sky. The weather had turned for the better, the pretty blue sky and the dissipating clouds, but the worst had still come to Peter, just the same.

Verlin came outside to tell Peter that he didn't show him the dog carcass because the dead animal might give Peter nightmares. The old man didn't want to scare the boy, he said, and he had a responsibility to protect him from harm's way, to keep him from losing his innocence any more than he already had. To any sentient being over the age of five, the thought would have been laughable that Verln cared about anything but his fragile ego and his rights to ownership of children and women, but it all seemed plausible to Peter, nonetheless. It made sense to him. He just didn't know why his dad would kill his only friend, his pet. Peter said that he understood and thanked his father even for being so understanding.

Peter crouched down on the ground, pushing his finger into the earth under the brown grass, Verlin going back inside. Peter knew that he would end up like Ramona Whitcanuck, dead and alone, and worse yet, he knew that there would be nothing that he could do about it. He had resigned himself to loneliness and shame there in the back yard...and hunger...and anger...and ultimately death. As he squatted down, numbly staring at the ground, at his finger, he had a warm sensation overcome his body, as if he were dipped into a warm, lavender bubble bath. Soothing and surreal, like a spirit had descended upon him out of thin air.

Peter looked up to see who approached him from behind but saw no one in the backyard. He could feel the presence of someone near him, as if someone were right there hovering over him, watching his every move and holding him in their gentle gaze, not the weighty gaze of his father. He stood up and looked around, thinking that the old man was playing 'games' again, giving him a run for the fun of it, but still couldn't see anyone near. The sensation continued to warm him from the inside out, and something else...what was it?..the sensation...was...calming...and reassuring in a way.

Peter realized that it couldn't have been his dad because he never felt peace and safety near him. That sense he got around his father actually felt a stark opposite to what he felt right then and there. The warm glow, like a couple of shots of whiskey, continued to build in his chest and then radiated out into his arms and legs, and then onto his fingers and toes, and out through his head...and then it was gone.

Peter instantly had the overwhelming thought that everything would, in fact, be okay and that he would be safe and home before he knew it. The image of Ramona Whitcanuck's bloody body and baseball cap, which he had never actually seen, like Simone's dead body, flashed in his mind, and then the thought of peace came again, stronger even yet, as if in some mystical, ethereal opposition to the thought of death and loneliness and suffering. You are going to be okay, the feeling spoke at a soul-level, where words were not necessary as if concepts and thoughts could be conveyed strictly through biophysics and chemistry alone, as if there were some elusive code that had been transmitted throughout his bloodstream, through the sinews of his body, which manifested in clear communication, as words to the ear might. The noiseless mental impression said, "You are going to be okay. Believe it."

Chapter 32

Fr. Ligero hung his head out the open window of Addie's old jalopy, the wind churning his gray hair like the Holy Spirit.

"That's a fancy car...boy, howdy!" Addie said, looking in the rearview.

"Yeah," Fr. Ligero said. "It's just a perk, Addie. We'll probably sell it after our mission's complete."

"You could buy a nice fuckin' trailer for the money that thing cost."

"We're on a mission from God. We gotta ride around in style."

"That boy went to prison, didn't he?"

"This is his first stop out of the can."

"Ain't that a pisser?"

"Yeah. Peter told me about some of your days of fighting crime."

"I ain't proud'a doin' a lotta the shit I done, you hear?"

Fr. Ligero puffed on his cigar contemplatively, rolling the ash off of the side mirror. He looked over at Addie, who looked like a little boy behind the wheel. "We've all done things we're not proud of, Addie."

"That boy done his time, I figure."

"He just wants to patch things up with his dad before it's too late."

"We already done buried my daddy," Addie said, "old bastard never was too good. He never did care nothin' of us. He's deader'n a kilt dog now."

"Did he ever give you his blessing?"

"What the hell that got to do with anything?"

Fr. Ligero patted Addie on the shoulder and said, "I guess not...but you know...you can have God's blessing right now, and I'll pray that for you."

"I need all the prayers I can get. That's for damned sure, ya know?"

"Me too."

Fr. Ligero said a comforting, to-the-point prayer for Addie as they went from one pocked blacktop road to the next and then onto the dirt roads. It still caught him off guard when some of the saltier characters he ministered to actually wanted him to pray for them. But then again, really, it always seemed to be the more clipper-cut, respectable types who would pass on prayer. Seemingly, the folks who had come to the end of every fruitless path in life and who had ended up rather scathed by life always proved to be the most open to his gesture.

Fr. Ligero gazed out the window over the pastures scattered with dilapidated, bleached-out buildings as he smoked his cigar. The burdened wood frames and graying clapboard sagged like old men coming in from the fields. All things come to an end after their usefulness has run its course. Fr. Ligero felt pretty good about how things were unfolding thus far, despite the fact that Peter probably felt scared and nauseous, that old anticipation of meeting his father yet again, after many years, gathering in his belly. Fr. Ligero had told Peter to take care of his 'side of the street', so to speak, and that all he could do was try to make amends for killing Verlin's wife. There would be no way to replace her. Verlin's girls grew up without a mom. Peter had to face the music.

Addie said they weren't going to be doing any of that hippy camping as they do in Colorado, with all of the fancy gear and tents and crap. They were going out to be one with the wild. Catching fish and getting good and drunk and sleeping under the stars was how they did it out there at Verlin's. Fr. Ligero told him that he didn't drink anymore after he left the gambling boats back on the Mississippi, to which Addie laughed and pulled out a bottle from under his seat. "You mind if I do, there, buddy?" Fr. Ligero smiled as Addie took swill. "You some kinda preacher?"

"I used to be a priest."

"How long it been since you got you some?"

"A long time."

Addie pulled his car up to an old, beat-up, rusty cattle guard and put the car in park. "You ain't gay, is ya?"

"I got kicked out of the priesthood because of my improprieties, directly related to a relationship with a woman."

"Well, I'll be..." Addie trailed off, looking in the rearview mirror. "So what happened to your impro..? What was that?"

"Impropriety."

"Yeah. Well, huh? What happened to that sweetheart?"

"She left the country with a sailor from Italy."

"Fuckin' bitch."

"I guess you could say that," Fr. Ligero said. "Sometimes people just need to find what they're looking for, Addie."

"Bullshit! I'd have gone out and shot the bitch."

"I thought about it."

"I'd have done it for ya if we'd been buds back then."

"I'll keep that in mind for the future."

Addie smiled at Fr. Ligero, who continued to puff his cigar, pointing to the road ahead. "Are we going in, or what?"

"I want you to go out there and stomp around on that cattle guard to see if you think she'll hold up."

"I don't think I weigh as much as a car."

"Just gitter done, will ya?"

Addie put the car into drive after Fr. Ligero got back in from checking the rusty, old pipes. "I guess we won't know until we drive over it, huh?" Addie said.

Addie pulled in through the opening of the leaning barbed wire and old tree post fence that ran from out of the woods on either side of where the gate should have been. Fr. Ligero turned in his seat to make sure the Beamer would make it over the deep ruts in the road. Peter waved them on from behind.

"She gonna be alright, buddy," Addie said.

"You know this place pretty well?"

"I told you, this is Verlin's land," Addie said. "We used to come out here and shoot guns and fish...ya know...get drunk. A long time ago. I ain't seen Verlin in a long time myself, ya know?"

"We didn't get any supplies, Addie."

"Verlin's got everything we need. He said to come on out, to hurry up."

Fr. Ligero flicked his cigar out the window, gazing into the blackjack oak and thickets of scrub-oak saplings covering the ground. The early evening sun poured through the trees above in thin, tall sheets, everything mottled with amber light and random shades and hues thereof. Addie crept through the trees and thicket like he was trying to sneak up on Verlin like some weekend warrior.

Addie said that it was all he could do to not bottom out on the deep ruts, the mound of grass in the middle of the road scratching from beneath. The trees closed in on the cars like palm fronds at the gates of the city, welcoming them home.

"Verlin knows that Peter's coming out here with you?"

"You bet your sweet ass he does," Addie said. "Them girls'a his are comin' too. He said it's gonna be a regular old family reunion."

"Do you know his girls?"

"They moved away as soon as they were old enough," Addie said. "After their mama died, they didn't want nothin' to do with their pissy old man. He ain't the cheeriest bastard in the woods here."

"I've heard some stories."

Chapter 33

Verlin brought Peter inside the house, scrubbed him down like a prize-winning horse, and set him at the kitchen table, where Louise had spread out a feast of a breakfast fit for a professional football team. The house looked to be totally in order now. Clinically clean, tidy, and fit for a surgeon…or a sociopathic father with a penchant for cleanliness, that is. Fresh-cut flowers and the gentle splash of sunlight coming through the window looked otherworldly to Peter, like seeing things through new prescription lenses for the first time. He had been outside for several days at that point, a new brand of camping, some might say, yet he now basked in his newfound hope, like a miracle, unfathomable.

Peter felt really nervous about all of the cheer and sunlight. The niceties felt awkward like the last time he got his hopes up, and he wondered how the old man and his automaton girlfriend would crush his spirits this time. Nevertheless, they were talkative…to each other, Louise and Verlin…and seemingly happy, genuinely chatty, and light. Peter kept his mouth shut and dug in while the getting was good.

"We're going to the parade today, Peter," Louise said, perky disposition and new clothes. Her open nightgown and her browning pink slippers had been retired for the time being, and she actually looked fresh and somehow younger. Peter had rather grown accustomed to her breast-exposing nightgown, yet he welcomed the fresh, new appearance of the new-and-improved, presentable Louise. He said a little prayer that she wouldn't become the creepy lady again.

Peter dropped his fork on his plate, sending a loud tang through the kitchen, and ran over to his shoes that lay on the rug near the front door. They had been washed and re-laced. Louise gathered herself and put out the last dish that she had been filling with blackberry preserves.

"Come on, buddy. Eat your breakfast, okay?" Verlin said, getting up from the table and walking over to where Peter sat on the floor and grabbing the boy by the arm. "You gotta get a good breakfast. It's a big day, boy."

"Come on, hon," Louise said as if she had just re-learned to talk, smiling, proud of her two cents worth.

Peter pulled both shoes onto his feet, not tying them, and went back to the table, where he continued to put more food on his plate. He loaded up as if his last meal lay before him. The old man and his creepy girlfriend might actually have been weirder happy than they were in their usual crappy mood, Peter thought, smiling, grabbing a little of this and a little of that, eventually running out of space on his plate. Peter realized that he would probably get more of the usual treatment once they got back home from the parade. He would deal with life in the backyard when the time came.

Peter ate some bacon, one-piece, two pieces, and then forked some hash browns into his mouth, and then some eggs. He crammed his mouth full like a teenager in a growth spurt, wanting to eat as fast as he could so that they could get onto the parade and funnel-cake and cotton candy.

Verlin and Louise went to the other room and came back with a card and a little basket.

"Here you go, buddy," Verlin said, "we thought you might like a little something for being so good." The gesture felt artificial and thin to Peter, like a crack head returning your totaled car after a joy ride might feel to someone a little older. If he had known the phrase "being obscenely placated," he may have used it. Peter threw the card to the side and tore it into the basket. "I hope you like the Army men," Verlin added. "Soldiers are real men, boy."

Peter dug through the basket, tearing into a Snickers bar with veracity, little green Army men flying about as if a bomb went off in the basket. "Thank you," he said, food spilling over the edge of his plate.

Verlin grimaced as each little morsel fell to the table, wanting to clean it up, his hand inching toward the food droppings without him even realizing it, the grease from the hash browns leaving little marks. Louise gently touched his arm. Verlin got up from the table and disappeared for a minute, possibly to do some shadow-boxing or calisthenics to burn off some of his frustration at having to deal with the little imperfections of Peter's slapdash dining habits.

Peter ate two plates full of breakfast and another Snickers bar. Verlin came back into the kitchen and went to the counter to turn on the radio. A commercial advertising the city parade came on. The parade was being put on to honor the work of Roland Stacks.

"Yeah, buddy! It's gonna be a fuckin' rip-roarin' time," Verlin said, going to the fridge to get a beer. He popped the top and lit a cigarette.

"My mama and daddy are gonna be there, Verlin."

Verlin held his beer up in front of him like he was toasting an invisible friend. "Well, well. That's just great, sweetie. I can't wait to see'em. They're gonna have to party down with me. Them sweet little fuckers, they are."

"Well, hon..." Louise began to say, sitting down at the table.

"That sum bitch ain't worth a turd in my book."

"Pinkie likes Roland Stacks," Peter said, looking up from his ransacked basket.

"That's real fuckin' nice, boy. She's gonna have a good time then, huh?"

"They're gonna be there?

Verlin nodded 'yes' as he took a drink of his beer, staring at Peter. "You bet your sweet ass, son."

"Sewell too?"

"Grandpa!" Verlin shouted and started laughing.

Verlin and Louise rode upfront as Peter sat upright in the comfy chair Verlin had put in the back of the panel van. He couldn't see out of the windshield because every time he tried, Louise would tell him to sit down, that he didn't want to get hurt if they got into an accident.

The parade was in town, Verlin said. That rat-bastard Roland Stacks had his own float with a bunch of tee-totaling retards that were coming along for the free ride. That old boy had all of Mississippi coming out to hear his bullshit. Peter felt light and happy, nevertheless, listening to his dad rant on about a man he didn't even know.

"Why do you listen to his radio show all the time, dad?"

Louise turned to Peter and put her finger to her lips.

"It's ironic, I guess, boy. I think someone's gonna shut that fucker up someday."

"Verlin!" Louise shouted.

"You know what ironic means, son?"

"No, sir."

"It means shit don't make no fuckin' sense." Verlin turned in his seat, swerving the van a little bit, to look at Peter. "Whattaya think about that?"

Peter had a look of serious contemplation on his face.

"What the hell's goin' through that little nut'a yours, boy?"

"Like our vacation?"

"What about our vacation?"

"It's ironic," Peter said, not so sure if he had it right by the look on his dad's face.

"Boy, you better watch that fuckin' pie hole!"

"Verlin!" she said again as if she were reminding herself of her boyfriend's name by some new method of forceful expression.

Peter sat back in his chair, soaking up that familiar vibration of the van rolling down the highway. He could see the tall pines and the hot blue sky out in front of them. He turned the transistor radio on, thinking of Ramona Whitcanuck and the end of that short life. Peter almost felt guilty that he was getting to go to a parade and that she had died at the hands of some dirty scoundrel.

Chapter 34

"Don't inhale it," Fr. Ligero said.

"Already did." Addie coughed, filling the car with smoke, and then continued gagging and slobbering all over himself like some St. Bernard chimera.

Fr. Ligero punched Addie in the arm, laughing. "Don't puke on me, now."

"Them things is pretty damned strong, ya know?"

They pulled into a clearing just beyond the opening of the canopy of trees perching over the road, the light dimming more, the sun beginning to simmer on the horizon in swaths of purple, pink, and orange.

"You aren't supposed to inhale them," Fr. Ligero said. "Here." He demonstrated how to puff the cigar deliberately, slowly savoring the flavor, smacking his lips a little bit after the long draw, and then letting the smoke curl out of his mouth in thick ropes, only to be snatched up by the breeze from outside the car. "See? Now you try it."

Addie took a long, deep pull off of the cigar, puffing his cheeks out, and then blew all the smoke out in one quick burst.

"You'll get it."

"It just don't seem right, not inhalin' all that smoke," Addie said. "You don't get that punch in the lungs that a cigarette gives ya."

"Yeah, that's why cigars don't kill people like cigarettes do. You'll get used to it. Not getting the punch, that is. Savoring the flavor." Fr. Ligero demonstrated the draw and the delay again, then held the cigar out in front of himself to inspect it, like he was examining a stogie for the first time in his life, surprised by the pleasing flavor, and compelled to see just what in fact he held in his possession. "That and the fact that many cigar-smokers don't smoke all day compulsively like cigarette-smokers do." He took another deliberate puff of his cigar and then looked beyond the smoke. "Look at that sunset."

"Purty, ain't it?"

"You betcha."

A white, mid-60s model panel van sat parked at the edge of a pond up ahead, a few citronella Tiki torches trailing through the brush down to the water's edge. Fr. Ligero felt his blood heat up and expand in his chest at first sight of the vehicle sitting there. The stories about that van, about the year or so that Peter had spent with his father back in Mississippi, with the dad who hadn't been much of a dad. The mere sight of that object from the past felt like some sort of talisman, attaching itself to the moment, conjuring another time and dimension altogether.

Fr. Ligero turned around in his seat and saw that Peter and Carly Jo were still behind him and Addie. The black Beamer gleamed in the evening light. Addie pulled in behind the panel van, Peter parking next to him. They both turned the cars off and sat there for a second. Looking at the water up ahead, over the brush.

"Has he had that van a long time?" Fr. Ligero said.

"Longer'n I known him," Addie said.

Addie got out of the car and held himself up by holding onto the door frame as he began to edge himself around to the trunk where his wheelchair had been stored.

"We didn't stop to get any grub," Peter said, halfway out of his car.

"Don't you worry 'bout all that, buddy," Addie said, "your old man said he gotter done, alright?"

"Sure."

Fr. Ligero could tell that Peter would have rather been anywhere else in the world right then but didn't want to ruin the moment with futile words, placating his friend with a shallow comfort that wouldn't do him any good anyhow. He wanted Peter to feel every moment of the situation, his life's culminating event, like the time he'd been preparing for in prison came to fruition and, ultimately, the moment that would finally allow him to move on without fear and doubt and curious wonder lurking after him for the rest of his life.

Fr. Ligero went around the back of Addie's car and met him at the trunk. "You need a hand, partner?"

"I ain't gonna be able to use my wheelchair out here."

"Can you walk?" Fr. Ligero said.

"I gotta damned cane that I sometimes use when I'm feeling adventurous," Addie said, working on getting the wired-shut trunk open. He jimmied where the lock used to be with a screwdriver that he pulled from his back pocket. "Come on, now. You gotta help me get this damned thing open."

Fr. Ligero pushed down on the trunk while Addie worked his magic. Peter and Carly Jo stood behind the two of them, silent, staring out over the shiny pond up ahead as if they were on a first date. Addie finally got the cane out of the trunk with a little help from his new friend. "Alright, dipshits. Let's get down there before that bastard falls in and drowns."

As they approached the pond through the saplings, thick underbrush, and ragweed, Fr. Ligero could hear a hissing sound up ahead. Hissing and releasing. Hissing and releasing as if some mechanical animal were dying at the water's edge, waiting for someone to come along and put it out of its pathetic misery. Fr. Ligero imagined that Peter's father had some kind of apparatus that simply pumped the fish into a basket and then spat the unwanted debris and water back into the pond, cycling over and over until he "caught" all of the fish that he wanted for the day. The thought was not only absurd but really flattering still that he would credit Verlin with such a level of ingenuity.

"What is that?" Peter said.

"I don't know," Addie said, mockingly holding his hand over his face. "The bogeyman, I guess."

"Addie, you ain't no good," Carly Jo said.

And then the four of them ambled through all of the ragged growth, standing behind an uncomfortably large man, oxygen tank pumping and cigarette smoke spiraling away from the side of his head, like burn-off from a refinery in the middle of nowhere.

"Hey, ya old rat-bastard," Addie said.

Verlin turned to see Fr. Ligero, Addie, Carly Jo, and Peter standing there behind him like four kids who had accidentally run up on a bear in the woods.

Chapter 35

Verlin parked the van on a side street, several blocks from the little downtown area through which the parade would be traveling. Louise patted Verlin on the arm and forced a little smile.

Verlin shrugged Louise's arm off and said, "Okay, boy. You ready?"

"Yes, sir."

They all got out of the van, Verlin going around the back and opening the doors. He moved some stuff around on the floor and then heaved a blue ice chest out of the back and onto the ground.

Peter stared into the back of the van for a second and then watched Verlin pull a beer from the ice chest, knocking the ice off, opening it, and then throwing the tab in the grass. Verlin held the beer up to Peter. "Wanna drink, boy?"

"Verlin," Louise said, pulling Peter by the arm as she started walking away.

Verlin laughed at Louise and lit a cigarette. He pulled a pint of whiskey from his back pocket and took a long swig of the amber courage, as well.

"Come on, Dad," Peter said.

Verlin shut the back doors to the van and said, "Louise, could you help me carry our drinks?"

Louise let go of Peter's arm, went back to where Verlin stood, and grabbed one of the handles to the ice chest.

"Did you get something other than beer?"

"I got some Mello Yellow, sweetie-pie."

Louise looked at Verlin as if he had just called her a stupid bitch.

The three of them ambled down the Magnolia and pine-lined sidewalk, still damp with morning dew. People up ahead were walking toward the crowds that lined the streets in front of the old brick buildings with their deep display windows. Peter held a couple of Army men tightly in his grip, walking up ahead of Verlin and Louise.

Peter couldn't shake the feeling that Louise had actually been replaced by a look-alike. She had become a totally different person altogether. Her levity and desire to help and communicate and engage felt very out-of-place to Peter. He thought that maybe he should ask his dad if she felt okay, but realized that would be silly, so he just accepted the new behavior, for the time being, fully realizing that some things are better left alone. He could accept the mystery for the sake of the mystery itself. It was a new day. God bless America!

"Don't you go running off now, boy," Verlin said, shaking Peter out of his morning meditation.

Peter turned and smiled as if he had taken that as a challenge. He felt strong and light in the new clothes that Verlin said Louise had bought him. New shirt with a race car on the front. New jeans. New underwear. Nothing with holes or dirt. Clean shoes.

"Hold on, woman," Verlin said, stopping to bend over and tie his shoe.

"What do you need that for?" Louise said, staring at the gun in the back of Verlin's waistband. "This is a parade, Verlin. A family affair."

"No shit? I thought we were in the fuckin' jungle or somethin'." Verlin sucked his teeth and rolled his eyes at Louise. "You outta mind your own damn business sometimes, woman."

Louise shrugged him off and grabbed her handle as Verlin stood up and grabbed the other handle, continuing on.

"Are we gonna sit with Pinkie and Sewell?" Peter said, stopping to let them catch up.

"Sure, boy. They're your fuckin' buddies now, huh? We're gonna have a damned good time today. I promise you that. Grandpa and Pinkie. My fuckin' heroes."

Peter started walking again once they caught up, fighting the urge to run off into the crowd ahead. The boy had manners and restraint, Verlin had told Louise one morning after he had let Peter in from one of his backyard slumber parties when she commented on the fact that Peter hadn't run away.

Verlin could hear the people ahead talking and laughing. He couldn't see what in the hell was so funny and interesting about being at another bullshit parade. He felt like walking into the crowd and smacking every last one of those stupid assholes for coming out to a parade honoring a fucking grifter who just wanted their money in trade for some empty, happy-clappy fairy tales. Louise's mom and dad were no better than the rest of those retards, he thought.

All of a sudden, Peter dropped his Army men on the ground, oblivious to Verlin and Louise standing behind him, and he darted toward the crowd ahead. He didn't look back.

"Boy! Don't you get lost up there! Hey!"

Verlin and Louise finally came to the edge of the street where everyone had set up lawn chairs and canopies to shield themselves from the already oppressive sun. Verlin scanned the area looking for Peter. He noticed a stage set up on the other side of the street about halfway down the block.

"That old dog ain't preachin', is he?"

"What do you think preachers do, Verlin?" Louise said, setting her end of the ice chest down.

Verlin sat his end of the ice chest down, staring hard at Louise. People walked around them, looking at Verlin with disapproval as he reached into the cooler and shook the ice off of another beer. Verlin lit his cigarette and rolled his eyes at a fat old lady with a cane who rubbed up against him, trying to stay on the sidewalk, edging around Verlin, who blocked the way.

"Maybe God'll knock some of the fat off that big ole ass, granny."

Louise slapped Verlin on the arm, and he laughed, having a good ole time. He continued looking over all the people, searching for Peter, who had blended into the pathetic crowd so quickly. Verlin wiped the sweat from his forehead and pointed over to the bank on the other side of the street, near the stage.

"There's the little fucker," Verlin said. "He already found your mama and daddy, right over there by where the preacher man's gonna be." Verlin bent to grab the ice chest, pulling the back of his t-shirt back down over his gun. "Come on, woman. You need a damn invitation or somethin'?" Louise didn't budge. "Louise! Come on, Simple Simon."

She just stood there as if she didn't want to be seen with Verlin in public, her hometown and all.

Verlin picked up the ice chest by himself and walked directly over to where Peter stood with Pinkie and Sewell. Public places usually scared the crap out of Verlin, yet he strolled across the street, through the throngs of parade-goers, like he was putting the dang thing on himself.

"Verlin," Sewell said, nodding his head as Verlin walked up.

Pinkie stood bent over, talking to Peter. Verlin set the ice chest down as Louise came up behind him, staring at his back. Pinkie looked up from talking to Peter and said, "Hey, hon."

"Hello, mama."

They hugged each other. Pinkie just stared at Verlin as he bent to get another beer out of the cooler. She looked away as he came up with another ice-cold libation.

"This is gonna be a Goddamn hell of a shindig, huh?" Verlin said.

"You outta watch that mouth in front of your boy, Verlin," Sewell said.

"Where's that fat friend of yours?" Verlin said. Sewell looked at Verlin, probably realizing that he meant Cow Town, but not wanting to dignify the slight with an answer. "Cow Town? Huh?" Verlin nudged him on the arm. Sewell didn't seem to be too entertained by Verlin's playful persistence. "You know his brother?"

"Yeah," Sewell said, pulling a pouch of tobacco from his back pocket. "He's a sheister lawyer."

"He's gonna help me out."

Sewell gave Verlin a tired look.

The parade had begun with a couple of burly motorcycle cops riding burly Harley Davidsons out in front of a burly drum majorette and a smattering of some of the members of a high school marching band. Verlin had taken a seat on the ice chest, almost sulking for a moment, as Pinkie and Peter, and Louise all huddled around a brochure that Pinkie had opened up before them. Sewell kept his eyes on the little parade.

Peter looked over at his dad and smiled. Verlin smiled back and then quickly got up and started walking down the street after he lit another cigarette.

The crowd continued to grow, the expectant believers pouring onto the main street from the surrounding area as they anticipated the coming of the man of the hour. Verlin pushed his way through the crowd, drinking his beer and smoking his cigarette amongst all of the mindless prudes who didn't have anything better to do other than stand out in the Mississippi heat waiting for some money-grubbing messiah on a late Saturday morning. Verlin felt at his back waistband for the gun, safe and sound, the closest thing to the faith he had ever known. He grabbed his half-empty whiskey bottle, opened it, and killed the rest of it before throwing it in the grass between the sidewalk and street.

Verlin had brought Peter to the parade to teach the boy a lesson, for shit's sake. A person has to stand up for what they believe to be true, and the boy needed his daddy to show him the way to fight for what mattered in life. Roland Stacks was gonna be preachin' his line of bullshit, sticking his hat out for money and lying and telling the good people that all they had to do was listen to him and give him money and get fat, and stay stupid, and the good Lord would take care of them and...and...fuck it...dammit!

Verlin tripped over his own two feet thinking about that crazy sack of shit. He'd fix that asshole once and for all; he would.

Verlin looked back to see if Sewell and the gang had stayed put. He didn't need no sorry kid of his or no old man following him around while he was taking care of business. Cow Town's brother had stood Verlin up twice now, and he had a thing or two to tell him too, but first wanted to scope the place out to see where that fucking preacher was gonna be coming down the road so that he could get a clear view of the old boy.

Verlin ducked into a little bootleg package store he had found by chance a couple of days earlier to get another pint of whiskey. The stress of everything had finally begun to press down too damned hard. He almost couldn't breathe. He had his boy safe in Mississippi where nobody could touch him, for the time being anyway, the court on his side, yet he had a lot of work to do to make things right. To get all of life under control, Verlin had to get control, dammit!

Verlin took a long, hard pull off of the whiskey bottle as he stepped out into the shaded doorway of the package store. He capped the bottle and moved to the sidewalk, just in time to hear the crowd go wild. He noticed Roland Stacks riding high afloat above the crowd, like God himself in the holiest of the holies, as all of his creation worshiped him with the fervor of a thunderstorm.

Verlin scanned the crowd again. He was looking for Cow Town. Cow Town's brother, maybe, not knowing what the guy looked like, sure, but...

Cops, Sewell, Louise. Whoever the hell might infringe on his liberties, keep him from taking care of what he came to do, he would have to deal with as it came.

Verlin opened the bottle of whiskey again and finished it in one more hearty, swift gulp. He threw the bottle into the doorway, smashing it against the concrete.

"Hey, mister!" a parade-goer passing by, wearing a 'God Loves Roland' shirt, said.

"Go fuck yourself," Verlin said and pulled out his Marlboro Reds. He lit a cigarette and started walking along the sidewalk, staggering now, following Roland on his float, the crowd totally immersed in the servant of God's presence. Verlin pulled the gun out of his waistband and pulled the slide. He aimed the gun at Roland Stacks and then quickly put the gun back down to his side. A little boy with a stuffed toy catfish looked up at Verlin with some concern.

"Go on, ya little shit," Verlin said to the boy, and the little boy looked away quickly.

Verlin continued to look around the crowd, his vision a little blurry, his gut-wrenching now. He thought that he saw a guy that looked like the boy's uncle, Lenny. Fucking paranoia, he thought and shook his head, trying to adjust his vision.

"Hey!" a little boy said, shouting at someone else altogether.

Verlin jerked, startled, and put his gun back into his waistband, spastically looking around the crowd. He sucked his cigarette down and tossed it in one of the doorways as he passed. He could see Sewell and Peter up ahead. Sewell was standing proudly, with Peter on his shoulders. Pinkie and Louise weren't anywhere to be seen, however.

Fucking bitch, Verlin thought. Just had to run off with her bitchy mother, didn't she? Huh? He looked across the street, past the parade, to see if the guy that looked like Lenny was still standing there. He wasn't. Verlin expected to see Peter's mom next, that damned whore-bitch. She had done her best to keep the boy away from Verlin. That didn't work out real well, did it? Who had the boy now? Who was the fucking hero now? Huh?

Verlin wiped the slick of sweat and grime from his forehead and pulled the gun out of his waistband again, picking up his pace to get next to the ornate float where Roland Stacks waved from.

Fucking hack, Verlin could almost be heard saying, the thought coming up from the deepest pit of hate and bitterness at the center of everything he amounted to. If anyone had been listening, the comment would have been audible. That was Verlin's eternal problem; nobody listened to him. Nobody!

Verlin put the gun to his side and then yanked it up in front of himself, aiming it right at Roland Stacks's chest, taking a steady, dead bead on the old man, the calm and stillness of his aim had come from deep within, the moment clear and clean and real, as if he stood outside of all space and time, like God himself.

Verlin had come on his own mission from God. He came to kill the imposter, and it really wasn't even premeditated. He was smart, and the weight of the gun felt good and solid, as he began to apply the slightest pressure to the trigger, and firmer still…but the safety was on, dammit!..the safety is never on…he thumbed the lever "off," and he reestablished his aim, and the next thing Verlin knew, his face was sliding across the pavement in front of his tumbling, drunken body.

Panic in the midst of that slow-motion kaleidoscopic vision hit him hard in the chest and neck, or was that a slab of concrete and a forearm?

Cow Town did show up. He sat straddled across Verlin's back, holding the back of Verlin's sweaty, hair-matted head down to the hard ground. That's when Verlin felt the first wave of searing pain spread across his face like hot oil. He tried to pick his head up but only felt more force come down on him when he did, pain in his knees and balls now too.

"Verlin," Cow Town said. "You gotta keep still, old boy. I don't wanna hurt you...but, you gotta chill the fuck out...okay." Cow Town fought to catch his breath as he held Verlin down. He had grabbed the .45 as Verlin fell forward, and he had already stashed the gun in his back waistband, trying not to draw any more attention than he had to.

A small crowd had formed around Verlin and Cow Town; nevertheless, women were gasping and children pointing. Cow Tow helped Verlin up and pushed him down the street. "Alright, people! Epileptic here! Move! Mind your business! Clear the way! Come on, now! Get the hell out of the way! Emergency!"

Cow Town continued to push Verlin in the opposite direction of the proceeding parade, looking around to make sure none of the city's finest closed in on them to see what the ruckus was all about. He pushed Verlin into a doorway, the one that Verlin had thrown the cigarette butt into, and reached for the doorknob.

"What the fuck are you doin'?"

"You ain't got the sense of cow, boy," Cow Town said, "you're lucky I took you out, man. You already got the heat on your dumb ass. You crazy?" he said with an added push on Verlin's back for emphasis.

They went through the door and into a plush reception area.

"This is my brother's office. He told me to bring you here. You got some serious trouble on your ass, dummy."

Chapter 36

Peter sat in the back seat of his uncle Lenny's car, his mom covering him with kisses and hugging him ferociously. He squirmed, trying to break free from the onslaught of affection. Something about the open road felt right to Peter, despite his mom's overbearing greeting, and he simply endured. He hadn't been on the road, going to God-knows-where since he and his dad left for their vacation. The days had dragged on like Chinese water torture, but the time, in general, had passed like a dream, and Peter was just glad to be with his real family again. A year older and a thousand wiser.

"Where are we goin'?" Peter said.

"For a ride," his uncle Lenny said.

Peter smiled at his mom, who continued kissing him, crying, petting him. He had been on Sewell's shoulders one second and in his loving mother's arms the next. Verlin didn't make a scene as the boy said his short, clipped goodbye to Sewell, who told him that he would see him later. He felt good that he had given Pinkie a hug before she walked off with Louise because he didn't see her right before he left the parade, being swooped up by his mom and uncle so swiftly.

"We're going home," Peter's mom said.

"Will I get to see Pinky and Sewell again?"

"I hope so, honey."

"They're nice, mom."

"Yeah, I think so."

Chapter 37

Peter had run the pick-up out of gas, filled it up, and nearly run it dry again before he went back to his new apartment, well after dark. Somewhere between his joyride and pulling into the parking lot of the apartment building, he finally realized that he would definitely have a psychotic, pissed man, his good ole dad, on his trail, and he started to get a little nervous. He rubbed his clammy hands on his dress pants and got out of the truck to go inside. The old man didn't have a problem smacking someone around a little, especially someone who should know better than to mess around with a guy's truck.

Peter didn't care when it came down to it. He wanted something real out of his father, anything, be it blood, anger, or love. He felt like that desperate, chubby girl in high school who would let Mr. Popular do anything to her, as long as she got the seeming affection, the date, no matter how superficial the attention might be. He wanted the old man to love him, to accept him, to tell him that he was doing the best that he could do, especially since he hadn't had a father around all those years. Peter had learned to be a man all on his own. Peter wanted to hear that his dad would now be there for him, no matter what. The way Peter saw it, his dad had a chance to redeem himself after years of being absent and indifferent. He would take rage if it came down to it, however.

Peter went around the building, pulling the little piece of paper out of his pocket that Perky had given him, the one with the building and apartment number on it, and unfolding it. When he got to the apartment door, he could hear loud music coming from inside. He looked down the little walkway at a group of kids playing in the grass next to the fence that butted up to the brightly lit parking lot. He looked the other way, already embarrassed to be going into the apartment that would surely soon be known as the new troublemaker's place in the complex. He let himself in the front door but didn't go any further.

Perky and her new 'friends' were dancing in the middle of the empty living room, boxes and paper scattered about like a storm. Peter stared at Perky until one of the other guys went over to the boom box that sat alone in the corner, turning it down as Perky started in.

"What the fuck are you doin' here?" she said. Peter had seen her drunk and high a million times and had never gotten used to the way her eyes seemed to belong to someone else, as she jerked around in her body like she was channeling some pissed-off, deranged mime. That mocking sneer deep down inside, like a demon, had gotten inside and taken the wheel, crashing into unsuspecting lives, ruining people's day, made him want to punch himself in the face for being so stupid as to get involved with someone as mindless as she could be.

"I thought I lived here, and..."

Perky stumbled over and hit Peter in the face before he could utter another word. He touched his nostrils to check for blood but came back with nothing. Perky stood in front of him laughing now, taunting him with threats that made no sense, while her retarded friends stood in the background like they were waiting to be released to recess. Peter stepped back, and Perky lunged at him, beginning to pound him in the chest.

"Come get your crazy bitch," Peter said through the barrage of punches and obscenities. He spoke to the brighter-looking of the two guys as if he had known him for a while, which only pissed Perky off more. She had just met the guys that day at the McDonald's drive-through down the street.

"Who the hell does he think he is, Peter, that fucking snob?" she had said to them as she picked them up for some afternoon fun.

The other guy, the dopier of the two, moved in to help get Perky under control as she kicked and screamed and scratched and bit at anyone within reach of her mouth and hands. There you go, buddies, Peter thought. Have fun with that one.

Peter stepped back toward the front door, looking down to make sure that he didn't get any blood or spit on his clean suit jacket. He smoothed the front of his jacket slowly, brushed a little lint from the front of his pants as if he were brushing Perky off for good, and then nonchalantly waved, heading toward the door.

As the three drunks writhed on the living room floor, Peter noticed a nice little baggy, stuffed tight with white crystalline powder, spilling onto a mirror on a coffee table in a little sitting area that had been fashioned out of boxes and the old table. He dumped a little more out onto the mirror and then took the baggy, closed it, and then stuffed it into the breast pocket of his jacket. Perky and her friends had stopped groping and slapping in anger and frustration and now appeared to grope each other in sexual hunger, or so it seemed, trying to get each other's clothes off and down to business. Peter let himself out the front door that he had never fully closed, hoping to never see Perky again.

Peter tossed the piece of paper with the address onto the ground as he walked back out to the parking lot. He felt like getting good and drunk. He took the baggy of powder from his pocket and opened it up. He dipped his finger in and tasted it, smacking it a couple of times. His mouth went numb instantly. Peter dumped a little cocaine into the crook of his left hand, in between his thumb and forefinger, and snorted it up, feeling better instantly, and then thinking about those idiots in the apartment, and then his dad, and then the truck, and then, and then, and then...whew!!! Off to the races, man! Time to get good and crazy!

Peter wanted to set the place on fire, to watch the whole miserable lot of them go up in flames. There were kids in the building. Normal people who worked and went to school. Leaving was the more reasonable thing to do, despite his feelings, to destroy and fuck and scream and eat and cry and run that damned truck off of a cliff somewhere at the edge of sanity.

Peter got back out to the truck and peered over the edge of the bed to see if there was a random ice chest filled with beer. Sure, he didn't hear it flailing around back there as he fish-tailed and spun all over God's creation earlier, but his dad was always prepared, he thought, and there should have been a treasure of beer bungy-corded to the side of the truck bed.

The only things in the truck bed were a quart of oil and a machete. He thought about grabbing the machete and marching himself right back into that apartment to hack the useless trio to pieces right there in that cramped living room. He realized that society would be better off without the three of them, their annoying music blaring loudly, their ridiculous theories regarding life and the meaning thereof, none of them contributing anything positive to the world.

Peter felt like he could put his foot right through the blacktop parking lot, his whole face numb at that point. He pulled the baggy out of his pocket again, unsealed it, dipped the truck key in it, and snorted a couple of little piles up into his nostrils.

He just felt betrayed again. Again, dammit!

But that's okay, he told himself. New day. New chapter. And a nice pile of coke, and some pain pills, and maybe a party with the girl in Pony Town, in his new truck and, yes!

Peter got into the pick-up and turned it on. He just had to get out onto the open road, blow some steam off, burn some fuel and rubber. That would make him feel better, clean him out! Maybe he could even go back to The Silver Stallion and see if Carly Jo wanted to do some blow and get naked. Have some damned fun! The roomie, some whiskey. That thick sensation in his crotch and throat surged. Sex and violence. Deranged ecstasy in the early sweltering evening.

Peter put the truck in reverse and pushed the pedal to the floor. The truck barely moved backward, spinning tires, billowing blue smoke all about, as he kept his eye on the walkway coming from Perky's apartment. He expected her to pop out at any moment with her friends bringing up the rear, realizing that Peter had taken their precious drugs, as she hurled dishes and bottles in the midst of all the smoke and noise.

Up ahead, there were some more kids playing in the orange glow of the high-pressure sodium lamps throughout the parking lot. Peter put the truck into 'drive' and floored it again. The kids froze for a second at the sound of the engine and then started running in Peter's direction as if they wanted to play chicken. Peter wanted so much to be a kid again, to have his whole life to do things differently, to not get involved with losers and drunks. Crazy, needy women always proved to be more work than they were worth, their looseness of morals not really the payoff he expected.

Peter slammed on the brakes just in time to let one of the grungy little kids safely pass. He ran on, oblivious to the fact that he almost got smashed like a rodent. Peter scanned the area around him, eyes a little blurry, to make sure there were no more little punks in his way, and he gunned the truck again. No Perky, no kids. In the clear and free to go.

All of a sudden, like some unruly divine fiat, a car came barreling into the parking lot up ahead. A hubcap spun off of the passenger-side front wheel and hurled across the ground like a disc-shaped rover on some imminent mission of destruction. Peter knew the old, blue Impala belonged to his dad after a long second or two, as his over-stimulated mind finally got a grip on the unfolding situation. It was the car Verlin drove when he wasn't driving his beloved '51, his baby.

Peter snapped out of his trance, tromping on the gas pedal, lunging him and the pick-up forward like a hungry bull, the challenge taken. Peter could see the old man behind the wheel, Louise riding shotgun, as they headed straight for him and Verlin's most prized possession. Peter knew the old man wouldn't run into his own truck and kept gunning forward. Alright, that's the way it is. An afternoon game of chicken. You got it!

Verlin bared down on Peter, and Peter bared down on Verlin, no more consideration for the neighborhood kids or old ladies, or the quiet of the night for that matter. The length of the parking lot became squished between the car and truck, and then at the last minute, reluctantly but quickly,

Peter turned chicken, tunneling through a space in the rows of cars, roughly clipping the front end of a car with the bed of his dad's truck.

Some of the kids running around the parking lot had congregated around the renegade hubcap that had come off of Verlin's Impala as if the thing were some alien artifact that possibly hold all of the missing answers to why the human race had so awfully gone mad and subsequently what had to be done to thwart the fate of utter annihilation. Dirty kids, trash flying in the heat. Peter honked when he went by, having fun with the whole cat-and-mouse, yet still holding the tension in his belly, that grind of excitement, as his face began to regain some feeling, him shouting unintelligible yelps at the kids. He turned again at full speed, all the way to the other end of the parking lot, as the truck went skidding along sideways because of the drainage dip that ran the length of the parking lot, down the center.

Peter looked into the rearview and...WHAM!

Verlin rammed the back of the pick-up with his car. Inconsolable now, it seemed to Peter, so he pushed the gas full bore, barreling out of the parking lot and out onto the side street. The dirt and the trash in the street fanned up behind him, swarming over his dad's car like a sandstorm in the desert. Peter could feel the old man gaining on him, and then...WHAM!..again. The pick-up went into a sideways slide in the middle of the street and then hopped the curb, spinning around a couple of times, where it finally came to a stop in the empty lot across the street from a neighborhood of tract homes.

Once Peter got his bearings about him, he could see his dad skidding to a stop about fifty yards away, out in the street. The pick-up was still running, the smell of oil, fuel, and dirt all around him. The group of neighborhood boys that had congregated around the hubcap had grown into a dirty little rag-tag mob, and they were running down the street like border-jumpers. Peter pushed the pedal to the floor and aimed the truck right at his dad's car that came racing down the street like a time trial, Peter picking up speed, their lines of travel forming an acute angle of heavy collision.

Verlin had lost another hubcap upon the last contact, which the boys had picked up and were holding up like a banner to their quest for adventure. The old, blue Impala raced down the street at full speed, as Peter too came at him full speed, hopping the curb, the boys at a safe distance and out of the line of fire, all coming together into a heaping crescendo, as Peter then slammed the rear end of the Impala at full-force, sending Verlin and Louise and the car up over the curb and into the side of a house, tearing through the brick-like a ragged saw. Verlin's Impala had come to its final resting place.

Peter turned the battered pick-up around and stopped out in the street. Damn, these old cars are tough, he thought. All of the boys were jumping and yelling and laughing, whipped into a frothy mess by the whole thing. Peter stayed put, pulled the pack of cigarettes out of his inside breast pocket, and lit up. The taste and punch to his lungs felt divine. Peter's adrenaline had reached a plateau, where he felt as if he had become one with the frequency of the earth's vibration, where everything around him and in him vibrated with energy so raw and consuming that he could do nothing but succumb to the force. He opened his little baggy again and poured more of the white powder into the crook of his hand, and snorted it up. And again. And again, until his whole face and throat, and chest were numb. His heart pounded in his chest so hard that he thought it would beat itself to death right in the middle of his chest.

Peter gasped for air, wiping sweat from his face with the arm of his blazer, as he stared at his dad's car, stuck in the side of the house up ahead, the crowd of cheering boys growing even more yet, as he sat there smoking and staring, waiting for any life to show itself inside the old Impala. Fucking jacked up!

He thought that there must have been some kind of boy's home somewhere nearby. All those dirty boys, with no fathers around to scoop them up, as they cheered Peter on like he were the role model of the year.

Glass and rubber went flying around his head like confetti. It took Peter a second to realize that he had just been shot at. The coke, the adrenaline was turning everything into a caricature of itself. A wicked, dancing rendition. The .45 slug had shattered the windshield, sending a huge slab of the safety glass into the cab, where it fell onto Peter like some archaic torture device, his hands over his face, scrunched down in the seat. Peter could feel a long section of the rubber gasket around his neck like a noose, and he quickly pulled it off and tried to throw it out the window.

Another shot came through the remaining part of the windshield, sending it into the cab like another unwelcome passenger. Another shot hit the hood. Verlin had made his way out of the car, staggering out onto the lawn, his old car sitting embedded in the house behind him, the dusty backdrop like a grainy still-life depicting a war-torn neighborhood that could have been anywhere.

Peter put the truck into gear and pushed the pedal to the floor. He couldn't see anything as he stayed ducked down behind the wheel, covered in glass and rubber and sweat now. Verlin emptied the clip of his gun, slowly limping, and then released the empty magazine, letting it fall to the ground, and pulled another from his back pocket and jammed it into the butt of the .45, pulling the slide to put the first bullet in the chamber. He started firing into the cab of the oncoming truck as if he could kill the heavy machine, given enough shots. The truck bared down on him like death itself until the last second when his .45 went click, resonating the end.

Verlin jumped out of the way, falling to the ground, as the '51 ran into the side of the old, blue Impala, driving it further into the house, bricks falling and more dust rising into the night summer air.

The cop cars ripped around the corners from both ends of the block. Four, five, six cars screeched to a stop, the officers descending on Verlin like a swarm of bees, forcing his ragged body further into the ground. The two biggest of the cops stayed on top of Verlin as one of the others wrestled the gun from his grip before the old man had a chance to reload and blast his way into oblivion.

Peter passed out in the cab of Verlin's bullet-riddled pick-up, while Louise never stirred, as she was cut short in her attempt at getting out of the car on the driver's side when the pick-up had struck the car. The coroner had later said that she had most likely been killed instantly. No pain, no suffering. Out like a light.

The police had to keep the crowd of boys and all the other neighbors from closing in on the scene, from suffocating the officer's efforts at dealing with the unwelcome mess on an otherwise innocent Oklahoma evening. The dust and the noise and the trash had finally settled all around them like dew. The neighborhood boys stood right at the edge of the police officer's prescribed boundary, waiting for Peter and Louise to stir in their respective vehicles in eager anticipation to see the grime and contusions.

Verlin screamed bloody murder in his futile fight. His broken body pumping to be heard, to have vengeance, as the cops made light work of him, dragging him to a cruiser. Peter could see his father being crammed into the car, still jerking his head and body, flailing his legs and elbows as if he could wriggle his way out of the handcuffs and straggle over to where Peter began to sit up in the truck, and strangle him to death, once and for all.

Chapter 38

"Well, looky there, will ya?" Verlin said, "Is that my boy?" he labored to turn just enough to get a straight-on look at every one. His neck and face were red with strain as he pulled himself up by his four-footed cane. Verlin stepped forward stiffly, then stood up straight with his arms out to his side like a cop or a wooden puppet, pants pulled high over stiff legs. "Hey, Carly Jo."

"Howdy, Verlin," she said. "Damn, you're fatter'n a sow boar."

Verlin tipped his ball cap to Carly Jo and then blew her a kiss.

"Catchin' anything?" Addie said.

"A couple of crappies' all," Verlin said, turning back to his chair to sit down again as if he had exhausted his allotment of energy for the day.

Peter stood there looking at the man who was supposedly his father, a four-footed cane and an oxygen tank keeping him company, like all of those silent, submissive women had all those years. Verlin had gained a hundred pounds or so since the last time Peter had seen him, his neck and face puffy with a bad diet and no exercise. He didn't look like he would give anybody much of a fight anymore. Peter could feel the pity welling up inside him, anger and remorse fighting it out in his gut, heart thudding, as he tried to force himself to say something. Verlin had been reduced to a fat paraplegic on supplemental oxygen, yet Peter wanted to kick the old man's chair out from under him, just the same. From where and why the thoughts had come mystified Peter, but for a moment. Verlin and his old panel van with a new paint job, sitting by the water, waiting for the fish to bite, the eternal fisherman, his dad. Peter shook his head at Fr. Ligero, who stood right next to him, puffing his cigar like a banker out to peruse a tract of land for which he might be in the market.

Peter felt hot all of a sudden, the old man acting as if they hadn't missed a beat, so aloof and casual. 'My boy' and all that happy horse shit. Fr. Ligero nonchalantly standing by like a tour guide didn't help matters either. Peter wanted his friend to take charge, to share his insights on life and death and sacrifice and suffering, to share his soothing perspective with Verlin like he had all those endless nights with Peter in the prison visiting ward. Peter felt like he had prepared his whole life, the last eighteen years anyway, for this moment, and all he could do was stiffly stand with his hands in his pockets, dreaming of revenge and redemption, his confidante standing by mute.

"Hey, Dad." Peter heard the words come out of his mouth.

"How long you been outta the clink, boy?" Verlin said, his broad back to everyone.

"I got out early this morning," Peter said, kicking at the dirt. He looked over to the others to see if they were as uncomfortable as him, but they had disappeared. "I wanted to come to see you first."

Addie had snuck off to Verlin's van, where he dug around in the back, eventually yelling out for some help. Carly Jo and Fr. Ligero hurried around the back as if Addie had gotten caught under the back wheel. "Help me get these chairs outta here, will ya?" Addie had said.

"Here, woman." Carly Jo grabbed the two chairs from Addie and handed them to Fr. Ligero. Fr. Ligero rested the chairs up against the side of the van and grabbed the other two from Carly Jo as she handed them over. The three of them continued to stand behind the van, whispering to each other, not moving around too much, as if they had decided to have their own little private party somewhere out of the way.

"I guess Mr. McDash was anticipating a party."

"Let's give them ole boys a couple of seconds. Whattaya think?" Addie said. Carly Jo and Fr. Ligero nodded, thick cigar smoke bunching up all around them.

Carly Jo scuffed her feet on the ground, looking over at Peter and Verlin as Addie perused the back of the van intensely as if it were chock-full of rare antiquities and enchanting objects de'art that only he could appreciate and must have. Fr. Ligero puffed on his cigar and inspected it again as if that cigar was the finest thing to ever reach his lips. The three of them acted out their individual vignettes of forced nonchalance.

"Where's your stogie, Addie?" Fr. Ligero finally said.

"Aw shit, I left it in the car. Will you go get it for me?"

"Sure."

Fr. Ligero started toward Addie's car to get the cigar when he heard the flat thud of something weighty, bulky, falling to the ground. He turned to see if Addie was still standing up, the sudden sound like a person falling over, and he saw Addie watching him like an expectant puppy waiting for a treat. Fr. Ligero looked over to where Peter and his dad had been talking and saw that they were both on the ground rolling around, both tangled in the fishing line from Verlin's fishing poles that had been pulled to the ground by the ruckus.

"You fuckin' little shit!" Verlin shouted, landing a couple of punches to Peter's face.

Peter kicked his feet and legs, trying to get the old man off of him, but Verlin's girth proved too much to heft. Verlin had wedged his cane diagonally across Peter's neck and held it in place with his left knee and opposite forearm. The old man got a couple more punches in, but then, just as soon as the fight had broken out, Verlin fell off of Peter, running out of gas again, as he rolled over into the mud at the edge of the pond like a bag of wet clothes.

Addie ambled up behind Carly Jo and Fr. Ligero, who had gotten to the two just as Verlin had fallen to the ground. Addie firmly pushed his cane to the ground.

"What the hell you idiots doin'?" Addie said. "Father, get that dummy's oxygen for him."

Fr. Ligero stepped over Verlin as Peter started to get up off of the ground. Verlin's oxygen tubes lay in the mud next to where the two had just been grappling, embedded in saw grass, tangled into a muddy mess that looked like greasy noodles. The tubes had come out of his nose when he leaped over at Peter from his little lawn chair, the chair giving in under Verlin's sudden shift, collapsing like an old cardboard box underneath a sugar-crazed kid.

"Here you go," Fr. Ligero said, wiping off the mud and water with the tail of his shirt. He put the tubes in Verlin's nose, who had begun to panic a little bit trying to catch his breath, and then let him adjust them so that they were delivering the oxygen just right.

"You're a pathetic old fuck. You know that?" Peter said to Verlin, dusting off his pants and shirt; brown-red smudges streaked across his clothes like messy war paint.

Verlin lay on his back at the edge of the pond, a dying fish out of the water, gulping at the air with his mouth, his oxygen tubes properly rammed up his nose again. He looked up at Fr. Ligero, who had taken a couple of steps back, as he slowly got his breath again.

"Thanks, old man."

"No problem," Fr. Ligero said, taking another step backward to give Verlin yet more room.

Carly Jo stood behind the others, holding Addie up so that he didn't topple over like his buddy there in the mud. Peter and Verlin stared at each other silently, intensely enough to keep the others quiet and on the periphery. Peter wiped his forehead and face with the sleeve of his shirt, continuing to look down at his dad.

"Where's the girls?" Addie said.

"They told me to fuck off, Addie," Verlin said as he started to laugh hysterically. He was still lying on his back in the mud, where one of his feet dipped into the edge of the pond. Peter couldn't help but take pity on the old man, even though he still felt like kicking him the rest of the way into the pond for the fish to feed on. All of those contemplative conversations with Fr. Ligero about redemption and reconciliation seemed so lacking, so awkward, and inappropriate right then.

Peter had taken the bait and bitten down hard when his dad started in on him. Peter was the murderer, Verlin had said. You went to prison, boy. You killed the woman who cared for your sniveling brat ass. Peter told the old man that he had never asked for any favors, if that's what you could call their involvement in his life. And as far as care…well…what?

Peter had gone to see Verlin so that he might be able to go in peace, once and for all, to forgive...and more importantly...to ask for forgiveness. Negligent homicide wasn't something you sent a card in the mail for which to apologize. Peter knew that. He felt something bubbling beneath all of his good intentions, nevertheless, as if there were some insidious force at work in his bloodstream, staining his insides like rust. He wanted to purge himself, to be done with it for good.

Peter bit his lip and bent over to give Verlin a hand after a couple of minutes had passed after they had cooled down. Verlin reached up and took his hand, saying, "You better get you some help there, hoss. I'm a heavy old turd."

"Yeah, yeah. Hold on," Peter said, waving over Fr. Ligero and Carly Jo, "you better stand back, Addie. I don't want you to hurt yourself too."

Addie flipped Peter off and grabbed one of the chairs leaning up against the van, shaking it to unfold it, and sat down.

"Where's my cigar, padre?" Addie said, shouting over to Fr. Ligero, who had grabbed one of the other chairs for Verlin.

"I'll get your smoke if you think you can handle it."

Peter, Carly Jo, and Fr. Ligero got Verlin back into an uncrumpled chair with a lot of combined effort. They stood by for a second to make sure that he didn't topple over into the mud again or simply crush the cheap aluminum piece of lawn furniture with all that bulk. "You going to be okay, Mr. Dernovish?" Fr. Ligero said.

"I ain't no fuckin' Dernovish, mister."

"Yes, yes. I'm sorry, sir. I forget. McDa..."

"McDash, buddy. Don't you forget that neither," Verlin said, "the one and only Verlin McDash. I sold more trucks to more old boys than fuckin' Ronnie Reagan."

Fr. Ligero didn't seem to be able to make the connection. "Impressive," he finally said, and then he cautiously made his way back to Addie's car to get his cigar for him.

"That your boyfriend?" Verlin said to Peter, nodding his head in Fr. Ligero's direction.

"He's actually one of the only ones that came to visit me in prison," Peter said. "A couple of old friends came through once in a while. People just get busy with life, I guess."

Verlin readjusted himself in his chair again, steadying himself, putting his arms out so that he didn't fall over. "Aww, little buddy, that's real fuckin' sad, ya know?"

Verlin stared at Peter, his face red like cloth, otherwise blank with icy eyes. Peter felt cold inside, sitting there looking at his dad with no real connection to speak of. He wanted to feel a spark, a glimpse of something real and eternal in the exchange, but he didn't.

"Maybe people don't like a stone-cold killer, huh? Ever thought'a that? Huh, boy?"

Verlin shifted in his seat again, from one hip to the other. "I wouldn't know about having too much family, boy. You talkin' to the wrong cowboy here. You know that?"

Peter stuffed his hands in his pockets, watching Carly Jo as she walked over towards Addie's car, where he and Fr. Ligero were leaning on the fender, talking intently about something. Peter thought that the conversation might have been about something other than he and his dad and their little meeting taking place, but that their minds were right there with him, their eyes darting over every couple of seconds just to make sure Peter and his dad didn't end up in the mud again.

Peter's mind felt muddy, murky, with nothing to say. He had to apologize. He would have to make amends for the rest of his life, more than likely, but what to say right then felt harsher than the prospect of an ongoing relationship with the guy who had tried to kill him as a kid. His dad. Daddy. Peter didn't come to blame his father for his childhood, his lack thereof, his struggles, and his confusion. He wasn't there to clear his name, per se, but to make something out of nothing, really, to let God mediate the situation, and come into their midst to begin the healing process. Peter could do nothing else but to allow healing, to allow intervention, but then again, it would be easier to just pick up and leave that place. Peter was a grown man who had paid his debt to society. He had done his time.

"I have thought and prayed and feared over this day for a long time, dad."

"Dad?" Verlin gave Peter a back-handed wave as if he were dismissing a pesky servant. "You think prayin's gonna get the job done, boy? Ain't you learn about them fuckin' fairy tales yet?"

"I think it helps," Peter said, grabbing one of the chairs and leaning on Verlin's van. "Is this the same van?"

"You bet."

"Looks good."

Verlin looked at the van like Peter hoped his dad would one day look at him, a bit remiss yet, but proud in an innocent sort of way. "Yeah, I got a custom paint job last year. Pearl-white, boy."

Peter looked at the van and back at his dad. "I'm sorry about Louise," he said, staring at the ground before him. He had to start somewhere, no matter how unsatisfactory the words might have felt. He didn't know what to do with his hands, so he just ran them down the fender of the pearl-white panel van. It hurt to look at his dad. He felt sorry for him and still angry, deprived of the old man's love, still, after so many years, brief interludes of something hopeful, nonetheless, along the way. "I would like to see if we could ever be friends. If we could ever have a relationship."

"Boy..."

"My name's Peter."

Verlin looked at Peter as if the boy had asked him if he had ever masturbated in the middle of a grocery store, Peter's statement sharp and off-putting. "Boy...I'm sorry, son...Peter..." Verlin readjusted in his seat again and pulled his cane closer to his side like he had to physically regroup before he could possibly say the right thing. "I didn't do too good, I know. Your mama wasn't no help, neither."

"You screwed that up."

Verlin looked down at the ground, tapping his four-footed cane into the ground a couple of times.

"Come on, man. You know you treated her like a dog," Peter said. "You were cruel to her and me. You deserved to get cut off. You would have really fucked me up for sure. Don't you think?"

Verlin didn't have anything to say. Peter got up to get a soda out of Verlin's ice chest, accidently knocking his own chair over.

"No Coors Original?"

"Quit drinkin'."

"Yeah, me too. It wasn't too hard being in jail all those years," Peter said. "I had a couple of cigarettes with Carly Jo. I can't say I've missed smoking all that much, either."

"I ain't never gonna quit smokin'."

"Isn't that dangerous?" Peter said, putting his chair upright again and sitting back down, "smoking while you're hooked up to that oxygen tank?"

"Shit, boy. I can just take bigger tokes now. Like the old days, ya know?"

Peter laughed at the stupidity of the remark but felt endeared just the same.

"You got any beer in that ice chest?" Addie said, ambling over.

"Just for you," Verlin said. "Ya old, crippled bastard."

Addie laughed, opening the cooler.

"The beer's still in the case in the back of the van, dummy," Verlin said.

Addie nodded over to the van, looking at Fr. Ligero.

"What?"

"Come on, man. Help an old man out," Addie said.

"I'm older than anybody here, mister," Fr. Ligero said, smoking his cigar, smiling, contently sitting.

Addie handed Fr. Ligero a soda out of the ice chest and said, "Pretty please."

Fr. Ligero went to the van and got the case of beer, and took it over to Addie to put into the ice chest. Addie grabbed himself and Carly Jo a beer, tossing hers over to her. Peter got up from his chair, patting Carly Jo on the leg as she reached for her warm beer.

Peter walked over to the van. He lightly touched the fender with his hand. The same hand that had been smashed in the door of that van over thirty years before. Peter stroked the smooth paint and looked over at Verlin, who shifted in his chair. Peter limped over to the black Beamer and got his cane out of the back seat.

"We're twinkies, dad," Peter said, holding up his cane for Verlin to see.

"That's a fancy one, boy."

"I made it in the woodshop before they closed it down."

Verlin turned a little more in his chair like he didn't want Peter sneaking around on him. "Don't scratch that thing, boy."

Peter laughed quietly to himself. He started laughing a little more loudly, taking his hand off of the fender. He walked around to the back of the van, widened the open doors, and began rummaging around.

"Hey, boy!"

Fr. Ligero and Addie had busied themselves with the task of getting a fire going. After Carly Jo had slammed her warm beer in only a couple of hearty gulps, she had slumped in her chair as if it were the first time in years that she had slowed down enough to actually rest.

Addie sweated over the pile of limbs and kindling that he and Father had formed into a little teepee in the middle of a ring of large rocks. "Peter. Your daddy got some gas back there?"

Fr. Ligero looked up from his handiwork.

Peter came out from behind the van, holding out a large red can of gasoline, smiling. "He sure does."

"Come over here and give us a little shot, will ya?" Addie said.

"Peter," Fr. Ligero said, standing up.

"You and Addie worry about that fire, alright?"

Fr. Ligero crouched back down next to Addie, keeping his eyes on Peter, who came over next to them and handed Addie the large red can. Addie made a messy little splash on the upside-down cone of sticks and then grunted to hand the gas can back to Peter.

Verlin had turned around in his chair, facing the pond again, as if he had suddenly grown tired of dealing with Peter and the others, everything was novel for a moment, but the fishing was ultimately the reason he had come out to the pond. He needed some time to stare at the water and think. Verlin watched his red and white bobber dip back and forth on the little waves stirred up by the gentle evening breeze. Carly Jo had pulled her chair up closer to where Verlin sat and was now fast asleep, ever-so-slowly slipping down further until she looked like she might fall all the way out and onto the ground below.

Peter went back to the van and sat the gas can on the ground at the passenger side, leaning his cane there too. He went around the back of the van again and grabbed a blonde brick from the floorboard. Everyone had finally become fully engrossed in what they were doing, business as usual. Peter walked around to the front of the van. He paused there for a moment, staring at Verlin's back to see if he would turn around. The old man had slumped in his chair like he was going to sleep too. Peter looked over at Fr. Ligero and Addie, now sitting by their little fire, talking to each other over their respective cigars. Peter pulled the brick back over his shoulder and then sent it reeling right at the windshield of the old van with the new custom paint job, the sound dull and sudden, shaking the three guys out of their trances.

"Peter!" Fr. Ligero shouted, standing up.

Addie pulled on Fr. Ligero's pant leg and gestured for him to stay put, to not interfere.

Verlin slowly turned to see what the commotion was all about; Carly Jo was deeply sleeping on his other side, snoring loudly.

"Boy!"

Peter went back to the side of the van and picked up his cane, looking it over carefully. "It took me a few months to make this thing. Lathing...carving...sanding...polishing." Peter turned the cane in his hand, over and over, as if he were carefully inspecting it for flaws, or perhaps in simple admiration. "More carving. You know, this thing was only for show in prison. People don't fuck with you as much if they think you're compromised somehow, you know what I mean?"

"Boy, you better think before you do anything else to that van, you hear?"

"...or they might really take advantage of you if you're compromised," Peter said.

"Boy!"

"You never know. Some folks are sicker than others, you know?"

"You better think long and hard before you go and do something stupid, son."

"I can't hear really well these days," Peter said. "What was that?"

Peter gently stroked the cane a couple more times and then looked out toward the pond. "You catchin' anything, dad? Huh? Maybe they just need a little excitement, huh? Whattaya think?"

And then Peter took the cane and smashed the passenger-side window out with one quick swing. He moved the gas can out of his way and slowly walked to the back of the van. He gently closed the doors at the back of the van and then peered around the side as if he were playing peek-a-boo with Verlin. Verlin didn't seem too amused by the gesture, trying to get his fat body out of the lawn chair again.

Peter took the edge of his shirt and wiped a smudge off of one of the back doors, and then breathed on the spot like a person might do to fog their eyeglasses before wiping them clean. He wiped at the imaginary spot again with feigned diligence and then smiled around the corner at Verlin again.

"Got it, Dad," Peter said. "Looks real good now."

Peter suddenly swung the cane, smashing one of the back windows. The dense, wooden cane broke in the middle, splintering into long fibrous sinews as it made contact. Peter opened the doors again, got into the back of the van, and grabbed a crowbar as he walked around to the driver's side, smashing that window too. He smashed the little wing window also and then went back to the front of the van and smashed out the headlights.

Verlin had gotten up out of his chair, bumping into Carly Jo, who didn't budge and tried to make it over to the van to stop Peter, but he tripped and fell, and then he simply resigned himself to sit on the ground where he felt safe for a moment. Father Ligero had gotten up to help, but Verlin waved him off, needing his space. The boy had made his way all the way around the van once, having already smashed all of the windows out, along with the headlights and taillights and blinkers.

Peter stood in front of the van for a moment, as if he had forgotten where he was, what he had been doing. He looked over at Verlin, sitting defeated on the ground like an infant who's about to throw a tantrum, and then back at the van. He contemplatively turned the crowbar in his hands for a few seconds and then swung away at the grill, tearing the thin metal raggedly, gashing it repeatedly. Peter pounded on the van's body, the front, then the sides, the back, then the other side...over and over, until he looked like he might drop from exhaustion altogether.

"You," Peter said, hitting the van, "are," hitting the van again, "the reason," again, "that," wham! "I fucked my life up...you fucking asshole!" Peter beat on the van over and over until finally looking like a railroad slave beating in that last spike for the day, his body slumping forward, sweat and red flesh covering his face. "You are mean and bad and stupid. You hurt me, and it mattered, and now I have come to forgive you once and for all. I don't give a shit what...you...think...anymore!"

Peter walked over to hand the crowbar to Verlin, who had managed to sit up nice and straight on the ground now, and then he went over to pick up the gas can. He started dousing the van with gasoline, pouring the fuel into the broken windows, into the back doors, and all about. Peter made it around the van again, using every last drop of the gas, what was left of the bulky five-gallon tank, and then threw the can in through the driver-side window frame.

"There," Peter said. "That oughta do it, huh, Daddy? Right? Gitter done, right?"

Verlin looked at the van and started crying.

Fr. Ligero and Addie sat next to their own fire, burning low and quiet before them, as they sat upright and forward, watching Peter and Verlin, both dumbfounded, both resigned to letting things play out unless someone pulled a gun at that point. Fr. Ligero thought that the scene which had unfolded was somewhat different than what he and Peter had rehearsed over and over in their evening prison visits, maybe a little more intense.

"This is for our vacation, Dad," Peter said, lighting a fresh cigar that he had gotten from the BMW. "Remember our vacation? Boy, what a year. I really thought you were gonna kill me. Remember? Like that little girl, they found in Birmingham, right up the road. Remember?"

Verlin trembled, trying to pull himself up with his cane, but he couldn't. He had become the helpless one, at the mercy of someone more powerful, more in control of the environment. If he had the chance, Peter thought, Verlin would have put a couple of bullets into him right there so that he could literally bury the past, bury his son. What did it matter anyhow, anymore? Lost cause, some might say.

"The way I see it," Peter added, hot-boxing the cigar and then throwing it into the open passenger-side window. "You owe me one."

Peter could feel the combustion of the igniting gasoline in his chest and head as it burst out of the busted windows, him flailing backward. The flames shortly engulfed the van like a violent embrace, the whole thing rocking to the force of the escaping energy from within, surreal and bright.

Carly Jo came to, lifting her head, not saying a word, as she looked around at everyone watching the flames lick the surface of the browning pearl-white paint job of the van. The paint bubbled on the surface like a dope in a crack pipe. Carly Jo hypnotically stared at the burning van as if the past were being put to rest for everyone, the bruised and tarnished and hurt alike, the sins of a lifetime being burned away in that refining fire. The melting and bubbling paint changed color and form, putting off an acrid smoke as it turned black. Metal clinking and vinyl seats crackling, the sounds of the conflagration sounded like some eerie ancient orchestra from the belly of the earth.

Everyone continued to stare at the flames like bones of divination. That massive heat and light, speaking to them like the ocean or mountains, eternally calling them into the heat and the light. The little fire that Addie and Fr. Ligero had built looked like a consolation prize next to the heaping blaze that had yet begun to calm a little bit.

Peter broke his gaze into the fire after several minutes and went over to his chair, and sat down. Verlin continued to stare at the van as if he had just seen his future play out before him from some obscure reel.

"Dad," Peter said. "I'm sorry about Louise. Can you forgive me?"

Verlin slowly turned, attempting again to get up off of the ground. Fr. Ligero got up from his chair and rushed over behind Verlin to help him up.

"I got it, old boy."

"Are you sure?"

Verlin shrugged Fr. Ligero off, even though the former priest followed him closely behind, just in case he took another spill. Verlin sat down with his son, two men, starting over, next to that fishing hole under the dusk light, as the old van burned behind them, the others nearby, like surviving members of a shipwreck, gazing into the dying flames of the last fire they would ever behold.

…and here's to new beginnings.

Amen.

www.ingramcontent.com/pod-product-compliance
Lightning Source LLC
Chambersburg PA
CBHW082126180726
48291CB00010B/2753